ALSO BY L. G. REED

The Maiden Voyage of the Maryann

Sydney Porter: Dog Girl

The Science of Defying Gravity

L. G. Reed

~

Olive Groves & Alibis

A Rose MacGillivray Mystery

First Edition

KEYES CANYON PRESS
SAN MIGUEL, CALIFORNIA

Published in the United States by Keyes Canyon Press
All rights reserved. For information, contact Keyes Canyon Press
https://authorlindareed.com/keyes-canyon-press/

Published 2026

Printed in the United States of America

Olive Groves & Alibis, A Rose MacGillivray Mystery -- 1st ed.
Names: Linda Reed (pen name L. G. Reed), author
Title: Olive Groves & Alibis/ L. G. Reed
Description: First U.S. edition / San Miguel: Keyes Canyon Press 2026/ Series: A Rose MacGillivray Mystery: 1
ISBN 978-1-7356528-2-5 (Trade Paperback)
ISBN 978-1-7356528-3-2 (eBook)
LCCN 2026904933

Book Layout © 2017 BookDesignTemplates.com

To Officer V. Gomez and all the officers of the Paso
Robles Police Department
Thank you for everything you do to keep us safe.

*Don't be afraid that your life will end. Be afraid that
it will never begin.*

—GRACE HANSEN

Chapter 1 Rose

~

"In wine there is wisdom, in beer there is freedom, in water there is bacteria."- Benjamin Franklin

Saturday, September 9, 10:30 PM

Riding shotgun in a police car, next to a young officer, had not been on Rose MacGillivray's wish list. At least, not until she moved to the sleepy wine-country town of Paso Robles. Situated halfway between San Francisco and Los Angeles, in a wide, fertile valley, she'd chosen it as the locale for her next chapter. Or maybe more as a place to end her last one, hoping this place would be far enough from the work stress and ignominy of her career in the end. No fault of her own, she told herself, although the long-term relationship that soured both her interest in men and her hard-won career could be at least partly her fault. Didn't everyone say to avoid workplace romances? Hadn't she ignored that advice?

She came to Paso Robles with no plans other than to rest, which she did for a month before realizing she also wanted excitement. Someone to share a glass of wine with, or even an immersive hobby. After two months, she could count one friend, several acquaintances, and five olive trees towards that goal.

So far, the late-night ride-along with an officer of the Paso Robles police department had been routine: mostly broken taillights or drunk motorists.

Rose judged Sergeant Gomez to be in her mid-40s, with deep brown hair pulled into a tight bun at her nape, olive skin, and small gold stud earrings. Her eyes scanned the road, sidewalks, alleys, and parking lots. Secretly, Rose was thrilled that the officer assigned to her ride-along was female. Though she wondered if that assignment came about *because* Rose was a woman.

The interior of the black police car was lit only by the dizzying array of computer screens and monitors that hogged the center console and dashboard. Streetlights and store illumination barely made a dent in the dark interior. It was like riding around in a shadow. One that had the new car smell of fresh plastic mixed with gun oil from the weapon strapped to Sergeant Gomez's duty belt.

"You have kids?" Gomez asked. The ubiquitous question asked of all women.

"No," Rose replied. She didn't feel the need to explain that she'd *had* a child but didn't keep it. That would only invoke more discussion on the topic.

The whole issue was fraught with too many emotions, conventions, and frankly false beliefs about what makes a woman a woman.

Rose had been involved in more of those confrontations than she wanted and hoped never to have to discuss it again.

A woman's voice squawked over the police radio.

"10-31, 5490 Main Street, suspect armed and dangerous."

Rose tensed.

Sergeant Nessa Gomez picked up the speaker microphone and pushed the side button.

"10-76, dispatch. ETA 5."

She flicked the siren switch. "Crime in progress, hang on."

The ear-splitting sound seemed to come from everywhere. Finally, Rose thought. She missed the adrenaline jolt of solving problems. Her old job had given her plenty of that. Would retirement?

The vehicle accelerated down Main Street, pushing Rose back into her seat. She held on to the door armrest. Tourists out enjoying the cooler night air after dinner cringed as they rushed by. Rose couldn't help but smile as a familiar rush raced through her. Drivers peeled off to the right as the police car wove between them.

Behind the front seats, a metal wall separated the vehicle, creating a temporary cell, known as the cage, where suspects would be held during transit. Mounted to that was the largest gun Rose had ever seen. She hoped that this weapon wasn't needed tonight.

Red lights strobed as three black and whites converged on a liquor store. A hooded figure dashed out the front door and jumped into a dark sedan in the small parking lot. Streetlights rendered everything in shades of gray and maroon. The sedan screeched away as they reached the shop. Sergeant Gomez had a straight shot.

Reaching for the radio handset, the policewoman pulled the device to her mouth.

"Dispatch, suspect is northbound on Main Street. I'm in pursuit. And…I have a rider."

There was a pause.

"Acknowledged, Standard protocol," came the reply. Gomez affirmed and replaced the handpiece.

"We're going to chase. No time to stop and let you

get out. Are you okay with that?"

Rose's muscles tighten. "Fine with me!"

The bad guys roared down Main Street toward 24th Street, weaving around slower drivers and nearly hitting someone in a crosswalk.

"10-31 is a crime in progress," Gomez said, and then turned sharply as she followed the suspect. Rose's shoulder bumped into the door. She righted herself and hung on.

The suspect's sedan careened into the right turn sign as it entered the southbound on-ramp to the 101 highway. Bits of plastic and metal from the front end flew into the air. The car kept going.

Gomez accelerated. The radio squawked with news that a fellow officer would enter the highway at an on-ramp further south of them, trapping the suspect between them. Rose's heart pumped like she'd run a mile. What would happen when they caught up?

Hadn't dispatch said he was armed? She eyed the large weapon again.

Headlights glimmered off something shiny on the onramp. Liquid. Probably from the fleeing car. The taillights flickered on the late-model Volkswagen; she knew a thing or two about these cars.

"His taillights were flickering, and his coolant is leaking. Probably damaged his ECM, um, Engine Control Module. That affects the electric water pump. He'll overheat quickly."

Gomez looked over at her as if surprised Rose had any intelligence at all.

"That's useful. Thanks," Gomez said. She relayed the message to dispatch.

"If that happened, he won't be driving far," Gomez said.

They flew down the highway, passing the fairgrounds and the big box store in the newer section of town. Gomez stayed about one hundred yards behind.

"He's slowing," she said. The car drifted side to side, like the driver was having trouble with steering, before coasting to a stop. They hadn't reached the cruiser in front of them.

Another squad car came up behind and pulled alongside. The driver waved.

"That's Hernandez," Gomez explained. "We'll box in the driver."

Hernandez drove ahead and positioned himself beside the suspect vehicle. Gomez pulled in close behind the sedan, boxing him in. She cut the siren off, removed her gun from its holster, and released the safety.

"Stay here," she told Rose. "Under no circumstances are you to get out."

Rose bristled at the command. Her ears rang from the siren like they would after a loud Bob Seger concert. The car idled with the AC on.

With her gun pointing at the stalled car, Gomez shouted, "Driver, throw the car keys out the window." A minute later, the keys flew out the window and landed on the tarmac at Hernandez's feet. Gomez nodded at him, then said, "Driver, with your right hand, reach out the window and open the door.

Rose wished she could see inside the car, but the driver's side headrest was in the way. She imagined him unbuckling the seat belt, because even bad guys should be using a seat belt, and then reaching out to pull the door handle. Sure enough, his hand reached out, and the door swung open.

"Driver, with your hands up, come out of the car slowly," she ordered.

A young person, no more than eighteen, got out with his arms raised and his fingers laced behind his head. A practiced move. He'd done this before. He wore dark pants, a black hoodie, and fluorescent yellow running shoes that glowed in the headlights. In his waistband, a chrome-plated 45 reflected the flashing lights. To Rose's way of thinking, he looked like he might try for the gun.

Officer Hernandez yelled, "Don't even think about it!"

"Screw you, pig!"

Rose shrank back into the safety of the police car, hoping that the front window was bulletproof.

Hernandez responded, "If you do it, don't blink, or you'll die in the dark." It was just like in the cop shows on TV.

"Go down on your knees," Hernandez ordered.

In slow motion, the youth sank to the highway, his hands still laced behind his head.

Both Gomez and Hernandez approached. Hernandez handcuffed the suspect and removed the gun. Then pulled back the hood to expose the youth's face and head, which was covered with tattoos. Rose could tell he was light-skinned, Caucasian, but there was so much dark ink it almost obscured that fact. Rose took a breath. Her first real deep breath in minutes. She opened the window so she could hear what was happening.

The guy was turned to face the police dash-cam to record the action, and Gomez read him his Miranda rights.

He glared into the lights with defiance. before ducking his head as he was led to the cruiser and locked in the back seat. Rose was glad that they hadn't put him behind her in Gomez's vehicle. She didn't want to be that close.

In addition to the skull cap of decorations, he had two teardrops tattooed on his face, one dropping from his right eye. She fought the urge to get out. While she usually followed rules, she couldn't help but want to be part of the inquiry. For twenty years, her job had been to investigate failures of high-tech hardware. How different was that from crime?

As Hernandez loaded the suspect into the back of his cruiser, Gomez donned rubber gloves and searched through the car's interior and trunk. From under the driver's seat, she pulled out another revolver. She carefully placed it in an evidence bag and walked it over to Hernandez so it would go with him to the station.

Almost without Rose's control, her hand reached for the door latch and pulled. It popped open just as Gomez and the young officer who drove past them earlier returned. She pulled the door shut. Hopefully, Gomez didn't see that.

"Rose, this is Officer Hernandez." He looked barely old enough to have graduated from high school. What must he think when he sees a petite, mid-sixties woman with silver-white hair? Young people thought anyone older than fifty was from Methuselah's time.

He smiled and saluted her with two fingers.

"Good catch on the ECM." His voice was friendly. Not challenging her or doubting her.

Gomez climbed back into the police cruiser. When Rose had buckled her seatbelt, Gomez looked over at her with grudging respect.

"How did you know that? About the ECM, I mean."

How could she describe an entire technical career?

Especially one she hoped to leave in her past. Ridiculous. Once an engineer, always an engineer.

"I'm a nerd," she said.

It wasn't an answer. Not really. '

But now wasn't the time to wax eloquent about an engineering career in the defense electronics field, working on everything from the Mars lander to Tomahawk missiles. A field that developed military components, which eventually made their way into the private sector, such as the ECM in that VW.

With a slight shake of her head, the policewoman said, "I suspect there is more to it than being a nerd, but thanks. And please call me Nessa."

Ten minutes later, a tow truck pulled over in front of the suspect's sedan. The ride-along was ending. Nessa climbed into the SUV and followed Hernandez to the station so she could help with booking. The hour was late, and Rose realized how tired she felt. Still, she wanted to keep going.

"This was fun. Have you always wanted to be a police officer?"

They reached the off-ramp. Nessa turned off the strobe lights.

"Yeah, I guess. I have relatives in various forces in the state: CHP and several PDs. When my husband left, I needed something that would pay well to support my son. This fits the bill. Plus," she flicked on the turn signal and navigated around the corner.

Using a powerful flashlight, she aimed the beam into a car parked alongside the lane. It was empty. She flicked off the torch and drove on.

"Where was I, oh yeah, it's like a calling. Policing isn't for everyone. But it gives my life meaning beyond being a mother."

The city park glittered with twinkling lights that dangled from the trees. Rose barely saw them, her mind spiraling on Nessa's words. Mother. Did carrying a child and giving it up for adoption count?

Would the baby have been a boy?

"It must be difficult as a woman in this business," Rose said. She'd certainly encountered her share of unwanted shoulder rubs and inappropriate comments, or times when her words were ignored in favor of a male colleague.

"Do you experience sexual harassment and things like that?"

When Nessa finally spoke, it seemed as if the answer was rehearsed. "I wouldn't say difficult, exactly. Different maybe. I can often diffuse a situation before it escalates to an arrest. Most of the guys come in too hot."

An SUV pulled out in an unwise left-hand turn. Nessa braked hard.

"Idiots everywhere. Who cuts off a police car? Anyway, where was I? Even after all my years with a badge, when I call dispatch for backup, every guy on patrol shows up. Like I'm their little sister in trouble. It's sweet, in a way, but not something I need—or want."

"No wolf whistles in the gym or 'babes' or 'honeys'?" Rose asked.

"They wouldn't dare. I can beat most of them in wrestling." She smiled. "Four brothers taught me well."

I'll bet they did, thought Rose. She couldn't help but admire Nessa's grit. They turned into the station's sally port.

"Thank you," Rose said as she gathered her purse.

"I've never done anything like this before. It's inspired me."

"Any time. Paso Robles can get rowdy, especially on Friday and Saturday nights. Fortunately, we don't get much big-city crime, like murder, because we're understaffed as it is. Pulling officers off to investigate violent crime would stretch us pretty thin."

"Well, it certainly brought some greatly needed excitement into my life," Rose said as Nessa escorted her out to the street.

Maybe Paso Robles wasn't as quiet as Rose thought. The gang member. The gun. Rose wasn't so sure this quiet Norman Rockwell town wasn't hiding something more sinister. As she drove home, she thought about her new friend, Natalie Patel. Natalie lived next door in a rambling house tucked up in a copse of trees. Rose couldn't wait to share the ride-along experience with her. The thrill of the sirens and the peek under the veneer of small-town tranquility. Nothing, it seems, is as it appears on the outside.

Her headlights caught the falling yellow leaves of poplars and oaks. October nights grew chilly. Her big house would be cold. Cold and lonely. In her favorite books, the Hamish Macbeth mystery series by M. C. Beaton, a change in the weather or a cold hearth foretold evil doings.

Sergeant Gomez's words played in Rose's thoughts. "We don't get much big city crime like murder."

Could murder happen in Paso Robles? The thought gave her a momentary shiver, as if the mere possibility threatened the life she hoped to create here. One full of friends.

Before going to bed, she double-checked all the door locks and opened the built-in gun safe in the hall closet and retrieved her father's old pistol. After loading a few bullets into the cylinder, she set it on her bedside table.

Just in case.

Chapter 2 Rose

~

Mission Olive – A cultivar developed in California by Spanish missions along El Camino Real in the late 18ᵗʰ century

Friday, October 7, 11:00 AM

Rose sat on the folding chair behind a plastic table under a pop-up shade tent. So much had changed. Three months ago, she would have been in an office with a hard-won window. Windows went to the executives. Cubicles for anyone less. At least he hadn't taken that away from her.

Meetings, problem-solving brainstorming sessions, and one-on-one interviews crammed her calendar. But even that became scarce as the magnitude of his betrayal became evident.

Like a snake shedding its skin, she left behind a job, an ocean-view condo, and a career. Pretty much everything that defined her. The experience didn't leave her with much. She even hated her name. Winifred Amanda MacGillivray. Too close to Winnie the Pooh. Most people stumbled over the words, afraid they were insulting her. That having a name similar to a children's book character, a cartoon character to top it off, meant that she was simple.

So, she changed it when she came here. At least as far as what she told people to call her. Her driver's license and passport held the name she left behind. New location. New name. New life.

With practice, the name began to feel more like her. Who she wanted to be. Rose. Sweet and innocent until someone gets too close. Then prickly and sharp. With thorns to shred.

Three months after moving into the two-story house on Chestnut, she felt comfortable saying the name, though the scars of her former life reminded her that the snake of the past hovered at the fringes. Some things you just can't leave behind. She'll change her name one of these days. Get a new passport and then tell her new friends. Not that they would appreciate the weight that revelation carried.

Now she manned a table at a craft fair, of all things. She took a deep breath and thought about her new house and her new friendship with Natalie Patel. At least you're not under all that stress, she reminded herself. Look where you are. In a beautiful small town in wine country. Full of welcoming people to get to know.

That's better. Right?

A police cruiser rolled down 13th Street on the north side of the park. Was it Officer Hernandez or Sergeant Gomez from her ride-along the previous week? The first time since retiring, she felt part of something bigger than herself.

She took another breath of gratitude and appreciated the stately Coastal Live oaks, Raywood ash, and Southern Magnolia trees that soared overhead, shading the old Carnegie Library, and sheltering a bandstand at the east end. Fresh, colorful awnings arched over outdoor dining patios on the streets on three sides of the park, and the scent of restaurant burgers and movie theater popcorn infused the air.

In the past, she would have laughed at the idea of

moving from Los Angeles to a small town halfway to San Francisco. That's the way life goes, isn't it?

"You have to express yourself or lose yourself," her therapist had said. "You've become a chameleon to mimic what *they* want you to be, not who *you* are."

Not they—him.

The hard metal chair-back pushed into her ribs. A young couple propelled a stroller past. Rose leaned forward to peer inside at the sleeping baby. Her heart tugged. The past is past, she reminded herself.

Instead, she focused on the tables laden with soaps, face lotions, and hydrating gel masks, along with lavender bundles, woodwork art, and boiled wool hats. If you could think of it, someone made it and tried to sell it at this monthly fair. Rose wasn't crafty. Had never even so much as sewn a button on a shirt. No, her skills lie in talking, problem-solving, and today, giving out stickers. She tapped the Fitbit on her wrist and checked the time. 11:15 am.

An old woman bent over a walker shuffled by, glanced at the stickers on the table, and waved. Would that be her in twenty years? *Oh god. Please, no.*

The day promised to be hot. She rummaged in the cooler sack and brought out a water bottle. Her new house had an air conditioner, though, and large shade trees cut the solar load on the roof. Two more hours and she could walk home, cocoon inside, and read. A stack of books awaited her eager eyes. Books bought over the decades to read on a plane or in a hotel room, but she never got around to them.

True, she worked in a world where secrets were kept, clearances obtained, and one didn't discuss what one did for a living. It had been exciting. But that was behind her.

Now she was applying her considerable experience to the task of taking care of the olive trees she inherited when she bought the charming bungalow. Her first hobby. The trees could live thousands of years, and she felt the weight of duty not to be the one who cut their life short. She joined the local Growers Association. And, to ingratiate herself among that esteemed group, she volunteered to sit at a table at the craft fair and give out stickers.

One had to start somewhere.

Sunlight shifted and sliced between limbs high overhead. Rose blinked in the brightness, eased her feet out of her shoes, and felt the warmth of the ground on her toes.

"Are you trapped at this table, or were you willing to undergo the torture?"

Rose looked up to Sergeant Gomez. Nessa.

"Nice to see you again," Rose said.

Despite having gone on a ride-along with the policewoman, an unjustified flush of guilt washed through Rose. Not because of any brush with the law, but out of a fear that she may have done something she didn't realize was wrong. And being wrong was the worst thing Rose could imagine.

"No," she said. "Believe it or not, I signed up for this."

The park had filled up with tourists. Nessa stepped aside to let a family pass.

"I hope you don't mind if I stand here a bit. Your table has an unobstructed view of this side of the park. The gala is a big deal for this town. Extra policing and everything. They have a night guard, but this is the Met we're talking about."

The art gallery sat on the east side of the park. To

Rose, it looked safe. "I didn't think we had enough crime to warrant a night guard."

She saw something in her peripheral vision. An irregularity. The thing she watched out for as a quality manager. The one thing that stood out, shouldn't have been, and led to a failure.

By the corner, next to a kid's playhouse, stood a man in a navy suit and government-issued aviator sunglasses. Everyone else wore jeans, shorts, flip-flops, or cowboy boots. She squinted. It felt like he was looking right at her. She decided it must be the policewoman.

"It's a new thing," Nessa said, drawing her back to the conversation. "Just in the last year or so. Maybe three. With all these tourists come some undesirable characters as well. There's the security guard now."

She pointed down the row to a man in a yellow, short-sleeved polo shirt and a baseball cap. He looked vaguely familiar. Muscles bulged on his upper arms, and the shirt strained across a broad chest. As they watched, he straightened. The black-suited man approached, and they exchanged words. Even from a distance, Rose could see the stranger's angular jaw and close-cropped hair. He looked like a central casting version of a government agent. Sergeant Gomez tensed.

"That's all we need."

"What?" Rose asked, surprised that the young woman was so congenial.

"The guy wearing the dark shades must be a tourist. The other one, Brad Knight, the security guard I was telling you about, has some history. At least that's the rumor. He works at Olive Heaven during the day."

Ah, that was it. She'd seen him at her first meeting

the previous week. As the two women both watched, the discussion between the men grew heated. Brad shoved the guard with one arm, then backed up and walked away toward the art gallery. The policewoman's hand moved to her revolver.

A shaft of sunlight popped through the leaf cover and beat down on Rose's head like a hot iron. "Whew, I wish this heat would break."

Nessa's stance relaxed as Brad Knight disappeared into the gallery.

"I agree," she said. "With this heat comes crime. Things heat up and cool off with the weather."

Rose picked up her bottle of water and drank down the last half of it. The cold liquid felt good as it slid down her throat. Across the park, the guy in the suit seemed to glare at everyone around him, then stalked off and vanished around a corner. A whisper of dread filled Rose. Nothing bad happened in small towns. Right? Hadn't Gomez said as much during the ride-along?

The man in the suit hinted at a dangerous underpinning to the small town. Rose felt that sensation when the chase started, and she felt it at the last growers' meeting when the topic of vagrants came up. A break in the peace she sought, but also a familiar charge of excitement. Did the policewoman feel the same?

"Do you know anything about an old ranch off the San Anselmo exit? There've been reports of squatters in the outbuildings."

"I heard something about that. I'll check into it and let you know." Nessa pulled a notepad out and jotted down the information.

"That would be great," Rose said.

Nessa tucked the notepad away.

"It's an ongoing problem. Any empty space is a habitat for animals, insects, and people. Most of the unhoused live along the river. That's not good either; they start fires and get swept up when the river swells."

Down the walkway, a kid screamed the beginning notes of a tantrum. Nessa turned toward the sound and grimaced.

"That's my cue. Have a good day."

She strode quickly along the path towards the harried mother. It didn't seem like a police officer's job to handle crying kids, but that didn't stop the policewoman from helping the child and mom over to a picnic table away from the crowds.

A cluster of teens, shoving and pushing each other, came toward her table. One kid grabbed a handful of stickers and tossed them in the air. They danced like confetti in the breeze. If the stickers were all gone, she could go home. Then a dose of responsibility kicked in, and she yelled, "Hey!"

The kids started to take off. Out of nowhere, Brad Knight appeared, like a magical genie that popped up whenever you needed help. He towered over the table, Rose, the kids, and even the pop-up tent. Over 6'5". Mid-thirties with blond hair and slashes of sun-bleached eyebrows.

He held out a hand. "Stop!" The authority steeped in his voice brought them to a halt.

"Don't make me execute a citizen's arrest."

The boys turned toward him and stood still. Several stared at the ground.

"Pick up the lady's stickers and put them back where you found them."

Brad stood watch over them until everything was returned to her table.

"Okay. Now, beat it. If I see you do anything like this again, I'm reporting you to the police and your parents."

They fled like wild animals. Rose felt a flicker of envy. To feel fear and release, with so much abandon. She sighed. How long had it been since she experienced anything like that? When the miscreants had gone, Brad turned back to face her.

"Thank you," she said.

"They were just being kids," he said. "But they need to learn, and their parents aren't around to see the trouble they get in."

"Well, I appreciate it. My name is Rose."

"Brad Knight. I think I saw you at an Olive Growers meeting. I was there for my boss."

Rose nodded. "Yes, I remember seeing you, too. You saved the day for me today."

Praise seemed to disturb him. Some people didn't know how to deal with compliments. She understood because someone saying something nice about her made her wonder what they were after. He nodded and strode off.

A weathered man dressed in authentic-looking cowboy duds with scruffy, muddy boots walked by. Lines on his face mapped out canyons from his eyes to the corners of his mouth, illustrating days spent in the sun, working cattle. He smelled of harsh tobacco and whiskey.

Her feet still ached from her walk to the park from her house, six blocks away. Silly that she'd chosen this pair of canvas sneakers instead of the pretty red leather pair with good arch support, but she admitted to herself, they went perfectly with the white capris and nautical blue and white striped tee shirt she had chosen for her stint at the fair.

Did looking good matter that much? Well, there was the possibility that Frank Terroso might wander by. Tall and slim with grey flecks in his chestnut brown hair. He'd sat beside her during the last presentation at the Olive Growers meeting and brought her some sweet tea after the question-and-answer period. She couldn't drink it, preferring her Earl Grey unsweetened. Even milk, which many Brits liked, was an abomination to her.

She still felt the embarrassment of her fumbled words as she remembered their first encounter.

I haven't seen you here before. My name is Frank." His voice was deep, worn around the edges, but strong.

"I, um."

Being tongue-tied wasn't a familiar feeling for her. Through her job, she honed her public speaking skills and could present to a room full of top executives. Eventually, she introduced herself and offered her hand to shake. He took it with a bemused look in his eyes.

The sound of a throat clearing pulled her back from the memory.

"Ahem."

There he stood, as if summoned from her imagination. Tall and slim with grey flecks in his chestnut brown hair. He wore navy "dress" jeans and a checked shirt. Rolled-up sleeves revealed tanned skin and the hint of a tattoo. Was it a lover's name? She hoped not.

He smelled of Dior Sauvage, with notes of bergamot and pepper. The corner of his lip lifted in a semi-smile when his eyes met hers.

"Nice to see you again, Rose."

A flutter darted through her chest. Don't do that, an inner voice warned. Once burned was enough.

"And you as well, Frank."

He picked up a sticker and turned it over.

"I've got lots of these, but one more can't hurt, I suppose." He tucked it into a pocket.

"You're the first taker I've had today."

"Any chance I could talk you into a coffee?" he asked.

"I, uh." It wasn't a date. Not technically, but her heart pounded anyway.

Frank shifted from one foot to the other, and she realized she had been staring at him with her mouth slightly open. "Sure. I'm sure they wouldn't mind if I cut out a bit early."

"Well, since I'm on the board, I can say they definitely wouldn't mind."

The coffee shop had one corner with comfortable chairs, tables in the middle, and a counter along the windows where people sat with open laptops.

Frank set down a cup of coffee and sat across from Rose. Bergamot vapor from her Earl Grey made her think of her mother, who had loved afternoon with the Earl.

"I love the aroma of this brew. It makes me think of England. I've always wanted to go."

"It's never too late," Frank said. He mixed a small container of creamer into his cup.

"Oh, I don't know. First, it was because of work. Now, I guess it's just a lack of inertia. I might plan something, once I get settled here."

"Are you going to the gala tomorrow?" he asked.

The special showing of paintings from the New York Met dominated the local gossip. No one could miss all the signs posted in store windows. How on Earth had the local art gallery managed to snag the traveling exhibition? Of course, she planned to go. It was the closest to the artistic excitement of Los Angeles since moving.

"My neighbor and I are going. She's an artist, so I'm hoping she'll give me an audio tour."

Despite being a regular at the Getty, Rose wasn't familiar with many of the well-known painters.

"Well, that should certainly help. I'm not much for fine art, although I do help the gallery with fundraising. Having culture in town is important."

She surveyed his face for any sign of sarcasm but found none.

"You sound like an advert for the tourist board."

He leaned back in his chair. "I do a little consulting for them."

"What? You're everywhere! Philanthropist, consultant, grower, board member. What else is there?"

An inner voice warned, 'too good to be true.' She'd thought that of David, too, before he betrayed her with a young secretary and proceeded to badmouth and damage her credibility. Perhaps she should listen to that internal caution.

Frank crossed his arms. "Inventor. I have a few patents that have proved to be valuable."

"Oh my god, and I thought I was an overachiever."

His easy manner put her at ease, despite herself. This was a man she wanted to get to know better. With his technical background, he might understand her nerdy tendencies.

"Have you always lived in Paso Robles, or are you a transplant like me?"

He sipped his coffee.

"I grew up here, left for college and a few decades of working for someone else, then returned, started my own electronics company, and planted olives. Haven't left since."

The skin around his eyes crinkled when he smiled.

"Tell me about you. Recently arrived?"

"Unlike you, I was never the big boss, but I did stay in the corporate world longer. I moved up three months ago from LA." An unplanned retirement, she reflected, but didn't say.

"I'm making friends and finding my footing."

The sparkle in his eyes said he'd like to be one of those friends. Rose felt a flush of something burning her cheeks. Nerves? Embarrassment?

"It still feels weird to sit in a coffee shop in the middle of the day and not feel guilty."

He chuckled. "I remember that feeling. Give it time."

Rose sipped slowly but eventually ran out of tea.

"This has been fun. I should get going. Natalie and I—she's the neighbor I mentioned—we're getting our nails done for the gala. It was her idea."

Why was she justifying a manicure as if it were something frivolous? Better question—why was she letting him rattle her?

"You'll be the belle of the ball," Frank said and stood. "I've enjoyed this."

Rose glanced again at the thin lines of the tattoo that peeked out. Please, let it not be a woman's name.

He held the door for her as they left. Generally, she

didn't like men to do chivalrous acts, but this felt different. A furnace blast of heat assaulted her as she passed through the door. As Frank strode off in the opposite direction, her first thought was that she couldn't wait to share this with Natalie. Her first true friend. A treasure she would do anything to protect.

Across in the park, craft marketers packed up their products and folded tablecloths. Officer Nessa had vanished, but the man in the dark sunglasses leaned against a light standard at the northeast corner, watching the crowds leave. She would have to pass him on her way to where she'd parked her car. Rose turned to stop Frank, but he'd turned a corner down Park Street. She drew her shoulders back and straightened her back.

It was hard not to stare as she grew closer. She felt his glare, though the dark glasses hid his eyes. Ignore him, she told herself. At the intersection, she stopped to wait for the traffic to stop. He left his post and stood beside her, a move that amped her heart rate up. Thoughts of a safe town seemed ludicrous now; danger was everywhere.

He crossed at the same time and followed her to her car, parked in front of the art gallery. A tall man, dressed in denim pants and a jacket so dark they must be new, walked with long strides towards the entrance. His dark hair was slicked back into a ponytail, and he wore wrap-around sunglasses.

The stalker, as Rose had come to think of him, pivoted and ducked into a winery. Funny, she hadn't thought he'd be the wine lover type. At the art gallery entrance, Ponytail glanced from side to side, as if checking to see if he was being followed, before wrenching the door open and disappearing inside. It all looked like something out of a made-for-TV mystery. Or if would have if she hadn't felt a pall of fear, both in herself and in both men.

In her car, Rose cried out when she touched the sizzling hot steering wheel. She was gingerly buckling her seat belt when the gallery door swung open, hitting the glass window behind it with a crash that should have shattered it. The dark-haired man stormed out, looking like he might kill someone.

Chapter 3 Rose

~

*Tempranillo A Spanish grape cultivar with medium to full body and
notes of cherry, fig and tobacco*

Friday, October 7, 7:15 PM

Sandwiched between a bar and a dress shop, the Galería
de Arte was bright and busy. Art from local artists filled
the large front windows. Lights glowed from within, a mix
of old school hanging barn lights and articulated desk lamps
hung from the walls to highlight works. It welcomed all in
without pretension.

Rose held the door open for her companion, who
swept into the lobby of the Galería de Arte as if she owned
the place. Natalie gave off the aura of someone who had
been everywhere, done everything, and elected to live in a
small town anyway. Rose envied her grace and wished she
could be as comfortable in her body.

The gallery had originally been an auto parts store.
Up lights illuminated the silver finish of insulation visible in
the ceiling, along with all the HVAC ducts and metal structure reminiscent of its former life. Polished concrete floors
still showed marks where service bays once changed oil and
fixed transmissions. This was a building transformed from
one purpose to another. The industrial aesthetic boldly
moved into the future and highlighted the colorful artwork.
Pottery sat perched on pedestals between galleries. A piano

and cello played a Serenade by Franz Schubert in the corner, though with everyone talking, it was hard to hear.

Taking a glass from the table at the entrance, Rose inhaled the leather and blackberry scent of the wine. Then she swirled it, sipped, savored, and slowly swallowed. Smooth. Velvet.

"I haven't been out to this winery yet," she said, making a mental note to add it to her list.

Natalie stood by her side, resplendent in a pale lavender pantsuit that complemented her long silver hair and golden skin. Layers of mascara created black lashes around sharp, seawater-colored eyes. An upturned nose and rosebud lips gave her the impression of an imp. Next to her, Rose felt frumpy and old. Her nose tended to hook increasingly as she aged, and her once honey-brown hair faded to a steely gray and white. A trip to the hair salon could fix that. The rest she lived with.

Natalie sipped her wine and nodded. "It is good, but with so many vineyards and tasting rooms, there's no hope of visiting them all."

"True, but I intend to give it a go." Rose chose a blue, floor-length skirt, a silk top, and two-inch, black-satin, St. Johns that pinched her toes.

"Good luck with that!" Natalie said and raised her glass in a toast to what Rose realized was an improbable goal. She probably thinks I'm a fool, Rose thought, for moving to this small town. In the middle of the night, Rose agreed with her. But staying in LA wasn't an option. Likewise, continuing at the company she'd given so much of her career to wasn't viable. Not after David's betrayal. It was time to put it all behind her.

"All this art is amazing," Rose said as they entered a

room with work from local artists. "Why don't I see your art in here?"

Natalie waved her hand in a dismissive gesture. "You're kind to say so. It's been a while since I've done anything serious. Any paint I have now came from my penchant for repainting the walls in my house. I dabble now and then, copying famous paintings for the fun of it."

A uniformed man approached them. She recognized Brad Knight. He may not be the law, but he sounded authoritative to those kids. His security guard uniform stretched across his broad chest; the buttons strained to keep the shirt closed.

"Evening, ladies. You look lovely." His booming voice cut through the loud hum. Brad turned to Rose. "No more trouble at the craft market, I hope."

"No. All was peaceful. Thank you again for your help."

"Trouble?" Natalie asked. Before Rose could explain, a small woman with blond highlights strode over in a teal-colored, tailored suit. Brad squirmed and waved a quick goodbye before dashing off. Natalie leaned in to whisper to Rose.

As the woman approached, Natalie greeted her warmly.

"Evangeline, please meet my friend Rose. Evangeline is the owner of the gallery."

The flamboyant owner flashed a broad, artificially white smile. Bangle bracelets jingled on her wrist. Rose reached out to shake hands, her first instinct when meeting someone new.

"It's nice to meet you."

Evangeline looked at the offered hand, and then,

ignoring it, took Natalie's and patted it. "Natalie is our best, hardest-working employee. She almost runs the place herself. Manages all the ins and outs."

She displayed her array of arctic teeth again, and Rose wondered how much whitener it took to achieve the effect.

A loud laugh came from a group of patrons gathered in the lobby, and Evangeline glanced over.

"Enjoy the show," she said and turned to greet a man in a tuxedo and a woman in a fox stole.

"She's very nice," Natalie said. "And always busy. Now tell me about what happened in the park. What trouble?"

Rose went to take a sip of wine and found the glass empty. Had she drunk it all down? With meeting Evangeline and seeing Brad, could she have been so distracted that she didn't remember the taste, or even the action of lifting her glass to her lips? She steered them to a table where they could get another drink. She remembered the kids tossing her Olive Growers stickers in the air.

"Nothing. Some kids having a bit of fun at my expense. Brad stepped in and handled it."

"That sounds like him," Natalie said.

"He seems like a gentleman," Rose said, hoping that would flush out any relationship between Natalie and Brad. Were they co-workers? Or was there more to it? But Natalie just dipped her head in agreement. Rose considered her new friend for a moment. Should she ask the follow-up questions, keep asking *why* until the root cause of the problem becomes clear?

Her thoughts drifted to a pivotal meeting where she had done that very thing and rankled a few of the higher-ups whose negligence turned out to be the reason the wrong parts ended up in the final units. It was far easier to interrogate a process than pepper people with questions. It wouldn't help her win friends.

Rose didn't have friends. Work associates, yes, but those disappeared when frequent contact ceased. She still exchanged holiday cards with some childhood acquaintances, but didn't count them as real friends. Grilling someone she had met a month ago was probably not the best approach, and she filed it away in her memory.

Wineglasses in hand, a nice Tempranillo, they moved to the second display room on the left. A sign on an easel at the entrance announced the collection.

Limited Showing - Early 20th Century American Impressionists from the Emmet Bathory Collection.
Courtesy of the New York Metropolitan Museum of Art.

Brochures on a table nearby described all the pieces. Rose glanced through the glossy flier and smelled the fresh varnish on the heavyweight paper. She felt the slick surface under her fingertips.

"Not that this isn't a local treasure, but how do you suppose they snagged an exhibit from the Met?"

Natalie's back stiffened as if Rose's question offended all artists in the community.

"We didn't *snag* it."

Without intending, Rose hit a nerve. "Do you have any paintings in the gallery?" she asked.

She knew the answer.

No.

During their first get-together over wine and pizza,

Natalie hinted that she avoided showing her pieces at the gallery. But Natalie surprised her once today. What more was buried?

"No, I um, nothing's ready," Natalie said without making eye contact.

Due to the special showing, the gallery moved much of the artwork by local artists to a back room. Still, what was left didn't compare to the pieces in Natalie's living room that Rose saw when she visited the only time she'd been in her friend's home. Due to the large front porch on Rose's house, Natalie came to her, as she had on the first day Rose moved in, carrying a wine bottle and a plate of cookies, dressed in flowing gossamer clothing, Natalie welcomed her to the neighborhood like an angel of hospitality.

Natalie took a sip of wine and then cleared her throat. "I work part-time, handling the technical stuff."

"Technical stuff?" Rose stopped and turned her gaze back at Natalie. She knew her friend spent her days here, but not much about what she did.

"Computers mostly. And I help with their security systems. The owner is hopeless with anything plugged into the wall."

As an engineer, Rose knew what it was like to deal with tech-averse people.

"You've never mentioned what you do. "

"Like you, I had a life before." Natalie turned to the next painting.

Part of that life before, Rose knew, involved a disastrous marriage.

Natalie closed her eyes and took a few breaths. "Anyway, you asked how the show came to Paso Robles. Emmet Bathory's daughter arranged it. All these works came from her father's collection, which he donated to the Met when he died. She told me it was the only way to see the paintings since the Met has locked them up in their overflow storage."

Her hand trailed along the bottom of the frame, hovering lovingly, centimeters from the wood. It felt like an intimate moment between a woman and an artwork.

The name Emmet Bathory was familiar. Her boss handed out the financier's books as mandatory reading, hoping his financial prowess would change how they ran their business. It hadn't, fortunately, because like all such management philosophies, they were useful only to the author's book sales. One company's ideas of best practices weren't always the best approach for others. In Rose's case, the actions resulted in the loss of good people through a mandatory 10% purge.

"He lived in Paso Robles," Natalie said, "Or at least had a house and olive ranch near town. Gave a lot of money to the art community."

That surprised Rose, though she supposed he had enough money that giving some away benefited his tax bill. Don't be cynical, she admonished herself.

At each canvas, Natalie provided an artistic commentary, noting the brushwork and color palette and explaining what all that meant. They stopped at a landscape painted in dusty blues and greens. Even the custom frame reflected the stormy skies, with swirls of federal blue and white paint. Mountains dominated the skyline, and a smattering of oak trees gathered in the near foreground. The title read *Gray Day, Montrose Valley*; the author's scrawl in the corner - *Nell Walker Warner*.

"Lovely," Natalie sighed. "I'd kill to have this one

hanging in my house." She stepped back to take in more of the painting. "Look at the deep hues and palette knife strokes. So forceful. I can't decide what the artist was trying to say."

The scene was a rural, empty landscape. Montrose was a bustling city, but not when this was painted. Whether brush strokes or color choice played any part in Rose's lack of appreciation for the piece was hard to tell. It made her feel lonely. Isolated.

"How about 'I have a lot of blue paint to use up before it goes bad'?"

Natalie rolled her eyes. "I can see you are going to require a lot of training."

Also viewing the painting was a woman the same height as Rose with long, rich black hair gathered in a ponytail at her nape. She wore a simple but elegant shift in midnight black with matching flats. She carried a gold-chained Gucci bag with abstract owls stamped into the leather.

Natalie leaned in and whispered in Rose's ear. "That's Liz Bathory."

Clad in a dress that clearly didn't come off a rack in any of the stores Rose shopped in, the woman looked like a rich financier's daughter. Rose recognized her outfit from a shop window on a business trip to Paris earlier in the year. It cost thousands of dollars. Strange to see something so haute couture in Paso Robles.

Over the voices and music, they could hear Liz sigh. A long, protracted exhalation of air that contained a world of meaning that sounded sad. Yet, because it had so much energy behind it to be heard, Rose wondered if it was intended to garner a response.

Unable to hold back, she leaned toward the woman. "Are you all right?" she asked.

The woman held a tissue to her nose.

"This used to hang in our house. I'd love to have it, but my father's will..." A tear descended over flawless foundation and blush. She sniffed and dabbed the corners of her eyes.

Penciled eyebrows arched over in a perfect semicircle and led to a longish nose and stern, thin lips coated with lipstick. And what mascara was she using? It held up to waterworks. Rose took another look at the piece, searching for something that would generate such an emotional response.

To her, it was merely a painting. It paled in comparison to the others in the collection. This must be the most insignificant piece, and yet, Ms. Bathory, daughter of the man who bequeathed the art to the Met, seemed to find this one the most important.

"Good evening, art lovers," thundered a male voice.

Two people joined their little assemblage around *Gray Day*. The man's face was long and angular, with black, close-cropped hair, and slashes of eyebrows glowered over penetrating blue eyes. He wore a black suit, white shirt, and black tie.

His physique reminded her of an army action doll, all broad and rippled across the shoulders with the waist nipped into slender hips.

This guy clearly spent too much time in a narcissistic soup of sweat. His shoes shone like they'd been coated with an oil slick. Despite all that, she had to admit he looked good. Dangerous but desirable.

In contrast, the young woman stood five-nine, with loose curls of brown hair that fell to her shoulders. About thirty years old, with irises the same crisp, sky-blue color as Rose's mom's.

Funny that thoughts of her kept coming up. Rose decided that the gala might be the sort of event Mom would have loved, and that was why she was so top of mind.

Like the man, the woman looked like she spent time in a gym, though Rose gave her a pass. Female unity and all that. Overall, she looked friendly and outgoing. Someone Rose could like as a friend, despite the age difference.

"Rose, this is our new neighbor. Stella, isn't it?" Natalie stuck out her hand to shake. Stella grabbed Nat's fingers with vigor.

That's why she recognized her. The moving van that had parked at the house kitty-corner from hers a few weeks ago. Stella directed the two college kids who carted furniture into the old Victorian.

"Nice to meet you. Welcome to the neighborhood. I'm new too."

Stella took Rose's hand with both of hers. They were warm and soft. "The pleasure is all mine." She spoke with a refined British accent. Little smile lines crinkled as she looked at Rose. Her smile felt warm. Sincere. With a hint of curiosity.

"Uh hem," her companion said in a fake sounding clearing of his throat. Stella flinched.

"Oh, pardon me! This is Slade Bolton. He lives across the street from me."

She pointed to Rose. "From all of us, I guess. We met a few weeks ago."

Slade Bolton stepped forward and gripped Rose's hand with a strong, authoritative handshake. She pulled her fingers away, stretching them to get blood flowing again. A handshake like that sent a message:

I'm bigger than you, so don't mess with me. I'm stronger than you, so don't test me.

Now, what warning was this man sending so soon after meeting her? She forced a smile.

He placed a possessive hand on Stella's lower back. Liz Bathory turned enough to see him. Her stern eyes flitted from Slade to Stella to Rose before she faced forward again, lifted the flap of her handbag, and pulled out another tissue. Rose could see the heiress's shoulders rise and fall twice as she dabbed tears from her eyes before turning to walk on. Rose felt sorry for her. The heiress probably lived her life in the public eye, and yet when she wanted a bit of privacy to mourn the loss of something she loved, she had an audience.

Something unspoken happened between Slade and the heiress. Almost as if they despised each other. Rose could see his eyes locked on Ms. Bathory's disappearing form as she blended into the crowd. His ears reddened at the tips. When Liz turned a corner, with one last glance back at their little group, a cryptic smile on her lips, he stiffened and then swiveled to Stella.

"Let's grab a cocktail at the place down the street."

Stella looked surprised but agreed. "I suppose this all will be here for a bit. I can come back when it's less crowded."

"For a month," Natalie said. "It's definitely more impressive when you have the paintings to yourself."

Turning to leave, Slade took Stella's hand and, in

doing so, bumped into Natalie. Her purse fell to the floor. A makeup compact, her security badge, house keys, and lipstick tumbled to the floor along with the fringed leather bag. He swooped down to pick up the contents.

"Sorry; that was clumsy of me." He scooped the items up and slipped them inside before he snapped the purse shut and handed it back to her. She murmured an embarrassed thank you.

As they stepped out into the warm night air, Natalie hitched the purse strap higher on her shoulder.

"That was weird. Not sure about him, but she seems nice."

Rose thought the same thing. Her mind returned to whatever unsaid message passed between Liz Bathory and Slade Bolton. What was their connection?

They wandered the rest of the exhibits without saying much. Natalie's enthusiasm for the artwork seemed to have waned.

Rose saw Frank enter a smaller, side gallery with a gorgeous woman. Willowy, with long blond hair and wearing a skin-tight red dress. A tang of jealousy flushed through her. Ridiculous. All he did was ask her for coffee. Not an official date. Anyway, a romantic relationship would only get in the way of getting her life settled down. A silver-haired man came up behind him and the woman. Frank backed up a step, and the man placed his hand possessively on the woman's lower back. Relief washed over Rose. Which annoyed her. Emotions made things difficult. She couldn't afford difficult right now.

The press of people had grown too great for them to spend much time on each canvas. After an hour, Rose's ears rang from the din of music and voices.

"It's time to go," she almost yelled in Natalie's ear.

Rose limped as they walked to her Subaru. The blasted high heels pinched her toes, and she couldn't wait to get them off. A big glass of wine would help, too. Who didn't relax with a glass of Chardonnay?

Restaurant goers passed by laughing and taking selfies. Natalie side-stepped them with the grace of a dancer.

"I can't get that painting out of my mind. The brooding one."

Yes. That painting stuck in Rose's mind, too. "Why do you suppose Liz Bathory hung around that particular one? It wasn't on par with the others in the collection and couldn't have been worth much."

Once they reached the car, Natalie sat down and pulled her purple pumps off, wiggling her toes. "What I want to know is whether the artist was trying to hint at bad things to come, or was she simply painting plein air on a stormy day?"

What was it about artists that they looked for deep meaning in everything? She saw it as a painting that captured a mountain immediately before, or after, a storm. Often, a storm is just a good soaking. But sometimes, she thought as she put the car in reverse, sometimes, those angry clouds indicated headwinds aimed right at you. Which would it be?

Chapter 4 Liz

~

Cabernet Sauvignon – The world's most popular red grape was formed from a natural cross between Cabernet Franc and Sauvignon Blanc. It is known for its rich flavor and powerful tannins.

Friday, October 7, 8:04 PM

Liz Bathory sat in deep shade in the corner of Pappy MacGregor's sidewalk patio, sipping a deep red Cabernet Sauvignon. The glow from the tree lights in the park didn't reach that far, nor did the dim lights from the bar's interior. The watch on her wrist buzzed, announcing a text. The final stage of an operation planned over five years ago was in motion.

The men she hired, gang members from Fresno who sought revenge against Brad Knight, weren't her typical approach. They made her uncomfortable, and yet, they were also willing to do the work that needed to be done and were prepared to do it free of charge. Now she needed everything to unfold as she had envisioned. She wanted that painting and would have it at the expense of everyone and everything else in her life.

She would fulfil her grandfather's wish and her mother's wish. Hadn't Grandfather Grossman stated it in his will? Hadn't Mother?

Only her father stood in her way, and now that he was dead, she'd have it her way. It meant disappearing once the job was done, but that was a sacrifice she was willing to make. *Gray Day, Montrose Valley* would be hers. And the secret it held would be safe as well.

She pulled a book out of her capacious handbag and set it on the table.

"Everything okay here? Did you want to order any food?" asked the waitress dressed as a Scottish wench.

"I'm fine," Liz replied, hoping the woman would leave her alone.

"I'll get you a candle so you can see that book," the waitress said and leaned over to another table to grab one no one was using.

"I'm fine," Liz said again, wondering how many times she needed to say it before the woman left.

"Okay, well, let me know if you need anything." She finally left. Liz laid her hand on the worn, smooth cover and tried to imagine the spirits of her grandfather and mother emanating from within. Seeing the words wasn't necessary. They had been memorized five years ago when the diary fell into her hands, quite unexpectedly. It was the last secret her father kept from her. His death proved to be the last barrier to the family legacy. The bastard didn't leave her his fortune, but it filled her with immense joy that dear old Daddy never understood the implications of the words her grandfather captured in the book. But she did. Maybe because she actually read the thing, and she knew as she finished the last page, that her father had never bothered.

Two women walked past, not five feet from her. The one with frizzy hair who had helped set up the showing spoke.

"I can't get that one painting out of my mind. The brooding one."

Liz knew exactly which canvas she meant. Her painting. Well, it would be. Soon.

"Why do you suppose Liz Bathory spent so much time on that particular one? It wasn't on par with the others in the collection and couldn't have been worth much," said her companion. Liz remembered that the tiny woman had asked her if she was alright when she was crying. A mostly staged waterworks, to make her seem emotional and weak, though she'd been strangely moved to see *Gray Day* hanging in the small art gallery. She'd only ever seen it hanging in her mother's sitting room.

The women moved on to a small silver sedan, climbed in, and drove off. Had she made a mistake creating a situation where these two, and possibly more, remembered her actions? No, she reminded herself. She never did anything without a reason, and the reasoning was sound.

Reasonable doubt.

A loud, drunk giggle announced a couple coming up the alley and onto the sidewalk. Liz shrank back a few inches to ensure her face was hidden.

Lights strung along a railing separating the bar area from the sidewalk illuminated their faces. Slade and that flighty thing he'd chosen as his cover. She knew his frame well. Had lived with it for the last five years. Seeing him with another woman did not affect her. Should it? Perhaps, but then their relationship had always been, for her at least, a business arrangement.

In fact, all her affairs, dalliances, and even family connections were financially driven. The only person in her life who meant anything to her was herself.

If he did his job right, he could have all the floozies he wanted. And she would have what she wanted. A few more days and she'd be free.

Chapter 5 Thief

~

Tannins - Naturally occurring polyphenols found in grape skins, seeds, and stems that create a drying, astringent sensation in wine similar to strong black tea.

Saturday, October 8, 3:07 AM

God, he hated rubber gloves. Despised how they made his hands sweat after a few minutes. They were a vital tool, though, if stealing things was part of your job. Avocation, really, not his vocation. The gloves snapped at his wrists as he put them on. The stolen key card slid into the slot on the security door in the rear alley, and the lock clicked softly. Now the real operation began.

They had it planned, down to the minute—the second, in some cases. Talked through the contingencies. This will not go like the botched job in Fresno. Lucky for them, the cop who investigated was willing to take money to say he couldn't solve the case. It was weird that he saw the same guy in the park today.

He wasn't worried, though. Everything was planned.

Dressed all in black, he slipped into the gallery. Half the overhead lights remained on, while none of the individual side galleries were lit, giving the place a moody, film noir look.

Folded tables leaned against a wall in the lobby.

Several boxes of empty wine bottles were piled against the reception kiosk. He crouched at the corner of the service area, out of view of security cameras, and pulled night-vision goggles out of my backpack. Overkill? Maybe..

The minute he stepped around into the main lobby of the place, the security guard came out of a side gallery and saw him.

Shit—this wasn't supposed to happen. Not that he saw him, but that there was a guard at all. The "conversation" in the park earlier in the day should have been enough for Brad Knight to call in sick. This was one contingency they hadn't discussed.

"Hey," Brad called out. His hand moved to the flashlight hanging at his waist. "We're closed."

Did he seriously think that pathetic torch was a deterrent? A gun would have been a better choice.

Easing the goggles behind his back, the thief stepped forward. Benches lined the center of the main area, along with stands displaying sculptures made of junk you'd find in a garage. Not his garage. He didn't have one. But someone's.

Should have used a balaclava, another item he loathed. The material snagged on his chin.

"So, I guess the money wasn't enough? What's your price?"

The painting he wanted was in the first gallery on the right. He moved toward it, staying out from under the few lights that glowed down from the high, industrial ceiling. This pushed Brad further toward the front of the room, further into darkness, causing him to squint.

"I told you, I'm clean." His hand grabbed the long, heavy flashlight.

The thief flinched and dropped the goggles. Wincing when the precious equipment smacked the floor. Damn. If those were broken, there would be hell to pay. Paperwork and explanations. Now he'd have to hurt Brad. No matter how hard he tried, someone always got hurt.

Brad's right hand finally found the flashlight and rested on the top end. That really did hurt when it made contact. Memories of bruises made Slade ease his shoulders down. Relax, he told himself, as he strolled further into the gallery.

"We didn't have a proper chat in the park. How have you been? I'm just checking up on things. This show is a big deal." He reached the wall with the empties and picked up a sparkling wine bottle.

"The winery didn't pick these up yet?" The weight felt heavy. It would do. Next time, they'll add a truncheon to the equipment list. If there is a next time. The relationship wasn't going anywhere, and he'd been thinking lately that their luck couldn't hold forever. Best to get out now, before it went south. Split up and…that's where his plan always stops. And what?

The winery name didn't sound familiar, but it didn't matter. What mattered was that it had been a sparkling wine, with a heavy glass bottle designed to withstand internal pressure. He tossed it from hand to hand, feeling the heft, then grasped it by the neck and let it hang down by his leg.

Brad's eyes followed it. "They'll stop by tomorrow to get them. Please put that one back in the box."

His right hand still rested on the flashlight, as if that might scare me off.

"Dude, you've got to go now. We're closed. Employees only."

De-escalation techniques. Standard cop stuff. Not gonna work, buddy. Slade could smell Brad's sweat. Acrid with fear.

"Now, Brad. That isn't any way to talk to a friend."

A soft click came from the rear of the gallery. That would be his partner.

Brad's left hand seemed to be hunting for a phantom revolver.

"Look, I'm not involved in that shit anymore." His voice came out husky, pleading. "Come on, man, you don't want to do this."

He made the mistake of turning to look at the unlit back of the gallery. In that fraction of a second, the thief swung the bottle into Brad's temple with a solid thwack. His body crumpled to the polished concrete floor. With a dull thud, his head landed.

His partner came up beside him, clad in black, head to toe, and wearing the balaclava he should have worn. With a sigh of regret, he stashed the bottle in the backpack and flexed his cramped fingers. Perhaps the hit had been a bit too hard.

His partner tapped their watch and nodded toward the exhibit.

They crept into the side gallery, which contained the special Met show, and lifted a painting off the wall. Just the one. That's what this whole thing was about. As they passed the security guard, he heard a soft pop and turned to see a silencer at the end of a Glock 17.

Blood seeped onto the floor in a halo around Brad's head. A dark circle sat centered on his forehead. His partner slid the Glock into a holster hidden under a black vest.

"What'd you do that for?" he asked. The guard hadn't moved since the wine bottle hit. Quite sure he was already dead.

"He saw your face. He knows who you are."

"We'll talk about this later," the thief said. The killing unsettled him. Was he getting soft?

Their gaze drifted up to the security camera in the corner. A silent sentry recording everything. That was next. Except for the guard, everything was going according to plan.

Chapter 6 Rose

~

Nebbiolo – An Italian red grape known for delicate aromas, strong tannins, and the flavors of cherry, rose, leather, and anise.

Saturday, October 8, 3:45 AM

Rose bolted upright in her bed, heart pounding. Her work nightmare dissolved into shadows. Breathe. That's all behind you. Mantras she used to shut memories out.

Even after three months, the room looked foreign. The dresser was hers, and the comfortable chair by the window was for reading all the books stacked beside it. And next to that, a woven basket containing skeins of alpaca wool and knitting needles. She had big plans to learn how to knit a sweater.

She got up and put on a light robe. After a trip to the bathroom, she stared out the window that overlooked the street. Nothing moved below. The winds that kicked up in the evening as the sun went down had ceased hours ago. A sliver of moonlight through the trees created silent silhouettes. If the artist who painted *Gray Day, Montrose Valley*, tackled this view, it would evoke a similar feeling. Loneliness. Isolation.

What had Rose been thinking, coming here? That by moving away, the anxiety would disappear? Not follow her? That friends would materialize out of thin air?

Even as a child, she didn't have many friends. It

usually took her so long to develop a connection with someone that by the time she did, it was time to start a new school, or later, a new job. It became too painful. As a result, she stopped trying. She was barely able to get a full breath into her lungs. Please don't let that happen here, she whispered to the night, before moving down the hall into another room. Another window.

Why is it that when you can't sleep, all the bad decisions you've made in your life come to haunt you? That evening's remembrances were of a friendship that turned romantic, before exploding into a career-ending mess. In hindsight, choosing to date someone she worked with proved why all the columns advised against it. But they'd been together for so long, and helped one another advance, that she thought they were unbreakable. Nothing is.

After that, getting as far away from Los Angeles seemed like the right thing to do. Less traffic. Peaceful nights. Find somewhere to reflect. And start over. Perhaps, she would have success with female friendships. None of the romantic entanglement problems, though she supposed jealousy could be a problem. Despite all that, she admitted to herself, Natalie seemed like the type of friend she'd dreamed of. Though in three months, she had one friend. What was wrong with her?

Something moved on the sidewalk. Two cats faced off in the street, tails bristling with feline fury. They circled each other with loud hisses. She crept back from the window, left the bedroom, and walked the whole upper floor of the house, her footsteps a whisper on the Berber carpet.

From the south windows in the guest room, she had a clear view of Natalie's house next door. The hulk of her neighbor's midnight-blue hatchback was parked on the driveway, blocking the garage door. The sight of the home eased the tension in her chest. A friend. Her new life was going to be full of friends.

Something moved. She'd seen it with her peripheral vision, but when she looked directly, nothing was there. Another cat, perhaps, coming to join the struggle for territory. It happened again. A shady, vertical pattern resolved into the figure of a man that crossed the street from Natalie's side and vanished into the shadows. She moved to another window. It didn't help; the figure disappeared, leaving her wondering if she'd imagined the whole scene.

A light flipped on in the house directly opposite hers, a fellow insomniac. A silhouette appeared in the window, and the light went out.

The night played tricks with the eye, but her gut told her it was Slade Bolton.

Hadn't Stella said he lived across the street from her? That meant he lived across from Rose, too.

Could the figure crossing the street have been Bolton?

She dismissed that thought as soon as it formed. Any thought that appeared during these midnight strolls didn't bear much reflection. Her muddled mind ranged from topic to topic, usually focused on some error she felt she'd made during the day. Or all the errors she'd made in her life.

Twelfth Street came to a dead end at Chestnut, with Rose's and Natalie's houses on the west side, Stella and Slade Bolton on the east. While Rose's house was a two-story, restored turn-of-the-century California rustic, and Nat's a one-story ranch, sat a relic of the town's early days—an authentic Victorian.

The style of the house both fit and contrasted with the British woman who now rented it.

Stella Richardson. The young woman was on the arm of the mysterious Slade Bolton at the gala. Perhaps he was going home from Stella's and had crossed the wrong street, headed to Natalie's, then corrected to head back to his own house. It was plausible. He was new to the neighborhood and could have gotten twisted around.

She chided herself for being suspicious. It must be the night spirits that spoke in her mind, dug up demons and anxieties.

Sleep was still fifty minutes away, at least. Rose returned to her bedroom and lay back down. While those minutes were generally filled with regrets and what-ifs, tonight she couldn't shake the image of the sinister figure crossing the street.

She glanced over to check that the gun was still on her side table.

Chapter 7 Natalie

~

Barbera – An Italian grape that produces deeply colored wines with low tannins and high acidity, often tasting of cherry and plum. Goes perfectly with pizza.

Saturday, October 8, 8:00 AM

Mornings were Natalie's favorite time of day. Birds chirped in the trees and fluttered around the feeders she'd hung around the patio. The street lay quietly in the pre-work or school rush. This particular morning, the air started cool, but she knew it would warm up soon enough. Dappled morning light danced on the patio. In her kitchen, she dumped a handful of herbs and flowers from her garden into her China cup, added water heated to 180 degrees Fahrenheit, and steeped the leaves for three and one-half minutes.

Some people used commercial teabags, but she couldn't imagine doing that. Homemade herbal infusion from her garden filled her with peace.

Out at the round wrought iron table nestled in a corner of the back patio, she sank into a chair, craving a few minutes of peace before the day started.

Evangeline expected her at the art gallery to go over the results of the first night of the Met art show. Crowds brought in for the exhibition will have bought artwork from local artists as well. After reviewing the security video, they would discuss tweaks to the camera positions to ensure they had covered everything.

Shadows still covered the side of the garage work-shop that opened to the back. No one knew she'd started taking a new art class. Online, but still, real. The instructor encouraged them to analyze the masters, so she printed copies of classic paintings and scrutinized them, mimicking the brush techniques and colors. Through them, she worked to hone her creative voice.

A terra-cotta flowerpot lay broken on the ground near the door to the garage. Soil spilled out over the wilted basil plant.

She dashed over to save the dying herb. Embedded in the mess, she saw a heel-shaped footprint. Bigger than any shoe she owned. Pedro, the gardener, wouldn't leave a mess like this. Flickers of her dream came back. The sense of an intruder. Maybe it wasn't a dream.

It was times like this that she wished Paul was still alive. Still her husband. Fortunately, that thought didn't come often and she could sustain her admittedly withered anger toward him.

Inside the garage, she flipped on the overhead lights. Tubes of paint were piled on the worktable fashioned out of sawhorses and a battered door. Her nose picked up the pungent smell of turpentine and paint thinner. Mason jars of the brushes she loved to use sat on the table.

Against the furthest wall, used canvases leaned against one another, creating a colorful hill town of stacked paintings, from the major disasters she never finished to decent replicas. Nothing looked out of place. Only a scuff of dirt on the sisal rug at the threshold. Had she done that?

Was anything out of place? One shelf held auto-related paraphernalia: windshield washer solution, motor oil, bug, and tar remover. Her trusty ladder leaned in the corner: useful for picking fruit from the citrus trees. Buckets, rakes, a box of ripped towels, and T-shirts to use as rags. Everything that should have been there was present and accounted for.

She pulled her cell phone out of her back pocket and dialed Rose.

"Can you come over?"

"I'm walking home now. Meet you in five minutes." It didn't take long for her neighbor to arrive. Rose's cheeks were flushed, and a damp circle covered the back of her shirt when she arrived.

"What's up?"

"I want you to see something. Maybe I'm being silly, but I had this dream…" She dragged Rose over to the back of the garage and pointed to the pot.

"I had a break-in last night. The garage. At least, that's what it looks like."

Rose tilted her head to the side to indicate she wanted more information. Natalie flushed.

"Hearing it out loud, it does sound daft, but I had this dream that someone broke into the house, and then I came out and found this."

Rose bent down to inspect the mess. "I heard a cat out last night making a ruckus. Could he have knocked it over?"

"I thought of that," Natalie said. "But a cat didn't make that mark. And no, before you ask, it isn't any of my shoes."

Rose got up. "I did see something odd last night. Around 2:00 AM. A man crossed the street from near your house and went into Slade Bolton's house."

"The guy we met last night?"

"Yes. Stella's boyfriend."

"Why would he be over here?" Natalie didn't like the implication.

"I guessed that he got lost, came out of her house, and turned the wrong way."

That could happen. There wasn't any other reason Slade Bolton would come to her house in the middle of the night.

"Should you call the police?" Rose asked, remembering her ride-along and the few stops they had at businesses worried about break-ins before the car chase.

"Nothing's missing. I checked the garage. Looks the same mess it always is." She smiled sheepishly. "It must have been the gardener. I'll have a word with him next week. And just to be sure, I'll change all the locks."

Rose jiggled the door handle.

"Let's check it together. Sometimes another set of eyes helps. You might be in some type of shock."

"NO!" Natalie moved to block Rose from entering. "I'm sure nothing's been taken."

Rose stepped back and looked at her neighbor. Natalie smiled and directed her to the patio.

"Want some tea?"

She looked back at the garage door as they walked. When the time was right, she would show her new friends the paintings, trusting that they would understand what she was trying to achieve. When she was ready.

For now, though. Only she would go into her studio. When they reached the back door into the kitchen, Rose massaged her neck and looked toward the garage.

"I don't like having something like this happen so

close to home. Though it might be the incentive I need to do something I've thought about for years."

"I'll bite," Natalie said as she filled the teapot.

Rose grinned. "I've always wanted a dog."

October was a petulant month in Paso Robles. Hot one day, temperate the next, and always the chance of a downpour. Today was warm, high eighties, but wispy clouds stretched like a lattice across the sky. Natalie reached the gallery at 10:30 AM after the calming five-block walk. The broken flowerpot seemed insignificant now. She'd been silly to overreact. Outside the entrance, she searched the inside of her purse for the security badge. It lived in a pocket and only came out when she used it on this door or the back one. Her fingers moved among keys, a makeup bag, pens, and pencils. No key card.

"Excuse me, ma'am," a police officer said.

She looked up and blinked. The cop moved to block her path. His brass nameplate read Gonzales.

Peering around him, she saw police tape across the room that held the Met exhibits and the bold word FO-RENSICS on the uniforms worn by people at the back of the gallery. They were gathered around something she couldn't see. A niggle of fear crept up her spine. He moved to block her view.

"You can't come in. The gallery is off limits."

"What's going on?"

"Move on, please." His hard-edged voice alarmed her. The local police department helped set up the security. She thought they had established a decent working relationship. Natalie shook her head.

"No, no. I work here, I have things I need to do."

He didn't move out of her way. Instead, he folded his arms across his chest in a move that made him look even more intimidating. Evangeline's heels tapped on the hard floors as she approached the door and waved him aside.

"It's all right, she's an employee."

Natalie noted her boss's wan face. Despite the always perfect makeup, new wrinkles creased in the corners of her wolf-gray eyes. Evangeline put an arm around Natalie's shoulders and steered her into the small front gallery where they sold woodblock prints. Nat pulled her hand out of her purse and zipped the bag shut. The small plastic security badge with the magnetic strip had to be in there. She could find it later.

"The police are here?" Natalie asked her boss.

"It's awful. They stole *Gray Day, Montrose Valley.*"

"What!?" Natalie felt the blow in her gut. How could that have happened, given all the extra security and all the care that had gone into setting up the show?

Evangeline clasped her hands in a pseudo-prayer.

"We'll be shut all day, at the very least. No one will be able to enjoy the show. I'm sure the police will want to talk with you at some point, but I suggest you go home."

She walked Natalie to the entrance and pushed her out. Like a small child in a forbidden room.

"Today is just ugliness." She pulled the door shut, and Natalie heard the lock click into place with a decisive thud. She stared, paralyzed, her mind wrestling with the situation. Paso Robles was a safe town. Things like this didn't happen here. People didn't break into other people's houses. Or steal art.

The sound of the dead bolt snapping into place made Natalie shudder. Evangaline's words that the police would want to talk with her repeated over and over in her mind. What could she tell them? She had no idea who could do this, or how. Extra security cameras captured everything except the restrooms. Natalie had drawn a line there. Even Liz Bathory, the old guy's daughter and the onsite representative of the MET, said she was satisfied with the security protocols. And what was up with Evangeline? Did she have something to hide?

Her hand instinctively went back into her purse, searching for the missing access card. Where had she put it? A pocket, maybe. Its absence unnerved her. She'd have to go through everything she had worn over the last week and find it.

Chapter 8 Rose

~

Chardonnay — A French green-skinned grape used in the production of white wine.

Saturday, October 8, 6:16 PM

Sunset clouds over the Sierra meant rain in the mountains. She set out paper plates, napkins, and two glasses and poured herself a drink from the bottle of Chardonnay cooling in an ice bucket. Natalie should arrive soon.

Birds rustled and sang in the bushes as they returned to their nests for the evening. A small shaggy dog padded out the front door and jumped on a seat. He turned a few times and curled up with a view toward the street. Rose smiled. Something about his presence felt natural.

Never one to let a promising idea go to waste, she had driven to the animal shelter that morning after returning home from Natalie's house. If someone had tried to break into her neighbor's house, having a watchdog would be an added layer of protection. The cacophony of dogs barking almost turned her back, but the woman at the desk seemed to recognize the look of panic in Rose's eyes and escorted her into a private room.

After a conversation about what type of pup she was looking for, some questions about her living accommodations, and the type of yard the dog would have access to, the woman left and returned five minutes later with a white and tan fluff ball. Coal-black eyes shone from underneath shaggy hair and Groucho Marx eyebrows. He was about the size of a large house cat, like the one Rose had as a child, until a delivery truck backed up over it while the feline hid in a stray paper bag. This dog would be her first pet since that accident.

"His name is Watson, but you can rename him anything you want," the shelter woman said.

Watson stood still momentarily, sniffed the air, and surveyed the room. Then he approached Rose, sniffed the leg of her pants, hands, and shoes, and thoroughly inspected her purse. Satisfied, he sat and studied her curiously. She stared back. Watson seemed like a perfect name.

"Do you want to come live with me?" Watson cocked his head to one side and wiggled his bushy brows. Then he barked.

The shelter woman laughed. "I think that was a yes!"

The first sip of the unoaked Chardonnay brought crisp hints of lemon and pear. A breeze brushed her cheek with a warm whisper, and Rose sighed the contented sigh of a woman at peace in her world. Granted, it wasn't the big, wide world covered by the news. And it wasn't the world she'd lived in for the last decades—a world of high-rise condos, traffic, and ocean views.

She had a second friend. A dog. And olive trees. She could walk into town for a cup of tea, something she'd dreamed of doing in LA but never had the nerve.

Contemplating her olive trees, she experienced a stab of guilt. Was there anything she should be doing in October to prepare for harvest? When was the fruit ready? She'd give Margery Wheat a call and ask. The woman had been kind to her at the first Olive Growers Association meeting Rose attended.

Dusk settled in the sky with peach and violet colors that washed the sky. Natalie came up the stone steps; her curly hair pulled back from her face into a loose ponytail.

"Rose, you won't believe what happened." Natalie's typically calm voice sounded strained, as if her vocal cords were fighting the words.

"What?" Pepperoni steam permeated Rose's senses. Her mouth watered. Someone had once hinted that she might be a super smeller, a person who could detect scents better than most people. She doubted that, but still enjoyed life through scents: peanut butter, Cabernet, and pizza. Anything that involves eating or drinking. Perfume gave her a headache.

Natalie zipped up a hooded sweatshirt against the evening chill. "I'm so upset I can't talk about it." When she glanced up, her gaze stopped on Watson.

"Who's this?"

"His name is Watson."

Rose scratched behind his ears.

Natalie reached over and rubbed her hand along the dog's back. Watson closed his eyes and gave a satisfied moan.

"Just this morning, you said you wanted a pup, and here it is."

"He. Here he is." Did dogs take offense at being called an it?

"My apologies, Watson. I hope you are as helpful to Rose as Watson was to Sherlock." Watson shook his head, which waggled his whole body.

"Fortunately for him." Rose scratched the little

dog's ears, "All he has to do is keep me company. Now, what is bothering you so much that you don't want to talk about it?"

Natalie sank into a cushioned chair. "The gallery's been closed. Someone stole that painting I liked so much."

Wine splashed over the rim of Rose's glass when she set it down hard. Her hand reached for a napkin.

"What? With Brad Knight on duty?"

Cars drove past. A Nightingale sang from a branch in the Oak tree. Natalie sat back. Her shoulders drooped as if the mere mention of the theft had placed a heavy weight.

"I don't know. Evangeline wouldn't let me in. Well, more to the point, she shoved me right back out. Like she didn't want me to see something."

The internal sensors that Rose relied on to detect problems on the factory floor flared to life. First, someone tries to break into Natalie's house or garage, then this. A theft. All in a twenty-four-hour period. One occurrence was a chance. Two became interesting. A third instance indicated a trend. Would there be a third event?

"Hellooo." A woman's voice called up from the street. Watson leaped up and ran to the top of the steps.

"With your trouble this morning and then an art theft at the gallery," Rose said as she praised the dog in her mind. "I'm glad I have him to announce strangers."

"All right? May I come up?" the voice said.

"Certainly!" called Natalie.

A brunette-haired woman came up the stairs holding a wine bottle out as an offering. Watson moved aside to make room for her and settled himself on the top step.

Natalie took the Chardonnay and led the stranger to the seating area.

"Now, Rose," she said. "Don't be mad at me, but I invited Stella to join us."

Rose recalled the noise of the art gallery. The young woman with clear blue eyes and Slade Bolton wrapped around her like a feather boa.

Her bosses used to mix things up like this. Adding an unwanted team member to an already established group. A familiar tightening of chest muscles crept over her. You're not there anymore, she reminded herself. Didn't she want more friends? You can't make them if you don't meet them.

Rose watched the newcomer sit. "This is Watson. He won't bite. I think. He's new."

Stella smiled at the dog. "Oh, I love dogs! Thanks for the invite. I haven't met many people in town, and really, I'm a people person, so this is wonderful! Oh, here, this is for you." She handed the bottle over to Rose, who noted that it was from one of her favorite wineries. Good taste in wine, at least. She cradled the bottle. "I'll get this open if you don't mind."

Stella nodded, and Rose left to retrieve the corkscrew. When she came back, Stella had kicked off her shoes and curled up on a lounge chair. Settled in as quickly as Watson. Natalie sat opposite.

Watson lay on the floor near Stella's chair. Traitor. But then, he must be a good judge of character. He came to live with her. Not that he'd had much to say about the matter, but Rose liked to believe the wag of his tail said more than words.

"I just love a British accent," Natalie said in a stage whisper as she held up her glass for Rose to pour.

Once everyone had a plate of pizza and a full glass of wine, Rose looked around at their little group.

The addition of the younger woman didn't feel as weird as she imagined it would.

"I'm glad you could join us, Stella. Gives us a chance to get to know you. I'm new here as well, arrived three months ago."

Natalie smiled and raised her goblet. "We have our own little Newcomers group." She raised her glass. "Here's to new friends." They clinked and drank. She winked at Rose.

"What's Newcomers?" Stella asked. Rose had to agree that the girl's, no, young woman's accent was lovely.

"We have one here in town, we could join to meet more people. It's an organization that helps new people, newcomers, to meet people in a new area," Natalie explained. "I used to be in it when Paul and I moved here."

"Paul?" Stella asked.

A slight smile lifted Natalie's lips, as if remembering a bittersweet moment. "Long story. Later."

"Well, that sounds good to me," Rose said. "Working didn't leave me time to have real friends, so, and don't laugh, you might be my first true friends. Assuming we actually like each other."

Natalie and Stella laughed. "Of course we'll like each other, how could we not?" Natalie said and then cleared her throat.

"Let's start with introductions. I have tons of questions for Stella, but I'll tell my sad story first. I am divorced and widowed." She held up her left hand to show the empty ring finger.

"Which is a long, sorry tale that I won't bore you with now."

"Slade told me you're an artist." The introduction

of a male name as strong as Slade Bolton dampened Rose's festive mood. What was it about that man?

Natalie sat back and took a sip of wine. "So, I am. But that's just a hobby. I work at the gallery in tech support. Computers and stuff like that."

All this was information Rose knew. Something in the way her friend had displayed her hand caught her attention. It wasn't the lack of a gold or silver band that intrigued her. It was the smudge of color. Artists aren't strangers to paint, but something about it struck Rose. When she looked up and caught Natalie's eye, her neighbor quickly covered the smear. It wasn't any of the shades on the walls in her neighbor's colorful house. Natalie repainted as often as Rose cleaned the pantry. Which is to say, about every other month. The bit of color seemed stormy, like the blues and grays on the frame of the stolen painting. What new path of artistic expression had Natalie chosen?

Stella took a generous sip of Chardonnay and set the glass down. Her left thumb rubbed the base of her ring finger as if feeling for an amputated appendage.

"What sort of art do you create?" she asked.

"Oil paints, mostly. Some acrylics. I've even used house paint. Starving artists can't be picky --"

"House paint?" Stella's voice mirrored Rose's confusion. She'd heard of acrylics and oils, but never plain old latex paint. I guess one's as good as the other, she thought. Maybe she could help pay for better paints. Natalie was a particularly good artist.

"She's too modest. I've seen landscapes and still life paintings in her house."

"Well, yeah, if that was your question. At one time or another, I've painted almost everything."

"Porn?" Stella asked with raised eyebrows.

"Nudes. Life painting." Natalie took a sip. "So, Stella, what do you do? I can tell from your accent that you're not from here."

"I came to the States because of a man. No, not a man, a cheater, and I stayed because I liked it here and refused to follow him to Australia, where his newly discovered child and her mother live. Like, how awkward would that be?"

A faint tan line on Stella's ring finger hinted at an extended period with a band blocking the sun. His betrayal must have hurt as much as hers had.

Stella took another swallow of wine.

"Besides, I'm trying to find my birth mom."

Here?" Natalie's forehead wrinkled with confusion. "Wouldn't she be in Britain?"

"My parents adopted me in the States, then moved to the UK. I got interested in genealogy in my late teens, but really dug into it a few years ago. I've traced my bio mom to the West Coast."

Stella's sapphire blue eyes looked over at Rose. "Specifically, California. Do you have kids?"

"Does Watson count?"

Rose tried to laugh at the cold feeling of someone seeing into her innermost being, the part she kept locked away.

Natalie lifted her wine glass in a toast.

"Of course he does! Kids can have two legs or four."

Stella's gaze hadn't changed.

Rose smiled and identified the uncomfortable feeling in her gut as guilt.

"Then I have one kid. A perpetual two-year-old, I suspect."

They all looked over at Watson, who had claimed a cushion and curled up into a ball. Her heart warmed looking at him. Then an old memory chilled it. Of a child, held briefly, before disappearing, held in the arms of a nurse.

Wind rustled the branches of the oak tree. *What branches have I cut off?* Lines from a favorite poem by Dina Elenbogen came to her. *The sky says remember your roots/The Earth says remember the wind.*

She'd followed the wind. Perhaps at the expense of her roots. Her child. Somewhere. She stifled the quick ache in her heart.

"What will you do when you find her?" Rose asked.

Stella sat back and shrugged. "She might not want to make contact. What would you do if a daughter you placed in adoption suddenly showed up?"

Rose looked down at her hands. *What would I say? I'm sorry seems so empty. And am I, really?*

Natalie took another slice of pizza.

"What about your bio dad? Anything on him?"

"No," Stella admitted. "Surprisingly, he's still a big blank. That just means none of his family has done one of the DNA tests. I'm sure eventually something will pop up. In the meantime, I bought a tax and bookkeeping business. It was cheap because the previous owner didn't do any marketing, but I'll overcome that."

She smiled sweetly at Natalie.

"I heard you work for the art gallery. I don't suppose they need a bookkeeper?"

Natalie winced. Stella's face flushed a charming pink. "I'll swing by tomorrow and make a pitch."

"You might want to wait a few days."

While Natalie filled Stella in on the break-in at the gallery, Rose sipped her wine and stared at the house across the street. She couldn't see it without remembering the dark figure crossing in the shadows. Something in the back of her mind tried to make connections. It was weird that he lived so close to the girl he dated, especially since she'd just moved in.

"I'm curious, Stella. Did you know Slade before you moved into the house?"

Stella giggled. "He's cute, isn't he? We met a few weeks ago at a winery event. My ex was a winemaker there, and I'm still a member. We hit it off."

"Hitting it off" seemed like an understatement. The way they clung to each other at the gallery, Rose would have thought they'd been dating much longer. Was this how relationships went now? Rose couldn't remember the last time she'd gone on a date, much less seen someone more than once. Not since… she shoved the thought from her mind.

"And then he rents the house across from you? You didn't think that was strange?"

"It does look odd, right?" Stella said with a self-deprecating laugh. "He says it's a coincidence."

Rose shook her head. "A coincidence is usually a chance event with an underestimated probability." She saw the blank look on the other's face. "Sorry. My old life waking up. I was a professional problem solver. Technical gobbledygook comes with the territory."

"Well," Natalie said. "At least there's no long walk of shame."

Stella leaned back into the chair.

"Oh, that's a good one!"

A smile crinkled the normally smooth skin around her eyes.

"He's originally from New York. Wanted to leave the big city. So, he came here."

"He came to Paso Robles from New York City?" The skepticism in Natalie's voice sounded obvious to Rose but seemed to sail right over Stella's head.

"It's not like this is the middle of nowhere," she said.

Natalie chortled. "We are almost the definition of the middle of nowhere. Except for wine lovers, most people don't know we exist."

Rose detected a change in both women's tone and didn't want the evening ruined.

"Let's talk about the art show. Natalie was instrumental in making the Gala happen. I thought the exhibits were lovely. Mostly early California impressionists, weren't they?"

Natalie pulled her gaze from Stella and picked up another slice of pizza. "Yeah, all from one collection. His daughter was there, remember? The tissue lady. We saw her near the stolen painting."

"I can't believe I stood so close to something that was stolen." Stella pulled her sylphlike legs out from under her and crossed them. A delicate gold chain embraced one ankle.

"I remember that piece. It's about the only thing I do remember. Dark, moody. It didn't strike me as being remarkable. Or worth much."

Natalie smiled as if remembering something pleasant from childhood.

"I grew up in Montrose. The painting shows what

the area near my house looked like in the early twentieth century."

The dark blues and greens of *Gray Day, Montrose Valley* materialized in Rose's thoughts, along with the memory of the little stucco house her mom rented after a heart attack reduced them from three musketeers to two. If Natalie's memories were as strong, Rose could understand that her friend had become attached to the stolen painting. She paused. Attached enough to steal it? No, don't be silly. She stood and went into the house to get a pitcher and some tumblers. Nonsense thought told her it was time to switch to water.

A cell phone rang on the porch, and Natalie answered.

"Speaking." Her voice sounded as tight as Rose's grip on the heavy pitcher.

She went outside and set everything down on the table.

"Oh my God." Natalie's voice sounded strained. Her face turned the color of the travertine table that held their wine. "Oh, God, no, yes, I'll be there." Natalie tapped the red phone button and terminated the call. Tears glistened on her lower lashes. Her breath came as a shudder.

"That was the police. The robbery last night that I told you about, at the gallery, they killed the guard. Brad Knight is dead."

Stella sat back with her hand covering her mouth, eyes wide. Rose rushed over to Nat's chair and knelt beside it. They hadn't had a chance to talk about Brad yet, but she'd seen the look on her friend's face at the Gala. She liked him. Maybe even more than liked.

"What happened?"

"They wouldn't tell me. I need to go to the station and give a statement in the morning. Why didn't Evangeline tell me this morning? I don't understand."

"I'm certain they'll find whoever did this," Rose assured her. How could something like this happen in out-of-the-way Paso Robles?

"Of course they will," Stella added. "Did I mention that Slade is with the FBI Art Crime team? He'll be on top of it."

Natalie dabbed at her eyes with the hem of her shirt. "I need to go, need to, to think." She got up and ran down the steps. Stella stood as well. The party was breaking up. The young woman smiled at Rose. "I look forward to the next time."

As they descended the stairs, Rose reflected on how quickly she made friends when she wasn't going to have to evaluate their performance or potentially fire them. Watson followed her into the house. The click of his toenails on the tile made her smile. His presence calmed her. She almost looked forward to her midnight stroll with him by her side. She was getting the hang of this retired life. New friends. A dog. All in the span of a few months. A murder to solve was icing on the cake.

As was usual for her, Rose couldn't get to sleep. She threw the covers back and got up. Upstairs held the day's heat and the air conditioning struggled to bring it down. Stella's face kept appearing in her mind. She'd never had friends, much less one so young. Yet the woman seemed to meld into the little group they were creating.

How brave of her to search for her birth mother. Rose wondered, for the millionth time, whether anyone wondered who she was. Her pregnancy had been an accident. Yet, many women didn't give such oops away. She wasn't strong enough, at least not then. Maybe now. But that time had passed. Was her child a boy or a girl? Healthy? Resentful?

It didn't pay to wonder too much. Water under the bridge, as her mother would say. Stella's face floated into her thoughts again. If she did have a daughter, a confident, bright woman like Stella would be wonderful.

Chapter 9 Slade

~

Koroneiki – A Greek olive cultivar used primarily for olive oil production

Saturday, October 8, 5:30 PM

Slade Bolton folded his legs into the folding lawn chair and groaned. The rental house came unfurnished, and he wasn't going to waste money on furniture. It meant he needed to keep Stella out. Shouldn't be too much trouble. Besides, it wasn't for much longer.

The old biddy across the street was having a party on her porch. His binoculars would allow him to lip-read if the angle from the street up to her house wasn't so steep. As it was, he could keep track of who came and went, but that's it.

At least there's beer in the fridge. The can fizzed when the pop top was lifted. The chair squeaked as his weight settled in to watch. And think.

It'd been ten years since he slipped into the American Wing of the New York Metropolitan Museum of Art on a blistering summer day. Humidity didn't usually bother him; it reminded him of days on the lake as a kid, but that day it felt oppressive.

He leaned on the wall inside the main door, soaking up the cool air and feeling the sweat run down his back. A group of school kids holding hands came past. They rustled restlessly as the chaperone bought tickets. He had a museum membership and waltzed in without waiting. That's the benefit of growing up, kids! Once in the main hall, he grabbed a brochure.

Ever since joining the Art Crime Team, he'd spent part of his lunch hour there a few times a week. The quiet. The art. Plus, it reminded him of his mom. She loved to wander and stare at the paintings, trying to imagine the artist's life.

He skirted students sketching the Masters until he found a spot under a vent in the pottery room. The frigid air felt good as it dried the sweat on his head.

Mom would have loved this. Her favorite was the Detroit Institute of Arts. It had the genteel atmosphere that she loved, offering her the chance to mix with a higher class of society than our lower-middle-class origins permitted.

They saw contemporary and European, African, and Asian paintings and statues. He wanted to play baseball, but all that art exposure came in handy on his FBI application for the Art Crime Team.

Once he cooled down a bit, he scanned his surroundings. Standard FBI protocol, know the environment. Gilt-framed paintings hung from dove-colored walls. In the center of the room, glass display cases housed pottery, bronze, and ceramic sculptures. Across the room stood a woman, more beautiful than anything in the entire museum, scrutinizing a piece of pottery. From the brochure, he learned that the artist's name was Adelaide Alsop Robineau, a pioneer in glazes and design.

The woman wears a black-and-white polka-dotted dress, black-and-white spectator pumps, and a ponytail so black it looks almost purple.

He finds he can't breathe. All he can hear is the tapping of her fingers on crossed arms as she ponders the vase.

She's the one. His father's last words echo in his thoughts.

He remembered how cold it was that night as his parents headed off to a Christmas party.

"Son, marry rich," Dad said. "If she's smart and good-looking, all the better."

Mother slapped his arm. "Honestly, Stu, you make it sound like you regret marrying me because I don't have any money. Though I am smart and attractive."

She winked at him and out into the storm they went. They died in a fifteen-car pileup. One car slid into another, then another. He went to live with an aunt and uncle and never forgot those last words. "Marry rich."

The woman in the polka-dot dress looked loaded. The kind of money that came from family wealth, not some high-paying Wall Street job.

He ambled around the gallery until he stood next to her. Yes. Ambled. He'd mastered the art of walking with purpose but seeming to wander accidentally. She smelled of expensive perfume.

With feigned interest, he read the card that describes the pot in case she asks for his opinion. Minutes passed, maybe ten, before she sighed and moved on to the next display.

What made it so fascinating to her? He didn't "get" pottery. Paintings were his interest. When he looked up, the woman had moved to another sculpture. He strolled in her direction, pretending to consider a figurine on the opposite wall. She's gorgeous. Like that girl in high school who aroused such hormone-driven lust that his ears reddened. Like the birds in a National Geographic magazine, signaling their intent to mate. He took to wearing a knitted cap to cover them up.

No cap that day and his ears felt hot. Damn it all to hell. He had stopped carrying the cap years ago, thinking he had things under control.

His practiced eye caught movement across the street. Natalie Patel ascended her front steps and walked over to join the party. Poor Natalie. Widowed and innocent. They always play the victim.

He sipped the beer and licked the foam from his upper lip. His thoughts drifted back to that day. With closed eyes, he was there again.

She's so far out of my league that she probably won't even see me. Me and my red ears.

She probably traveled the world as a kid, while I spent summers working for my uncle on a truck farm, picking lettuce and pulling carrots to earn money for college.

Her perfume wafts on the air-conditioned breeze, and my head spins. She's the femme fatale to my Joker, never mind that that makes me Batman, and I'm no caped hero. Far from it.

At the Vase with Queen Anne's Lace, she looks at me and gives me a dainty Mona Lisa smile. The pottery has a spray of flowers with an uneven opening at the top formed by bracts of wild carrots. I know this because I read the card.

"Brilliant, isn't it?" she says. Clear, delicate bells sing when she speaks. I look around to make sure there wasn't someone behind me that she had aimed her comment at.

No one.

Pale blue-gray eyes wait for my answer, and a claw of fear grips my chest.

"Sure, I mean, such creativity to make something that looks like it's fashioned out of weeds."

Her eyes widen, then narrow. She thinks I'm an idiot, no match for her good breeding. The heat in my ears ratchets up to blow-torch level. It takes all my willpower not to cup them with my hands.

"Steady," I mutter. "Don't blow this."

Lights in the gallery flicker. An alarm blares. Instantly, automated roller shutters unwind from the ceiling and coil down the walls, covering the art with a protective barricade. This happens when there has been a theft. Or fire. I don't see evidence of either.

"What's going on?" one mother demands of the nearest security guard. She has a squirming six-year-old held tightly by the wrist. Another woman takes the hand of her elderly companion. "Let's get out of here. Something's wrong."

Everyone in the gallery hurries toward one of two exits. With all the confusion, I can't see the raven-haired woman.

"Please exit immediately," a security guard urges us in a tone that sounds stern. The normally hushed voices were shouting now, people telling each other to get out of their way and to move faster. There isn't any smoke, and an old fear surfaces that my ears radiated so much heat they triggered the system. That doesn't seem possible, but right now, that doesn't matter.

A fine mist of water rained down, dappling my jacket. There she is. The mystery woman walks with long, fluid strides to the entrance. I follow and am the last to leave before a guard pushes a large red button that activates the metal mesh gates. The glass display cases and wooden benches where art students had been sketching minutes ago are bathed in a cooling shower.

Security guards move to stand across of the room's entrance, their shoulders touching, a human wall of muscle and batons. What exactly has happened? As an FBI agent, should I make inquiries?

"Move on, folks. No need for panic." One of the staff is herding everyone through into the European Paintings Galleries. The woman vanishes into the crowd. I'm tall, which comes in handy in crowds like this. With the advantage of height, I scanned until I saw her as she moved through the hall's exit into the European Sculpture and Decorative Arts rooms.

Dodging mothers with strollers and old folks wielding canes and walkers, I follow until I see her leaning on a railing overlooking the Great Hall. Checking her phone. No panic reaction for her. I stop short and catch my breath.

"What do you suppose happened?" I ask, leaning casually on the rail beside her. She turns her head a bit and her pale, blue-gray eyes check me out. Not to be boastful, but I'm not bad to look at. Some women have told me so, even comparing me to a certain James Bond actor.

"Museums have thermal monitoring systems to maintain climate control. With this humidity and heat, the room must have warmed up too much with everyone in there." Her voice is deep and smooth, like good Scottish whiskey. Despite the wetness evident on her shoulders, she didn't appear concerned about what had happened or that her clothes might be ruined.

I knew about thermal monitoring but kept quiet, as I didn't want to come across as a pompous ass. Better to hold back some cards.

"But drenching everyone? That seems extreme to me."

She gives me a sympathetic smile as if my lack of knowledge about how art protection technology had progressed over the last one hundred years was an indication of a lack of character.

"Priceless artifacts require extreme measures to protect."

In truth, I made a detailed analysis of the science when I moved to the Art Crime Team. So extensive that I know my ears couldn't have triggered the whole thing, but that doesn't stop my internal demon from telling me I was responsible.

The woman put her phone back into her Hermes purse and began to walk away. I was about to lose my chance of finding out her name. This babe looked way beyond rich. I needed to get a phone number, at least. I fell into step beside her.

"Would you like to get a drink or something? There's got to be someplace close by that has decent coffee." Hopefully, my desperation didn't come across in my voice.

She looked at her Cartier watch.

"The Great Hall Café is right here. I could use a coffee."

She turns and heads in that direction. I grabbed my ears with cold hands to chill them down and follow. She'd be sure to notice if they were flaming red.

The café is bright. The conservatory ceiling lit the statues and sculptures scattered around on plinths. I don't generally eat in the museum because of tourist prices. But this was different. We sit at a small table with cups of coffee. I introduce myself. In a situation where I plan to lie, I've found that starting with the truth disarms people.

"I just moved to the city for work."

And the truth is, a promotion from the FBI Detroit office to the Art Crime Team relocated me to New York with a commensurate salary increase so I could afford a small apartment.

She sips her cappuccino. "Have you always been interested in art?"

"Art thieves are my main concern. The things they steal are relevant, but not my focus. I'm after the human element that perpetrates the crime." Her eyebrow arches upward.

I'd been practicing that line since I started. It sounded sophisticated. Plus, it cut short any lengthy conversations about art.

She doesn't say anything. Just sits cooly appraising me. Damn. My ears start to burn again.

"That's not to say I don't appreciate art. Some art." You, for instance. That part I didn't say out loud. I'm not a complete idiot.

The corner of her mouth curves in a small laugh.

"Good save. How is it that you know about art theft?"

I allow one more truth to trickle out. "I'm with the FBI Art Crime Team."

That may have been a mistake. Her eyes widen, then narrow as if assessing a fact and determining it useful. The coffee has grown cold. The AC system, which had been a blessing when I entered from the muggy street, has rendered a cup of steaming café mocha into a cold brew. For the record, I think iced coffee is an abomination.

"You haven't told me your name," I said.

She smiles that enigmatic expression again.

"Liz Bathory. Pleased to meet you." She extends her hand; long delicate fingers with a ring that screamed wealth. Not to shake, but more of an eighteenth-century kiss my hand gesture. So, I did. Planted a kiss right on them. It was a move my dad, the master at flirting with women, taught me. Dad didn't tip well, but he always made the servers smile.

The name Bathory is a legend in the art world: the family had a collection valued at over $600 million. If I could score with the old guy's daughter, my career at the FBI would soar. Or is she his wife?

"Is that your maiden name or your married name?"

There aren't any tan lines or indentations in the flesh to indicate a ring. Her fingers are slim and delicate with red nails in a discreet oval shape.

"Family name." Her voice has a harsh edge to it. The beating organ in my chest adds a few thumps.

"As in Emmett Bathory, Wall Street mastermind and financier?"

"Yes. Dear old, recently departed, Daddy. Scheming, narcissistic bastard that he was." Her tone tells me that she didn't like him more than her harsh words.

"I read that he passed away recently. I'm sorry for your loss."

She drains her cup and places it back on the table carefully. As if deciding whether to prolong the conversation or not.

She stands.

"The world is better off without the selfish bastard. Thank you for the coffee." She lifts her Hermes purse to her shoulder and turns to leave.

"Dinner, tomorrow night? 8:00 PM. Per Se on Columbus Circle," I call out.

She stops. Pivots back. Those pale blue-gray, almond-shaped eyes evaluate me from the top of my cheap haircut to the scuffed but shiny loafers. Not up to her standard, but hopefully she sees me as a diamond in the rough. Good looking but in need of some of her feminine touch.

She nods.

My ears flush as thoughts rush to what life would be like with this beautiful woman.

A Harley roar woke him at the same moment as Stella crossed the street toward the MacGillivray woman's place. Stella is the type of woman his mother would have loved. Genuine, smart, attractive (for pretty babies, his mother would say), and unpretentious. His father would approve of Liz Bathory.

Elizabeth "Liz" Bathory smirked as she left the museum. Slade Bolton was a bit rough around the edges, but she could polish him up to her standard. An FBI agent fit in perfectly with her plans. Yes, he would do nicely to get what she wanted. And she always got what she wanted.

Chapter 10 Rose

~

Syrah/Shiraz — A dark-skinned grape variety grown throughout the world. Generally called Shiraz in Australia.

Sunday, October 9, 7:00 AM

A shard of sunshine blazed through the tree boughs and into Rose's bedroom on Sunday morning. She put on jeans and a striped shirt, bright red canvas shoes, and pulled a purple beret over her hair. As she arranged stray, gray strands, she remembered a Kurt Vonnegut quote she read in an airplane magazine, back when airlines had their magazines in the seat pocket and not on an app. *We are what we pretend to be, so we must be careful about what we pretend to be.*

"What am I pretending to be?" she asked Watson. He shook his head. Funny how he almost seemed to understand her. She stared at her reflection in the mirror, and with a sigh, she turned off the bathroom light and went downstairs.

Morning was her favorite time in town. Most of the tourists were still sleeping off the effects of wine tasting the previous day. Locals headed to work; shop owners dusted display windows, and people walked their dogs. She thought about snapping the leash on Watson's collar and taking him with her, but today she and Natalie planned to go to the gallery together.

"Sorry, fella, no walk this morning."

The house Slade Bolton rented looked, at first glance, like a single-story bungalow. But as she walked down the hill, the second floor and a garage revealed themselves. In the three months since Rose moved to Paso Robles, the house has been empty. Now it housed Stella's new lover. A worrisome development. Dependable men didn't rent houses adjacent to girls they wanted to date. It smacked of stalking.

In contrast to the boxy dwelling Bolton rented, Stella lived in a Victorian with a historical designation. Blue and white with a black painted wrought iron mailbox; a toned-down version of the more flamboyant Victorians in town. Rose thought it seemed like the perfect home for a displaced Brit: a bit of London in Paso Robles.

Down the rest of the street, she passed a mixture of Craftsman, Victorian, and Mission-style houses. Fences lined the sidewalk, which was concrete in some stretches and dirt in others, hinting at a city that wanted to stay true to its rural, small-town origins.

Redolent with the scent of coffee, the cafe buzzed with people. There was the mom with two youngsters who couldn't resist strumming the strings of a piano's inner workings that the café owners had hung below the counter. She held a third child strapped to her chest. Rose decided this woman was the type of mother she could never have been. Though in truth, she hadn't given herself the chance.

"Hot chamomile," the barista called out. Rose carried the cup to a seat by the back wall, a comfortable armchair where she could see the entrance, and settled down to read her book. Around the shop, people's eyes were glued to a phone screen or a laptop computer.

"Rose?" A young woman dressed in a police uniform and utility belt loomed over her. Rose recognized her at once.

"Officer Nessa," she said as an unnecessary introduction. "I thought it was you. May I sit?"

Rose set her cup down. "Certainly. Nice to see you again, Sergeant Gomez. I'm not in trouble, I hope."

"You were at the art gala Friday night," She said it like a statement, but an accusation lurked under the surface. "What time did you leave?"

She dragged a chair from a nearby table and sat down, then pulled a little flip notepad from her vest pocket.

"Why are you asking me these questions?" Did they think Rose killed someone? The policewoman clicked a pen and stood poised to write down whatever Rose said.

"There was an... incident. We're asking everyone who attended about their movements that night."

The call Natalie received and the reason they were going to the gallery later. One person is dead, and a stolen painting. Rose let her thoughts drift to Friday night.

"I left about 8 PM, with Natalie Patel. Am I a suspect?"

Nessa made a note. "At this point, everyone at the gala is a suspect."

Her gaze locked on Rose's, giving Rose the feeling that the policewoman was rummaging around her thoughts, looking for guilt. "Were you alone? That night, I mean."

Her face reddened.

Rose smiled at the implication. "Yes. Yes, I was. I heard about Brad Knight. I suppose it doesn't matter if I say I didn't do it. But other than showing you my Fitbit's sleep tracker, I can't prove anything."

"A Fitbit?"

Rose pulled back her sleeve and showed her the watch. Then she pulled out her cell phone, tapped the app, and held out the sleep results for Friday night. The police-woman stared at it, then took out her cell phone and took a picture. "I'll ask legal, but it should be good enough for now."

The equipment belt squeaked as she tugged down on the vest that held handcuffs, radios, a baton, and who knew what else. "Enjoy your tea."

As the policewoman was leaving, Natalie slipped into the coffee shop, stopped by the counter and ordered a double espresso. Coffee-colored circles stained the skin under her eyes.

"Did you sleep at all?" Rose asked. It didn't look like she had.

"I just came from the police station. Giving my statement. I must be the number one suspect, based on how they treated me. Rose, please believe me when I say I didn't."

The barista called her name, and she went up to retrieve her shot of energy. When she returned, she sat, placed the cup down, and rubbed her forehead. "I'm beat."

Rose reached across the table and touched Natalie's arm. "They suspect everyone, at least at the start. A young policewoman was here asking me about it as well."

"It didn't help that I didn't get much sleep," Natalie said after sipping her coffee.

Rose had adapted to her nightly routine of waking up, wandering the house for a bit, then lying down until sleep returned. If you weren't used to it, though, it left you feeling hollow.

"What kept you awake?" she asked.

Natalie pulled a tissue out of her purse and blew her nose.

"A house is so loud in the middle of the night, have you noticed? Every creak, every leaf against the window, the hum whenever the fridge turns on. I jumped at everything. Last night, I just couldn't relax. I did call the locksmith, by the way. So that's taken care of."

"You might want to take something tonight," Rose said. "Going without sleep can make you crazy."

They drank tea and espresso and watched the shop's patrons around them. Ten small tables, two of which were side by side for a regular morning's group of men who gabbed their way through cups of coffee and bagels smeared with cream cheese. Two real estate agents dressed for show-ings went through multiple listings on a laptop. A trio of women, walkers no doubt, back from a few miles' hike in the local hills. The place smelled of coffee, toast, and after-shave lotion.

The family with small kids snapped covers on their cups and escorted their ebullient charges outside. With them gone, Rose could hear the soft rock music playing on the PA system. Her shoulders relaxed. She'd never been com-fortable around small children. Had Natalie had any? Rose couldn't remember whether they ever talked about it. It wasn't the sort of thing you asked about directly.

She stood. Time to get her thoughts back to today

"You ready to go? I want to see this crime scene for myself."

Chapter 11 Rose

~

*Nero d'Avola - A full-bodied red grape with dry red and
black cherry to prune flavors*

Sunday, October 9, 10:30 AM

Sunday mornings were quiet in Paso Robles. Tourists weren't generally early risers, and those few who were out were window shopping as they sipped café mochas. Stores, bars, and restaurants still slumbered as Rose and Natalie walked the two blocks to the Galería de Arte. It was one of those warm fall days with wispy clouds to hint that the coast was enshrouded in fog. Here in Paso Robles, it was lovely, with no hints of the crime scene they walked toward. The trees still held on tight to their leaves, and the grass seemed a fresher green now that the scorching sun had abated.

Inside, portable tripod-mounted lights brought in by the police washed the gallery walls with a clinical, blue-white sheen, accented periodically by camera flashes that bounced off the shiny silver surface of the ceiling insulation. Yellow police tape blocking the exhibit's opening almost appeared as a contemporary performance art piece. The air smelled of oil paint, linseed oil, and the vinegar tang of turned wine.

A box of empty bottles by the back door was the obvious source of that last scent. Rose also detected the metallic scent of iron, typical of paper cuts and scraped knees. Rose was often accused of smelling something that wasn't there, but she knew that what she detected was the scent of blood. A knot of police officers surrounded a chalk outline on the floor at the rear of the gallery where Brad's body had fallen. Rose pulled her phone from her back pocket to snap a photo. Everyone died, eventually. But an unexplained, unnatural death violated the social agreement needed to live in a civil society. Death left her feeling violated. Weak-kneed.

Dressed in crisp dark blue jeans, a gray T-shirt, and cherry red stilettos, Evangeline Abbott hurried over.

"This is horrible. All the work we put in…"

Natalie put her hand on Rose's shoulder. "This is my friend, Rose. I introduced you on Friday night."

The gallery owner squinted at Rose. "Dreadful business. As you can see, we've had a bit of trouble." Her gaze drifted to the back of the gallery.

"They stole *Gray Day, Montrose Valley*. Tragic. Now no one will trust us with their collections."

Her hands never stopped moving, fidgeting with her ring, and fluttering around. Rose thought she seemed more concerned about the art theft than the demise of an employee.

"How long had Mr. Knight worked at the gallery?" she asked.

The gallery owner stiffened. Fine lines radiated from her lips. "Why do you ask?"

"I'm a naturally curious person."

Evangeline closed her eyes, as if thinking, Why must I suffer fools? She opened them with a defiant glare. "I've already provided Brad's employment records to the police."

From the corner of her eye, Rose saw her friend

wrinkle her brow as she looked at her boss. "Three years," she said. "I remember when he started."

"You don't speak for the gallery," came a curt reply. "All communications will be with the police or the FBI. Well, I'm busy. Natalie will see you out."

With a huff, Evangeline tottered off toward the gift shop, her heels clicking on the concrete floors and echoing in the lofty ceilings, leaving Rose with the sense that whatever the woman was, she wasn't busy. Rude, nervous, overbearing, narcissistic, hiding something, but not busy.

So, the guard was a sensitive topic. Natalie leaned close to Rose's ear.

"There's been a rumor she's been fooling around with Brad. I didn't think it was true, but now I'm not sure. She was acting weird. Come on," Natalie said and took Rose's hand. "I want to see it for myself."

Rose's red tennis shoes squeaked on the cement floors as they walked to where Brad's body had lain. Thankfully, his body had been removed. A rust-red halo of dried blood stained the polished concrete floor in a wide circle. A group of official-looking men and women closed ranks as they approached. Officer Nessa stepped back from the circle to block Rose and Natalie.

"No photos. And no civilians at a crime scene."

Natalie stared at the empty outline.

Rose looked at Natalie, who was staring at the empty outline. Her face was the color of chalk, and not the pretty kind kids used to draw on the sidewalk.

"Can you tell us what happened?" Rose asked the policewoman.

"It would help my friend. She knew the guard. The dead man."

Nessa looked over toward the circle of officers and forensics specialists, then turned back to Rose.

"I shouldn't be telling you this, but you helped catch the suspect on your ride-along. Forensics has the official word, but it looks like he was hit on the side of the head, then fell and cracked his skull on the floor. The bullet seems unnecessary, but they shot him, too." Her voice was soft. Conspiratorial.

"Did you find the casing?" Rose asked.

"Not yet." The policewoman crossed her arms as if to say, I've shared enough. They all stared at the outline on the floor.

"Send that report to my phone," said a deep voice. They looked over to see Slade Bolton talking to the police chief. The FBI agent hadn't wasted any time.

Natalie leaned toward Rose and whispered, "What is he doing here?"

Across the room, the chief nodded, made a note of Bolton's phone number, and walked over to join Rose, Natalie, and Sergeant Nessa.

"We certainly don't need that distraction," Chief Donnelly said and rolled her eyes in Bolton's direction. Then she saw Rose.

"Who's this?" Her tone held a strong note of disapproval. Her shoulders stiffened.

Natalie placed her hand on Rose's shoulder.

"Police Chief Donnelly, please meet Rose MacGillivray. My neighbor and friend."

Sargeant Nessa added, "Rose was instrumental in catching the liquor store robber last week."

The chief's posture relaxed. Nessa had said that a murder would stretch the small police force.

No wonder the chief was under stress.

"With the FBI here…" she said, then cut herself off, obviously due to the presence of civilians.

Nessa finished the sentence. "We'll be under scrutiny. Who called them? I mean, we're barely getting started and he's on the scene already."

The police chief flashed a look of annoyance. "This is police business."

"He lives across the street," Natalie said. Rose contained a grin. The police chief looked up with wide eyes but gathered her composure quickly.

"Oh, really. Tell me more."

"I'm afraid that's all I know. He's dating a neighbor. I haven't spent any time with him, just saw him briefly at the gala Friday night."

Nessa's eyebrows bunched together in a look that Rose interpreted to mean, What the….? Before Rose could agree with her, the chief took Nessa's arm and pulled her away, turning their backs as they moved.

Rose shifted her gaze to the walls and floor around the body. Fifteen years ago, she sat on the jury of a murder case where the perpetrator used dumbbells to beat a guy to death. The panel spent days listening to a blood spatter expert explain angles and density.

The medium-sized blood droplets on the walls of the art gallery were easy to see once she found the first one. They dappled the wallboard and speckled the floor. The roundish shape with splattered edges could mean that the blow to Brad's head had not been enough to kill him. Though enough to bruise his brain and render him incapable of living a normal life. Shooting him was either an act of fear, mercy, or hate.

The police officers finished talking and turned back to them.

"When will we be able to clean this and reopen?" Natalie asked. "Eve's going to be frantic about lost sales."

"Another day or so," Nessa said. "We have an outside art theft forensics expert coming in. He'll want to see everything firsthand."

"No wonder Eve's in a snit," Natalie said.

Slade Bolton walked with a police officer to the main entrance of the gallery. Rose heard questions about fingerprints but couldn't hear the answer. She remembered the ghostly image of a figure crossing the street, appearing in the yellow pool cast by the sodium vapor security lights and disappearing in the shade cast by the trees.

She turned back to Nessa.

"Will you tell us when this happened?"

"The coroner's preliminary estimate puts it between 2:00 and 4:00 in the morning. We're hoping the security tapes will narrow that down, but they've been having trouble accessing the system."

Natalie straightened. There was a fresh spark in her eyes.

"I can help with that. I work here, and that security system is my baby. I know every inch of the monitoring room and all the backup procedures."

Nessa took out her radio and spoke into it. She waited for an answer. Rose heard a loud static sound followed by one word.

"Approved."

She turned to Natalie and nodded.

With a sense of determination that Rose understood, Natalie walked over to a door in the back, opened it, and disappeared inside. Her friend had something she could do to help, and that meant she wasn't powerless.

A buzzing on her wrist from her FitBit reminded her to move. Rose slid the screen until her sleep times were visible. Her nighttime wanderings fell dangerously close to 2:00 to 4:00 in the morning.

A young male cop approached, holding a sheaf of papers. "I've got the list of attendees." He fluttered the pages. Nessa smiled at him, showing straight white teeth. The last time Rose had been to the dentist for a crown, the color selected to match her other teeth was a disappointing yellow-gray. Natural aging was the reason, the dental assistant said. Nessa had years before that would mar her grin.

"Hernandez, this is Rose MacGillivray, and the person entering the security room is Natalie Patel."

"Yeah, I remember you. The tech genius. Nice to see you again."

He glanced at his list and winced.

"Yes, we were there," Rose said. His eyes flicked over to Nessa's. She shook her head, which could mean any number of things. No, they aren't suspects, no, I haven't cleared them yet, or no, don't say anything in front of civilians.

Slade Bolton strode toward them and stopped when he reached them.

"Does the Paso Robles Police Department have civilians investigating crimes now?" His voice dripped with sarcasm. The face that had looked so handsome last night when smiling at Stella now had a harsh, ruddy quality of a schoolyard bully. Rose clenched her jaw to prevent herself from uttering the curse word that sat ready to spew out. Pretend to be calm.

Nessa put her notepad away. She addressed Slade with crisp efficiency. "Natalie Patel is an employee at this gallery." She looked back at the open security room door. "She's working on getting the system up and running." He smirked, but Rose thought she saw a flash of fear.

"Don't bother," he said. "Small towns like this one aren't set up to deal with art theft. The FBI will take over in a few days, and our skilled technicians will want all the evidence. Untampered." He stressed "untampered" as if the SLPD didn't know how to do it. Was he accusing Natalie of altering official material?

"Shouldn't the murder, not the theft, be front and center? And that is the jurisdiction of our local police. Right, Chief?" Rose challenged.

"That's correct, as the FBI well knows. The murder of Brad Knight falls within our jurisdiction," the chief explained.

He held up his hand and wiggled his fingers. "You have five days." Then strode off. Nessa let out a huff.

"Try not to let him get under your skin, Sergeant," the chief said. "I remind you that this case is a chance to show what you can do. All the detectives are otherwise occupied, so make the most of this opportunity."

"Yes, Ma'am."

Voices from the technicians in the lobby distracted the chief, and she headed in their direction, leaving Rose and Nessa alone.

Rose lifted her eyebrows. "She didn't say I had to leave."

"She didn't say you could stay, either."

"Well, let's call it a draw, and I'll stick by Natalie as emotional support."

"Don't get in the way, Rose. I mean it. The police department will handle this."

Natalie called out to say that the video was ready.

A moment later, Evangeline hurried by from the gift shop where she kept a desk.

In the interest of keeping all options on the table, what reason could the gallery owner have had for staging a theft? Publicity? Brad's reaction when Evangeline had joined them Friday night played in her mind again. He had stiffened. Shut down and left in a hurry. If they were having an affair, he might have known what she planned, had inside information on the planned robbery, and now he was dead.

Entering the back room, Rose saw multiple monitors, each with a different view of the interior and exterior. It seemed a lot for a small-town art gallery, but then Natalie had said that the Met required increased security for the show. Now she sat at the console, hair pulled back into a puffy ponytail and her mouth set in a thin line. Evangeline stationed herself near the door, and Officer Hernandez pressed in beside the console.

Officer Nessa joined them and stood next to Natalie. "Let's start before the event begins. I want to see everyone come in."

Rose leaned against the doorjamb, surprised the policewoman hadn't booted her out. Natalie typed commands, and the video started.

"Can you make it go faster? I'll flag you if I want you to slow it down," Nessa said. A few taps later, the figures sped up like Keystone cops and zipped across the monitors.

Rose saw herself and Natalie enter and move from

the entrance camera to the lobby view at 7:15 PM. Liz entered at 7:20, and Stella and Slade at 7:31. Figures dashed by until 7:40 when Liz strode out, and 7:45, when Slade and Stella left. It wasn't until 8:03 that Natalie and Rose departed. By then, the number of newcomers had slowed.

Nessa bent next to Natalie. "Okay. Let's shift to after the front doors were locked at the end of the night."

Natalie keyed in the time, and the view on the monitors changed to the cleaning crew. The cleaners left through the back door at 12:03 AM, leaving only Brad and Evangeline. They had a discussion with lots of hand-waving and defiantly crossed arms. No one needed words to know that this was an argument.

Nessa put her hand up, and Natalie paused the video. Evangeline cleared her throat.

"We were, uhm, discussing an employee issue," the gallery owner explained.

That's a lie, realized Rose, remembering Brad's reaction to his boss's presence at the Gala. That hadn't been a give me more vacation time discussion.

With a slight nod, Nessa indicated to continue. On screen, their argument seemingly over, Evangeline turned and stormed out the back. Brad watched her go; then he began to walk from one screen to the next as he patrolled, before returning to the guard station.

Natalie progressed the video forward at double speed until something flickered.

"What was that?" Nessa asked, pointing to the screen.

Natalie moved the video back and forth around the blip in the tape, and a person popped into the frame. The video stream was black and white, and the figure had dressed in black from top to toe, so they appeared as a shadow on the screen.

Evangeline inched her way to the door opening and squeezed by Rose. The police officer leaned close to the middle screen and pointed at the mysterious apparition. "How did that person just appear?"

Natalie fiddled with the playback again. "The only explanation I can come up with is that someone tampered with the video. See how the time stamp jumps here? We're missing fifteen minutes of video." She scrolled forward and backward in time again.

"Hold there." Nessa pointed to the figure. "Can you zoom in?"

As the person increased in size, the picture got blurry. In the lower right-hand corner of the screen, a time stamp glowed in white letters, 1:00 AM SATURDAY

"Who is that? Do you recognize them?" Nessa asked. Natalie leaned toward the monitor, her nose crinkling as she squinted. "That's Evangeline. What is she doing back?"

"Good question. Let's ask." Officer Nessa turned around, but the gallery owner had gone.

"She left about five minutes ago," Rose explained, guessing what the questioning look on the policewoman's face meant.

Officer Hernandez took a step toward the door. "I might be able to catch her if she's walking."

"Find her," ordered Nessa.

Rose sidled over to Natalie. "Are you okay?"

"I can't get the image of Brad lying on the floor with blood around his head out of my mind. I didn't have to see it to know what it would look like."

Rose could imagine what her friend was picturing: an artist's vivid imagination would have filled in the gaps and assigned hues and tone to the brick-red blood, pale tones for the dead human flesh. She wanted to wrap her arms around her friend, to protect her from the pain of losing someone. Natalie had lost a husband, but—and her friend would admit this herself—it wasn't a painful loss. Paul announced his intention to divorce her two days before dropping dead on the driveway while washing his prized Aston Martin DB5.

Some people would have called it poetic justice, but Natalie, full of reserve, buried him, sold the car and moved on. Brad had hit a nerve with her. For him, she would grieve.

"I'm sorry you're having to do this," Rose said quietly.

Nessa reentered the tiny room. "What other security measures did the gallery add for this event?"

Natalie thought for a moment. "We went from one security camera to three and added humidity sensors and humidifiers. And we've always had mag strip key cards for the doors. Those records would be available."

The police officer noted this in her notebook.

"Please pull the mag strip info and get it to me as soon as possible," she said then pulled out her phone and dialed.

"Dave? I'll need the forensics guys to look at some security footage. It's been tampered with. I want to know what's missing. Thanks."

She turned to the small group crammed into the security room.

"We'll get to the bottom of this." Rose let her eyes

drop to the monitor still showing the blurry figure of Evangeline. When she looked up again, the policewoman had gone. Rose bubbled with questions. Why was there a gap in the footage? Who doctored the system? Where was Evangeline coming from and going to at such a late hour?

Rose caught up with Officer Nessa as she was taking quick strides toward the main front door. "Any chance you have time for coffee? Or lunch?" An altered video and a gallery owner who'd made herself scarce begged to be discussed.

Nessa tucked the notepad into a pocket in her police vest. "I really can't discuss it with you. I probably shouldn't have mentioned anything or let you see that video. Let the police handle this."

The door to the gallery closed with a quiet click. Yes, she should let the police handle it; that was their job. But. Rose couldn't let it go. Her mind whirled with why, where, how, and who. The basic tools of an investigator.

Chapter 12 Rose

~

Barolo – A wine from the Piedmont region of Italy made from the Nebbiolo grape

Sunday, October 9, 6:45 PM

Impromptu parties were always the best. A cool, fall breeze called for a hearty red like Barolo. Rose gathered plates and napkins as Stella and Natalie talked on the veranda. How long could her waistline handle it? She'd need to diet soon. A four-letter word she hated even to contemplate. Right now, though, Stella had brought a veggie pie with every topping Rose could think of scattered over the cheese layer.

Crickets chirped as she came out the door, and Natalie spoke. "Stella, we need to discuss the kind of men you find interesting."

Stella's eyes narrowed.

"I mean, look at her, Rose, she's a beautiful woman, smart, accomplished—"

Stella was all those things, but her shoulders inched up toward her ears and her lips clamped in a straight line.

She didn't need them telling her how to live her life. Rose felt a maternal pull to the young woman, but recognized that she had boundaries, and if Rose didn't jump in and stop things, their congenial night would screech to a halt.

A cool breeze rustled the leaves of the Sycamore tree, and Rose felt the first hints of colder weather.

"I think what Natalie means is that we want to make sure you are attracting the best."

Echoes of her mother's words when Rose was fifteen.

Gooey cheese dripped down Stella's fingers as she folded a slice of pie. "And Slade isn't the best? He's got a fantastic job, he's fit, eats healthy, and is respectful to me. Okay, so he isn't the most open person I've ever known, but no one is perfect. Right?"

Rose took a slice of pizza and looked away from the conversational train wreck. She bit down on the crunchy crust, the hot cheese burned her mouth, and she pulled it out and dropped it onto her plate. Stella must have cast-iron fingers.

"How can you eat it that hot?" she asked.

"Don't overthink it," Stella said as she set her glass down on the table. "It's like with dating. I don't think about it. I know the fling with Slade won't last, especially since—"

Rose eyed her new friend. She didn't know the woman well, but well enough to sense something was wrong.

"Since what?"

"Since, oh god, I went into his house. The whole time we've dated, he'd only come to my house. Earlier today, I marched over and rang the bell. When he answered, I barged in."

She gulped down some wine. Rose glanced over at the bottle and wondered whether to open another one. Stella twirled the stem of her glass between her fingers.

"It's like no one lives there. No furniture except a folding lawn chair and a sleeping bag on the floor. No wonder he doesn't invite me over."

"That's it? A chair and a sleeping bag?" Rose asked. Slade Bolton was an annoyance and gave her the creeps, but was he dangerous? Normal people didn't live like that.

"I agree it's weird, thrifty to the point of obsession, but why did that make you think you wouldn't be dating him much longer?"

"Well…I haven't told you the worst of it," Stella continued. Natalie moved forward to the edge of her chair.

Tears gathered in Stella's eyes. This guy had gotten to her. Rose handed her another napkin. "Sweetie, it won't go beyond us."

"It was on the kitchen counter." Stella blew her nose and then sniffed. "A framed picture of Slade and that woman we met the other night, Liz Bathory. They were all lovey-dovey."

Natalie and Rose looked at each other with widened eyes. It seemed clear from how they acted Friday night that they knew each other. Perhaps more intimately than any of them had guessed.

Love can rip you up. Rose lacked much experience in that department. But she'd read lots of romance novels and imagined that her one affair was an anomaly in the world of love. Like in the books, she'd been breathless and weak-kneed. Until he left her devastated and broken.

That was twenty years ago, and yet the sting still burned.

Stella's sniffle brought her back to the veranda. Natalie handed the young woman another napkin.

"Could be from a long time ago. He did say he knew her, and she didn't seem happy to see him. Probably ended badly."

"He still has her picture." Stella blew her nose.

"It was the only personal thing there. It must still mean something to him. I could never compete with her. Rich and beautiful. I don't know why I'm getting myself so worked up. I knew it wouldn't last."

"You can definitely compete with a cold woman like Liz Bathory," Natalie reassured her. "I think it might be the other way around. He needs you. You don't need him."

Rose wasn't sure she agreed with Natalie. If Bolton was filling in a gap with Stella, all the while hoping Liz would come back to him, that didn't bode well for Stella.

"What did Slade say when you pushed your way in?" she asked.

Stella tucked the crumpled napkin into her pocket. "Oh, he was furious. Tried to block my view, but I slipped around him. I didn't see his expression at first, but when I did, I realized what a mistake I'd made. His whole face was red, even his ears." She sipped her wine. "When I saw the picture, I stopped. He grabbed me by my shoulders, spun me around, and shoved me out the door."

Natalie gasped. "Did he hurt you?"

"No, thankfully." Stella rubbed her left shoulder. "But I got the sense that if I didn't get skedaddle right away, he might."

Rose fought the urge to go over to Stella and put an arm around her like her mother had done but wasn't sure how Stella would respond. It might be too personal, especially to someone seeking her own birth mother. It might feel like Rose was trying to fill that role.

"Do you still consider it a good idea to date him?" Rose asked instead.

"Despite that nasty photo, he's a decent man." Stella's voice grew petulant. Rose had been like that as a child, stubborn as the day is long, her mother used to say.

It was time to move to another topic, and the one Rose wanted to talk about was the murder. Parse it out. Could the guard's death and the theft of the painting be separate events? A macabre twist of fate? Or the dreaded word, coincidence? Rose didn't believe in those.

"Is it possible that Evangeline stole the painting?" she asked.

A murmur of blackbirds descended on the sycamore tree to the left and cackled so loudly they couldn't talk. It was just as well. Rose herself believed Evangeline would steal, but that was precisely why she asked the question. Natalie knew her better. Though would she let the boss/employee relationship color her thoughts?

Natalie appeared to ponder the question until a souped-up Camaro roared down the street and the birds flew away.

"Maybe, but not that one. It was too somber. Evangeline's words, not mine. I think it's lovely. I've got a perfect spot to hang it in my house if it weren't already in the New York Met's collection."

That was the second time Natalie had said she'd love to have the painting. Did she want it badly enough to take it?

Stella crisscrossed her legs, tucking one foot under the tangle. Rose wished she could sit like that. Her thighs were too substantial to make that work.

"Slade mentioned that there might be a dangerous art theft ring behind this," Stella said.

"In little Paso Robles?" Natalie's forehead lifted in surprise. "We're not exactly the hub of the art world here." She paused. "Though that might explain his presence. If the

FBI got a tip in advance. I mean, he just materialized a few weeks ago, swept Stella off her feet, and settled into the routine of a small town. That picture is incomplete; the color is all wrong."

Stella's smile stiffened. She took a sip of wine and nodded as if deciding on some compilation of the facts. "Or maybe he's decided the bustle of DC was getting old and read about wonderful Paso Robles. For him, it all adds up to a better life."

The image of the figure crossing the street on Friday night remained in Rose's mind. Would Stella defend Slade if it had been him?

"Natalie, did you call the police about the break-in?"

"No." Natalie fished into her pocket and brought out two keys. "But I got you a key. For emergencies." She handed one to Stella and one to Rose.

"Someone broke into your house?" Stella slid it into a pocket in her yoga pants.

Natalie settled back into her chair and picked up her wine glass. "Garage. I'm probably being paranoid. It may have been a cat, but something knocked over a plant and left dirt tracks."

"You said footprints earlier," Rose said.

"It must have been the gardener. I realized that later. Anyway, the door locks are all changed."

A black Mercedes rolled past, turned left, and eased into Slade's driveway. Perched high above the street, Rose could see the car, but the driver couldn't see her. Stella sank into her chair. Perhaps there was hope that she'd dump him.

The sedan slid into the garage, and the door came down.

They ate in silence before Stella straightened up and said, "More wine," then reached for a new bottle of Peachy Canyon Zinfandel.

Rose held out her glass for some as well. "If the FBI got a tip and sent him, Evangeline should have known about it."

"She didn't mention it," Natalie said. "We did put in all sorts of new security equipment. Maybe the FBI required it. I'm going into the gallery again tomorrow. I'll do some poking around. See what I can learn."

Rose remembered how she investigated a quality problem at work. First, she gathered all the facts, interviewed everyone involved, and sorted through available data. Difficult with this theft and murder, considering she had no official role.

Difficult, but not impossible.

"Stella, you can help too. Can you find out about the FBI tip that brought Slade here and about his assignments over the last year or so? We need all the background we can find."

There was a tense minute before Stella replied. "I can do that. You won't find anything, but if it will stop you both from picking on him, it will be worth it."

Natalie chewed and gazed at the mature oak that anchored the corner with its thick, deeply ridged trunk and massive canopy that shaded the sidewalk. "I've been pondering the security video."

Rose looked up. "And?"

"The cleaning crew left at around midnight. They have their key cards. Suppose someone waited in the alley and stole it from them?"

Stella's brows furrowed.

"Wouldn't they have reported the theft?"

Nothing had been said about the cleaning crew other than when they arrived and left. Rose pictured the lobby of the art gallery.

"The cleaning folks didn't toss all the empty wine bottles?"

Natalie shrugged. "The winery came back for them. They get credit for recycling or something like that."

That made some sense. "Is that normal?" Rose asked.

"They cleared it with us before the gala, so I don't think it's anything to worry about."

"Still…" Rose said, wondering about it anyway. Anything out of the ordinary could be a clue.

"Have you been able to figure out if there is a way to get to the missing security footage?"

"The security company we lease the equipment from will be here tomorrow." Natalie lifted another slice from the cardboard box. "Between them and the police forensics guys, hopefully, they can trace it back and figure that out."

Rose nodded and took a bite of the pizza she had held for so long that the cooling cheese congealed. "Do you trust them?"

"Who, the security people? Yeah, I do. We worked closely with them for several weeks to get it all set up. There are backups, so if anything looks fishy, we can double-check."

Later, as Rose straightened the veranda and kitchen, she thought about the tape.

If the cleaning crew left at midnight, and Evangeline came back at one AM, the altercation had to have taken place after that but before she arrived back in the morning to find the body.

Rose tossed two empty wine bottles into the blue recycling box outside her back door. The tapes didn't show Evangeline leaving, so one of two things was true: either she was the killer, or someone wanted it to appear that way.

Chapter 13 Rose

~

Zinfandel — a black-skinned wine grape also known as Primitivo in Italy

Monday, October 10, 8:00 AM

Watson bolted out the door as soon as it swung open. He made straight for his favorite rosemary bush and lifted his leg. A doggy expression of bliss settled on his face. Rose marveled that something so simple as watching a dog relieve itself could give her such peace. If Watson felt safe enough to lift his leg and pee, she should feel that same sense of security in this new town. She didn't. Perhaps, with time.

Rose made herself a breakfast sandwich and took it out onto the back patio. Even during her working days, October was her favorite month. The days were shorter, which meant less time for the heat to build and a longer evening for the house to cool. The sun moved further south, which softened the glare and made the oak leaves greener, even as they began to yellow, and the sky bluer.

Thanks to the people whose house she bought, her garden was still in full swing. The tomatoes needed picking, the Japanese eggplants were ready for veggie lasagna, and the herb garden was a riot of blooms and bees. Watson rooted around until he found a spot to dig and then went at it with gusto.

A row of stately Mission olives grew along the back.

Her fingers brushed through the silver-gray leaves. Fragrant oil seeped out when she dug her nail into the hard, round fruit. She'd need to harvest these soon. That brought a rush of nervous energy as she thought of the imposing equipment in the garage that she'd need to figure out to press the oil.

She nibbled the sandwich, and her thoughts drifted to the killing. How could she use her quality assurance skills to solve a murder? It couldn't be that different from a mechanical failure in hardware. There would be people, processes, and circumstances that caused the problem, although calling murder a problem seemed insensitive. And an understatement. Still, one followed the same steps. Interview the people involved, develop a timeline of events, and figure out what really happened.

When she finished, she brought her plate into the kitchen and clipped the leash onto Watson's collar. Years ago, if someone were to walk along a street and talk to no one, everyone labeled them a kook. Now, with cell phone earbuds and hearing aids that rang directly in your ear, *everyone* looked crazy, and thus no one did. Rose discovered that she liked talking to Watson. He was a great listener. Anything that bothered his new owner was fair game for discussion on their strolls around the neighborhood.

As they strolled, and he sniffed bushes, she told him all about the killing in the gallery. His ears swiveled back as she spoke, and he sniffed shrubs and weeds along the way.

"I met the guy, Brad Knight. Such a shame. Natalie's devastated. And why shouldn't she be? She knew him. Between us, she had the hots for him."

Watson turned and looked at her.

"I know what you're thinking, he's married. Or was. But that isn't important right now. The time of the crime was when we were wandering the house looking out windows, and I used my fitness watch as proof, which sounded good at the time." They stopped so Watson could spray on a lamp post. Rose waited until he was done to continue talking, not wanting to distract him from his task.

"Now I'm worried they'll arrest me. And, for the record, I'm innocent."

Good lord, she was defending herself to a dog. Is this what happened when one moved from the city to a small town? Innocent people don't have to worry. No, that wasn't right. They should worry because innocent people get arrested all the time.

And thus, the reason she needed to dig into things and clear her name.

"I'll have to figure out what happened, give the information to the police, and be done with it. And maybe I'll get lucky, and they will solve it before me."

Watson gave an all-body shake, which Rose decided meant he agreed with her.

They went six blocks in one direction, one more block over, and then made their way back. With hills over that stretch, she got her heart rate up. Her doctor would be happy. Watson explored every shrub and marked quite a few. Leaving breadcrumbs, Rose thought of it as she watched him dart from one to the next.

When they turned into her driveway, a police car passed by and stopped in front of Natalie's house. Paso Robles's black vehicles looked more imposing than the many tourist SUVs that crowded the roads. At least five cruisers had already parked in the street. Her chest tightened.

What could command such a response? She scanned for a coroner's van and relaxed somewhat at not finding one.

At the corner, Slade Bolton stood on the sidewalk with his arms crossed over his chest and the smug look of an overpaid government employee on his face. Rose's hands went clammy. Watson growled a low rumble, and the fur on his back ruffled up, a response Rose wished she could emulate.

Next to Bolton stood Stella. When her gaze drifted to Rose, she hurried over to stand next to her, her hair bouncing against her shoulders with each step.

"I can't believe it!" she said. Rose noted the elevated voice like an excited schoolgirl might have when finding out she made the cheerleading squad. Something Rose had never done. Not that she hadn't tried.

"What's going on?" Rose asked. "Why are the police here?

One cruiser blocked Natalie's vehicle, and her front door hung open. Three police officers milled around in the middle of the street, one holding the leash of a police German shepherd. Watson sniffed the air and tugged at the leash.

"Not now," Rose said. This was not the time for a play date.

A forensics tech came down the front steps carrying a large, flat object the size of a coffee table wrapped in furniture blankets. More techs entered the front door with cameras and equipment satchels. Officer Nessa marched Natalie down the driveway, her hands handcuffed behind her back, and her head drooped. Natalie's stilted steps suggested reluctance, which was understandable.

It also might be that her friend couldn't believe what was happening, and her feet were even further behind.

Stella gasped. "Slade said they were going to do it, but I didn't believe him. She's seemed so nice."

Fear tightened Rose's gut. "Going to do what?"

"Arrest Natalie for the theft and murder."

"That's insane!" Rose handed Watson's leash to Stella and took off at a jog to intercept the procession. Everything jiggled as she went. Yet another thing to add to her goals for the year. Get in shape.

"I didn't do it!" Natalie cried when she saw Rose. "You have to believe me. I didn't put that painting there!"

"What painting?" Rose asked as the policewoman guided Natalie into the back seat of a squad car. Was that what the techs were carrying in the moving blanket? Natalie was an artist; naturally, her house and garage contained canvases, paint, and brushes. Nothing strange about that.

Nessa didn't answer; she just placed her hand on Natalie's head and guided her into the back seat.

"It wasn't me! I swear!"

Nessa shut the door and patted the roof twice. The engine started.

"Step back, please," she called out. Several cops who stood in the vehicle's path moved to the side, and the car pulled away.

"I don't believe this," Rose said. "She couldn't have done whatever you think she's done."

Nessa pulled her notepad out and jotted down the time. Then she turned to Rose.

"Sometimes people surprise us. Not always in a good way."

The policewoman's mouth pressed together in a

line that was more of a scowl. The glare a teacher gave when a student asked a question they could easily have answered themselves. At that moment, Rose wondered how she could have ever liked this young woman.

"She's not guilty, I'm guessing you know that." Rose's voice cracked with strain. "I'm going to get this cleared up."

"We received an anonymous tip about the painting. And her key card was used to access the gallery at 3:06 AM." The policewoman's tone was flat and direct.

"And did you find that key card in her house?" Rose asked.

Could someone have duped Natalie's card without her knowledge? In her own working days, Rose guarded her security pass with extreme diligence. Had Natalie done the same?

"Not yet. But we will," Nessa said, then moved away to talk with a colleague. Slade Bolton crossed the street and stood beside Rose.

"Looks like it didn't take long at all. I thought I'd need to step in, on behalf of the FBI, but it turns out small-time crooks are as simple as this town is backwater."

Rose pulled her gaze away from the disappearing police cruiser and turned to stare at Bolton. *How dare he?*

"So, you aren't planning to live here and set up house with Stella? Escape the hustle and bustle of the big city?"

He grinned. "With this solved, I'll be gone."

It seemed unlikely that the FBI sent him to a small art show in Paso Robles, even if it was a traveling show from the Met. Yet, his presence didn't feel random.

Rose knew from their brief discussion during wine

and pizza that Stella was strong. She'd move on, though the sting of rejection always hurt.

Government employees didn't frighten her. Rose smirked back at him.

"Go back to your big city, Mr. Bolton, and your petty little job. Natalie didn't do this, and I'm going to prove it."

He squinted. "You?"

She straightened to her full, just-over-five-feet height. "Me."

He shoved his hands in his trouser pockets. "My advice is to stay away. This is a dangerous business. Art thieves can be ruthless."

Rose took a step back. "Is this how the FBI works? By threatening citizens?"

Was a slap too outdated?

He sneered. "Consider yourself warned. A geezer like you could get hurt. Or worse."

Did he call me an old lady? Her fist clenched. She could slug him so hard he'd regret calling her anything but ma'am.

"I am not —." She paused and took a breath to steady herself. "I am more than capable of protecting myself."

Which was almost the truth. At ten, her father taught her to handle firearms, and she had taken self-defense classes at the company gym. How long had it been since she handled a gun?

He laughed a sharp "ha" and walked away.

Nessa approached, and together they watched as the FBI agent strode away.

"Don't let him get to you."

The policewoman acted like she hadn't arrested Rose's best friend in the world.

"Why did you even look at Natalie's place?"

After a silent moment, Nessa said, "I suppose it won't hurt to tell you. We got a tip."

That sounded like something from a TV detective show.

"A tip? That the stolen painting was in Natalie's garage?"

Nessa nodded. A squawk came from her radio, and she pulled it from her belt and stepped away to answer. Slade Bolton stood in the opening of Natalie's front door. What was he really doing here?

When the call ended, Nessa turned back to Rose.

"Yes, it came in on the tip line. And we found the painting. So, it looks like we've got our killer."

Rose couldn't get words out fast enough.

"You can't, no, seriously? Natalie couldn't have killed anyone; she's, well, this can't be true. I could call in a tip that I saw Bolton cross the street in the middle of the night from her house to his. Would you raid his house?"

"Did you see him do that?"

Nessa hugged her arms across her chest, waiting for an answer.

"I'm not sure."

"No evidence, no raid."

Rose pointed to Bolton. "Did you hear him? He threatened me. Arrest him, too."

"What threat?"

Rose forced herself to unclench her hands. "He called me an old lady. I wanted to punch him."

Nessa chuckled. "I'm glad you didn't. "

"You didn't answer about arresting him." Rose lifted her eyebrows to indicate she expected the policewoman to address her question.

"As much as I'd like to, I can't arrest an FBI agent without proper authorization." Nessa gave a quick nod as if reassuring herself that that was so and left.

As the last police car drove away, Rose retrieved Watson from Stella, who had held onto the leash the whole time. The younger woman's face was the pallid shade of someone about to be sick. Watson seemed reluctant to leave her side, as if he sensed that he was needed for emotional support.

"Thank you," Rose said. "I'm pretty sure—" Stella put up her hands to stop her from saying more.

"I can read lips. And body language." She straightened up, took a deep breath, and marched home without looking in the direction of the man she had defended.

Rose glanced up at Natalie's place. Everyone had left. The house looked strangely empty. Knowing her friend wasn't in there made it exude hollowness.

Who had called in the anonymous tip? That question piled on top of all the others that filled Rose's mind after talking it over with Watson.

What had the fight between the guard and the gallery owner been about? Why did Evangeline come back after leaving in the first place? Whose footprint was on the carpet? Who might have a grudge against an ex-cop? And, lastly, what had the argument in the park between Brad and Slade Bolton been about?

How would she ever figure it all out? It didn't seem that any of this was connected.

Rose tugged on Watson's leash.

"Come on, boy. We're going home."

As she ascended her stairs, she thought about how people could surprise you. Shock you. But they rarely turned out to be murderers and thieves. Rose went to her desk and pulled a new spiral-bound notebook from the far bottom drawer, along with colored pens. She drew a line across the top of the first page and put a dot at the beginning. This she labeled *R&N Arrive* and drew a box around the words. Then she noted the time and date. *7:15 PM Friday*.

She added arrival and departure times for Stella, Slade, and, for good measure, Liz Bathory, mainly because the woman had cried over the painting. It seemed a trivial reason, but she was grasping at anything that might prove useful. Toward the end, she put another small circle. This she labeled *Body Found, 8 AM Saturday*.

Sitting back, she stared at the paper. Somewhere between the dots, a killer entered the gallery and hit the guard. Then shot him. Whether the intent had been to kill him or incapacitate him, either way, the guard died.

No. Brad died. A human being. Not an inanimate piece of hardware on a test technician's bench; a living, breathing human being, with a wife and a worthwhile life.

She shook her head as if to rattle doubt away. Who, what, when, where, and how were important. But motive, the last W, felt most elusive. And the key to learning who committed the crimes. If she kept her inquiry along those lines, she was confident the process would work.

So, after the thieves entered the side gallery with a special traveling show on loan from the Met, probably worth millions, they stole one insignificant painting.

Why that one?

Memories of the night of the gala filled her mind. Classical music filled the lobby. The air was redolent with the smell of peonies in a large display in the lobby and the swish sound of long dresses. A woman's emotional response to the painting *Gray Day, Montrose Valley*.

Liz Bathory. The woman whose family bequest was the center of the exhibit and the center of the crime. She had come across as aloof and despondent until Slade Bolton arrived. In an instant, she wound up like a panther ready to fight. Jealousy? No, it didn't feel that way. Maybe betrayal. She turned and walked away with her shoulders stiff and her chin lifted. Bolton and Stella left immediately after Liz departed, leaving Rose and Natalie looking at each other with raised eyebrows. What had that been about?

Chapter 14 Rose

~

Sauvignon blanc – a crisp dry white wine varietal originating in Romania

Monday, October 10, 11:00 AM

A strong knock on the door startled Rose. Where had she been? Oh yes, contemplating the events of Friday and Saturday. Stella waved frantically through the peephole, followed by another pound on the door.

"Come on, Rose. Open up!"

Rose hesitated. Could this young woman be a plant? Ingratiating herself into their little friendship circle to gather intel for her boyfriend/co-conspirator? Perhaps. Rose's hand hovered over the doorknob, feeling a mix of guilt for even thinking it and fear. Fear that she might be right.

Still, at this point, any morsel of information could be useful in constructing the puzzle of who killed the guard and stole the painting. If she kept her emotions under control, Stella might be helpful.

She opened the door.

Stella pushed her way in and slammed the door behind her. "What was that all about?

Rose wasn't sure if she meant the delay in opening the door or the whole scene earlier at Natalie's house. They had seen the same thing; watched the spectacle unfold. Before Rose could produce a response, Stella marched from the hall into the kitchen, opened the refrigerator, and pulled out a bottle of sauvignon blanc.

"I'll have one too," Rose said as she followed her into the kitchen.

The refrigerator door slammed shut with a rattle that sounded like the overpriced bottle of local olives tipping over. That would be a mess to clean if the top came loose.

Stella reached for the open shelf that held stemware, twisted off the bottle cap, and poured to the rim.

"I mean, arresting Natalie? Based on what?"

Rose watched in amazement. Stella had been in Rose's kitchen once and yet knew the location of alcohol-related serving ware. Almost like a sixth sense. Stella stopped and stared at her.

"What?"

"I'm amazed that you knew where everything was."

Rose perched on a stool and accepted the full goblet Stella slid her way. A bit of wine slopped over the side.

"Easy. You've set up your kitchen the same way as I have mine. It makes logical sense, doesn't it? To have the glasses in that cabinet?"

It did make sense, and yet the idea that they both thought that amused Rose. It was like they were cut from the same bolt of cloth. Enough of that, she thought. We have other problems to solve.

Rose pulled a napkin from the holder and wiped up the spill. "We need to focus on helping Natalie."

"Damn right. That son-of-a-" Stella poured herself a serving, almost draining the bottle.

"I take it then that you're no longer seeing Mr. Bolton?" Rose asked.

Stella took a long drink, swallowing several times, and didn't spill a drop.

"I don't know. I'm not sure I want to. He had Natalie arrested!" She gazed out the window. "I mean, the sex is great and—"

Rose took a quick breath, felt an urge to intervene. If this were her daughter, if she had a daughter, she might have. But what right did she have to judge someone else's decisions? It wasn't like her slate was clean in that regard.

"Stella?"

The younger woman stopped talking.

"What happens if you find your birth mother? Have you thought about that?"

If the change in conversation startled Stella, she didn't show it.

"I think of nothing but that. I don't know what I'll do. I guess it depends on who it is."

"You won't be angry that she gave you up?" Rose wanted the answer to be 'of course not' - it's what she hoped would happen if she ever ran into the child she gave up. Stella came from a younger generation, though. One that didn't see out-of-wedlock birth as something to be ashamed of. Something to hide.

"I want to know why, of course. But, no, I wouldn't be upset. More like relieved. I've been looking for so long. It will be a miracle if I do find her, and I don't want to waste time on negative emotions."

Rose spun the stem of her glass between her fingers. "Thank you for being so open about it. I mean, we've only met, and I'm grateful you feel comfortable talking about something so personal with me."

Stella's smile radiated acceptance. "From the moment I met you in the gallery, I felt like we would be good friends. I know my mom, back in England, would love you. You're very much like her."

Tears stung Rose's eyes, and she sipped her wine to cover the slight napkin dab to dry them. Having friends was such a wonderful feeling; she couldn't believe she'd gone so long without.

And she had another friend. Natalie. Poor Natalie. What was going on with her?

"I saw them take what looked like a painting. The police must think it's the missing artwork. And it makes sense they will charge her with Brad's death as well."

Stella's mouth dropped open for a moment before it snapped shut in a lip-lined scowl. "I saw her at that art show. She practically drooled over the guard. She wouldn't—"

"Kill him? No. Though she did love that painting."

"Then who?"

The same question ran around in Rose's mind. Could they be looking at two different crimes? One a murder and the other a theft, which happened to occur on the same evening, between the same hours?

Stella set down her wine with a clang on the granite. Her eyes widened, but she relaxed when it was clear the stem hadn't broken. Rose made a mental note to move the stemless glassware to the front of the shelf.

"What if someone planted the painting?" Stella asked. "That night, Friday night, after the art show."

Rose sat up straight.

"Natalie did say she found a broken flowerpot the next morning."

"I'll bet that's what happened."

Rose sipped her wine, a lovely Viognier from Bon Niche Cellars. She cast her memory back to that night.

"A cat was out making a racket; he could have knocked the pot over. Natalie checked - nothing was missing, so no evidence of anyone entering the garage or house. I saw someone crossing the street, but I can't prove that. I mean, whoever it was did go by Franklin's old house, but I didn't see a face. It was dark, and the trees cast shadows, so all I really saw was someone cross and disappear. To top it off, she's already had the locksmith out, which will have destroyed any evidence that did exist."

Rose felt empty, as if this recitation had drained her spirit. Natalie had said how much she loved that painting. Why was it such a shock to learn that the police had found it in her garage?

"But..." she said. "Following your theory that someone planted the painting, what is the motive?"

"Why did they even look in Natalie's garage?" Stella asked.

"The police received an anonymous tip. Maybe the same person who put it there in the first place. Unless Natalie..."

Had she made a copy for herself, and the police found it? Nothing illegal in that. Rose couldn't believe her friend would kill for a painting.

Stella's brows wove together like a Knit-purl stitch pattern. "Slade couldn't have done it. He was with me."

"All night?" Rose sat up straight.

Stella paused. "Well, no, I can't say for sure."

"You realize that's a red flag. Don't you?" Rose asked.

"I wouldn't say—"

"He gives the word 'creepy' a whole new definition. Face it, he's good-looking but scary. And he said you were just a cover story."

Stella turned away, then drank a long slug of wine. Rose pushed hers away. Already she felt the warm relaxation of her muscles and the effortless way her thoughts slipped from one idea to another. She needed all her faculties sharp. Tall people could handle wine better.

"Okay, you're probably right, but for now, I don't know." Stella gazed across the room. The hands on the clock on the kitchen wall ticked off the minutes. When her focus returned, it blazed with resolve.

"Screw him! You said you saw someone cross the street in the middle of the night, from Natalie's house to his?"

"Yes. I did see someone." Rose didn't trust this sudden shift from defender to prosecutor. "He didn't say anything to you? Like, why is he here? Why did he pick a house across the street from you?"

"To be honest, I never asked. I'm sorry." The blush on Stella's cheeks was the same color as the ranunculus growing in the back. Rose felt a rush of maternal protectiveness. No, that wasn't right. It wasn't maternal, it was woman to woman. They needed to stick together to solve this.

"I'm sure Natalie didn't do this. It's up to us to rescue her. I don't trust anyone else to get it right."

"That settles it," Stella said. "We need to get back into Slade's house."

She picked up the bottle and drained the splash left into her glass. "It shouldn't be too difficult."

"You're talking about breaking and entering. Unlawful and dangerous." Rose felt compelled to say that, even though she contemplated the same thing.

"Who said I'd be breaking in?" Stella asked. "We're not officially broken up. So, for now, we're together. I'll show up in see-through cling wrap and push my way in."

That should set the pompous Mr. Bolton back a step. Though if he was dangerous, it could be an invitation to abuse.

"He might not be as receptive as you think."

He'd said she was a distraction. Yet, it could work. No. The idea of seducing someone suspected of murder didn't feel like something she should be encouraging. But then, he was a man. Of course, he'd let Stella in. The real question was, could she get out?

Chapter 15 Rose

~

Viognier — a white wine grape variety, originating in the Northern Rhone of France

Monday, October 10, 3:00 PM

The voice that answered the phone at the county jail sounded distant and gruff. Rose wasn't sure what to say to speak with a prisoner. It was difficult to think of Natalie that way.

"Natalie Patel, please."

"Inmate or officer?"

Inmate sounded so permanent, but the alternatives, convict, jailbird, lifer, were worse.

"Inmate," she finally said, though the word felt dirty in her mouth.

The line clicked as the call was transferred, then went quiet before another voice asked her whether she had set up a funded account to pay for calls to this inmate. When she said no, they politely told her the call could not be put through.

Disappointed, she thought about Natalie's skill as an artist as she ate a late lunch of a turkey and cheese sandwich on the back patio and sobered up. Young Stella may be able to handle drinking so early in the day, but it wasn't Rose's habit to imbibe before noon. With a clearer head it was easy to imagine her friend had created a version of a painting she loved. But who knew about it? Who called in the anonymous tip that the painting was in Nat's garage?

She ran through the list of suspects. Of all the people in attendance at the gala, who would have a motive? Or was Brad the target and the painting a mask?

A hummingbird hovered at the scarlet red feeder hung from a shepherd's hook. Her pen hovered over a fresh notebook page.

Slade Bolton, the conveniently placed FBI agent.

The people in the government she'd worked with during her career were competent, trustworthy, and dependable. None had ever given a reason to doubt their intentions. The FBI bureau recruited the best and brightest; that's what their ads said.

They had even contacted her about a position, which she declined because it meant leaving California. On the one hand, it didn't make sense to include a federal agent in a suspect list, but Rose remembered the feeling of menace in his handshake. And he had called her *old*, which in itself was criminal. She wrote down his name. If he were innocent, he would be a quick target to eliminate.

She should add Natalie and Stella but somehow felt the laws of girlfriends forbade thinking of them as guilty. And despite just meeting Stella, she felt a motherly concern for her. So, if Natalie had painted a copy of *Gray Day*, it was for an innocent purpose.

The tip of her pen touched the paper and bled a black blob. A mistake her literary hero, Hamish Macbeth, frequently made was overlooking those closest to him. With a heavy sigh, she wrote down the two names. Her first task would be to clear them.

She wrote down Liz Bathory and Evangeline Abbot. Both were present on Friday night. And Brad's wife.

Spouses were always high on the suspect list in murder mysteries.

It made sense to start with the Abbot woman. What was behind that tense exchange between her and Brad at the gala? Could she have known about the paintings in Natalie's garage and called the tip line?

Rose cleaned up her lunch things, grabbed her purse, hat, and sunglasses, and gave Watson a treat on her way out the door.

The bell at the gallery entrance jangled, and the aroma of cinnamon and cloves from freshly brewed coffee greeted her.

Evangeline sat hunched over a laptop in the gift store, which occupied an old car bay from the days when the building was an auto repair shop. She didn't look up.

"We're closed."

Mascara smeared around Evangeline's red, puffy eyes. Rose felt an urge to console the woman, suspect or not, but reigned it in. As an investigator, she needed cool dispatch.

"Did you hear me?" the owner said, looking up finally. "We're closed."

"Just looking," Rose said as she wandered around the shop. Evangeline resumed tapping on the keyboard, clearly not interested in selling merchandise. Artistic earrings, note cards, scarves, and necklaces adorned every nook. Rose didn't like that sort of thing—most art eluded her. A nice silk scarf might brighten up a corner, but nothing interested her.

She fingered delicate earrings with silver teardrops that dangled from hoops. Either Stella or Natalie would love these for their birthday. When were they? She'd have to ask.

But right now, she needed to steel her nerves for what was sure to be a confrontation with the owner.

Tears trembled in the corners of Evangeline's eyes as Rose approached. She reached into her purse for a tissue to hand to the woman. The gallery owner hesitated, then took the offering.

"All this... mess. We finally got the forensics team to leave." Evangeline swept her arm to indicate the entire space. "Will buyers come back?"

The gift shop itself was tidy and showed no signs of catastrophe. But Rose knew what she meant. Out in the main lobby, the body outline remained on the floor. A macabre tourist draw.

"I wouldn't worry about that. People love death. It intrigues them."

Evangeline sniffed into a tissue. "I remember you. Natalie's friend. They arrested her, you know, and I thought I knew her."

Okay, so either this was a magnificent acting job, or Evangeline didn't call the tip line.

Rose set the earrings down on the counter. With restraint, she looked straight at the woman.

"I don't believe she would, or could, do something like this."

Evangeline closed the laptop and placed a black lacquer stylus beside it. Rose gave her a sympathetic smile in the hope that their previous connection gave her permission to probe for information.

"I'm hoping you could help Natalie by answering some questions." Rose waited. The woman said nothing. Okay, so that's how this is going to go.

"At the gala, Friday night, I noticed that you and

Brad weren't on the... best of terms."

Evangeline's bloodshot eyes narrowed, and she spoke in a voice so low Rose had to lean in to hear. "That is none of your business." Then a flush of tomato red crept across her cheeks.

Rose tried to convey understanding through her eyes, though she didn't feel any sympathy. She was beginning to suspect the whole tear thing was an act. "I would appreciate your help."

"We had a fling. Okay?" Evangeline looked up at Rose with a defiant glare.

"How long did it last?" Rose could see all the tears for a long-term relationship, but not a "fling."

"A while. A year, maybe. But I called it off. My husband became suspicious, and I can't afford to lose him. So, I told Brad it was over, and he didn't accept that. He threatened to quit. Then this happened."

"Your husband never found out?" Rose asked.

"Oh, he knows all right. It was better to rip the band-aid off than always wonder what he knew. He was angry, of course. But it's over. Finished."

Death had a way of making the word "finished" sound redundant. Rose tried to recall every detail from the gala. The guard had been all smiles until his boss arrived. In hindsight, it would have been more valuable to remember Evangeline's expression. Either way, two spouses had every right to be furious at Brad Knight.

Which one might have been mad enough to kill him?

"If you don't mind me asking, why would a successful woman like yourself have an affair with Brad Knight, a security guard?" Rose asked.

It was a personal question with a tenuous connection to the theft and murder. Rose hoped it would lead to a motive.

Evangeline's eyes glared with anger.

Rose slid the earrings closer to the register.

"Your husband wasn't at the gala, or did I miss an introduction?"

Evangeline picked up the plastic card that held the delicate dangles and peered at the price tag. She set the earrings down.

"I wouldn't let Carlos come after telling him about Brad. He's hot-blooded, he was ready to kill him right in front of everyone. It would have ruined the whole evening. He fools around, why shouldn't I?"

Her words sounded genuine for the first time.

"When did you tell him?" Rose asked. Wondering if the tall man she'd seen leave the gallery in a huff was the mysterious Carlos Abbott. Evangeline's eyes glared at her. "Not that it's any of your business, but it was Friday."

So, it was the guy. Was he angry enough to kill?

"Did Brad really threaten to quit if you ended the affair? Rose asked.

Evangeline slid the computer to the corner of the counter. That small action told Rose that Brad had no reaction at all, and that angered his boss or offended her.

"He asked to be moved to days. Actually, he's been asking for that since I hired him. I guess that should have told me something."

"Did Carlos kill Brad?"

"Of course not! It's an expression."

Rose's intuition said that Carlos had nothing to do with the death. It was easy to check whether he was there or not, so why take the risk of lying? There remained the matter of the missing minutes of tape. Carlos Abbott could have gone in and out undetected. Would he have killed to protect his honor? Or his wife's?

With as much nonchalance as she could muster, Rose set her purse down on the counter to pull her wallet out.

"I was here when the police viewed the security video. You come back at around 1 AM. Did you kill Brad?"

Evangeline's head snapped back as if Rose had struck her. Her eyes had the wild look of a trapped animal. She dropped the earrings on the counter.

"How dare you ask me that. My gallery was robbed. My employee was killed. The person you should be talking to is Gloria Knight. I'm sure she's an unpleasant woman if Brad felt free to cheat on her."

The irony of Evangeline saying Gloria must be unpleasant didn't seem to strike the woman as applying to her husband, too, if she felt free to cheat on him. Evangeline stormed out, her heels clicking on the concrete as she pounded her way back to the rear of the gallery. She was a haughty woman, but that didn't make her a killer. Or a thief. Yet, she hadn't answered the question about the video. Instead, she tossed Brad's wife into the mix before stomping away. Smooth. It was one more thing to ask Gloria Knight about when Rose went to visit. Because, of course, she had to meet the woman.

The earring still lay on the counter. Rose pulled out two ten-dollar bills from her wallet and left them next to the computer. Then she slipped the earrings into her purse.

She passed Hernandez in the lobby and remembered him questioning why the FBI had a man on the scene.

Hopefully, Nessa was actively pursuing that line of inquiry. In a failure investigation, it was wise to consider anything that smelled like a coincidence as a contributing factor. An anonymous tip and the FBI's presence were two such factors that Rose didn't intend to ignore. They would fit in as facts, eventually.

Rose wandered off toward the blocked-off gallery and studied the blank space on the wall, with the white card listing the artist's name. Nell Walker Warner. Natalie had said she wanted the painting. What was it about that piece that inspired such longing? It couldn't be money. The artist wasn't famous. Rose needed to start over with a different question. Or a different answer than greed. Even with Natalie's reaction to Brad's death, could she have killed him to get the painting?

She had said that something woke her up in the night. What if she were already awake and at the gallery? With her key card for entry, she could have hit him with the baseball bat she normally kept by the front door of her house for protection. Evangeline described Natalie as someone who knew the place inside and out. If anyone could trick a security system, Rose's money was on Natalie.

Could she believe such a thing of a friend? True, she'd only known her for a few months. Then there was the bullet. Did she even own a gun? Rose knew from her time as a quality investigator that you couldn't overlook someone just because you knew them.

Her cell phone rang as she exited the gallery. Nessa identified herself when Rose answered. "What can I do for you?"

The policewoman's voice sounded light, upbeat, and conversational in the way people talk about the weather.

"I received a rather angry call from Evangeline Abbot about some questions you asked her."

So that was where she stomped off. To tattle.

There was a pause before Nessa spoke. "I'm officially supposed to tell you to cease and desist. Leave it to the police."

Rose shook her head, though Nessa couldn't see her. "I can't do that. My friend is innocent. The FBI as much as threatened me for sticking my nose in where they didn't want it, which tells me something's not right. It's not that I think you won't solve the crime, it's just…"

Rose searched her mind for the words she wanted, then continued. "I'm confident you'll get there, eventually, but an innocent woman is in jail, and I'm going to do everything in my power to help her. I'm sorry if that steps on your toes."

The line went silent, and Rose looked at the screen. The green button still showed an active call.

The Sergeant cleared her throat. "I understand. So, unofficially, I wanted to tell you that the CSI team came back with a potential weapon that matches the blow that may have killed Mr. Knight."

"May have killed him? There's a question? I mean, they shot him."

Rose sensed reluctance in the young woman to share too much information. After a pause, Nessa continued.

"The question is whether the blow to the head killed him, or the bullet. One could be accidental; the other is intentional. Unfortunately, the bullet was a 9-millimeter. Common ammunition. Ballistics is working it, but I don't expect much to come from that."

Brad hadn't stood a chance against armed thieves. What was so special about that painting? Even if the injury to Brad's head was accidental, it didn't seem to matter. The bullet killed him if the fall didn't.

"Let's focus on the object they hit him with," Rose said. "It might lead us to the killers."

"A cylindrical object, like maybe a wine bottle."

Rose chuckled. "It was a gala. One of the wineries was pouring. Has anyone checked all the bottles? The trash?"

Using a wine bottle as a weapon was genius. It might be impossible for the police to be able to tell one from another.

"Hernandez did that this morning. All the bottles he found were clean."

Rose closed her eyes. Clean bottles could mean one of two things.

"As in only having prints from the winery employees along with cardboard dust from the box?"

"Rinsed-out-and-wiped-with-a-towel-to-remove-any-residual-fingerprints clean. We didn't get to them until after the winery picked them up."

An unfortunate turn.

"Since we're talking unofficially, has anyone done a background check on the guard? Could someone have wanted to kill him and then stolen the painting as a cover?"

There was a pause, and Rose wondered if Nessa regretted saying as much as she had already.

"That's being done, and we'd appreciate it if you shared any info you come across."

"Are you saying you welcome my help?" Rose's tone was tentative, hopeful.

Rose heard Nessa take a deep breath and let it out slowly. "If the Chief finds out, I could lose my job, but yes. I welcome your assistance."

It felt like a tap on the shoulder with a ceremonial blade, anointing her into a secret society. A responsibility that gave her purpose and a mantle that might help get some of the suspects to open up and talk with her.

"Thank you," Rose said. "You won't be sorry."

At the end of her walk, Rose stood on Slade Bolton's driveway, looking into the front window of the house. Her thoughts rambled. Brad had worked for Olive Heaven. His employer might have useful information. With luck, she'd see him at the Olive Growers' annual dinner that night. She took one last glance at Bolton's rental house. It would frost Mr. Bolton's cupcakes when he learned she had the blessing of the police department.

That thought made her smile.

Chapter 16 Nessa

~

Pinot Grigio – aka Pinot gris creates a variety of flavors depending on where it is grown, ranging from light and crisp to full-bodied.

Monday, October 10, 6:00 PM

Sergeant Vanessa (Nessa) Gomez waited until the door to her apartment shut before undoing the top button on her uniform shirt. At least they didn't have to wear a tie. A wall safe received the handgun she carried. Talking the landlord into allowing that had taken some doing.

She walked through the small hall, passed her son Danny's bedroom, to her bedroom, her personal hideaway, and removed the sweaty shirt. A tentative sniff told her it would last one more day. She hung it carefully on a hanger and moved it to the bathroom.

After slipping on a tank top and a gauzy overshirt, she poured herself a glass of Pinot Grigio and opened the door to the small balcony.

The strident buzz of her cell phone made her close her eyes and exhale with frustration. The caller ID showed the call was from Police Chief Elizabeth Donnelly.

She didn't waste words on small talk.

"Is that MacGillivray woman still asking questions?" Nessa put the call on speaker and took a sip of Pinot Grigio. Grateful that this was a voice call and not a video conference.

"Not officially, of course. Her friend is in custody, and she wants to help. I didn't see any harm in it."

At the other end of the line, the chief moved some papers around. Her voice sounded tired when she finally spoke. "We need to tread lightly. Keep the focus on the murder."

Nessa didn't say anything. She was surprised the chief felt the need to say that the killing was her primary concern. Nessa didn't care about the painting. Brad Knight had been a member of her community. She took his death on her watch personally.

Chief Donnelly sighed heavily.

"Between Evangeline Abbott and Special Agent Bolton, my phone keeps ringing with complaints about her. I don't want it to ring. Understood?"

Clear as day. Her job was on the line if Rose got in the way.

After confirming that she understood the message, the Chief hung up. As a rule, Nessa liked Chief Donnelley. Liked the way she ran the department. For her to be so abrupt on the phone indicated stress.

Nessa knew what stress felt like. Danny was visiting his father in Oregon, giving her a few days to be herself. Not a cop, not a mom. A woman who needed to unwind. Danny loved spending time with his dad, his dad's new wife, and their baby bump. His college classes started in September, and since that first day, she barely saw him. That didn't stop her from worrying. When he went north to see his Dad, she let go. Another parent had the job of keeping him safe. Although he would always be her little boy.

The cool wine tasted like summer at the pool. Nessa closed her eyes. Leaves blew in the breeze. She could hear them rustling as they landed beside her on the lanai. That's what her mom called anything outside now that she lived in Hawaii. Does the Honolulu PD have any openings? Warm weather and beaches. That sounded nice. It also sounded like a big city. She loved the calm of Paso Robles. Their main problems were drunks, break-ins, and an occasional gun discharge. Not the gangs and murders she read about in other cities.

Until now, that is. Add art theft and murder to the list.

Maybe this was her chance to prove she had what it takes to be promoted. Someday, she might even be the chief of police.

That is, if Rose doesn't get in the way. She sipped the wine. And yet—Rose had been helpful, and despite herself, Nessa trusted her. If she could help, why shouldn't SLPD take advantage of her skills? Still, caution was warranted. If something happened to Rose or her friend Stella, the blame came back to Nessa.

The anonymous call bothered her. Who knew about the stolen painting in the artist's garage? And the key card. Had Natalie Patel used it to gain entrance Friday night, or had she given it to someone else?

The evidence was too strong. They had to bring Natalie in. If for no other reason than to sort things out. She'd be transferred to the Sheriff's lockup. Unfortunate, but necessary. SLPD didn't keep anyone longer than six hours due to regulations regarding feeding prisoners, which they weren't set up to do. Even so, Natalie was in for a rough go. Prison isn't a hotel. The smell alone could haunt you for months.

She took another sip. Better get some crackers or

something to buffer her stomach lining. She poured some salty chips into a bowl and carried them out to her chair.

Besides the anonymous call, something else bothered her. The same thing that was giving the Chief so much grief. The Johnny-on-the-spot FBI agent, Slade Bolton. Dealing with the FBI required a gentle touch. Last year, when threatening social media posts started popping up centered around the high school, the FBI signed a Memorandum of Understanding with SLPD and sent a team. Nessa understood. Federal crimes bring federal officers. That didn't bother her. Their holier-than-thou attitude got under everyone's skin, including the chief, who finally spelled out a few rules for them. That, plus a call to their bosses in New York, caused them to back off a bit. The day they left town, the station had a potluck to celebrate.

A mockingbird landed on the balcony railing.

"Why didn't the FBI let us know about Bolton?" she asked. The bird flew away.

Special Agent Bolton materialized one day, and Nessa remembered now when that was. The dark glasses in the park when she spoke with Rose. Had she seen the guard and Bolton talking? She thought she did. With luck, security cameras will have caught their exchange. Not words, but a lot can be learned from body language. She bet anything that it wasn't a friendly chat.

Chapter 17 Rose

~

Arbiquina Olive – a cultivar of olive that produces a small, round and sweet olive used for making a mild, fruity oil

Tuesday, October 11, 8:00 AM

Rose opened her eyes to a sunny Monday with one thought: How little progress she'd made in her investigation into the death of Brad and Natalie's arrest. Despite her normal midnight ramble with Watson, she slept well. Guilt flooded her mind as she thought of Natalie sitting in a concrete and steel cell.

She grabbed a notepad by her bedside, clicked the pen, scribbled circles to get the ink going, and paused with the tip ready to capture — what? What did she have to write down? What brilliant thoughts had crept into her mind overnight that would help Natalie?

They had met when Rose bought her house. The big house had been in foreclosure and was way more than she needed, but the light in the kitchen was beautiful, and the garden was perfect for flowers, veggies, and herbs. As a bonus, it came with five gorgeous olive trees.

That first night, Natalie came over with a bottle of wine and a plate of cookies. They sipped, ate cookies, and forged a friendship that transcended any Rose had ever had.

With Natalie, she made up for lost time. And Natalie came with her own set of tragedies to chew over with pizza and wine. And now her new friend was in jail.

An intolerable situation if there ever was one.

Clouds accumulated in the sky outside her window. In a murder mystery, that meant trouble brewing. But this was the real world. Clouds were formations of water vapor in the sky. She scratched Watson's ears.

"No headwinds for us, my friend, we've got cold, hard facts in our favor. Just need to figure out what they are."

She dressed, fed Watson, and let him out in the yard while she gathered her phone, a notebook, and the plastic badge from a recent Central Coast Olive Growers Symposium on crop yields in a drought. If one didn't look too closely, it appeared official enough.

When Watson realized she was going without him, his ears drooped until she opened the treat cabinet. He perked up and sat with his tail swishing side to side against the tile floor.

She needed someone to brainstorm with and generate crazy ideas that might lead to real, solid steps forward. As she walked into town, Rose went over all the people she could discuss Natalie's arrest with and, to her dismay, came up with only one name: Stella. They'd made a pact the previous night to solve the murder, but wine had been involved.

How serious was Stella about helping? She turned left at Vine Street and walked to the bungalow that now holds several small businesses, including Stella's bookkeeping service.

An antique bell jingled over the front door. An older gentleman with bushy eyebrows and suspenders over a white shirt peered around the open doorway of an office when she entered.

"I'm looking for Stella Richardson."

His eyes registered surprise before he pointed to a door at the back of the building. When Rose reached it, she could hear Stella talking on the phone.

She was dressed conservatively, for her, in tight jeans, a frilly, low-cut blouse, and gold jewelry. Should Rose mention that a more sedate, higher neckline would emit professionalism instead of sexuality?

Maybe if Stella were her daughter, her advice would be more welcome. As a friend, perhaps not. Rose bit back the words.

The office was basic, with beige walls, a metal desk, and a faux leather swivel chair.

"I'll need computer access if you want me to input the data directly," Stella told whoever she was talking with.

After an 'okay,' and one or two 'I sees,' she signed off the call with, "I look forward to hearing back from you."

Rose knocked on the door. Stella looked up.

"Oh, hi, Rose. Do you need a bookkeeper?"

"Got time for coffee?" Rose asked.

Stella looked at the calendar on her desktop, which Rose could see was clear of any appointments.

"I do, seeing as my day is nothing but cold calling."

The large desk left little room to move in the small space. A window looked out at the back at what once had been a garden and small yard and was now a parking lot. Rose pulled a guest chair away from the wall and sat down.

Stella's auburn hair shone in the morning light that streamed through the window. So much like Rose's mother, it made her heart ache.

"I was thinking of Amsterdam Café. Are you still willing to help?"

Stella closed the laptop.

"Are we sure she wasn't involved? I mean, she works at the gallery, her key card was used to enter just before the guard was killed. It doesn't look very good for her. How well do you know her?"

Rose pushed the chair back and stood. Her hands shook. As did her voice.

"Well enough to know she wouldn't steal or kill. You're right that the facts are stacked against her, but there are so many clues pointing to one person it makes me suspicious. If she planned to steal the painting, she wouldn't use her own key card. She runs their computer system; she'd know they would figure out how the thief got in." She sat back down.

"I'm going to prove she's innocent with or without your help."

There was a quiet moment while Rose practiced a yoga breath designed to lower her blood pressure, and Stella rolled a pencil back and forth on the desk top. Then she stood.

"I don't want to believe it of her either, so I won't."

Five minutes later, they arrived at Amsterdam Café. Rose ordered a jasmine green tea. The girl behind the corner wrote down her order.

"I was shocked to hear about Natalie Patel and can't believe she'd do something like that."

"She didn't," Rose said. "How did you know I know her?"

"This is a small town. She comes here all the time and told me you'd moved in a few months ago. She described you well. Chamomile tea is her favorite drink. I start making it as soon as she comes through the door. Tell her hi if you see her."

There was so much about Natalie Rose hadn't known. Maybe Stella was right to question her innocence. Stella stepped to the counter and requested their strongest brew. "Black. No sugar. Just coffee. Strong."

"Didn't sleep well?" Rose asked when they sat down. She nodded toward the steaming cup.

Stella's hands hugged the ceramic mug. She closed her eyes, then opened them with a coquettish smile.

"Slade came over, and it was," she paused, as if deciding how much of the sex to share with a woman twice her age.

Rose glanced away, showing moderate interest, but inside, she hung on every word.

Stella finally chose a safe adjective. "Intense. And to answer your question from last night, of whether we are still together, it would appear the answer is yes. At least for now."

Rose grimaced. "Mr. Bolton is a handful, then?"

Stella grunted. "The bloke was so full of himself over Natalie's arrest. Made it sound like he was personally responsible. I'm sure he wanted the cops to fail so he could swoop in and rescue their reputation. When they picked up Natalie, he needed to find a way to take the credit."

It would appear the plastic wrap idea wasn't needed after all. Despite how little she knew about the man, Rose could see him reacting this way.

She watched as Stella sipped her coffee and thought about what her friend said. Maybe Bolton was responsible. Definitely a possibility. And it made sense. His brooding stare in the park still gave her a shiver.

"The police said they received an anonymous tip. Could he have...?

Stella shook her head so hard the curls quivered.

"Oh, no. He's with the FBI; they could have gotten a warrant."

"But he didn't. Sounds like from what you said that he knew that Natalie was guilty all along."

"Male ego. He was taking credit, so he didn't look bad. Local police caught the criminal." She paused, then flushed.

"Not that Natalie is a criminal. That didn't come out the right way."

Rose thought it came out exactly as the younger woman had thought it. Still, the ego thing made some sense. That man had an overabundance of testosterone-enhanced self-importance.

"Doesn't sound like a very romantic evening with him bragging."

"Well, no. But it did make him frisky. "So," she picked up her ceramic mug. "A little stimulant helps."

The aroma of strong coffee overwhelmed the Earl Grey in Rose's cup. She'd been up as usual in the middle of the night. Last night had been tranquil, though, not like the night—

She stopped mid-thought.

"Do you remember what he was like Friday night, after the gala?"

Stella frowned in thought.

"I remember going out to the speakeasy and getting plastered. Then we went back to my place, shagged a bit, and then I took a sleeping pill. Helps with the hangover."

She stared down at her steaming cup.

"I'm aware of how that makes me sound."

Rose leaned back in her chair. She learned long ago not to judge people by their lifestyle. It fell under her "do unto others" rule.

"Do you always go back to your house? Not his?"

"Yep. Like I said, he's not into furniture. If this does last, I'll have to buy him a bed at least."

"Stella…" Rose started to say. Words her mother had blasted at her during high school rushed to her tongue. Maybe that was why she never married, her mother had convinced her she was unable to make good choices when it came to men.

Stella held up her hand to stop Rose from going any further. "You don't have to say it, you think he's going to leave. I read his lips, and you might be right. But he might not. I choose to believe he'll stay."

There was no way Rose could convince her that Mr. Bolton didn't plan on staying long. Even though he said as much, it was clear that Stella refused to see it.

A man and a woman sat down at the table next to them and pulled out Bibles. Why people thought a busy café was the best place to have a religious discussion was something she never understood.

"Have you talked with Natalie yet?" Stella asked.

Rose sighed and shook her head.

"I tried, but she wouldn't take my call. Something about an account. I'm almost afraid to talk with her. It must be horrific, and I need to keep my head clear. I keep mulling over the broken flowerpot near the door into the garage."

Stella stirred her drink with a wooden stick and then stuck the stick in her mouth and sucked it dry.

"You think Slade was trying to break in?"

Rose shrugged. "If we assume that he was responsible, that he made the call, then he might have been staking out her garage as the most likely place to store stolen goods."

"What if he didn't tip off the police?" Stella asked.

Rose didn't have a ready answer. Did he suspect Natalie of being the thief and go looking for the painting? It didn't add up. If Natalie were an art thief, she'd pick something more valuable, though she had said she loved that particular piece.

"Something I don't understand. If he were looking for the stolen painting, he should have been able to find it. The police found it the next day; it had to be there the night before. We need to get inside that garage. Maybe we'll find something that will clear her."

Stella finished her coffee. "How do we get in? She probably locks it when she's not there."

"She gave us a key, remember? We'll swing by and get mine. I need to let Watson out anyway."

Stella shouldered her purse and stood. "Let's go."

"Don't you want to finish?"

"I've had enough to hold me. Besides, we'd better leave before I pour what's left into the lap of the guy at the next table who keeps misquoting Bible passages."

As they walked, Rose pondered what they would find in Natalie's garage and whether this was a violation of her privacy. Well, if it was, too bad. They needed to do something to help, and this seemed the logical next step.

Chapter 18 Rose

~

Chenin Blanc — a high acidity grape with flavors of quince, apple and honey and produced in a range of styles from dry to sweet

Tuesday, October 11, 10:00 AM

Cracks ran up Natalie's concrete driveway to the garage. White flakes of paint peeled off the wooden door. A dusty blue car sat parked in front. The rest of Natalie's house wore a similar ramshackle appearance. Not run down, but not well-maintained either.

"Someone might call the cops on us," Stella said. "I mean, we are planning to break in."

"We're her neighbors," Rose said. "We're checking on her plants, seeing if everything is okay."

"She's only been gone one day," Stella admonished.

"Oh, hush."

They walked up the steep driveway and followed the walkway around to the garage side door. The flowerpot still lay shattered on the ground, which surprised Rose. "Strange. She called the locksmith out, so I assumed this mess would be cleaned up."

Rose snapped a picture of the broken terracotta and plucked a wilted geranium leaf. Dirt dusted a two-foot area. A perfect place to look for evidence of a break-in if Natalie hadn't walked around the area, and then the search team when they came with the warrant.

She didn't see any footprints as Natalie had said.

She pushed her key into the lock and prepared to turn the bolt when she noticed Stella leaning towards the corner of the building with her ear against the wall.

"Stella? What are you doing?"

"Shush." She held up an index finger in a wait-a-minute gesture. After a moment, she stood straight and came back to Rose. "Thought I heard something."

Rose peered through the dirty glass window in the door but saw nothing in the dim light. How could an artist stand such a dirty studio?

A crash came from inside. Rose jumped back, and the two women retreated to the other side of the walkway.

"Should we call the police?" Stella asked. Her tone clearly said, No way am I going in there. Rose heard her blood pounding in her ears at aerobic levels.

Watson trotted around a corner of the house with his tail wagging and his tongue hanging out. She put out a hand to stop him, but he ignored her. If he even knew what it meant. They'd have to work on that command.

"Stay!" she whispered. He stopped and looked at her until another sound from the garage made his head swing around and his ears spring up. He sniffed the threshold at the bottom of the door, making a further mess of the dirt from the flowerpot. Stella backed up and mouthed the word police.

Rose looked at the key in her hand. We could call, she thought, or we could open the door and stand back.

She took a step toward the door. Stella grabbed her arm.

"What are you doing? You can't just unlock it!"

"Why not?"

The key slid in, and the tumblers clicked.

Rose eased the door open.

"You're relentless," Stella said.

A ball of yellow fur flew out, hissing and spitting as it passed them. Watson took off after it.

The Ceja cat. Down one life but breathing. It had knocked the pot over, then somehow ended up locked in the garage.

Rose reached her hand out and pushed the door. The ammonia odor of cat pee stung her nose.

Stella pinched her nose shut. "How long do you think that thing has been in here?"

"Hard to say. Days maybe?" Rose said.

The smell of linseed oil, mineral spirits, paint, and used motor oil worked hard to overcome the essence of feline urine. Blank canvases leaned against one wall, covered with a paint-splattered sheet. An easel stood in the center, a tall table next to it covered with tubes of paint and a mason jar of brushes.

Rose circled in place. An ancient lawnmower, a bicycle with flat tires, and a wheelbarrow tipped up on its point.

Her eyes kept going around the space. Rose recognized several of them from her high school humanities class. Girl with a Pearl Earring, Mona Lisa, the Portrait of Madam X by John Singer Sargent. She peered at the corners of the paintings. All unsigned.

Copies. Or forgeries?

"She really is a painter!" Stella said.

Rose turned and saw that Stella held a canvas painted with colorful hydrangeas and peonies. It featured bold brush strokes and something between an impressionist and abstract arrangement.

Rose picked up another piece depicting a lilac bush in morning light. "She doesn't share her work much."

Luminous light emanated from the painting, giving the lilac flowers a dewy blush. Simply gorgeous.

Next, Rose saw cans of paint splattered with federal blues and deep olive greens. Natalie had written the word HOUSE in bold marker pen on the blue can and BATH-ROOM on the green one.

Natalie repainted her rooms often. Some colors worked; others didn't last a month. In the time Rose lived next door, Natalie repainted three rooms. These two colors must have proven winners. It seemed to Rose that Natalie spent more time painting her walls than actual artwork.

The colors felt familiar. The moody frame of *Gray Day, Montrose Valley* swam into Rose's mind.

The same blues and greens covered the scene.

"I'm surprised that Natalie has all these paintings hidden in here," she said.

Stella flipped through a stack of canvases leaning against one wall. "She should be in that art gallery. She's good."

In her head, Rose agreed. Good enough to have re-produced any painting she wanted. Rose closed her eyes to the chaos around her and tried to come up with a rational explanation.

"Maybe Natalie painted a copy of Gray Day, her own version, and the police think it's the real thing."

Stella held the copy of the Mona Lisa in her hands when Rose opened her eyes. "A forgery?"

A copy didn't qualify as forged unless sold with the intent to defraud. Natalie might have changed something in the composition, thus making it original.

To hang in the front room, where she envisioned it going perfectly with the view out the window. Could the painting the police took from the garage be one of Natalie's experiments?

"The police don't know what they have," Rose said. She locked the door, and they walked around to the front.

"I need to get back to my office. Those cold calls won't dial themselves." Stella smiled. "This was fun, in a creepy stalking in someone's house sort of way."

They walked down the driveway to the street. Rose's thoughts were muddled. Was it possible that Natalie took that painting and killed the guard? She stole a glance at Stella to find the younger woman watching her with the same look of concern Rose's mom used to have. Knitted brows, a squint with a crinkle in the corners of her eyes and firmly set lips.

Then, as if she'd read Rose's mind, Stella replied, "No. Not possible. She couldn't have killed anyone."

"How did you—?" Rose asked.

"I could tell by your face. The same question ran through my mind."

Stella still watched her. Rose tried to smile, to reassure her new friend, but couldn't pull it off. "Let's take it one day at a time."

Stella reached out and hugged Rose. Rose stiffened, then relaxed. "We're a team. You tell me what to do," Stella said. Directing a team came naturally to Rose. Together, they stood a chance of helping Natalie. As Stella headed back to her office, Rose proceeded to her house. Stay neutral, she told herself, collect data, and let the evidence point the way. She needed facts to prove Natalie's innocence. Facts she didn't trust herself to find.

Chapter 19 Natalie

~

Aglianico — a full-bodied, high-tannin, high-acidity red wine from Southern Italy with flavors of leather, white pepper and black fruits

Tuesday, October 11, 3:45 PM

The horrid orange scrubs Natalie was forced to wear made her feel dirty. They'd better take loving care of the cute outfit she wore that morning. The whole "booking" nightmare alone had humiliated her. Sheep, during fleecing, had more respect shown to them. She supposed that was the point. Criminals lost rights, but she didn't do anything that deserved this. Her biggest offense? Not rinsing bottles and cans out well before tossing them in the recycling bin.

The concrete cell walls felt cold. The steel platform they laughingly called a bed smelled like sanitizing cleaner. That she didn't mind so much, since it eliminated whatever lowlife had occupied this prison cell last left behind.

A hard, flat pillow. Nothing soft or calming. Nothing long enough to permit her to hang herself. She shuddered. Overhead lights made her skin look dead. She felt dead.

And the odor. The steel toilet in the corner made her nauseous to look at. Since childhood, smells evoked colors in her mind. The sour rankness of body odor -- lime green. The sharp, astringent synthetic-lemon smell of the cleaning solution appeared bright yellow, and the burnt-linen odor of the scalded-in-the-dryer stripped scrubs looked brown. The scrubs themselves were orange and white stripes. Hideous.

They gave her one phone call. She used it to reach a lawyer she once dated. They broke up after three dates. She couldn't stand how he ate, talking while chewing, and food spilling out. Hopefully, he wouldn't hold that against her as a client. He came right away, an expectant smile on his face.

"Don't speak to anyone," he said. She wondered if that included Rose.

"Anyone," he repeated.

Rose couldn't have had anything to do with this, though. Could she? They were sisters, not by blood, but by choice. Then again, how had that painting gotten into her garage? She didn't put it there. But someone did. Canvases didn't magically appear and land in one's garage. Rose was the only other person with a key to her house. She could have stolen the key card and planted the evidence. Maybe even killed Brad and took the painting herself.

The flat pillow didn't bend into something that looked comfortable. Natalie punched it. She didn't want to believe her friend would frame her, but she couldn't shake her doubt.

Chapter 20 Slade

~

Corvina – an Italian red grape variety with a sour cherry flavor

October 11, Tuesday, 7:00 PM

Slade ordered an IPA at The Crooked Kilt and selected a table with a clear view of the TV screen carrying the Detroit Tigers. Years of living in New York hadn't changed his favorite team. They were playing the San Francisco Giants, making him a silent Tiger fan among the many decked out in Giants' team merch.

Maybe he'd retire back in the Midwest. Something on Lake Michigan. Though Liz wasn't a lakeside kind of woman. But then, the polish was nearly off that apple. He'd begun to sense her pulling back. Talking about the heists, or the art, brought a light tone to her voice. The rest of the time, it seemed she was surprised to find him there at all. To be fair, he had been working a lot and traveling. They'd become partners in crime more than lovers in life. It wasn't that way in the beginning.

"Another beer," he shouted at the waitress in the short tartan skirt. "And some onion rings too." He'd have to cut back soon; his shirts were starting to feel tight. The game paused for the seventh inning stretch, and he closed his eyes, feeling the beer in his system. Alcohol always made him nostalgic and drowsy. In seconds, dreams filled his mind. Memories of the hope he'd clung to at the beginning.

The elevator up to Liz's floor-through apartment was miles more elegant than the one in my old building. There, the sides are all scuffed from moving trolleys and smell like urinals most of the time. Liz's has mirrored walls, brocade wallpaper, and plush red carpet. Lighting infused the box instead of glaring down, and Zen music hums in the background, making the whole experience feel like a transport to heaven.

The doors slide open with a sophisticated hush onto an elegant corridor. The scent of gladiolas smacks me in the face from a vase sitting on a hall table. His battered suitcase and three boxes sealed with duct tape looked lost on the brass rolling cart the doorman had loaned him.

"But hey, I live simply," he reminded himself. The FBI has a dress code, which limits the number of clothing items needed, and that suits him fine. He didn't have free time, and what little unstructured minutes he had these days were spent wooing Liz.

It turned out you didn't have to have fancy couture to snag a beauty like her. But he still hadn't figured out what it was about him that appealed to her.

Liz's apartment was fourth on the left. A pile of books props the door open, and he pushes it with his shoulder. Lavish smells hit him: leather, exotic flowers, and the tangy punch of oil paints. Liz doesn't live the simple life.

"I'm home!" He knew it sounded like a corny '50s situation comedy. But he couldn't help himself. His small studio never felt like home.

This place has views clear out to the edge of the city. With two bedrooms and baths, it's a massive luxury in the city. He stood for a minute and took it all in. This is a place he belonged, his first step to a life of high society and wealth, of fitting his sense of self and having a woman who fit together with him like the pieces of a puzzle. His career with the FBI will soar when his superiors learned of this new situation.

"Stick your stuff in the second bedroom," Liz says as she comes around the corner from the kitchen.

Wait. What? They'd been sleeping together for a month. Had he misread the invitation to live with her? Given that he let the lease expire and didn't have much choice. Plus, the apartment was amazing. He rolled the cart to the second bedroom and deposited his worldly belongings on the bed, thus creating a reason he should be sleeping in her room. With her. Smelling the clean scent of her shampoo and spooning against her back.

On the way to the kitchen, he passed a small room, more of a closet really, with a canvas propped on an easel and a small folding table covered with tubes of paint. Several jars of liquid with a sharp smell held brushes. Turpentine? Paint thinner? Printouts of paintings by Monet and DaVinci lay on the floor.

In the kitchen, she handed me a bottle of Cabernet Sauvignon. "Give that to Ned, the doorman. To thank him for loaning you the cart."

Seriously? Slade looked at the bottle. The vintage was old. Pricy. The glass felt hefty in his hands. It would do some significant damage if you hit someone with it.

"Isn't that his job?" he asked. Did they need to reward him every time he opened the door for them? Or called a cab?

Liz put her hands on her hips as if lecturing to a small child. "Be nice."

"That's it?" he demanded. "Be nice and let the working class walk all over you?"

"Despite my meager inheritance, I still believe in thanking people." Her tone made his blood feel cold. What did she mean by meager?

Back in the elevator, he marveled at how quickly his mindset had leapfrogged social lines. His mother would have slapped his hand if she heard his thoughts now. He handed the bottle to the doorman with a mumbled thanks and returned to the elevator as quickly as possible before he changed his mind and ran the bottle out to his car. The only thing stopping him was knowing that any heat would destroy the wine, and he wasn't that much of a heathen that he didn't know not to do that.

When he got back to the apartment, she had set a glass-topped table with real China and sterling silver flatware. The table's position was dangerously near a floor-to-ceiling window, and his head swam when he peered down at the street. It will take some time to get used to that.

An old book, tied closed with a string, sat on an antique side table.

"What's this?" he asked. The cover is leather and looks like it's been carried around for years. Ink blots mar the surface.

She closed the distance between them in two steps, grabbed the book, and hugged it to her chest.

"It's personal," Liz said.

Then, as if realizing she'd overreacted, she smiled and pulled open a drawer, deposited the book inside, and locked it in. The small skeleton key was tucked into her bra.

"It's nothing. A gift from my grandfather." She handed him the wine. His memory triggers an internet search he'd done on her when they started dating. Couldn't be too careful these days. Maternal Grandfather Grossman was rumored to be a Nazi sympathizer with unsubstantiated ties to Goring. Just the sort of secret in the closet most folks would prefer kept locked up. It made me want to see the manuscript even more. He'd have to get that key.

She poured Chateau St. Something into two Riedel stemware glasses.

"To beginnings," she said with a raised glass. "And opportunities."

"Opportunities?"

"We can talk about that later. Tonight, we celebrate."

Her eyes shone as they had when they first met.

"I am sleeping with you, aren't I?" he asked. Putting his stuff in the guest room weighed on his mind.

She smiled with a toothy, Cheshire cat smirk. For a second, it appeared sinister before morphing into a seductive grin.

"Of course," she said. "I didn't want your clutter all over tonight. You can unpack tomorrow while I'm out at lunch with the family lawyer."

Always with the lawyers. Dear old Daddy must have had a stable of them. He'd been a Wall Street financier and frequent A-list topper of the wealthiest individuals. The old man had died two years ago. What did she need to discuss with the lawyers at this point?

"Anything serious?" he asked.

"On top of leaving me essentially nothing, I want to make sure dear old Daddy doesn't screw up Mommy's will again. He gave that painting away, which by rights, and Mom's will, belongs to me. I want to make sure he didn't do anything else underhanded. That's all."

Liz slices into the medium-rare porterhouse steak and smears some horseradish on before opening her delicate mouth to insert the food. She even chews delicately. Such care, such artistry. Except sex. There, she resembled a wild cat.

"What do you mean by essentially nothing?" Slade asked after swallowing the first bit which seemed to grow in his throat.

"I have this apartment, a place in California, an olive farm, for the love of god, and the yacht, thank god. But most of the estate went to museums, libraries, and NGOs if you can believe that. Found God, he said. I don't believe that for a minute."

She swirled her wine and sipped. "When does the rest of your stuff arrive?"

His hand stopped halfway to his mouth with a forkful of

roasted carrots. The abrupt change of topic confused him. Plus, he may have led her to believe he had more in the way of financial reserves than he genuinely did. Did she think he had gobs of money to solve her inheritance problem?

"I decided on a fresh start. With me, what you see is what you get. Nothing hidden behind the curtain."

She tipped her head a fraction of a degree. They hadn't been together that long, but he knew that look. It usually preceded a drilling for information. Liz set her fork down.

He'd been careful not to bring her to his apartment if you could call a ten-by-twelve closet an apartment. A high-cost closet that held his life, hidden from the world. This next step in their relationship meant opening that door and hoping the contents didn't scare her away.

"Don't get me wrong. I've been living simply as an experiment. But now, I plan to expand my lifestyle to accommodate yours."

He gave her what he thought of as his charming smile. It had done the trick before.

The corner of Liz's lips curls up. "Oh, don't do that on my account. Once the genie is out of the bottle, it's hard to stuff it back in there."

Was she telling him that this was just a fling? Not to get too comfortable because the world was cold outside the blanket of wealth? The tips of his ears warmed. This conversation wasn't going well at all. Time to get back on track.

"Speaking of things expanding and not fitting in . . ." He winked. She sighed. Not a happy sound, but a here we go again exhalation. She'd said they were celebrating — so let's celebrate.

She looked down at her barely eaten meal, then back up at him. He stood; his hand held out for her to take. As she takes it, he knows that he will love her till the day he dies. Or longer.

A loud cheer awakened him. The Giants scored in the ninth inning to win the game. Typical of the Tigers. Well, maybe next time. He stared at the wall the bar shared with the art gallery and thought about Brad Knight. He didn't have a next time.

How long ago was that heist? Two years, he thought. Fresno Museum of Art for a modern piece, nothing he'd buy. The job was simple, swapping out the forged version with the original and disappearing. It had worked, too. The museum security was laughable, and they'd got in and out without setting off any alarms. A docent noticed something off, hard to say what, but they checked security footage for surrounding buildings and saw us enter. The police sent Detective Brad Knight to investigate, and that son of a bitch was smart enough to figure out the gig and track us down. It took $10K to keep him quiet. Too bad he didn't stick his hand out for a payoff this time. Slade should have killed him outright instead of just hitting him; then Liz wouldn't have had to shoot him, making Slade look bad in the process.

Slade set his credit card in the tray on top of the bill. He chuckled. Going straight. That's what Brad said he'd done. Not possible. At least not in his experience, though the idea was beginning to sound attractive to him. Poor Brad. Did he have a family? For the first time in his life, Slade Bolton felt guilty. What would his mother or grandfather think if they knew what he was doing now?

Chapter 21 Rose

~

Riesling – an aromatic grape with high acidity used to make dry, semi-sweet and sweet wine

Tuesday, October 11, 5:00 PM

Sunlight dappled on autumn-tinged Sycamore leaves, and west-facing windows gleamed like polished gold in early evening sunlight. People flowed through the entrance to the two-story brick building on the grounds of the Paso Robles Inn. The venue was part of the original 1890s hotel. Rose carried a salad for the Olive Growers Dinner potluck. Hopefully, if the night went as she planned, she'd have more information on Brad Knight. And Frank might be there. Certainly, he must be. He was a key member of the board.

She wore her red leather walking shoes and carried dressier pumps in a bag. Cream-colored pants and a pale-yellow top fluttered around her body in the light breeze.

Rose placed her dish on the buffet table. Most contributions contained the grower's olive oil. Rose's dressing was a bottle from the store. Hopefully, no one figured that out.

She surveyed the room, looking for Frank. In addition to the buffet, there were ten round tables with seating for eight scattered like drops of water on a pond. People tipped chairs to claim a spot and wandered off to find a drink.

Two tables over sat Evangeline and a man Rose assumed was the hot-blooded Carlos Abbot. He sure looked like the same guy who nearly smashed the gallery door on Friday afternoon. Rose glanced over until she saw the glare in Evangeline's eyes. Their encounters at the gallery after the murder and theft were contentious, if Rose was charitable. Hostile if she wasn't. What was it about? The gallery owner acted guilty of something more serious than an affair with a security guard.

"I'm so glad you made it," said a woman beside her. "Sometimes these things can scare people off."

Rose jumped, then sighed in relief at finding someone she knew. Margery, a master gardener, had answered many of Rose's initial questions about how to care for her new olive trees.

"Hi, Margery. Quite a crowd."

"Thanks to home growers like you. Have you found a seat yet?"

"I want to change my shoes," she held up the bag that contained a more fashionable heeled shoe. Margery led her over to a table with several chairs still available. She hung her handbag over the back and placed a shawl on the seat. Rose sat down in the next chair to slip on her pumps. Every little bit of heel helped when you were slightly over five feet tall.

This was her first of these quarterly events. Everyone in the local olive world would be there. Including, she hoped, the owners of Olive Heaven. And Frank. She scanned the crowd.

"Looking for someone in particular?" Margery asked.

Well, yes, Rose thought. "I love the wood and the architecture."

"We used to hold these dinners at the Elks Lodge. This place is nicer and better able to handle the size of the crowd. Rose," she paused and moved closer. "I wanted to say I'm distressed over Natalie's arrest. She's always helpful to us with web-related matters. I'm sure they will clear her soon."

"I didn't know she worked with the Olive Growers Association, too."

"Oh yes. Has for years." Rose was learning more about Natalie from the townsfolk than she was from the woman herself. They headed over to get a glass of wine, an essential ingredient for surviving a dinner like this. Evangeline and Carlos passed her without acknowledging them.

Margery leaned over to whisper.

"That's the queen bee, Evangeline Abbot. More money than brains when it comes to olives. Fortunately, they've hired a friend of mine to manage their orchard and handle harvest."

"Why queen bee?" Rose asked.

"She's on every charitable committee in the county, dominates, and pushes her own agenda. Everyone is afraid to kick her out because the flow of donations might stop. I don't care for her style. Which means I don't kowtow, and therefore she doesn't give me the time of day."

Rose reflected on her visits to the crime scene.

"I went to the gallery to ask questions about the murder and theft. She stonewalled me at first, but then told me all about her affair with Brad Knight and how she refused to let her husband, Carlos, attend the gala because she was afraid he might kill Brad."

Margery took a few steps forward as the line moved.

"Oh, THAT secret that everyone except Brad's wife knew about. Poor thing. She works at the Shop and Bag. I've wanted to mention it to her several times, but it's not my place. Maybe I should stop by and see if there is anything I can do to help. Oh, hi Joan, how have you been?" Margery struck up a conversation with the person in line behind her.

Evangeline didn't have to worry about Rose taking her place in philanthropic organizations. That wasn't her interest. She gave to causes she supported, but attending meetings was something she wanted to shove to the past. Was that why the woman had been so cold when Rose spoke with her? Or was there something deeper, something related to the stolen painting that Evangeline didn't want to talk about?

Behind Rose in line was a long-time grower with a family history in the area, which she recognized from a seminar she attended. He wore cleaned-up farmer gear: Carhart pants, a plaid shirt, and a newish blue jeans jacket. His name was Carl something. Next to him was a man with shredded jeans, a rock and roll T-shirt, and dirty running shoes. Did no one dress up anymore?

"Good to see you, Jeff," Carl said. "Down for the weekend?"

Jeff shifted his wine glass so he could shake Carl's hand.

"Yeah. I'll be switching to remote work. Janice and the kids are moving here full-time."

There was something about waking up in the country, inhaling the fresh morning air that soothed an ancient ache in your bones. Rose felt it every morning as she breathed in the scent of sage and lavender.

Jeff leaned around Carl. "Rose, thanks for taking booth duty. Janice came down with a cold, and with all the germs running around now, well, it seemed prudent that she stay at home."

Ah, that explained the last-minute call for her to sit at the booth in the park.

"It was interesting. I didn't give out many stickers, but they knew I was there." She smiled at the memory of the kids tossing the pieces of plastic in the air and then Brad Knight stepping in to corral them and give them a stern word.

Across the room, a group of men stood in a circle around a man named Jenkins. His years as a grower had made him an icon in the industry. Everyone wanted to hear his opinion on things.

Rose reached the front of the wine queue, asked for an Alberino, and, taking her glass, crossed the room to join the cluster around Mr. Jenkins. She slipped in between two people. He expounded on how the weather had changed his watering scheme, and Rose listened with great interest. As a child, she managed to keep a tomato plant in a pot going all summer, and that needed daily watering in the summer heat. With a tree, she had no idea what to do. Jenkins did, and she planned to soak up any knowledge he was willing to spill.

Frank slid into an opening next to her as a chime rang out announcing dinner was to start.

"Ah," he said. "I'll catch you later."

Diners moved to their tables. Rose drifted over to her seat next to Margery. To her delight, Jenkins and his wife sat at the same table. A metal stanchion proclaimed that this was number eight. On the other side of the circle, to Mr. Jenkins' left, sat Dave Acer and his wife. She couldn't have asked for a better seat. Beside them came another couple she didn't know, yet, but they were too far away to greet them other than with a smile and a wave. Margery Wheat was the last to join them.

"Gracious. So many old friends to say hello to, I almost didn't make it back here," she said.

An announcement over the speaker system called tables one and two to the buffet line. Chairs scraped on the floor as sixteen people rose at once.

The woman to her left smiled, her eyes crinkling in the corners like crinoline.

"My name is Daphne Jenkins."

Rose offered her hand, and Daphne squeezed the tips of her fingers, providing an unsatisfactory shake. "Do you grow olives, dear?"

"I have five trees. Trying not to kill them," Rose said.

Daphney laughed. "Aren't we all?"

"Rose is being modest," Margery said. "She's an ideal steward for her orchard."

It gratified Rose that these two women thought she could take care of her trees as well as they could. With a start, she realized she owned an orchard. Something she never suspected would give her such satisfaction. Still, there was so much she didn't know about olive trees, and she was afraid to admit her incompetence; being a technical expert had been her business, her reputation.

Daphne sipped her wine and appraised Rose over the rim of her glass.

"This group will help you succeed. Even one olive tree bestows a duty on you to protect it. They can live to over a thousand years, you know."

One thousand years? The fact intimidated Rose and yet gave her purpose. With a pang of guilt, she reminded herself that clearing Natalie's name was purpose enough.

"Have you met Cindy and Dave Acer of Olive Heaven Farm?" Daphne asked, indicating the couple on the other side of her husband. Rose had recognized Dave from a seminar. His tousled dark hair and bushy walrus mustache made him unforgettable. Rose wondered if it tickled Cindy when they kissed. Cindy, in contrast to every other woman in the room, looked like a runway model. Tall and slim, with sun-kissed blond hair pulled back in a bun. She looked as contrary to Dave as possible. They both leaned in toward Daphne as she told them Rose's name.

The distance was too great to shake hands without reaching across Mr. and Mrs. Jenkins. 'Dears' didn't do that sort of thing. She smiled and dipped her head in an across-the-table greeting.

"Tables eight and nine," came the announcement, and they all stood. Standing in line for the buffet, Rose found herself behind Dave.

How to ask about murder? Rose considered that it might be rude to start with that. She turned around.

"How is your harvest this year?"

"Was going gangbusters," Dave said. "Until we lost an employee. Had to find another worker, which at the last minute was a challenge. We rallied, though. Got everything in and processed. Not as much as last year, but enough to keep the lights on."

"Brad Knight," Rose said.

Standing behind her husband, Cindy Acer raised sculpted brows. She and Dave exchanged a look before turning back to her.

"You knew Brad?" Dave asked.

"I met him last Friday night. My friend Natalie worked with him at the art gallery."

Cindy's face relaxed. "It came as a shock. We knew he had a night job, and that seemed like such a safe one to have, but then..." her voice trailed off.

They must have done a security check on an employee they let onto their premises. A quick look at Dave's face told her they had, and that it uncovered something distasteful. Something that might have come back to haunt Brad.

Should have brought my notepad, Rose reflected, one never knows when valuable information might be spilled. "Was there anything in his file that might explain what happened?"

"Well," started Dave, though he seemed reluctant to continue.

Should she mention that the police knew she was investigating?

"They've arrested my friend Natalie for his murder. Anything you can tell me might help me clear her name."

Cindy put her hand on Dave's shoulder and whispered. Rose could barely hear her say, "I don't see any harm." He nodded.

"We did run a check. He had some things in his past he wanted to get away from. And, well, I believe in second chances."

Could there be someone who felt Brad didn't get what he deserved and wanted to even the score?

"Did you ever meet his wife, Gloria?"

He was married?" Cindy asked. "He didn't wear a ring."

"He wouldn't, around all the farm equipment, though. He was smart about that," Dave explained.

Rose reached the buffet, picked up a plate, and began to sample the salads, main courses, and desserts. All the while, her mind raced. Brad Knight had a history. The policewoman had hinted at that on Friday in the park.

"May I see your files? I'm not officially an investigator, but Sergeant Gomez knows I'm digging into this."

"Give me your email, and I'll get them sent over," Cindy said.

Rose felt a thrill of discovery. She was good at this!

"Having fun?" Frank's voice cut through the maelstrom of thoughts that swirled in her mind. She looked up from her plate, piled with food she didn't remember taking, and froze. He looked even better than he had on Friday. Tonight, he wore a gray and blue checked shirt with a heather gray blazer over those crisp blue jeans.

"Hi, Frank." His gaze dropped to her dinner selections. Rose felt a hot blush on her cheeks.

"Everything looked so good," she said with a timid smile, "I couldn't decide, so I guess I took some of each."

He stepped beside her and reached over to the table to straighten two of the dishes. When they met his standards, he turned to her.

"Yeah, I've done that. Stay away from that brownish lump of stuff there, though," he pointed to a scoop of what looked like potato salad. "Take it from me, you'll regret that decision."

The offending lump seemed to grow in proportion. In fact, she'd piled an enormous amount of food on her plate. She flushed with embarrassment and looked for a trash can.

"Thank you."

Frank cleared his throat. The dinner he carried showed restraint and a tendency toward vegetables over meat. Did this guy have any flaws?

"There's a show at the college theater this coming Saturday. A musical. I have two tickets. Do you like musicals?" His gentle voice cut through the hubbub in the room. She swallowed and savored the moment.

"Um, yes. My favorite is South Pacific, though I doubt it has held up to modern times."

A smile spread across his whole face.

"Would you be my guest?"

His question hung between them. Was she ready for a real date? Rose noticed his eyebrows were a mix of chestnut brown and tarnished silver hairs. Bushy, but not inclined to a mono-brow. He owned his own company, had patents, and liked musicals. He was asking her out. Of course, she should say yes. But getting the words out proved harder.

"Um…"

Going on a date during a murder investigation seemed wrong, with Natalie sitting in jail while Rose went out with a man.

Behind her in the food line, Margery scooped some potato salad onto her plate.

"The correct answer is yes," she whispered.

This was supposed to be a new life. Time to embrace that idea. Rose looked up at Frank and felt a slight heat in her cheeks.

"I would love to. What time? I can meet you there." Driving herself would allow her flexibility if he turned out not to be the nice man he appeared to be.

People can surprise you, as Sergeant Nessa said.

They arranged to meet at the entrance to the theater at 7:30 for an 8:00 p.m. curtain. Rose returned to her seat with a gentle hum of excitement and outright amazement buzzing through her.

--

After dinner, Margery gave Rose a ride home. "Come out to the farm. We'll have lunch and talk. I'll want to hear all about your date with Frank."

"Have you known him a long time?" Rose asked.

"Years. He's salt of the earth. Nice guy. Steady. And he's been through a lot."

Rose translated that all to not a serial killer but has a story. Don't we all. Then she admonished herself for going so dark. Give yourself a chance, she thought.

"What do you mean?"

"You need to ask him," Margery said and waved goodbye.

Walking up the front steps, Rose wondered why Margery hadn't snatched Frank up if he was such a great catch. Maybe they had dated, and it didn't work out. Maybe the lot of whatever he'd been through involved her.

She turned and glanced at Slade Bolton's house. Lights were on in the front room. Two figures moved about, silhouettes in a black-and-white movie. It looked like Stella had been successful.

She slid the key into her lock. A door slammed. The loud bang startled an owl perched in an oak tree. It swooped along the street, then disappeared into the night.

Only one figure showed in Bolton's house now. The other figure walked briskly over to Stella's house, up the short steps, and through the front door. The click of heels on the concrete, then wood, sounded like faraway gunfire.

Inside, Watson greeted Rose with a robust tail wag.

"Doesn't look like a satisfying end to a date for Stella, Watson. Should we give her a ring?"

He shook himself all over.

"I guess you're right. Let's give you a run in the back. I'm too tired for a walk. Then we'll crawl into bed."

As she closed her door, she saw a lone person standing in the window of Slade Bolton's house, facing her direction.

The figure could be a cutout; it was so motionless. Granted, it was late, but it stood so still it didn't feel real. Could he see her? Rose glanced behind her. With all the lights off, there was no background glow to silhouette her frame. Seeing him stand there gave her the chills, and his words echoed in her memory.

Consider yourself warned…you could get hurt. Or worse.

Chapter 22 Rose

~

Albariño – a white wine grape tasting of rich stone fruit flavors, a hint of salinity and a light body with no tannins

Wednesday, October 12, 11:45 AM

The drive to the Knight house wove through streets overhung with yellowing trees and swirls of red and gold leaves on the road. Rose found Brad's widow in a garden resplendent with irises, cosmos, and lavender. The woman perched on a padded garden kneeler and pulled at weeds, aggressively dumping them in a hardware store bucket.

Gloria Knight was as short as her late husband was tall. She wore cut-offs, a dirty white T-shirt, and rubber garden clogs. A broad-brimmed hat covered a mass of unkempt, wavy, auburn hair.

When Rose pushed the squeaky gate, Gloria stood and stretched her back. Rose's back ached in sympathy. Gardening was such an unergonomic activity. Gloria straightened and rolled her shoulders.

"Can I help you?" Her eyes left Rose's face and dropped to Watson, who pushed in and stood with his tail wagging. Rose shielded her eyes from the sun with her hand, wishing her hat had a broader brim.

"I'm Rose MacGillivray. Please accept my condolences for the loss of your husband."

An expression of confusion passed over Gloria's

face as if she wasn't aware that her husband had been murdered. Rose froze. Had the police not been here? Did the woman not know?

"I'm so sorry, I assumed you knew."

The woman took off her gardening gloves and dropped them to the ground. Despite her disheveled appearance, her nails were bright red and quite pointed. "Who are you again?"

"My friend is Natalie Patel. She used to work with Brad, your husband. I met him in the park on Friday for the first time."

I'm babbling, she realized. Trying to fill space while Gloria grappled with this intrusion. Rose knew the look in the woman's eyes. Confusion. Disbelief. Rose had felt it when her mom died last year. Take a breath and let the silence speak. Finally, Gloria's eyes focused on Rose.

"You're a cop?"

"No...I'm a consulting detective." Rose liked the sound of that: No gun. No rules. Like Sherlock Holmes, free to ask questions and deduce motives.

Gloria let out a long, deep breath, likely one she'd been holding for a long time.

"I got a visit from the police Saturday morning. 'Hello, ma'am, I'm sorry to say your husband is dead. Where were you between the hours of...? I hadn't even processed the shocking news before they were accusing me of killing him!"

As the wife of a police officer, Gloria must have had some idea of how this went. Of course, knowing and experiencing it were two vastly different things. She bent over, picked up the gloves, then dropped them again.

"I thought if I pretended it didn't happen, then

maybe it didn't." Gloria plopped down on the grass.

"Every time he left for work, I didn't know if he'd come home. That's why we moved here, and he took that job. Less stress. Less danger. He's been on night shift since he started, but was going to move to days next month."

Pulling her notebook out, Rose lowered herself to the lawn next to the distraught woman.

"Mind if I let Watson loose? He'll behave."

Gloria waved her hand, which Rose took to mean consent. She unclipped the leash, and Watson ambled off to inspect the row of bushes along the front of the Craftsman-style bungalow. Gloria's tears turned into full-on gushers. Rose was willing to listen, and that was all it took to open the tap on the other woman's grief.

"It's just…this was supposed to be different." She sniffled. Tears streaked through a smudge of dirt on Gloria's face. "It was supposed to be temporary."

"Which one? The security guard or the olive farm?" Rose asked. Had Brad managed to keep his second job a secret?

"Or did you mean living here?" Rose went on. Were they on the run? Brad Knight must have done something he wanted to put behind him. Working as a security guard at a small art gallery wasn't a high-risk position that needed his criminal justice background. But it could have been a good place to hide. If the Fresno death wasn't the result of police brutality, then something else must have been going on. Sexual misconduct? Theft? Excessive force? Any of which would result in an investigation and termination.

"The olive farm was mostly seasonal." Gloria's forehead gathered in deep furrows as the words sank in.

"The guard job was why we came here. He was supposed to start the night shift and move to days in two months. Then Evangeline took a liking to him, wanted him to stay on the graveyard shift. At least that's what he told me."

Rose closed her notepad. This woman needed a confident, not an investigator.

Gloria leaned over to pick up her gloves and then laid them down again. Rose wanted to grab the distracting things away from her.

"I thought he changed. He never wanted to go out to lunch with me. Kept sneaking off and wouldn't tell me where he was going. She looked up at Rose with tears in her eyes.

Rose softened her tone in sympathy. "Have you met Evangeline Abbot?"

Gloria laughed. "Oh yeah, I met her all right. She's a petty, treacherous woman who stomps her feet and pouts when she doesn't get what she wants."

That summed up Evangeline Abbott nicely, thought Rose, but there was a big gap between bitch and murderer.

Gloria was crying. Great sobs with shaking shoulders and tears. "What do I do now? I don't think I can afford to stay here; my job doesn't pay enough. It's too much for me."

What could Rose say that would ease this anguish? Assuming it was real. Gloria could be an accomplished actor. Had she killed Brad because of an affair? If she did, why steal the painting? Maybe she wanted it to look like a theft. That made sense.

Gloria retrieved her gloves and clippers and then stood, signaling that the interview was over. Rose got up awkwardly as well and mentally added squats to her fictional workout routine.

"Come!" she called, and the little dog appeared with alert ears and a nose covered with cobwebs. She clipped his leash onto his collar.

"Out of curiosity, where were you Friday night between 2:00 and 4:00 AM?"

"Mind your own business!"

The change startled Rose. Brad's widow had been surprisingly open about answering Rose's other questions. But this one angered her. Why? Was it one too many inquiries, or was there more to it? As if Gloria heard the questions running through Rose's mind, she uttered a resigned sigh.

"I was cooking roast beef, so my adulterous husband had something delicious to eat when he got home from work in the morning. Waste of money. Nearly burned it to a crisp after the call. I tossed it in the trash."

A large, blue rolling trash can was pushed up against the garage door. Someone had painted it with a riot of pink, oranges, yellows, and blue flowers. How would the woman respond if she went over and opened the lid? Not well, Rose guessed.

Gloria put on her gardening gloves and resumed pulling weeds. Rose retraced her steps to the front gate and back to her car. Two doors down, an elderly gentleman stood with a hose in his hand, watering an herb garden of rosemary, basil, and oregano. He wore a battered fishing hat with stains along the brim, Bermuda shorts, black socks, and scuffed bedroom slippers.

"That smells nice," Rose commented as she walked past. The man smiled and waved.

"Cute little dog," he said.

Rose paused, then doubled back. Watson sniffed a shrub.

"I'm thinking of buying a home in this neighborhood. It's so peaceful, and that's what I need for my nerves. Is it as quiet as it looks?" The ease of lying surprised her.

He walked over to where she stood and watered a dry patch of grass. His T-shirt read "Old Guys Rule."

"There isn't anything for sale around here."

She took a quick breath. "Yes, well, I've got my eyes open." That seemed to appease his curiosity.

"To answer your question, yes, most folks are older, so no kids barreling up and down the street, though we do have some residents who come and go at odd times and more vacation rentals than I like."

"Oh?"

"Couple doors down, the husband works both days and nights, and she's in and out. They never seem to sleep."

Rose visualized this busybody peering like a spy through the curtains to keep an eye on his neighbors. Then she realized she did the same thing. He must have insomnia, too.

"Any loud fights?"

He tipped his head and squinted at her. "You in real estate?"

When she shook her head, he shrugged and turned off the water flow. "Well, anyway, seems a weird way to live, if you ask me, which no one does."

"I appreciate you sharing your thoughts. Have a lovely day." Rose turned to walk away.

"Widowed?" he called after her, his face beaming with hope. She thought of Frank and their coffee at the park. And he then asked her out again for a show. What was his game? It felt odd to have a man paying attention to her. Odd but nice. A smile spread across her lips, which was not for the man with the hose, though he didn't know that.

"Happily single for the time being. Have a wonderful day," she said and tugged at Watson's leash to get him going again.

She opened the doors to vent the heat out before letting Watson hop inside. After setting the AC to Arctic Blast, she buckled her seat belt and checked the rearview mirror. Gloria Knight stood in the yard, watching. Had she seen the conversation with her neighbor? They didn't seem to be on speaking terms.

Her husband had caught the eye of Evangeline. Had Gloria got so fed up with his fooling around and finally eliminated the problem? She might qualify for his police pension, assuming he got one. She'd need to check into that.

Gloria watched as the nosy woman drove away. What had the neighbor said about them? Something vile, no doubt. Brad kept to himself, and she followed suit. They didn't talk with their neighbors and wanted to keep it that way. It kept them safe. Or had done, until this.

She turned to look at the house. Should she go back to Fresno? They didn't have any retirement saved up, no pension to lean on, and Social Security was too far away.

That left her finding a better-paying job that would allow her to stay. Or a second job.

Some fresh start. All the danger, unknowing, and difficulties had seemed to follow them from Fresno. Would they leave her alone now that Brad was dead?

And who was this prying woman? What right did

she have to poke at open wounds? If the guys Brad ran from came after her, she'd point them to Rose. That would shut the bitch up.

She would need sleeping pills again tonight.

Chapter 23 Stella

~

*Muscat — an overarching term for a family of grapes used to make,
among other wines, Moscato*

Wednesday, October 12, 5:00 PM

Stella let the lace curtain close on the front window and leaned against the wall. She had watched Slade Bolton roll his trash to the curb, climb into the black Mercedes, and drive away. The framed picture of him and another woman on his kitchen counter swam through her mind: the beach umbrella, bathing suits, and snogging. She'd seen Liz Bathory at the art gallery and remembered the straight, dark hair. So different from her brown curls. What did he prefer?

A tempest of emotion threatened, but she stopped herself. Get a grip. Look what happened to Natalie. He caused her arrest, she felt sure now. Just as she was confident that her birth mom was somewhere nearby. No proof of either, but she trusted her intuition.

That trash bin looked heavy. Weird, since he never cooked there and barely slept in the house. She waited to make sure he didn't double back before opening her front door.

The sturdy black receptacle sat in the street against the curb. No blue recycling box like hers, full of jars and bottles. She lifted the lid. Inside, she saw a black plastic bag. He hadn't even pulled the plastic straps closed around the fast-food wrappers, chip bags, and crushed soda cans.

The In-N-Out Burger wrappers tattled that he traveled to San Anselmo, the closest location. Groping through someone else's trash might be illegal, but then, who was going to complain? Using the hem of her shirt to keep her fingers clean, she lifted the bag out.

At the bottom, nestled on top of bubble wrap, lay a cylindrical piece of concrete or stone. She held her breath and dove for the object. Even clean trash containers smelled like rot. Seconds before her hand touched, she stopped. Think this through. Don't put your fingerprints on whatever it is. And what it looked like was a miniature one of those Easter Island heads.

She straightened up, pulled her phone out, and dialed Rose, who arrived moments later with Watson at her heels.

"What's up?"Stella pointed into the trash bin.

The aroma of sunbaked garbage made Rose gag. Then she saw a solid object at the bottom that looked like a statue.

"What made you even look in here?" she asked.

"A feeling." Stella leaned over to view the object again. "It doesn't look like the type of thing normally found in someone's trash."

Rose peered over the edge again. "Maybe he bought it at a big box store to class the place up."

Stella rolled her eyes. Honestly, doesn't anyone listen to her? There was NOTHING in the house. No pictures of pretty scenes, no plants, fake or otherwise, and certainly no statues.

"And put it on what? The lawn chair? Nestled in the sleeping bag on the floor?"

She knew he didn't buy this thing. Stole it, maybe.

If it were real art, someone who made a living finding stolen pieces wouldn't throw it out, right? One of her two clients was a sculptor, and he wouldn't toss work like this.

"What do we do with it?"

Rose snapped a photo. "We need to call the police. You'll have to explain what you were doing. You didn't touch it, did you?"

"Give me a little credit." She was glad her conscience had pinged her in time.

Rose dialed.

"Sergeant Gomez." The policewoman's voice over the speaker sounded businesslike. Startled, Stella couldn't imagine why Rose would call that particular policewoman. She had arrested Natalie. That made her the enemy.

"Nessa. There's something that I think you should see. You might want to bring a forensics team with you." She gave her the address and rang off. Stella marveled that the two women were on a first-name basis. In her experience, that didn't happen. Respect and distance were the watchwords of police-citizen interactions.

Watson lifted his leg on Bolton's trash and peed.

Nessa didn't waste any time getting to Slade's house. It helped that the police station was only eight blocks away. She did, however, show up alone. Stella showed her the trash can and the object nestled at the bottom in the bubble wrap.

Nessa leaned in and then looked up. "Is this yours?"

"No. I live over there." Stella pointed to her house, but her eyes stayed riveted on the gun holstered at the officer's waist. The casual way police in the States carried a weapon amazed her. British Bobbies didn't have them.

"Then why were you looking in your neighbor's garbage?"

A flush of red moved up Stella's face. "Going through the bits and bobs, looking for recyclables. The guy doesn't use the blue bin."

Nessa tilted her head as she considered this.

"Don't do it again. Okay?"

Stella agreed.

"So, the guy has an odd thing in his trash. And you thought to call me?" Her voice lifted at the end of the sentence to imply a question.

"Because," Rose said. "You told me that the potential murder weapon was a cylindrical, hard object. This is a rounded, hard object, which also happens to be a piece of art and is an unusual thing to find in the trash of an FBI Art Crime agent."

As she spoke, her tone got hard and clipped.

"We thought you might want to take a look."

Nessa looked back into the can, then straightened with a sigh.

"The chief isn't going to like this, but I see what you're saying, and it doesn't hurt to take a look."

She pulled a two-way radio off her belt, turned her back on them, and spoke. While they waited for the crime scene guys, Nessa looked from Slade's house to Natalie's.

"Strange that this is on the same corner as Natalie Patel's house, maybe that's how…" She didn't finish the thought. A white van with SLPD stenciled in bold black letters drove up and parked.

A small man climbed out. He looked about thirty years old, with such thinning hair that his pale scalp blazed through the strands of fading brown. He wore a yellow jacket with CSI on the back and black pants with a sharp crease.

He took photos and bagged-and-tagged the statue, then took the black plastic bag for good measure. With the bin returned to its spot on the curb, the FBI agent would be none the wiser.

When the forensics tech had packed all his gear into the van and pulled away, Rose approached the policewoman. Stella hovered to hear what they said.

"Any word on bail for Natalie?"

Nessa smiled with one of those empty, lifting-the-corners-of-the-mouth smiles. "With a murder charge, it's unlikely."

Rose looked as if she expected this but was still disappointed. Stella counted herself lucky that she had no experience with law enforcement since immigrating to the U.S. Some things, though, were self-explanatory. Murder suspects weren't sent home to await trial.

Rose cleared her throat. "Did she mention that someone broke into her house Friday night?"

Nessa scowled. "No."

"I'm sure she is in such shock that things like that aren't occurring. She mentioned it Saturday morning when we were at the coffee shop. She didn't see anything missing, so I suggested she get her locks changed, but not to report it, as you guys couldn't do anything."

"We would have taken the report. But you're right; there wasn't much we could do."

The muscles along Rose's jaw flexed, and her finger moved side to side as she pondered. Stella could imagine the tumble of thoughts running through her friend's mind.

"What if…" Rose stopped and squinted up at Natalie's house again. "What if nothing was taken, but instead something was left? Like a stolen painting?"

"You're saying someone planted evidence?" The officer's tone made it clear she didn't think that was likely.

"I'm saying keep an open mind. Natalie didn't do it."

The policewoman placed her hand on Rose's shoulder in a maternal fashion, despite their ages being reversed. "I know this is upsetting to you. We'll figure it out."

Rose's stare could melt glass. "So, you'll be talking with Gloria about Brad's police department history?"

Nessa's eyes widened. "How do you find out about that?"

"I have one of those faces that people like to confide in. They tell me things. You did say I could help."

"We'll follow every lead," Nessa said. She closed her notepad and slipped it into a zippered pouch on her vest. Stella eased over next to Rose. This new neighbor had hidden depths, visible only when something pushed her. She hoped she had the same inner strength.

They both glared at the policewoman. Stella asked, "And once you've sorted it, you'll let Natalie go?"

A car door slammed. Crows cawed in the trees overhead. The cop sighed. "That's not up to me." She looked like she wanted to say something more, but instead, turned and walked back to the squad car and drove away.

The air seemed still after all the commotion.

"Come on." Rose took Stella's hand and led her toward the stairway up to Rose's veranda. "I want a glass of wine, and we need a plan."

Chapter 24 Rose

~

Pinot Noir — a French grape from the Burgundy region also known as Pinot nero. Light to medium-bodied with flavor of red fruits like cherry, raspberry and strawberries, and earthy notes of mushroom or forest floor.

Wednesday, October 12, 6:00 PM

A cool breeze skittered leaves across the veranda. Stella took a sip of an earthy Pinot Noir and sighed. "Alexander Hamilton had the room where it happened. I'm starting to think of this as the porch where it happens."

Watson jumped up onto Rose's lap and snuggled in. She scratched behind his ears. "We certainly have a view of everything happening on this corner."

On the sidewalk below, the neighborhood tomcat strutted by. Watson tracked its movement with a low growl.

"Do you remember hearing a nasty skirmish between two cats the night of the Gala?"

"Yes, well, maybe not. Slade suggested I take a sleeping pill; I might have dreamed it."

Rose felt the muscles in her neck tighten. "Slade suggested...? I remember you saying you took one, but not that he had anything to do with it."

Stella closed her eyes and rubbed her forehead. "I feel like I'm getting close to figuring out who my biological mother is. I've felt a stronger pull since I got to California. She's here somewhere.

Getting involved with Slade and trying to salvage

my bookkeeping business has slowed me down; I haven't had time to search. Thinking about it keeps me up, so I've been using them to get some sleep."

Rose studied the young woman. Was Stella angry? Or sad? She thought about her own mother, recently departed, and couldn't imagine growing up without her calming presence.

Would Rose have been a calming presence? No chance. Not with all her worries and anxieties. With her eyes closed, she let the emotions wash over her. Somewhere, a child wondered who she was.

She wrenched her mind back to the problem at hand. The figure she saw crossing the street when the cats were hissing and spitting. When she opened her eyes, Stella was watching her.

"Was he with you when you woke up?"

Stella sipped her Pinot Noir, leaned back, and closed her eyes. "He never is."

No question about it, the guy was a creep, though she suspected Stella had already made that discovery herself. Then a thought occurred. A knocked-out Stella couldn't have returned to the gallery, killed the guard, or stolen the painting.

"Do you have any proof that you took the sleeping pill?"

Stella sat up.

"The pop-out pill pack is still in my basket. I can't prove I took it that night, but maybe where it is in the can would say something."

TV crime shows trained viewers in the rudiments of forensics. Hopefully, what they saw was real enough. Rose relied on it.

"Don't touch it. The police might want to take the whole can. This could be your ticket off the suspect list."

They kept it to one bottle of wine, though it went straight to her head. Rose watched as Stella strode home with a youth's confidence of not falling and kept an eye out until the porch light went out and the bedroom lamp switched on.

Rose locked the doors, checked the windows, and headed for the kitchen. A nice, hot cup of Earl Grey might help with the headache that was brewing. Not from wine, though; the strain of Natalie's arrest and her inability to do anything about it had built up.

Tea in hand, she settled in her comfortable chair with a notebook. The first page listed possible suspects. She drew a line through Stella Richardson. Sleeping pills would have rendered her unable to get to the gallery. One down.

Brad Knight and his wife, Gloria, were a puzzle. She thought he was having an affair but it might have been because he was working more at the Olive farm. Harvest season was approaching and there was prep to do in advance. If their work schedules didn't align they may have never seen each other. If Brad was having an affair with Evangeline, as everyone seemed to think, how did he have time between his two bosses to fool around?

Gloria could have gone to the gallery, knowing he would be alone to confront him. But that would mean she would have arrived sometime after Evangeline's visit, and the footage lost when the video was tampered with.

She seemed like any shell-shocked widow, a bit calmer than most, but everyone handles grief differently. The murder was on Friday evening. Today was Tuesday. Pickup wasn't until Thursday. There was a chance the burned roast could still be in the trash. It might not be if she waited for the police.

Neither of them needed an alarm at midnight. Dog and woman arose, walked from window to window, and watched the silent neighborhood. One thought kept circling through her mind. Could a forensics tech get any information from a charred piece of beef?

It would corroborate Gloria's story, but would Nessa laugh if she showed up with a scorched hunk of beef and asked for analysis? The fear of embarrassment flushed an uncomfortable tightness through her chest. Of all the fears Rose accumulated over her career, failure and public humiliation were the worst. But no one could fire her now. The worst thing might be that the policewoman stopped sharing information. She took a deep breath; there was only one way to find out.

She threw on a pair of jeans and slipped a navy-colored hooded sweatshirt over her pajama top. Watson bound over to the car. In the short amount of time since he came to live with her, she'd grown so fond of him that leaving him behind didn't feel right. Besides, he made a good lookout.

"Okay, you can come. But you must behave."

He panted his agreement.

Without the usual tourist traffic, they arrived in minutes. She switched the headlights off as she rolled down the block, stopping on the opposite side of the street, across from the Knight's driveway.

Rose eased her way out of the car. Watson followed, and she softly pushed the door closed. She didn't bother with his leash. Overhead, the Milky Way shone brightly despite the half-moon overhead and the ambient city glow. A perfect night for sleuthing.

The house was dark. The neighbor had said Gloria was in and out at all hours. She could have reverted to a normal sleep schedule with Brad gone. Rose crept up the driveway. The garage was set back from the house, and three cans stood before the wide door. A large green one, an equally large blue one, and a smaller black one.

A blaring car alarm almost made her faint. She slid into a slice of shade near the garage door and held her breath. What the hell was she doing? Skulking around in the middle of the night like a thief? And, to her horror, she realized she hadn't thought through what she'd say if she got caught. Never in her life had she done something so impetuous. Was this the result of retiring? Or was some inner personality defect bubbling up now that she didn't have a corporation shoving it back down? Whatever it was, she was there, and she might as well get on with it.

Inching over, she could make out the yellow flowers best, as they best reflected the small amount of street light. She removed the bungee cord that kept critters from rampaging into what they would see as the gourmet delights in the black can. The second time that day she'd examined someone else's trash. The smell of putrid garbage hit her. *Good god!* Tears burned her eyes.

What would a scorched, week-old roast smell like? Using her phone's flashlight, she peered in. Under a scattering of tissues and used makeup cotton pads, she saw the outline of a football-sized chunk of roast. Black char covered the outside. Maggots crawled over the crenelated surface. The acrid smell stung her nostrils, and the wine and tea in her stomach threatened to come up.

Staggering back, she dropped the lid with a crash that echoed in the stillness.

She froze, waiting for floodlights. Watson sat at her feet, looking up. Nothing happened. She let out her breath.

No doubt about it, that was a burned dinner. But was it proof that Gloria had been home when she said? Or did she hurriedly flambé a dinner to cover her tracks? Crouched down behind the blue bin, she typed an Internet search and selected the most reputable site that appeared in the list. Maggots, it turned out, could hatch within forty-eight hours, and the larval stage could be three to nine days. Add that fact to the things she never thought she needed to know.

She counted on her fingers. Saturday. Sunday. Monday. Tuesday. Four days. The chances were good that Gloria tossed the roast the night of the murder.

A loud bang rang out. She threw herself against the garage door. Watson cowered and tried to crawl up her legs.

Was that a door slamming? Someone putting more waste in their cans? Nessa wouldn't be pleased if she was caught prowling around Gloria's back yard. Her neighbors might even have a doorbell camera and be watching her now.

What if Brad or Gloria had a hand in something bigger than the theft of a painting? Someone could have followed him to Paso Robles and taken the opportunity to kill him for retribution. Maybe he hid stolen goods in the building behind her.

How stupid could she be? Hiding behind a trash can. A cramp seized her left leg, sending searing pain to her foot. She reached forward to grab the muscle and dropped her phone with a clatter.

Shoot! Someone might have heard that.

A shadow moved along the house. It was there for an instant and then gone. She let a long-held breath out slowly to avoid making a sound. Something rubbed against her. Soft but solid. She clamped her hand over her mouth to stifle a scream.

The pressure on her leg returned. She tensed, not sure whether to react or freeze. Watson shifted on her makeshift lap. Then she heard the rumble of a cat's purr. Watson catapulted toward the sound. Normally, he would have known it was there, but the smell nose-blinded him.

The cat arched its back, hopped up on the container, and then disappeared over the garage roof with Watson scrambling along at the base of the building. At least he didn't bark.

She stood slowly, testing her legs to see if they would support her. "Watson, get back here. Come!" She called with a hoarse whisper. Hopefully, he will be there when she needed to leave. That left her to decide the next step.

No way was she going to dumpster dive into that cesspool to retrieve the evidence. She had seen and smelled the decaying dinner. Mission accomplished. Feeling like a shredded dog toy, she crept back to her car and eased the driver's side door open. Watson materialized and darted inside.

Despite the fright, she had learned that Gloria's alibi held solid. Rose felt good about moving her name to the bottom of the list. On the other hand, a deep dive into Brad's background might generate a whole new roster of suspects.

Chapter 25 Rose

~

Manzanillo Olive – Used for table olives and oil. Frequently seen as canned black olives.

Thursday, October 13, 10 AM

When Rose pushed the doorbell, a deep gong echoed on the cavernous veranda. Gallery owner Evangeline Abbott and her hot-blooded, contractor husband Carlos lived in an Italian-style home on a hill surrounded by a vineyard. They weren't just doing well; they were doing exceptionally well.

Towering Mission olives shaded the drive. Columns of pale, golden sandstone supported the roof of the two-story building. A heavily carved wood entrance gave the impression that the Abbotts didn't want anyone dropping in.

Rose hadn't called ahead. That might have given them time to slip out or collaborate on a cover story to explain Evangeline's reappearance at the gallery. Rose also wanted to ask about the painting, which seemed to get lost in the tragedy of death. Why would someone take it? Why, if it turned out to be true, would Natalie steal that one?

A tall man with jet-black hair opened the door. He wore a soft shirt over relaxed jeans that hung low on his hips. He leaned against the jamb and crossed his muscled arms. The skin on his biceps glowed like he'd recently stepped away from a bench press. Small crinkles around his sky blue eyes indicated he was older than his hair color might suggest. Fifty-ish, she guessed. And smoking hot.

"May I help you?" His European accent sent a shiver down her spine.

"Good morning." She held up an old conference badge. She'd decided on a cover story as a survey taker for the olive growers. Something she knew just enough about to fake. All the good detectives on TV used cover stories. "I'm with the Central Coast Olive Growers Association and have some questions about your orchard practices."

His gaze swept her from head to foot.

"Is this a joke?"

Rose put the badge away and pulled out her notepad.

"What species do you grow and what is your expected yield?"

"How the hell should I know? I hire people for that. My wife handles the contracts."

"Is she home?"

"Who are you?" he asked.

"Rose. Rose MacGillivray. I'm new to the area and the Association." She smiled at him. "I missed seeing you at the gala."

"You are a nosy woman. I don't like nosy women. Leave. Now. He reached for the door handle. Rose didn't move. Carlos shifted from one foot to the other.

She pulled herself up to her full five-foot-one-inch height.

"I will ask questions over and over again until I find the right ones to clear my friend. It will be less bothersome if you answer truthfully, now. Then I won't have to return and ask again."

"What do you care?" His tone turned defensive, though the flex in his biceps said something else. Something threatening. "Look, you didn't see me because I wasn't there."

He casually examined his fingernails and pushed a cuticle back with his thumb. From the look of his manicured digits. A classic stalling technique. He was wondering how much to tell her to make her go away, she thought. Or coming up with a whopper of a lie.

"Look, we had a suite at Allegretto, and I enjoyed a massage and a soak in the spa tub." His smile gave her the hint that the massage involved more than oils and candles. She tried to keep her voice conversational.

"That sounds lovely. I imagine Evangeline enjoyed that after the stress of the event. What time did she finally get there?" How long could she keep him talking?

"I believe she locked up around 11:00 and joined me for a late dinner."

If Evangeline had gotten to the hotel at 11:00, there would have been time to eat dinner, spend time with her husband, and return to the gallery by 1:00 AM. But why? Could the painting have been valuable?

"Did you meet Brad Knight?" she asked.

He drew himself taller as if he found the mention of the name distasteful and beneath him to discuss. "I am familiar with him. My wife knows him well; you should ask her." Then his face brightened a bit. "Was he the guy who died? I hadn't put one and one together."

She felt a thrill that she might weasel a clue out of him.

"One and one makes …?" She let the question invite him to fill in the blank.

"I give her everything she needs. Now, I grow tired of your questions."

"That must have upset you," Rose said. "I heard she was fooling around with him."

He threw his head back and laughed. "Look at me! That guard couldn't compete with this body. Eve saw the error of her ways and ended it. So that's done and done."

What an arrogant bastard, Rose thought. She could see why Evangeline would want to have an affair. Her one experience with Brad Knight showed him to be considerate and personable. Would she have killed him if his reaction to her ending the affair wasn't despair and anguish, but more of a Carlos response? Cold. Arrogant.

A Range Rover pulled into the driveway. "Ah, here she is. Ask away." He walked back into the house.

Moments later, Mrs. Abbott exited the driver's side and rushed up the walk. "I've already complained about you to the police chief." She charged by and entered the hall. Rose followed.

"Yes, Sergeant Gomez told me. Then she said I could help."

Evangeline's eyes narrowed. Rose pulled her shoulders back to make herself look taller.

"You were so forthcoming at the gallery that I'm back with more questions. In a more "official" capacity."

This development stopped Evangeline. "The police are aware you're here?"

Technically, Nessa knew that Rose intended to investigate. Had, in fact, given her permission. So, how specific did she need to get?

"Earlier, we spoke about the guard but not about the stolen painting. Was it worth a lot of money?"

"Not as much as the others. Interesting, isn't it, that they took that one and not one of the more important works?"

Now that she'd tapped into the woman's gossipy side, the gallery owner rambled on. "I noticed Liz Bathory lingering at that painting. Maybe she stole it herself!"

"You're saying she orchestrated the entire show so she could steal one not-so-valuable painting?" Not likely. The rich could be eccentric, but that took it too far. She moved the gallery owner up a spot on her who-did-it list. Not only had she immediately thrown shade on someone else, but why would a wealthy woman conduct an affair with a security guard?

Rose looked around and considered the vineyard, the Tuscan landscaping, and the heavy wrought-iron furniture with plump cushions. Not to mention the steamy husband.

"I understand you had a suite at Allegretto. What time did you get there last night?"

Gray eyes glinted with anger, and Evangeline replied through gritted teeth. "I left at eleven PM, after closing, and joined Carlos at Allegretto. You can check with them. We booked a room for the night, so they kept the dining room open for us as a special favor. I'm good friends with the owners. We're done here. You would be wise to stop asking questions. You might get hurt."

Exuding as much swagger as she could muster, Rose walked to her car, her brain swirling on what she'd learned. On the surface, her husband supported her alibi. Though the chances were high that he'd lied. There would be security videos of her entering the lobby and eating in the hotel dining room. Would those same cameras record her if she slipped out in the middle of the night? Both Abbots had hinted at danger to her person. Rose didn't think they would actually follow through, but then again—

Evangeline watched the little gray Honda descend the driveway. That woman wouldn't stop sticking her nose into things she ought not.

Her marriage was her own business. It was unfortunate that things blew up the night of the Gala, but with Brad gone now, Carlos' anger had subsided. She'd committed to him that she wouldn't stray, and surprisingly, he'd done the same. That was the first indication that he'd been diddling around as well.

She placed the bag of groceries she'd been holding on the table, reflecting that Rose MacGillivray's presence had rattled her enough to forget all about it. A baguette stuck out of the top. They would enjoy a lovely Italian dinner of pasta, salad, and fresh bread with garlic butter, reminiscing about where they met at a little café in Rome.

Carlos leaned on the foyer wall and glared at her. Damn, she thought. His good mood had vanished already. Hopefully, dinner will restore it.

"I picked up some fresh linguini. Do you want to cook or should I?" she asked.

He shifted from one foot to the other, crossing muscled arms in front of his chest.

"What do we do about her?" he asked.

Evangeline closed her eyes and took a steadying breath. She didn't want to have this argument now. She wanted romance and her Latin lover tonight.

"There's nothing to do. The manager at the hotel will vouch for us and confirm our stay."

"I don't like it. She may stumble onto something related to my business, and I can't emphasize enough that we don't want that."

A frisson of fear rustled in Evangeline's mind. What was he talking about? He was a builder. End of story. At least as far as she knew it.

"I'm going to put this stuff away and then go for a swim. Coming?"

Carlos grunted and left by the front door.

Back at her house, Rose let Watson out and entered the garage. Seeing the Abbotts' elegant estate had intimidated her. Harvesting in their orchard would be a large affair, with quarter-ton bins and hired labor, resulting in hundreds if not thousands of gallons of golden oil. But Rose had a beautiful home too, with five stately olive trees, and a robust crop of blackening olives she needed to pick soon.

She pulled off the white sheet that covered the olive press and stared at it. Despite reading the instructions for using the steel tower, the idea terrified her. According to the directions, stacks of olive paste and screens slid between two quarter-inch plates, and a hydraulic jack applied the force necessary to squeeze out the liquid. The whole structure never moved from its spot along the wall, being too heavy and unwieldy for her to manage.

Gathering buckets, scrapers, and spoons from the shelves at the rear, she took them into the house to wash. With clean supplies, she set up an equipment assembly line on a long table in the garage. Next came the crusher, constructed from a garbage disposal and a steel can at the top to funnel the whole olives, pits and all, into the blades. Ground-up fruit paste oozed out of a tube at the bottom into a bucket. She would take the mashed-up olive paste, spread it on the screens, stack things as tall as she dared, and slide the tray onto the press. A car jack would press the tray, and oil would ooze out.

Rose decided she'd taken a big enough step toward harvest. She shut off the garage light and closed the door. Once in the house, she thought about Carlos. Maybe the suite at the fancy hotel was a place to rekindle a troubled marriage. Overcome a difficulty named Brad Knight. And with him gone, they could return to life as it had been.

Thinking of the Abbotts' marriage reminded her of two things. One pleasant, the other painful. Shunting the painful memory of Richard and his deceit, she focused on her upcoming date. Four days. Not that marriage was in her plans. Frank didn't have Carlos's overwhelming masculine aura, which she realized was good for her. Rose didn't have Liz Bathory's looks or Evangeline's sophistication. Rose and Frank fit each other. That thought gave her a little shiver. Don't get ahead of yourself, she reminded herself. He could be a serial killer himself. A serial killer she had a date with in two days. What had she gotten herself into?

Chapter 26 Rose

~

Sangiovese – an Italian red grape variety grown in Tuscany, also called Brunello and Sangiovese grosso. It is used to make Chianti Classico.

Thursday, October 13, 12 PM

Rose reviewed her notes over a bowl of tomato soup. Everyone on her suspect list had been interviewed except Slade Bolton and Liz Bathory. Bolton would be hard. She hadn't seen him at home and didn't relish the idea of hunting him down. He called her old. The insult still stung, and besides, what level of honesty would she expect from him?

Liz was another story. The heiress's reaction at the Gala had been strange. Why was she crying? Time to find out. The heiress's address had been easy to find. A simple internet search turned up the house address on the far west side of Paso Robles, in the hills and vineyards of valuable wineries.

Rose hoped an interview in the woman's home would lead to some morsel of information she couldn't get over the phone. A feel for Liz's life and motivations. How likely it was that she'd kill to steal back a painting from one of her father's collections.

Gravel crunched under Rose's red sneakers as she approached the Italian-style villa perched on a hillock surrounded by grape vines. Pale yellow stone walls reached up into the sky, as if screaming the cost to anyone who passed by. Columns marched along the front porch. Did you call something so imposing a porch? Was this her design or her father's? It had the grandiose feel of a financial wizard whose words made CEOs around the country jump.

Liz stood at the edge of the vineyard holding a shotgun. Pop! A shot rang out. Rose peered down the row and saw a dead pocket gopher lying in the dirt. Growers hated the buggers because they ate the grape vines from the roots up.

Dressed in blue jeans and a denim work shirt over a white tee, the heiress's hair tumbled down her spine in a loose ponytail. Rose approached and reached out her hand.

"I'm Rose MacGillivray."

Liz removed a leather glove and cracked open the shotgun to remove the spent shell. Rose could tell the woman didn't remember her.

"We met, briefly, at the art gala in Paso Robles. I was with my friend Natalie."

At that, Liz nodded. "Did we have an appointment?"

The benefits of catching the woman unprepared outweighed the social niceties of not showing up without calling first. "I just need a few minutes of your time. I'm assisting SLPD in their investigation of the death and theft at the art gallery."

"May we go inside?" Rose asked.

Liz looked over her shoulder at her home. Then she turned back. "We can talk here."

"Perhaps on the front porch. In the shade."

Liz thought about that for a moment, then agreed. They stepped onto the flagstone walkway that led to the front veranda.

This was to be a hostile witness interview. They settled into the cool shade behind a column. Through the floor-to-ceiling picture windows, large oils framed in carved, gilded frames could be seen covering a wall at least twenty feet high. A two-foot-tall vase that held sunflowers sat on a round table with carved legs. She needed to get in there, somehow.

Liz pushed her sunglasses up onto her head. Her pale, blue-green eyes looked almost translucent. "I heard what happened from Evangeline," she said. "They took *Gray Day*."

They. Did the police know that there was more than one person? It would have been more natural to say he. Statistics say most thieves are male. Odd. Rose stored that thought away for reflection later.

She shifted over a few inches. Another wall came into view, covered with a collection of impressionist art, and in the middle was a blank space the size of the missing painting. It wasn't a smoking gun, but it was curious.

"And killed the security guard," she said, not wanting Brad Knight to be lost in the discussion.

Liz flinched, then shut her eyes as if not wanting to see the body spread on the ground. Rose understood. Even covered with a sheet, Brad's cause of death was apparent in the pool of blood around his chest and head. After a long minute, Liz looked up. Her voice was steady, but the muscles in her neck stood out.

"That is horrible. Did he have a family?"

"A wife." Rose noticed that Liz already knew the guard was male. Perhaps Evangeline mentioned that fact.

"I must send a card. Something gracious…"

Her comment seemed more to herself.

Despite the shade, a trickle of sweat slid down Rose's back. She blamed the heat, but her nerves were so tight she could strum them like a guitar. She pressed on.

"What time did you leave the gallery?"

Liz looked up; a flash of anger lit her eyes. "I left immediately after speaking with you. Is that why you came here? To ask me if I killed him? That's outrageous."

Rose made a quick mental calculation and determined that Liz's outrage felt genuine. She also noted that Liz didn't say she hadn't stolen the painting.

"Of course not. I'm sorry if it sounded like I said that."

Liz's anger seemed to lessen, and her shoulders lowered. Okay, so let's say she didn't kill Brad. She could have stolen the painting, and someone else committed the murder. Neither she nor the police had settled on an order for the two crimes.

"I understood that you worked with the gallery owner to make the show happen."

A fresh shotgun shell slid into the chamber. Rose flinched when the gun stock closed with a crack. Liz certainly knew how to handle a firearm with assurance. She leaned the gun barrel down against the house.

"I did not expect it to … to affect me so much. I certainly did not expect to draw Slade's…" She stopped. Her cheeks flushed red.

This guy's name popped up everywhere.

"Slade Bolton? The FBI guy? What is your connection to him?"

Liz took a deep breath and slowly let it out as her face calmed into an emotionless mask.

Her voice, though, turned strident—confident.

"This was a small show in a small town. Insignificant as far as the FBI is concerned."

This woman really embraced the whole yoga breathing thing. Rose would have to look into it for herself. She could use some of that calm. This murder rattled everyone, including her.

Liz Bathory didn't come across as a thief. She had everything she could need. Why put herself at risk? Maybe life was boring, and a little larceny and murder spiced things up. Rose looked through the window at the blank space on the wall.

"You seemed particularly drawn to *Gray Day, Montrose Valley*."

"Of all the paintings in the collection, that is the one I wanted. My father knew that, yet he included it in the bequest anyway."

Rose took note of the possible motive. Revenge. She pointed to the awaiting space on the wall, visible through the large plate-glass window.

"Is that where it goes?"

Liz leaned to see where Rose indicated.

"What? No. I have many paintings that fit there, I haven't decided which to hang."

Well, la-de-dah thought Rose. "Does the fact that your father made sure you didn't get the painting make you mad enough to steal it?"

A thin line of sweat beads formed on Liz's upper lip.

"I would not and did not steal. Quite the contrary. I tried to purchase it from the Met." Her eyes darted from Rose to the window and the blank spot beyond.

"But you thought about it," Rose pushed.

"I will not stand by while you accuse me of something so heinous. You would be wise to keep out of this whole affair. Leave it to the professionals. Art theft is the domain of the FBI. Let them investigate. You don't want to go around angering the wrong people. Besides, the person you want to interrogate is Evangeline Abbott. She was overly cooperative with all the extra security the Met demanded. She'd be the first to know how to work around it to steal my painting."

With that said, she picked up the gun and strode away.

Despite all her protestations, Liz was hiding something. Just what, Rose hadn't figured out, but that would come. Slade Bolton's name had been an unwelcome intrusion into the conversation, and there was something unexplained about it that bothered her. He should be someone everyone could trust; he represented the U.S. Government. Yet, she didn't think trusting him was a smart idea.

Rose slid her sunglasses on.

"Thank you for your time. I hope you didn't mind me following up with you after I've spoken with a few more people."

"My answers will not change," Liz said defiantly.

We'll see about that, Rose thought as she climbed into her car.

As she drove home, she reflected on the heiress's denials and the threat implied in her 'leave it to the professionals.' Her cell phone rang through the car's audio system. She pushed the button on her steering wheel to answer. Nessa's voice came over the speaker.

"Rose? This is Nessa. We have a problem with the

FBI. Slade Bolton is demanding we terminate your involvement." What was it about that man that set her feathers on edge?

Liz Bathory watched the silver sedan pull away. Had she said enough to convince Rose MacGillivray that she was innocent? Why would she steal an insignificant painting when she could paint a Rembrandt and pass it off as authentic to the best art historians in the world?

True, forgery was illegal, but no one other than Bolton knew that was her specific skill set. The reason for their partnership. She hadn't painted anything in over a year. The paintings she inherited from her father more than covered the walls, and she'd lost the drive to apply oils to canvas.

Chapter 27 Rose

~

Grenache — a Spanish grape with spicy, berry-flavored notes that produces a wine with a relatively high alcohol content.

Thursday, October 13, 5:00 PM

Who was it that said that a busy mind needs a nap to come up with great ideas?

Rose's ringtone jolted her awake from a late afternoon nap, the interview with the prickly heiress having worn her out. Stella's voice sounded like a hoarse whisper laden with excitement.

"Rose, you've got to come over, quick!"

The sun still had hours before dropping behind the hills and bringing blessed shade. Only then was there a chance the temperature would drop. A deathly silence enveloped the street as Rose crossed to Stella's house. Even the birds stilled.

The lead-glass door hung open a crack. Rose let herself into a tiled foyer. Stairs climbed up on her right, and the dining room lay on her left. Down the hall was the kitchen and a breakfast nook. The whole place was tasteful, though sparsely furnished. "Stella?"

She heard a faint "Upstairs."

Rose took the steps two at a time, her footfalls muted by the thick carpet. Breathless, she stood on the landing.

"Where are you?"

"Guest bedroom." Stella's voice didn't sound injured, which reassured Rose.

She found her crouched at a window, looking out with binoculars at Slade's house. Rose herself used to do the same as a kid, watching the neighbor's cat stalk birds. Rose crouched down and peered at the scene on the street.

"What are you doing?" Rose whispered because Stella had.

"This room has a bullseye view into Slade's garage." Stella held out the field glasses to Rose. "Look."

The two-car garage door was up, affording a view of the dark interior. The black Mercedes sat parked in the middle. A ladder and some buckets leaned against one wall. A large, flattish, wooden crate was propped against the opposite wall.

"He drove up a few minutes ago, and I thought I saw something in his garage," she said as Rose held the binoculars to her eyes and squatted down so that she could balance her elbows on the sill of the window. Her knee pinged with a painful jab. *Can't do that like I used to.* She stood and handed the binoculars to her young friend. Was this another Easter Island head conspiracy theory?

"Something, what?" she asked.

Stella leaned against the frame to steady herself and raised the glasses to her eyes.

At that moment, Slade reentered the garage, climbed in the black Mercedes, backed out, and the door slowly rolled down. The car sat in the driveway, not moving.

Rose squinted to see the action.

"Oh, my god." Stella's voice was soft as breath.

A chill ran down Rose's spine.

"What? What do you see?"

The garage door finished its descent. Stella rocked back on her heels, then sank to the wooden floor, leaning against the metal-frame bed. Rose sat down on a chair. Her muscles were tense.

"What did you see?"

"He has it."

A breeze blew in and fluttered Stella's hair. Rose had never seen her new friend so inarticulate without the benefit of a few glasses of wine. "He has what?"

The driver's side door opened, and Bolton stood up. Rose watched as he came down the driveway to the street. Stella's head shook as she mumbled something Rose couldn't hear.

"Are you expecting him?" she asked.

Whatever Stella planned to say, he shouldn't be privy to it, and sound had a strange way of carrying.

Stella looked up. Her crisp blue eyes were unfocused. Rose put a finger to her lips, but Stella didn't seem to register. Meanwhile, Slade crossed the street and came up Stella's front path. He stopped at the first step up to the front door, just below them. Rose couldn't see him but knew he stood right below them, close enough to hear anything they said.

Rose waved her hands and again put her index finger to her lips.

"Shhhh!" She pointed to the steps. "He's right down there!"

Stella still looked dazed.

"I saw the painting in his garage." She didn't whisper this time.

"Don't. Say. Anything." Rose hissed.

"Natalie didn't steal the painting." Stella spoke with

her normal, boisterous voice. "I wasn't sure before, but now, I'm sure."

They heard the tap tap of footfalls move away from the door. Rose held her breath. Together, they watched as he crossed the street, entered his house, and closed the door without looking back. Rose exhaled.

"How long was he down there?" Stella asked.

"Long enough."

"Why didn't you tell me?" Stella's voice had an angry edge.

"I did. You didn't listen." Rose rolled her shoulders to loosen tension.

Had he recognized their voices? Stella's, he would because it was her house. Rose rewound the conversation. Had he heard enough to know she was there, too? Why had he come over anyway? Stella should have been at work. Maybe he saw something that indicated she was home and came looking for afternoon sex.

Stella closed her eyes and rubbed her forehead. "I saw a crate."

"We can't go accusing people of crimes just because they have stuff stored at their house."

Across the street, Slade's car drove away. Stella lifted the glasses to her eyes again and moaned, "It's gone."

Chapter 28 Rose

~

*Bordeaux — a region in France that grows six main red varieties —
Merlot, Cabernet Sauvignon, Cabernet Franc, Malbec, Petit Verdot,
and Carmenere, and three whites — Semillon, Sauvignon Blanc, and
Muscadelle*

Friday, October 14, 3:00 PM

The phone rang while Rose was sifting through clothes on a rack at the town's only department store. She needed something for her date with Frank, and after everything that had happened, she felt the need for a distraction.

An operator asked if Rose would accept a collect call. She'd never had one before, and in this day of smartphones, who would ever call collect? She hung the frilly top on the rack and went to a corner for privacy.

"I can only talk for a few minutes." Natalie's voice sounded strained.

Rose's heart hurt to hear her friend's voice. Actually hurt, which she didn't think happened outside of having a heart attack.

"We'll get you released, I know it sounds trite, but hang on," Rose assured her.

"I hate it in here. The police are being as nice as they can, but you wouldn't believe the stench, oh my god, it's worse than anything I've smelled before."

Worse than turpentine, linseed oil, or motor oil? Rose remembered the stack of art along the wall.

"Stella and I went into your garage. We saw all your pieces." She wasn't sure how to ask the next question, then decided the straightforward approach was always best.

"Are they forgeries?"

Rose heard Natalie take a quick breath in. "God No! It's an art school technique. Copy the great masters and learn how they use colors and brush strokes. Then apply it to your work. I'll eventually burn them." Natalie's voice rang with indignation. Rose wished she could hug her friend.

"I was hoping you painted a version of *Gray Day, Montrose Valley,* for yourself, and that was what the police found."

"No. I thought about it, but no. My lawyer told me that the key card used to get into the gallery that night was mine. That's why they arrested me. That and the artwork they found. I swear, I don't know where that came from!"

Rose had used a restricted access card at work for the front doors and special security areas. You guarded it with your life.

"How could someone get it?"

Natalie's voice was subdued. "That Saturday morning, it wasn't in my purse."

"Did you ever find it?" Rose asked.

There was a long pause. "I didn't get a chance."

They said their goodbyes and hung up. Rose missed her friend more than ever. Thinking over the call, Rose realized she had a key to Natalie's house. She could go over, check the houseplants, and search for the card. But first things first, new clothes for her date with Frank.

Rose returned home with several bags. One casual ensemble and another dressier.

She couldn't decide what a musical theater date required. Stella's youthful help was what she needed. She glanced out the front window across the T-intersection at the Victorian house. The front door hid in the shadows.

The bam-bam of someone hitting something heavy came from the street. A man was pounding a For Rent sign into the yard. Mr. Bolton was gone. Only that morning, she and Stella watched as he drove away. Good riddance, Rose thought.

Rose glanced over at Natalie's empty house. It felt strange to be at an intersection with two empty dwellings.

Stella's car sat in her driveway.

"Oh, good. She's home. Come on, Watson. Let's go say hello."

They reached Stella's front door, and Rose knocked. The door pushed open a bit with a groan. As an original, turn-of-the-century home, it wheezed and moaned like an old man.

"Stella?" Rose called out in a polite voice. She didn't want to enter unannounced, but the unlocked door raised the hairs on her nape.

Hearing nothing, she entered the hall. Watson trotted in and went down the front hall. Stella's purse hung on the hook behind the door, along with a denim shirt and a wide-brimmed straw hat perfect for the farmer's market on Saturday mornings.

Where could she have gone without her purse? Rose pulled her phone out and dialed Stella's number. She heard it ring and followed the sound to the kitchen. Watson padded after her, his toenails tapping on the tile floor.

Stella's smartphone vibrated as it rang on the granite counter.

Rose disconnected the call. No purse and no phone. Maybe she went for a run.

Unable to restrain her sleuthing nature, Rose crept up the stairs. She peered into the room from where they had watched Bolton's garage. Then she went to Stella's bedroom, hoping she wouldn't catch her neighbor doing something compromising.

Running shoes peeked out from under the bed. She proceeded to the bathroom, but that too was empty, with no damp towels to indicate recent use. Rose's palms grew clammy, and a creak from the stairs caused her to jump. Watson sat on the top step with a cocked head.

"Where is she?" she asked the little dog. He gave himself an all-over shake, which she interpreted to be, "Why are you asking me? Do you have any treats?"

They went downstairs. Car and house keys hung from a cup hook. Everything was where it should be. Rose couldn't think of anywhere Stella would go without her purse, keys, and phone. Hairs on the nape of her neck rose. She didn't have a good feeling about the situation. Don't get ahead of yourself, she admonished. But it was hard not to.

A buzz in her pocket startled her. Then the ringtone started. She grabbed the phone and answered. The speaker's voice had a raspy, altered sound like someone was using a computer to mask their identity on one of those 60 Minutes interviews. Her heart beat hard in her chest.

"Drop your investigation, or your friend dies."

Rose tried to swallow the lump that formed in her throat.

"Who is this?" Despite efforts to sound indignant

and full of authority, her voice squeaked with strain. Was there an accent? Foreign? No, it sounded American, but maybe that could be changed in the software that disguised the sound.

"The killer is behind bars, forget about the painting."

"Who is this?" She repeated, this time with a forceful tone of anger.

"Back off, or else."

A scuffle and a loud crash resounded over the phone line, then the line went dead. Had that garbled voice been a male or female?

She stared at the silent device in her hand, then opened the phone app, pressed the "Recent" icon, and found a nugget of gold: the caller's phone number. No doubt a burner phone, but the police might be able to find out where the call originated. She dialed Nessa's cell number. When she answered, Rose's words rushed out.

"Stella's been kidnapped. I got a call saying to stop investigating or she dies."

There was a pause. Then, "Oh, god, bring your phone to the police station. I'll meet you there."

Fifteen minutes later, a computer expert was tracking down the number and location of the call. Rose replayed the voice in her mind.

"He had a muffled voice, like someone talking over a tin-can-and-string phone, but underwater."

Nessa and the IT kid frowned and mouthed "tin can," with quizzical looks on their faces. Honestly, kids today can't imagine a world without the Internet, video games, and cell phones.

"Never mind. It was a man. I'm quite sure about that. American. Can they alter that?"

Rose ignored the tight knot in her stomach, which reminded her that it could be someone from Brad's past. But those types of people committed the crime and evaporated into the ether. Slade Bolton's words from the day Natalie got arrested rang in her thoughts. "A senior citizen like you could get hurt. Or worse." Was this something worse? He overheard them this morning, she was sure of it. But was it worth this?

"I think it was Slade Bolton."

"FBI Special Agent Bolton?" Nessa asked. "Why would he kidnap Stella Richards?"

Rose felt her cheeks flush. "She, we, were sort of spying on him yesterday. Stella thought she saw something that looked like a crate that would contain a painting in his garage. The missing painting. He might have overheard us."

Nessa let out a long breath. "We've already confiscated the painting, Rose."

Rose knew that. Was painfully aware of that fact and the harsh light it threw on her friend. And yet. Something nagged her. Some niggling little detail she couldn't put her finger on hinted that things weren't as they appeared.

"You've already proved it is the original?" She asked.

A ruddy blush colored Nessa's cheek. "Well, no. Not yet."

A computer chime made them both turn to the IT guy. He typed, clicked a couple of buttons, and then swiveled the laptop around so they could see.

"The call came from a one-mile radius around this spot."

A dot blinked on the map above the name San Anselmo. So close to the In-N-Out Burger place that Stella would be able to smell the hamburgers cooking. Hadn't Slade's garbage been full of wrappers from that fast food restaurant?

Sergeant Nessa picked up her phone and dialed. "I need a search team right now. Yes, I'm coming too." She stood and turned to Rose. "I know you want to help, but I need you to stay home."

Rose bit her lower lip and tasted blood. The salty, metallic flavor in her mouth startled her. How had she bitten through her skin? More worrying, it reminded her that Stella could be injured. Oh god. Why would this happen? How could she let this happen?

The station lights gave her a headache. Visions ran through her mind of Stella, crouched in the front window, peering through binoculars at Slade's garage.

"Nessa, have you investigated the FBI agent? It is weird that he was in town when a painting was stolen."

"We've checked with his office. He's legit."

"Oh, I don't doubt that he's real. But there's something about him that I don't trust."

Words couldn't describe the ominous feeling when they shook hands at the gallery. Or the way he slunk up to Stella's front door and eavesdropped. "They'd been dating, you know."

Nessa's brows arched up. "No, I didn't know. Anything else you haven't told me?"

"No," Rose said. She had suspicions based on her conversations with the Abbots and Gloria, but nothing concrete. Nessa returned Rose's cell phone and adjusted the heavy utility belt around her slim middle.

"Whoever this person is, they have proved themselves to be dangerous. Go home. Lock your doors. I'll call later."

"Isn't there anything I can do?" Rose asked.

"You have one friend in lockup and a second missing." Nessa gave her a "What do you think?" look and left.

The threat of defeat hovered over her. Natalie was the friend she never had the time for during her career. And Stella, well, she'd grown fond of Stella.

When Rose returned from the police station, the forensics team swarmed through Stella's house. A forensics van blocked the driveway. Inside the house, men in white clean room suits milled around. Rose wanted to go over there and see what they had found. Sergeant Nessa would understand, and Rose would be safe from whatever danger had befallen Stella with all the cops around. After that, she would go home and lock the door until she could figure out the next step.

That decision might require a glass of a nice, aged Bordeaux.

She approached the yellow crime scene tape that surrounded the house.

"Hello?"

Officer Hernandez walked over. He wore full SWAT regalia: Kevlar suit, bulletproof vest, military-style helmet. What were they expecting to find?

"Sorry, Ms. MacGillivray. I can't let you in." His crooked smile looked strained under the pull from the thick strap of his helmet.

"I understand. You might want to search the house Slade Bolton rented."

She pointed at the one-story building that had held

so much of her attention for the past week.

"Stella and I thought we saw a box that could be a painting in his garage."

"That FBI guy?"

Rose peered around Hernandez to see if she could get a glimpse of the CSI team inside. Her fingerprints were on railings, the doorknob, and the kitchen counter. Should she tell them?

She glanced back up into the tall police officer's eyes.

"Don't you think it's strange that Natalie suddenly has a painting in her garage, then Stella is kidnapped, and then Mr. Bolton magically disappears?"

She pointed to the For Rent sign.

"Last Friday, you said you thought it was weird that he came to Paso Robles in the first place. I think your instinct was right."

Hernandez twisted to look at the house and the one next door to Rose's home. There wasn't anything that gave a reason to elevate this. Rose leaned in toward him.

"Remember how I knew the guy's car wouldn't make it far when I went on my ride-along? I know there is something strange in all this."

He squinted as he looked down at her. Then he slowly nodded. "I'll call it in and see what we can do." He stepped away and spoke into his walkie-talkie. Rose stared at Stella's house. Guilt swam in her thoughts. She couldn't protect her friends. What use was she?

A fresh start. That's what the move to Paso Robles had been intended to accomplish. A new home. A new identity. She'd played about interviewing people and thinking she was a detective.

But was she just an old woman, as Bolton said? Age didn't have to define her. A simple number that chronicled years lived, not capability, nor years left. At sixty-five, she felt younger than ever. And smarter. The police would get there eventually, but she couldn't wait that long. Her friends depended on her, perilous or not.

On the front porch, Watson begged for a scratch behind his ears. She bent down to oblige.

"We've got to do something, boy. I can't sit here and watch."

Even with the threat of danger, she knew there was no way she would stay locked up in her own home. Not with everyone who mattered to her taken away.

Chapter 29 Rose

~

Merlot – a dark-blue colored grape used for blending and varietal wines

Friday, October 14, 5:00 PM

In the final year of her life, Rose's mom hadn't seen much of her. Rose was at work. Now that she had the time, she felt the loss of that valuable time viscerally. How was it that knowing that someone no longer existed on the planet delivered more pain than not seeing them but knowing they were still alive? Would anyone feel that way about her when she died? Murder brought too many morbid thoughts to Rose's mind. She collapsed on the living room couch and watched the scene out of her front window.

Watson jumped up next to her and curled into a donut. Down the street, doors slammed. Yellow tape fluttered in the breeze, and two officers leaned against a squad car talking.

Time to get her brain busy. If Slade wasn't the kidnapper—and she wasn't ready to say that, but just to play devil's advocate—who on her suspect list could be?

Gloria Knight's alibi had been thoroughly checked. Rose had smelled the rotten roast herself, but she wasn't ready to let Gloria off the hook all the way.

Even so, Brad's widow had nothing to gain by kidnapping Stella and didn't seem to have the disposition or strength to pull off something so bold.

Evangeline was such a tiny thing, but she could have held a big gun. If Carlos Abbot had been in cahoots, then anything was possible. He was strong, looked like he worked out daily, and could easily have overcome Stella's objections or carried an unconscious woman down a flight of stairs. Despite that, her money was on Slade. His vanishing at the same time couldn't be a coincidence. Proving that was another matter.

Taking down a wineglass, she filled it and went to the dining table and her laptop. She typed "Brad Knight," "police," and "security" into the browser and pushed Search.

Pictures of various Brad Knights popped onto the screen. Black, Asian, White. Scanning down the page, she found an article from a Fresno newspaper about Brad Knight's departure from the department under suspicious circumstances.

The article described how an anonymous caller had reported that landowners were selling water to out-of-county buyers. As implausible as it sounded for a farmer or rancher to give up any of their water, many officials assumed that some were guilty. Fresno police assigned the case to newly promoted Detective Brad Knight. Although his actions led to charges against several farmers, a persistent rumor circulated that he was accepting bribes to look the other way at certain ranches.

Some good came of it, but Brad was a liability to the politically motivated Chief of Police. The ranchers were a large voting bloc he couldn't afford to lose.

Picking up her phone, she pushed the "Recent Calls" icon and saw that Dave Acer had called earlier.

"Hi, Rose. Sorry for the delay. I'll text you the info.

The guy is dead, so I suppose it doesn't impact anyone's privacy rights."

She checked her email and opened the files.

"Well, Watson, what will we learn about the dead guard we didn't learn in the article on the internet?"

Watson padded over to her and pushed his head under her hand. She scratched his ears. Like Sherlock Holmes's companion, Watson had a gift for listening that made him an invaluable partner. He looked up at her and panted.

The computer finished its start-up routine and dinged. Rose located the email from Dave and clicked on the attachment. A PDF opened with multiple pages of photocopied documents.

"Okay, here we go." She enlarged the first page and started to read.

Bradley Knight, born in 1985 in Woodlake, California. A city in the San Joaquin Valley.

He grew up on his father's olive farm. That undoubtedly made him an attractive hire for Dave and gave him a reason to ignore the less stellar aspects of Brad's background.

He'd finished the police academy and entered the Fresno police force twelve years ago. That made it 2007. There was a distinguished career record with medals for bravery until the shooting led to his departure. The picture of him in uniform showed a fresh-faced young man with a smile that transmitted the joy he felt.

"This was a man who loved what he did. What happened, Watson?"

He married Gloria Radcliff in 2009, two years after he joined the department. She had to know what sort of life she was getting into. No children. Dossiers like this didn't go into whether that was a choice or a disappointment.

The officer-involved shooting had occurred at the twelve-year mark in his career. They assigned him to the sheriff's task force to halt the county's drug trade. Police had gotten word of a shipment and wanted it stopped. Things didn't go according to plan. There was a shootout. Everyone scattered, and according to interviews, order broke down. In the fray, one lieutenant received a bullet wound to the arm, and one target lost his life.

The dead man, aged thirty-two, was a local gang member. An attached picture showed a sinister-looking white guy glaring at the booking room camera. Tattoos covered a bald head such that it looked like the guy was wearing a hat. Rose didn't recognize the branding tattoos. But then, she told herself, gangs weren't something she had encountered, ever. Two dark teardrops fell metaphorically from his right eye.

Where had she seen that before?

A quick Internet search informed her that it represented a lengthy prison term or that the wearer was a murderer. In his defense, Brad maintained that he feared for his life. Rose stared at the picture.

"I'd fear for my life, too, if that man approached me." She tilted the computer screen so Watson could see.

Watson lifted one eyebrow. She swore his look said, "I would bite him."

Rose agreed with the little dog's assessment.

The investigation concluded that he should have handled it better, but the outcome was inevitable: fired for police brutality. Rose suspected that Brad had become a liability for the Chief due to his work on the water issues, and the drug raid incident gave the department an excuse to fire him. The gang members' buddies vowed revenge.

That sounded like a motive. Paso Robles had gangs. There might be reciprocal agreements; we'll take out your target if you return the favor.

"Did someone come to Paso Robles seeking revenge against Brad for taking a life? Or was the guard just in the wrong spot at the wrong time?" Watson jumped up into her lap. He didn't answer her.

Gang killing? Art theft? Could the two even fit together?

Rose lowered the screen of the laptop, shooed Watson away from her feet, and went into the kitchen. After arranging a plate of wheat crackers and smoked cheddar cheese, she poured another glass of Merlot and stepped out onto the veranda. Granted, not the most nutritious dinner, but easy. Watson jumped up onto the cushion next to her and rested his head on her leg.

She picked up a cracker with cheese, leaned against the cushion, and studied the trees. She couldn't call Natalie. She couldn't call Stella. Anyone else would think she'd lost her mind. Maybe she had.

Streetlights amplified the glowing yellow leaves. Fall hovered weeks away. She thought again about those copies of old masters that Natalie had been so vehement that they were not forgeries. Art school assignments. But they had been so professional. The back-and-forth questioning of Natalie's innocence wearied her.

"Pick a side, Rose." She said it aloud. Watson picked up his head and studied her with alert ears. "That would be best," she heard Watson say in her mind.

Great, now she was going crazy.

Pick a side, she berated herself again. So, she did. And the side she chose was that her friend had nothing to do with the gala crimes. That done, she sipped Merlot and nibbled while the sunset dimmed. A cold breeze whipped around the side of the house and drove them inside. She sat on the corner of the sofa in the living room and picked up a book, but it was no use. The words floated on the page.

"What should I do, Watson?" The little dog sighed and rolled onto his side.

Nothing made a difference to Natalie sitting in jail. Rose had more questions than answers. She didn't have the skills to figure out who murdered someone or stole anything. Nessa was right. The police knew what they were doing. She should leave it to them. She resumed reading.

The words disappeared, replaced by the image of the key card on the table and the sound of a raspy, altered voice warning her to stop asking questions. Or else. Stella's life hung on her decision.

Two police cars remained on the street below, along with the CSI van. Did Brad's background have anything to do with Stella's disappearance? His troubles couldn't have gone over well with Gloria. They relocated to Paso Robles, and Brad started work at Olive Heaven and the art gallery. They adapted to the new situation.

Rose knew that humans could adapt to almost anything. It was that resilience that ensured the survival of the species. Each loss increased elasticity. Rose had some experience with this. She'd gotten pregnant. Not intentionally and not to anyone she had any interest in spending the rest of her life with, but she couldn't end the pregnancy. Someone adopted the baby, and Rose went on as before.

Yet, you never got over something like that. You

went through it and emerged changed. You adapted to the new reality. And, if you were lucky, you came out of it better able to adjust to the next earthquake to hit your life.

The crime scene technicians moved about with sloth-like speed. A single police car remained parked in front of Stella's house. Rose went into the kitchen, Watson following close behind. He sniffed his food bowl while she held the wine bottle over her glass and considered pouring in the last bit. Instead, she dumped it down the kitchen drain. A clear head was important.

She stepped out the back door to drop the empty into the blue recycling can. The trash trucks would be by early in the morning, but she hadn't taken the bins to the curb yet. Still time, though she'd need to be quiet. Glancing down, she noticed a label she had never seen before, perched on top of the pile of empties. Not that her memory was photographic, but she did know the names of the wines she drank. The container sat at a jaunty angle as if someone had placed it there rather than tossed it into the bin. The sinews of her neck tightened. Could she have put it there and not remembered? Maybe Stella brought that brand, and Rose hadn't paid attention. Her thoughts swirled. If she told the police, they might see her as a hindrance, and Nessa wouldn't share information with her. That said, if she ignored it, and then it turned out to be important, they might never find Stella or clear Natalie.

When she thought about it, she had one choice. Pulling out her phone, she snapped a photo of the bin, then carefully removed a few of the discards and placed them in the regular trash bin. No need to broadcast how much wine she drank. Then she hurried over to the police cruiser. Watson dashed in front, doubled back to her, and then ran forward again with the exuberance of a kid. Was age starting to slow her down? She reached the officers out of breath.

"Excuse me!" Her voice had enough hysteria in it to get their attention right away.

"What's wrong?" the one in the driver's seat asked.

Rose pointed to her own home. "There is a wine bottle in my recycling bin by the patio door that I didn't put there. Someone would have to open the gate to get to it." As the words came out, she heard how stupid that sounded. Had she gotten so drunk that she didn't remember? "I know that sounds lame, but could you send someone to dust for prints?"

He stared at her, then turned his gaze to his partner and shook his head. Not a no, she decided, just amazement at the request. He surveyed the crew working inside the house and then checked his watch. "They're about done. I'll send someone over as soon as they've finished. Don't touch it." His sigh said more than his words. Crazy lady, but weirder things have happened.

"I know this sounds nuts, but given what's happened to Stella… well, you know."

Twenty minutes later, a bunny-suit-clad woman with transparent plastic goggles and an N95 mask stood at her door. A toolbox sat on the ground by her feet.

"You have something for fingerprinting?" Rose took her to the recycling bin and pointed to the evidence.

"Could you have touched it when you threw it away?" she asked. Rose felt her spine stiffen. Yes, she drank wine, but she wasn't a drunk.

"It's not mine," she said firmly.

The tech held the bottle with black latex gloves and studied it. Then she opened the toolbox and removed a camel hairbrush in a plastic sleeve, a pot of white powder, a roll of adhesive tape, and a black 5x7-inch card. She twirled the brush over the inside cover of the pot and spun it over the neck.

"I think we've got something here. I'll need yours to rule you out." She didn't look up as she spoke.

"No problem." Rose would gladly stick her finger in ink to prove she wasn't responsible. Her gut tightened. Had she replied too quickly?

After the print was visible, the tech took some of the clear adhesive tape and cut a portion that she attached over the print. When she pulled it up, the swirls of a fingerprint stuck to the adhesive; she attached this to the card.

Finally, she placed the glass vessel into an evidence bag and wrote the date, location, and a brief description of the item.

"There! Gomez will let you know what we find."

Rose and Watson walked the technician around the garage and down the driveway.

"Thanks for indulging me. I know it sounds crazy, but something tells me this will help."

The tech crossed the street, probably thinking about how she would spin this story over beers that night. She stepped into a van that pulled away as soon as the door closed.

Rose's phone rang.

"Rose?" It was Sergeant Nessa.

"I'm here." As per instructions, she thought.

"No luck with the search. No one saw anything, heard anything. There are many empty outbuildings and an olive orchard back there. Officers drove around the area for several hours. No indication of where Stella is being held.

I'm sorry to be the bearer of bad news."

Their best lead on Stella's location was a bust. Rose was sorry too, much more than sorry, but there wasn't time for that. What they needed was another lead, another call. Something to help pinpoint where the kidnapper had taken Stella.

Chapter 30 Rose

~

Hojiblanca Olive – A Spanish olive cultivar known for a slightly sweet, almond flavored taste with a pleasant bitterness

Saturday, October 15, 8:00 AM

The banging sound of a garbage truck woke Rose as it hauled the can into the air and bounced it up and down a few times with a racket that would wake the most ardent sleeper.

The sun inched its way up in the east. A breeze ruffled the oak leaves, and the sky was clear. Mockingbirds greeted the morning with echoes of chickadees. She thought about the blue recycling can as she hugged her pillow around her head to drown out the sound. If she hadn't noticed the bottle, the evidence would have vanished. Was that someone's intention? Or was it meant to be found? Would the police think she killed Brad?

The truck moved on, and she rolled out of bed. Watson jumped down and waited for her to slip on moccasins and a light robe. He ran and sat at the back door, waiting for his turn at a morning constitutional.

Her thoughts drifted to Frank. This stay-at-home order had better be over by Saturday so she could go on her date. A date. It still felt weird to think. In the crisp light of an October morning, the idea that he might kill her at a musical production was ludicrous. A bigger issue was whether she should even go with Stella missing and Natalie in jail?

Would Frank want anything to do with someone tied up in this mess?

A small boy and his mother passed by the house. The kid rode a bright red bike with training wheels that barely touched the sidewalk. His mother waved one hand as if conducting an orchestra and held a phone with the other. Her voice carried up to the porch in broken phrases. The mother probably saw it as multitasking. While Rose saw it from the child's perspective. A distracted parent who doesn't care. What sort of mom would I have been?

The smartphone in her pocket vibrated. Sergeant Nessa again. "Sorry for calling so early. May I come over?"

"Of course. I'll make some coffee." She had a machine that made any hot beverage one drink at a time.

Moments later, a black and white turned the corner and pulled into Rose's driveway. Nessa must have been out of sight, waiting. She bounded up the steps and arrived, not even slightly out of breath. Deep wrinkles creased the young woman's brow. Rose handed her a mug of coffee.

"What's wrong?"

The police Sergeant took a deep breath. "Let's sit."

When they were both ensconced in chairs, Nessa flipped open her notepad.

"You were right about the wine bottle. The one in your recycling bin. It was from the gala. Fingerprints matched a winery employee." She consulted her notes. "Chad Warner. Had a brush with law enforcement a while back for drunk and disorderly. We checked, and he has a rock-solid alibi for the murder window."

Rose narrowed her eyes and squinted at the police Sergeant. "Then how did it end up in my recycling?" Nessa put up her hand to stop Rose from saying more.

"There's more. We found another partial finger-print, not enough to be admissible, and we found DNA trace evidence."

"Do you have a match?"

Sergeant Nessa nodded. "The print matches FBI Special Agent Slade Bolton."

Everything kept coming around to him. Rose looked for holes in the logic. "He was at the gala. Could he have handled it then?"

"Chad Warner says that the only way Bolton could have gotten a hold of that bottle was to take it that night. They count empties for inventory tracking purposes. Chad checked. They retrieved one less than they allotted for the event."

"You wouldn't think an FBI agent would be sloppy. He would have wiped the bottle clean."

Nessa's eyebrows raised as if surprised at how much Rose knew.

"Agreed. The print was on the lip, at the top. He no doubt thought it wasn't enough to implicate him."

And it was in my trash, Rose thought. Just like the painting was in Natalie's garage. Someone was going to a lot of trouble to plant evidence.

"That was item number one that I wanted to tell you." Nessa ticked off the first line of her notes. "I did some digging on our FBI friend."

Nessa's notepad lay open on her lap, with multiple lines of neat printing. Was there so much that she needed reminders?

"Slade Bolton has been with the FBI for fifteen years. Eight of those are in the Art Crime Team. In those years, fifteen art thefts or attempted thefts were deemed worthy of the FBI's attention. Of the stolen works, about seven were never found. That isn't unusual. Art theft is tough to resolve. In the cases where the thieves were thwarted, the guard was killed or injured."

"You mean they didn't steal the art?" Rose asked.

"No. The target painting remained in the gallery or museum. The suspects had been deterred by the guard."

A heavy weight settled in Rose's chest. If Bolton was involved in some way, could a killer have lived so close? A shiver ran down the length of her spine.

"Did you guys find anything on the stone statue?" The strange object matched the technical description of the murder weapon. Cylindrical and hard.

"Forensics pulled a partial print that matched Natalie Patel. We showed a picture of it to her. It matches a set that she threw out. She only tossed one this week because of the weight. How it got into Bolton's trash is unclear. He may have thought it was valuable, took it, then researched and realized it was tourist junk."

So, Mr. Slade Bolton, super-agent, was a garbage thief.

'With all this new information, we're bringing in an art expert to verify whether that painting from Natalie's garage is real."

Finally. Rose closed her eyes and said a silent thanks to whoever looked over her. When she spoke, her voice sounded raspy.

"Anything else?"

Sergeant Nessa closed her notepad and tucked it into the special pocket on her belt.

"I saved this for last. We discovered traces of Brad Knight's blood and hair on that bottle you found. The killer got sloppy. Looks like you found the murder weapon."

Rose felt a moment of success, then a thought occurred.

"What about the gun?"

Chapter 31 Nessa

~

Cabernet Franc – one of the major black grape varieties   originating in the Bordeaux region of France

Saturday, October 15, 8:30 AM

Nessa sipped coffee from her *World's Best Mom* cup, courtesy of her son, Danny, and surveyed a pile of paper stacked on her desk. At least she didn't need to work the night shift. Saturdays got crazy with wineries, restaurants, and breweries serving until the early hours of the morning. During the day, things were usually calm.

Between the heat and the murder, everyone was working overtime. Her desk sat at the edge of ten cubicle-style stations, each desk occupied by an officer or detective. The room buzzed with talk.

Natalie Patel had been officially charged with the theft and, by extension, the murder, but Nessa was growing worried that Rose might be right about Natalie's innocence. It wasn't anything she could point to, but something in her gut told her that the anonymous call was leading them in the wrong direction. That would mean that someone stole Natalie's key card. The image of Slade Bolton in the park wearing sunglasses popped into her mind. She'd searched for security video that covered the kid's playhouse and the rest of the park and found nothing. They couldn't prove Bolton and Knight knew each other. If they did, they may have been collaborators on a job that went wrong.

She typed art expert Paso Robles into her search bar and pushed Enter. With any luck, she'd find one close and capable enough to get a quick-and-dirty evaluation. An expert from LA or SF would flag anything suspicious, but that would take more time than she had. It had already been a week since the murder and theft. The more time that passed, the less likely it was that they would catch the killer. For all anyone knew, the person could have fled the country by now.

Several hits appeared on her screen, mostly galleries in town. Hearst Castle popped up in the second position, but it listed only art restoration. She imagined that such a person might be able to detect forged work; she needed someone who would be considered an expert in a courtroom.

The third listing was for the Art Association. Bingo. She picked up the phone and dialed the number. A pleasant voice answered with a "Hello!" The woman sounded thrilled that her phone worked. Nessa guessed that not many people called the association.

After identifying herself, she asked about experts. "I'm looking for someone who could tell if a painting is a fraud. A forgery."

"Oh, dear. You don't think one of our local artists would do such a thing, I hope. Let's see . . ." Nessa could hear fumbling through a drawer, papers moving around, the splat of a notepad or file folder hitting the ground. "Here we go," the woman said.

Nessa clicked open her pen to write the name down.

"Evangeline Abbot," the woman said. "You can find her at the gallery on the park square."

"Seriously?" Nessa asked, surprised that someone who dressed like the Abbot woman would be an expert in anything.

"Oh, yes, dear. We're lucky to have her here in Paso Robles. She's an art conservator. Studied at the University of Pennsylvania for her master's degree."

What were the odds that one of the suspects just happened to be an art expert on forgery? Add another check to the column for Mrs. Abbot as a suspect.

"Anyone else?" Nessa asked.

"Well, many of our painters know a lot about those sorts of things, but Evangeline is the only one with experience in the field. I remember her saying that before she moved here, she worked at the Getty. Can't get better credentials than that!"

No, you couldn't. At least not anywhere close by, and she needed an answer quickly.

"Thank you. I appreciate the information. Have a lovely day."

Nessa could hear the woman's smile through the phone.

"You too. And good luck."

With an abduction on top of theft and murder, there wasn't time to run up to the Bay Area or down to LA to track down another expert. She dialed Police Chief Donaldson and explained the situation. The only local art expert she could find was also one of the main suspects. Three and a half driving hours to a better answer.

"What do you think you should do?" Chief Donaldson asked.

Was this a test? Could Nessa demonstrate she was detective material? Well, bring it on.

"Use the opportunity to learn more about Evangeline Abbott and see if she can give us any useful information on the painting. We can schedule a consultation with an expert somewhere else at the same time. This would give us a head start."

There was silence on the other end of the line. Nessa knew the Chief was thinking about the options. What would work legally? What were the pros and cons of engaging the Abbott woman?

"Proceed on that path. Keep me posted." The line clicked dead. Test passed.

Nessa called the gallery and set a time for the art expert to come to the precinct. Evangeline didn't sound surprised at all when Nessa called for an appointment.

When the duty officer at the front desk called to say the art expert had arrived, Nessa retrieved *Gray Day, Montrose Valley* from the evidence locker and placed the crate on a dolly from the maintenance department. It wasn't far to push the load to a conference room, but the box was bulky and heavy.

Once inside the room, Evangeline pulled a rolled towel from her handbag and spread out the contents on a table.

Brushes, bottles, a small conical magnifying glass called a jeweler's loupe, a palette knife, and a sharp blade lay on a towel. Her manner was professional. She wore a white smock over her jeans and a sparkly tank top, and totally looked the part.

They lifted the painting from the packing case and laid it face up.

Evangeline picked up the loupe and began a thorough inspection of the canvas's face.

"I take it you didn't do this when the paintings arrived?" Nessa asked.

"Correct. We didn't question the authenticity of the Met collection. That's their job," the art expert said as she narrowed in on a tree. She finished her examination by gazing at the signature in the lower right corner. Nell Walker Warner, now deceased, had not been a famous painter. However, she had a Wikipedia page, which said something about her.

The gallery owner looked up. "I'd like to take the frame off. Look at the edges."

The idea of damaging the evidence made Nessa nervous. "Is that something normally done to a piece of art like this?"

"There are several ways to identify fraud." Evangeline set the loupe down on the table. "Some forgers paint just the front, the part people see, inside the frame. If so, then when you remove the frame, there are straight lines, which is not the case for an originally painted canvas. Thus, the need to take the art out of the frame. Then there is the provenance of the paint."

Evangeline spoke as if lecturing a class. She stood with her hand on the frame, her gaze challenging Nessa.

"Go ahead then. Take the frame off," the policewoman said.

They carefully pried off the staples and nails that held the canvas to the frame.

"Hmmm," Evangeline said as she slid a screwdriver under a staple.

"What?"

"The staples look old," she said. Nessa squinted at the dull gray metal pieces. She'd done enough DIY projects to know that metal tarnished or rusted with time.

"Uneven paint edges, again pointing to an original," Evangeline said, pointing to the sides of the canvas with the knife.

"That's a good sign. Many forgers use high-end printers and dab color over the print, like a paint-by-numbers set. When they do that, the edges are straight. This was painted. But when, we don't know."

She picked up the loupe again and examined the painted surface before resuming her lecture.

"The varnish is crazed. Here look," she handed the loupe to Nessa.

Holding the small, cup-like instrument close to the canvas, she saw a web of little cracks across the surface.

"So?" she said, handing the loupe back to Evangeline.

"Varnish does that with age. So, at first glance, this is an older painting."

"I suppose it could be an old forgery," Nessa said as she wrote a note about the crazing."

Evangeline nodded. "That, or it's the original. Nell Walker Warner worked in the forties. She probably used natural resins, and seventy years is plenty of time for the varnish to age."

She stood and put the loupe back into a pocket in her tool caddy.

"Back then, paint had lead in it. The EPA outlawed in 1978. Knowing that would help date the piece."

"How do we check for lead in the paint?" Nessa asked, hopeful that a quick answer might be possible.

"The easiest way is by using a mass spec. I don't have one, obviously, but that would be your best bet."

"Is there anything else you can tell without that?"

"I could take off the backing paper."

With Nessa's assent, Evangeline picked up a palette knife from the blue cloth and gently peeled the aged brown paper off.

Several yellowed stickers identified the original gallery that sold the work. Evangeline examined them carefully, then stood up and pushed her glasses to the top of her head.

"This is the name of the art dealer, who is most likely out of business by now, but his or her records would be available somewhere. The art world is careful about those sorts of things."

"I'll leave that up to the experts at the de Young in San Francisco," Nessa said. "We'll be calling them today. I need a quick assessment from you. Is this genuine or a forgery?"

Evangeline looked down at the artwork, lifted it, and turned it over so the painted side was facing up.

After what seemed like an eternity, the gallery owner straightened. Was that a look of satisfaction Nessa detected on Evangeline's face? If she had stolen the original, she had a personal stake in this being a forgery.

"As you said, I'm not the expert you need. However, I suspect this is not an original Nell Walker Warner. I've seen some of her work, and the brush strokes don't look right."

Evangeline gathered the implements together and rolled them up in the caddy.

Nessa moved the frame closer to her and looked at the blue-gray hills, the olive-green trees, and the reddish ground.

"Any idea of who would have a mass spectrometer around here?"

Ms. Abbott tucked the roll of tools under her arm.

"Edgar Wine and Grape Analysis has the equipment you need."

"And that will tell me if the painting was painted seventy years ago or last year?"

Evangeline heaved a sigh as though she were talking to a brick wall.

"It will tell you that, but not who painted it."

Nessa closed her notepad and tucked it into a pocket. "You're an artist, aren't you?"

Evangeline nodded.

"Could you paint something like this?"

The gallery owner's eyes widened. "Are you accusing me of forging this painting?"

Well, that certainly hit a nerve. Nessa made a mental note to revisit the Abbotts' alibis. "I'm simply curious how difficult it might be."

"Either this was painted by Nell Walker Warner or someone else, but both artists are highly skilled. However, that person was not me." With that, she turned and strode out, leaving Nessa with the job of wrestling the canvas back into the wooden storage box.

This wasn't a famous painting that justified significant documentation. But was it an original that the artist herself had done in the 1940s or a forgery painted in the twenty-first century? And why would it be in Natalie's garage?

Chapter 32 Nessa

~

"A bottle of wine contains more philosophy than all the books in the world." Louis Pasteur

Saturday, October 15, 2:15 PM

The bright, modern lobby of Edgar Analysis was sleek in a way that implied efficiency and scientific accuracy. A sandy-haired guy with hazel eyes and the name Kevin embroidered on his white lab coat greeted Sergeant Nessa.

"Thanks for opening up for this," Nessa said as they shook hands.

"No problem. I like it here when it's quiet, so I'm often here on the weekend. Bring it back here." He indicated a hallway and helped her push the trolley into a large laboratory. Nessa counted four people working at a variety of machines or tables. Racks of glass vials awaited testing. When they reached an empty counter, Kevin stopped.

"May I?" He extended his hand toward the painting. Nessa helped him lift it onto the countertop and slide *Gray Day* out. He slipped latex gloves over long, elegant fingers and gently touched the surface of the canvas.

"I'm going to need to scrape a small bit of paint off to run the tests."

She hesitated. She hadn't thought about all the damage they might do to verify authenticity. If it were a fake, it wouldn't matter. If it were real, then hopefully a restorer could repair whatever loss there might be.

"You'll need to sign this first," she said and handed Kevin the chain of custody paperwork.

Using a sharp blade, he scraped the surface of the canvas until small blue flakes fell onto white paper. These he swept into a vial and repeated the process three more times, capturing each of the main colors of the composition from multiple places. After fifteen laborious minutes, he had a half dozen vials with dust on the bottoms.

"It will take a while. I'll call when the results are in."

"How long?" Nessa asked. Not days, please. They needed to wrap this up.

"An hour or so. I've got to process this, separate the proteins; then the samples go into the machine, and the magic happens." He helped her slide the painting into the protective box and lash it to the dolly. "I promise. I'll call," he assured her.

On her way to her desk, she stopped at the chief's office. "Mass spec chemical analysis is underway. Evangeline Abbott thought there was something off, but wouldn't say for certain it was a fake."

The chief nodded. "I've made an appointment for you to take it to the de Young Museum in San Francisco the day after tomorrow. We'll need a certified expert's assessment for our files, either way."

A day in San Francisco would be a nice break from the investigation. Perhaps she could have lunch on the wharf.

Nessa sat down at her desk and took a long swig of water from the large refillable bottle. Regardless of what she'd learned from Abbott or what they might learn from the analysis, Nessa couldn't see Natalie Patel killing the guard. She closed her eyes and let her mind run through the suspect list. Her fingers hovered over the keyboard, and she typed the name of the person she suspected most. Someone who should be above reproach.

There was Slade Bolden, a football player for Alabama. A Slade Bolton, health insurance agent. No Slade Bolton FBI. Unusual, but not unheard of, for someone to have no digital footprint. She closed the browser and switched to the background check software that SLPD used. There she found him.

The photograph showed a rakish headshot. Maybe they had a beefcake calendar. She'd buy that. She read down the page. His record appeared squeaky clean. Was it happenstance that he was in Paso Robles at the same time as the Met show, or had the FBI sent him to cover it?

She jotted down the name of his direct supervisor, William Jenkins, the head of the Art Crime Team. It was before noon, Washington, DC time. And it was Sunday. Unlikely that anyone would answer at all.

The phone rang three times before a perky woman said, "Good Afternoon. You've reached the FBI. How may I direct your call?"

"William Jenkins, please."

Without another word, the phone clicked and went silent, then a whirring sound and a ring. Of course, they would record all calls.

"Jenkins." The deep, firm voice conveyed authority with tone alone. Nessa found herself taken aback.

"Mr. Jenkins, I'm Officer Gomez with the Paso Robles Police Department, in Paso Robles California. I'm calling about one of your agents."

"Which agent?" Jenkins didn't sound surprised.

Nessa explained the situation and then asked. "Was he assigned?"

"There are currently twenty-two agents around the country, and each office has a high degree of autonomy. Mr. Bolton is out of our New York office. We would send someone from the LA area."

So, he was not sent in advance as he'd implied. Had Stella Richards misunderstood his words?

"I'm going to need a history of his notifications to you. Where he was, when."

Jenkins' voice turned icy. "Highly unusual. Do you have a warrant?"

"If I need one, I can have it within the hour. I hoped agency-to-agency cooperation and professional courtesy would extend to this request."

She'd never stuck her neck out like this. Which judge would give her the search warrant? An hour might be ambitious, but she'd have it by the end of the day.

"Certainly, if art theft is involved, the FBI is interested. I can have something sent to you in a couple of hours."

Nessa clenched her fist in a silent pump.

"Much appreciated."

"In return, you'll notify me if you find anything anomalous."

A click and then silence. Her phone beeped to indicate the terminated call. He hadn't even waited for her response.

Her cell phone vibrated. " Sergeant Gomez? Kevin here. From Edgar Analysis."

"Done already?"

"Yep. Ready for the results?"

"You bet," Nessa said and picked up her pen to take notes.

"We didn't find any lead, but we did see polypropylene in the results. It was from the lower left corner. It was invented in 1950 and first used in 1957."

How would there be polypropylene in the paint?

Kevin continued as if he'd read her mind. "The forger might have been wearing it when they worked, or it floated by and got stuck while the paint was drying."

"Did you say forger?" Nessa felt her heart quicken. Rose's theory that the painting was in Natalie's garage because someone planted it there popped into her mind.

Kevin's voice sounded apologetic. "Sorry. Probably shouldn't have said that. All I'm able to tell you is that the mass spec didn't find any lead, but it did find polypropylene. We found it embedded in the original paint, not in any restoration varnish layer. Which, interestingly, is the same material they used in the forties, a soft natural resin, called dammar varnish and was artificially aged to look seventy years old."

"Let me get this right. The paint wasn't from the forties, but the varnish layer was. How does that work?"

Kevin chuckled. "You know I usually do this for plants, right? Whoever painted this did their research and found out what varnish they used then. You can still buy it online. We could run some more tests, but I don't think I can narrow it down much more. You have good old exterior latex house paint and a varnish layer not typically used today, but not impossible to find."

Nessa drew little circles on a piece of paper. Her mind moved in similar spirals. Something bothered her. Had he been wearing latex gloves?

"Common misunderstanding," he said when she asked. "Latex gloves contain natural rubber, and paint is synthetic. Shows up different on the mass spec."

Satisfied that the evidence hadn't been cross-contaminated, Nessa thought about this news. A painting from the New York Metropolitan Art Museum contained house paint. Did that even constitute fine art?

"This sounds like a big forgery ring I read about," Kevin said.

"You read about art?" Nessa couldn't keep the surprise out of her voice.

"There was an article in the American Society of Chemistry magazine. I'm interested in anything that could expand our business. These guys did much the same thing, even artificially aging the varnish to pass as hundreds of years old."

Nessa liked this guy. Was he married? She'd have to check into that later. She thanked him and rang off. Now they had hard data which supported Evangeline Abbot's assessment that something was off about *Gray Day*. She picked up the phone and requested a new search warrant for Natalie Patel's garage and house based on the test results.

Rose and Watson waited at the foot of the driveway an hour later when Nessa arrived at the Patel residence on Chestnut Street. The crime scene van was parked in front.

"I saw the cars. What's happening?" Rose asked. Watson sniffed the policewoman's regulation boots before wandering off to mark the cruiser's tires.

Nessa wanted to tell her. She liked Rose, but duty stood in her way. "Just following up on some leads."

Rose tilted her head and frowned at her. Nessa felt

like squirming but held her composure, turned, and walked up the driveway, leaving Rose and the little dog at the curb.

The search team was lining up all the artwork against one wall of the garage. Several looked familiar. Hadn't she seen those in her high school humanities class textbook? She picked up one of the canvases and saw a handwritten notation on the back that credited the original artist. Not a crime. Others, mostly still-life paintings of flowers in a cyan glass vase, had Natalie's signature in the lower right corner. All the blank canvases looked new. Bright white with clean staples.

"Any sign of varnish?" she asked the nearest technician, a dark-skinned guy with a Jamaican accent.

"Over there." He pointed to a table on the far wall. Nessa donned gloves and picked up the jar. Synthetic. Not the Dammar Kevin mentioned, so not the stuff on the painting.

The kitchen door stood open. Inside, she found a bright, cheery room with dead roses in a vase on the counter. The same cyan-colored vase in the paintings.

Cotton towels draped from the oven door handle. In a drawer, she found more of the same, plus knitted hot pads, also made of cotton. Shelves held glass storage containers and metal bowls. Wool coats in the hall closet.

No sign of polypropylene.

Upstairs in the bedroom closet, the same. Natalie Patel favored natural fibers and materials. No sign of a fleece jacket or a tracksuit. No plastic bags or packaging. Nessa wondered what it took to get rid of everything in her house that contained poly.

The stuff was everywhere in Nessa's apartment.

"Anything?" she asked a junior tech.

"Nothing matching the fiber found in the painting. We'll keep looking."

Nessa nodded and wandered through the rooms on the second floor. A master bedroom with a floral comforter. Hardwood floors and throw rugs. She pulled off her glove to feel the material. Wool. The guest room was nice but sterile, the kind of accommodation you keep ready, but then you never have anyone visit. The place felt lonely.

In the office, she found a profusion of art books, seed catalogs, an overstuffed chair — wool and cotton — and a desk covered with framed photos of flowers and trees.

She had an anonymous tip, a forged painting, and a key card. Why would someone want to frame Natalie Patel?

Chapter 33 Rose

~

Port – a Portuguese fortified wine produced in the Douro Valley of northern Portugal. Can be dry or sweet. Only wines from Portugal are allowed to be labelled Port.

Saturday, October 15, 5:30 PM

Watson sat by Rose's heels in Natalie's foyer and listened to the silence. Those Groucho Marx eyebrows arched high on his forehead as he watched her. He seemed to understand they were on a covert operation.

Evergreens scratched against the window in the late afternoon breeze. Sergeant Nessa told her to stay put. She tried. Spent the day cleaning out her fridge and organizing spices. She fretted about Stella and longed to go over and inspect the crime scene herself. What a way to think of a friend's house – as a crime scene.

Then she remembered her pledge to check houseplants and look for the key card.

A semi-circular, marble-topped table held a cobalt glass bowl for sunglasses, mail, and miscellaneous necessities. Natalie's leather purse, featuring a bohemian fringe, hung on a wrought iron hook beside a mirror. Rose poked a finger around the contents, but didn't see a rectangular plastic access card. Taking the purse into the kitchen, she dumped the contents on the counter.

Wallet, lipstick, pen, hard candies, and a small sketch pad.

"Nothing," she told Watson, who wagged his tail and scratched on the door to a small patio.

"Okay, we can check there, though I know what you want."

She let him out, following behind and inhaling the rosemary and lavender that circled the lanai. In the center sat a wrought iron table with two chairs. The top of the table was an open-weave mesh. And on top of that, stark in the golden light of sunset, lay a small rectangle of plastic.

"Well, Watson. What's this?"

Rose approached the evidence with the type of caution reserved for huge spiders. "Natalie's missing key card. How do you suppose it got here?" Watson trotted over and gave the table a sniff.

"Smell anything?" They had only been together for a week, but already she knew what he thought.

"Where do I start?" she voiced on his behalf. "People, flowers, a cat, no two." Rose chuckled.

"I'm going crazy, aren't I?" Watson shook his head with such vigor he stumbled. Rose turned back to the table.

Had Natalie taken it out of her purse and forgotten she had laid it there? A strong wind could have blown it into the bushes, which would have made it impossible to find, but it sat out in the open, easy to see. Rose glanced at the garage door. Had it been there when she and Stella came over?

Counting her steps, she took six strides and stopped at the creaky door into Natalie's studio. She turned to view the table. The card was visible, but only if you knew what to look for. It could have been there three days ago.

Some detective she made. She overlooked important evidence, and the police arrested Natalie.

No, that wasn't quite true. Someone used it to get into the gallery on Friday night.

Did Natalie lie about losing it? No, someone had stolen her access credential, used it, and then returned it. A locked-up Natalie couldn't have done that last bit.

She stared at the incriminating plastic, uncertain what to do.

"Come, Watson." He crawled out from under a lavender plant. They went back through the kitchen and out the front. She stopped, thought for a moment, retraced her steps to the patio, and snapped a picture. Then she returned to the front, carefully locked the door, and they walked home. Rose thought about her suspect list, and Watson leaped through the ground cover between the two houses.

Once home, she pulled out her phone and dialed Sergeant Nessa's number. The call went to voicemail.

"Nessa? This is Rose. I was at Natalie's checking on plants and saw something you should know about. Natalie's key card is on the patio table. I didn't touch it. Anyway, thought you'd want to know."

She hung up and silently hoped she hadn't made things worse for her friend.

Chapter 34 Stella

~

Montepulciano — An Italian red grape grown in the Abruzzo region of east-central Italy known for flavors of blackberry, plum, and cherry flavors balanced with licorice, pepper, or tobacco.

Saturday, October 15, Time Unknown,

Oh my god! Stella struggled to quell a surge of panic.

Calm down. Think your way out of this.

The cloth around her eyes smelled like it came from a bag in a mechanic's garage. Machine oil and antifreeze. The odor amplified the headache that felt like it involved her entire skull.

What had happened? She'd passed out. It was the only explanation because she wasn't in her bedroom. Someone snuck up behind her, she remembered that now, and held an almond-scented rag over her mouth and nose.

Oh god, her head hurt.

It wasn't worth wondering who it was. Her shady boyfriend, Slade, was behind this. He'd overheard her talking to Rose.

Boy, I know how to pick them, don't I? Killer, probably a serial killer, art thief, womanizer. What else is there? She ransacked her mind for epithets.

It had to be Slade. Who else had any reason to kidnap her? It could be some random bad guy. *I couldn't have been that wrong about Slade.*

No light penetrated the gloom.

That could mean it was nighttime. Or she was in a deep hole somewhere. Ropes chafed her wrists. No gentle treatment like when they had sex. *Oh, god. I could die and never find my birth mom.*

In the end, that could be her biggest disappointment.

No. Get a grip on yourself. You are too young, too hot, too ledge to die. I should have noticed Rose shushing me when I jabbered on. He was standing right below the window. Of course, he heard everything.

He attacked late at night. She'd been sitting at the dressing table in her bedroom. There was only one door to lock, and Stella, like a ninny, didn't. He crept up the stairs without stepping on the squeaky tread. Only someone familiar with her house would know that. Her eyes burned when the cloth covered her nose and mouth.

A deep voice next to her ear said, "Don't scream."

The voice was deeper than Slade's, but he could be masking. Anyway, she couldn't see whoever it was, and it wasn't like she could say a word with his hand clamped so hard she could taste her lipstick. Pink Surprise. Well, color me surprised. She wouldn't have screamed anyway, having seen enough cop shows to know that never helped. Her head went woozy. Blackness closed in, and she was barely aware when he pulled her back and dragged her toward the door. Her feet slipped out from under her, and his arm circled her waist to support her weight. *He's about six feet one. Like Slade.*

She didn't make it easy on him, though. Oh, yeah, she could have stumbled along and tried to walk, but why? Deadweight was harder to carry. Her head bashed on the door jam on the way out. Her feet whacked on the steps, and he huffed and puffed enough to blow down a brick building. She struggled to stay alert, to remember what he sounded like during lovemaking.

He got away with her. And there she sat.

In the gloom.

When he took off the cloth, everything looked blurry. She tried to turn in her chair, but her range of motion was limited.

"Who are you?" No answer. Just the sound of footsteps behind her. "Why have you done this?"

She heard a chuckle from across the room. It took a few minutes before she saw a desk. A chair. A lamp so decrepit that the Salvation Army probably wouldn't take it. In the corner, she could make out the outlines of an ancient radiator. Being from the UK, she didn't know they even had those in California.

Ropes lashed her feet together, likewise her wrists, biting into the skin. A cord around her middle shackled her to the chair.

Grime covered the windows, and it was clear that she wasn't going anywhere, but at least he hadn't threatened to kill her. Yet. He stayed behind her. Hid his face, though she knew it was Slade.

She prayed. Asked any gods listening to give a girl a helping hand.

She wasn't as freaked out as she thought she should be. Blame her analytical brain. That was what a guy, two or three boyfriends ago, had said: that she wasn't emotional enough because she was too smart. He hadn't understood that her priority was to find her birth mom, not shag him.

They hadn't lasted, and she was fine with that.

Her captor brought her a burger and fries.

God, it smelled so good and she was hungry.

The blindfold went on, and he fed her, even guiding the straw in a soda to her mouth.

This could be sexy if it weren't for the fact...oh god, he's going to kill me!

She thought about spitting the food out, but decided against it. Even junk food gave the body energy, and she needed everything she could get to survive. The sounds of traffic outside meant she was near the highway. The smells of searing beef and fried potatoes spoke of a burger place, which narrowed it down to one of several locations. No way to tell which, though, and even if she knew where she was, what could she do about it? So, she sat there thinking about the painting. About why someone had killed the guard. And about how anything could have ended up in Natalie's garage. But mostly about her search for her mom.

Both moms. She felt like she was close. A hint from an ancestry website where she sent her DNA indicated that she had distant cousins in California. She got herself to the West Coast. Paso Robles sits between Los Angeles and San Francisco. It seemed as good a place as any to use as a base. She started assuming everyone she met might be a distant relative. Things would be different when she found the mysterious woman who had given her life.

Then she thought about the mom who raised her—a strong woman named Emma. What she would give to have Emma with her at that moment. She'd say, "Keep your wits about you, dear."

Stella's thoughts drifted to the painting in Slade's garage and the stone statue in his trash. At the time she and Rose found it, they thought it might be the murder weapon. But who went around carrying something that heavy?

It wouldn't have fit in a jacket pocket or a briefcase. No, he would have used something closer at hand.

Killing the guard was probably not the goal; the criminals had needed to get him out of the way. And why that painting? Others in the collection were worth more. Slade had even told her that when he gave her the tour. What was so special about *Gray Day, Montrose Valley*? The name itself was boring. It was just a view of mountains on a cloudy day. Maybe the artist hid something under the paint or the backing. What made that painting worth all the bother?

She couldn't do anything but think. At least it kept her from focusing dying at the hands of a monster. A monster? How had she not seen that? Is he going to kill me?

Chapter 35 Rose

~

"Wine is bottled poetry." Robert Louis Stevenson

Saturday, October 15, 4:00 PM

Standing at her closet, Rose wiped her sweaty palms on her t-shirt. Silly to be nervous about a date at her age. Was she too old for this? Stella's words echoed in her head—*You're never too old.*

The reminder of Stella's disappearance caused a sharp pain in Rose's chest. She could be dead, or being tortured, and she was surely scared out of her mind. Rose closed her eyes, slowed her breath, and repeated what had become a mantra for her. "She'll be okay. She'll be okay."

Her pulse thudded in her neck. She shook her head as if that would remove negative thoughts and turned her attention to her wardrobe. She'd gone shopping and now hated the things she bought. The rest of her closet was filled with work clothes. Not the type of thing you wear on a date to a musical theater production. Had Frank mentioned the name of the show? She didn't think so. She'd been so focused on getting information about Brad Knight at the Olive Growers dinner. She didn't remember much else about the night.

A loud pounding from the front door startled. Would a killer knock? Probably not, but best to be prepared. She picked up the gun from her bedside table and descended the stairs silently, her fingers tight around the grip.

Holding the gun ready to fire, she approached the front door.

"Who's there?"

"It's me, Rose. Natalie."

Rose set the gun on a hall table and unlocked the door. Natalie stood holding a bottle of champagne and two glasses.

"Oh my god, you're free!" Rose screamed. "I can't believe you're here."

She held Natalie by the shoulders at arm's length and assessed her friend's condition. Wet hair. Face a bit thinner. Eyes bright.

"I had a shower before coming over; you wouldn't believe how good that felt. I brought some bubbly to celebrate." Natalie waggled the bottle.

"I want to hear all about it," Rose said, sure now that Frank would be seeing the show alone.

In the kitchen, Natalie expertly popped the cork on the bottle, poured two glasses, and held a full one out to Rose.

"A toast. To persistent friends."

Rose sipped. "So, they finally figured out the painting in your garage wasn't the original?"

Natalie nodded and topped up her glass. "It's a good forgery, I'll tell you that, but not by me. Sergeant Gomez apologized but said the initial evidence looked conclusive. I like her. She has heart."

They went into the living room and sat on the sofa.

"Wine and pizza tonight?" Natalie asked.

Rose put her arm around Natalie's shoulders. "Of course! I had a date, he'll get along without me. You're home now. I want to hear everything."

"Oh no, you don't! Who is he, and what are you going to wear?" Natalie set her glass down and pulled Rose up. "Let's go. We need to get you ready for the ball."

"Are you sure? I mean, you've been through so much…" Rose wasn't sure she even wanted to go out tonight. Not with her friend back home.

"Yes. I'm sure. Come on."

Natalie led the way to Rose's bedroom. Rose watched as she rustled through the hangers of tops and pants, peered into drawers, and poked through the almost empty jewelry box.

"We're going to schedule a shopping trip for you when this is all over, but for now…" She pulled out a silky pink blouse and a pair of black slacks. She held them up against Rose.

"For now, let's go with this."

Once Rose was dressed, Natalie stood back and assessed.

"Yes, that will work. How tall is Frank?"

"He's um," Rose held her hand about five inches above her head.

Natalie selected a pair of black wedge sandals and then rummaged in the jewelry box until she found silver earrings and a simple silver chain.

Rose studied herself in the mirror. Dressy but not over the top. Fun and feminine without being frilly.

"I love it."

"Well, you bought it all at some point, so you have a sense of style. When was the last time you went on a date?"

How long had it been? "Maybe fifteen years. Big hair was in."

"Then it's time to get back in the saddle again," Natalie said with a laugh.

Side by side, they sat on Rose's bed, leaning against the padded headboard. Watson planted himself on Natalie's lap, as if he sensed that something bad had happened to her and would prevent anything else from occurring.

Natalie looked tired, but who wouldn't be after spending time in jail? How tired Stella must be. If she's alive.

"You heard about Stella?" Rose asked.

"Sergeant Nessa told me when they released me. Being kidnapped is way worse than what I had to go through."

Rose felt bad for holding that information back. "I wanted to tell you, but I couldn't add that to your troubles. Plus, I couldn't figure out the county phone system. I hoped she'd be home by now."

Natalie sighed. "Why would anyone want to kidnap her?"

"Something happened when you were gone. Stella thought she saw the stolen painting in Slade's garage. He overheard her talking about it. The kidnapping occurred that night."

"You think he took her?" Natalie asked.

"I don't know. I mean, it sure looks that way." Rose glanced at her watch. "When you invited Stella over, I didn't realize how much I would like her. You know, our ages are so different; she could be my daughter. It's made me think about..." her voice drifted off.

Was now the time to reveal the fact that she often didn't acknowledge herself?

"About what?" Natalie probed.

Rose slid to the edge of the bed and stood, brushing dog hair off her pants. "We can talk later; if I'm going to do this, I need to get going, though it feels a bit cruel to go on a date with Stella in the hands of a kidnapper."

"Are we sure someone kidnapped her? Could she be working with someone?"

Stella suspected Natalie, even though she said she didn't. And now Natalie suspected Stella.

"I'm sure," Rose said.

Natalie stood and took her hands. "Well then, there's nothing you can do tonight. Maybe a date will spark a fresh idea."

"I hope so," Rose said. Thanks for the help getting dressed. You can stay with Watson if that's more comfortable."

"And risk being here when you lure him into your love nest? No, thank you! I'll come over in the morning and get all the details, assuming you're alone, that is." Natalie winked.

Rose felt her cheeks blush.

Chapter 36 Natalie

~

"Give to the world the best that you have, and the best will come back to you." Madeline Bridge

Saturday, October 15, 5:00 PM

Natalie gave herself a tour of Rose's upstairs. Her friend radiated caution when it came to her personal life. There must be trauma there that she hasn't talked about yet. Peering into each room she didn't see anything that gave even the slightest hint. Watson followed her as she went, his expression quizzical, as if he was saying, "why are you spying on my Mom?"

Why was she? Natalie had never taken Rose upstairs in her own home, so why would she expect it from Rose? She shouldn't. that didn't stop her from checking every room and deciding she'd need to get below Rose's veneer another way.

Watson padded after her over to her house and settled himself on her sofa.

"Not going to leave me alone, are you?"

His eyebrows toggled up and down like a canine version of Groucho Marx. Growing up Natalie had wanted a dog, but her parents refused.

"I don't want dog hair everywhere in my house," her mother had said.

"Just another mouth to feed," her father added. Along the line, she'd incorporated those sentiments into her thinking. There was no reason she couldn't get a dog now.

Maybe a friend for Watson, too.

Armed with a glass of champagne, because getting released was as good a reason as any for drinking bubbly.

"What do we do about your Mom's reluctance to date?" she asked the little canine listener. Watson tipped his head.

"True," Natalie said. "We don't know enough history, and from what little she's said, some guy has done her wrong in a big way. We'll just have to be patient with her."

Watson shook his head and laid his muzzle on her leg. His trust made her smile. Patience wasn't a strength of Natalie's. She'd burned up whatever stock she'd been born with dealing with Paul and his med school studying, followed by an affair with his receptionist. A cliché if there ever was one. So, really, she wasn't in a good position to criticize anyone for being shy about dating. In the twenty years since Paul dropped dead, she'd dated only a few men, and four dates was the most. Did she attract losers? Or did her fear of commitment lure partners with the same problem? Or married men. Not that Brad had been interested in her, but if he was, would she have had an affair?

A sob built in her throat. Poor Brad. He didn't deserve what happened to him. Rose seemed convinced she could figure out who killed him. Natalie would do whatever it took to help her do just that.

Chapter 37 Rose

~

"Gewürztraminer-- an aromatic, full-bodied white wine known for its intensely floral, spicy, and fruit-forward profile, frequently featuring notes of lychee, rose petal, and ginger.

Saturday, October 15, 5:30 PM

Frank stood outside the theater in a tan sports jacket, khaki pants, and a white shirt. He'd left the cowboy hat at home. He exuded cool sex appeal, and Rose felt both nervous and terrified. Why did men age in a way that made them more attractive, and women sagged and wrinkled? She tugged her blouse down, hoping it would make her look thinner. Not much would make her look younger. A new hairstyle, maybe?

"I wondered if you'd make it," he said when she approached.

"Oh?"

"I know you're tied up with the theft at the gala. You look nice." He didn't know about the kidnapping yet. No one did. Should she tell him and possibly ruin the whole evening? Rose wanted to put it all in a room and close the door for the evening, as Natalie suggested, but having someone to talk with would be nice.

She decided she needed a Watson that spoke back.

"Thanks. I'm sorry, I was a bit late. Things are a bit chaotic. My friend, Natalie, was released from jail, and another friend has been kidnapped.

Frank didn't seem put off by this.

"Kidnapped? And yet you're here. I'm flattered. So, the person they arrested wasn't guilty?"

Rose tensed at the notion that people thought Natalie had done such a horrible thing.

"No, she was most certainly not. There are plenty of people around who could have done it, though. I just need to figure out which one."

"I'm surprised you're that involved in the investigation. It sounds too dangerous. Whoever is responsible has already killed someone and is probably behind your friend's kidnapping."

"I can't sit by and leave it to the police. They have so many other things to focus on."

He placed his hand on her back. "Please be careful. I'd hate to see anything bad happen to you." His voice leaned toward pleading. She smiled, pleased that he was willing to show he cared.

"I can defend myself, and yes, I'll be careful."

They walked through the main doors of the theater. Red curtains covered the walls, creating a dramatic atmosphere, as if the patron was backstage. Gold and red swirled carpet accented the mingling crowd. A large placard announced the name of the production. *Music Man.* A tale of corruption and transformation told in song.

Theatergoers thronged the lobby, imbuing the space with a thrum of voices. Frank took her arm and steered her toward the door into the auditorium. He'd shaved, leaving smooth skin where he normally wore a slight stubble. What would it feel like to run her hand along his jawline? Too soon, she told herself. Besides, her palms were clammy again. Nothing worse than sweaty hands in a romantic setting.

They found their seats in the second row, minutes before the orchestra started playing the overture. Frank leaned closely and whispered.

"What about motive? It sounds both premeditated and a crime of passion. Don't you think? And what about the security cameras? Did they show anything useful?"

"Let's just enjoy tonight," she said.

He nodded, as if that had been his thought all along, despite asking questions. As the music began, he leaned toward her once again.

"The growers have been worried about the Old Bathory place. Down in San Anselmo. Reports of unsavory characters hanging about. I'm wondering if they are involved."

The music drowned out any further conversation. Had he said the Bathory place? As in Liz Bathory? She closed her eyes to focus. Was that the abandoned ranch she'd asked Nessa to look into? If it belonged to Liz Bathory's father, that meant it now belonged to her.

Their arms touched, and Rose smelled bergamot and pepper. She sniffed the air, trying to locate the source.

"Too much cologne?" he whispered. She shook her head as the overture swelled. The aroma calmed her. A deep breath brought additional notes of lemon and patchouli. As the lights dimmed, Frank stretched his arms forward to settle back into the seat, and the mysterious tattoo peeked out again. Just a few lines. What was it? One of those geometric ones? Or something nautical or religious? The lights went dark, and on stage, the performers began singing about trouble in River City. Rose mused that there certainly was trouble in Paso Robles. Stealing that one painting made little sense other than that someone passionately wanted it. Liz

Bathory hated that her father gave it away. No one had mentioned that Liz had a place here. She seemed more like the New York type. Could Liz and Bolton be working together?

A horrible thought gripped Rose's mind. Had Stella really seen the crate that day when she called Rose over, or had she and Bolton performed an elaborate charade, then run off together, laughing at their ruse? Rose wondered if Stella was as young and innocent as she seemed. She and Slade entered Rose's life together at the gala, and Stella defended him at the wine and pizza party. The breakup could have been an act. But why? Was the kidnapping a ruse?

Frank shifted next to her as the first act closed with the cast singing the *Wells Fargo Wagon*. The curtain closed, and he stood and held out a hand to help her.

"Let's get a drink in the lobby."

As she got up, only one thought ran through Rose's mind. Was Stella Richards a thief?

Chapter 38 Slade

~

Lambrusco — An Italian red wine grape used in both dry and sparkling red wines

Saturday, October 15, 8:30 PM

Slade realized he'd let his guard down, thinking this podunk town couldn't investigate its way out of a paper bag. Or was it Liz? She wasn't returning his calls, a sure sign the romance was over. The whole thing was making him sloppy, not up to his typical professional standard. Slade's informant in the police department let him know that his prints showed up on the wine bottle. If he wasn't careful, he'd overlook something, and they'd get caught. At least the guy had taken a c-note to keep quiet about it. And they'd eliminated their presence on the security video so he could always claim he'd touched the bottle during the gala, being his generous, helpful self.

His "anonymous" tip had Natalie in custody and her credibility seriously damaged. She wouldn't be in the gallery to work on the security system. Not that he thought she could do anything helpful. He was safe for the time being.

He sat in the lawn chair in the middle of the living room, dangling a beer bottle by the neck. Light from the streetlamp illuminated the interior of the house. Not like that night in New York, where the flickering traffic lights had reflected on the walls of the apartment. The night his grand expectations crashed around him.

The night should have been special. One they would remember for years to come. Forever, maybe.

*S*lade boiled up spaghetti, the fresh kind from the little shop on the corner. He diced bacon and added it to a hot pan. It sizzled and spat as the fat rendered, sending tendrils of salty, meaty goodness into the air before the exhaust fan whisked it away. When it crisped to his standards, he drained the excess fat and added garlic.

In a bowl, he whisked two eggs and a generous handful of Parmesan cheese together. The pasta boiled until al dente, and he lifted it out with a strainer and dropped it into the pan with the bacon and garlic. Then he added the eggs and cheese mixture, tossed it with the heat of the pasta and residual heat of the pan, and dressed it with chopped parsley.

A quick sniff filled his head with the garlicky fragrance that drew a smile.

"Liz, darling? You're going to love this dinner." She didn't respond. He smiled, knowing how the surprise would make her frisky. He didn't cook often, true, but the effort would be worth the reward.

With a nice bottle of Montepulciano d'Abruzzo breathing in a decanter, he lit candles and called her to dinner. The black velvet box sat next to his wineglass, ready for presentation and the bended-knee proposal.

They had drifted apart in the last year. She spent her time immersed in art, and he built a career with the FBI. Tonight, they would hit reset. An evening to restart the romance.

"Liz?"

No response. He tracked her down inside the corner of a room she called her studio, her ponytail bobbing as her head moved in beat to whatever music played on the headphones. She hadn't heard. Fair enough.

He tapped her on the shoulder.

"I've made a special dinner for us. Are you at a stopping point?" She looked from him to the canvas, then back at him, then at the canvas. It wasn't a trick question. With a stab, he realized she saw him as an interruption. An inconvenience. The box in his pocket felt heavy.

She checked her watch and shrugged. "Yeah, I guess it's getting late."

The night wasn't going as planned. Not at all.

He pulled her chair out with a flourish and indicated that she should sit. Her hair was still damp from the shower she insisted on taking. The cheese had hardened on the cooled pasta. Not ideal, but he didn't want any further delays. He poured wine into their glasses and raised his in a toast.

"To us. And new beginnings."

Slender, paint-stained fingers picked up her glass by the stem. She studied the rim of the wine, holding up a white napkin against the side of the glass, looking for the brown rim along the top of the liquid that indicated oxidation, low quality, and a cheap product. Did she think he couldn't purchase an adequate vintage? Not finding that, she lifted her glass and met his eye.

"To new beginnings."

They sipped. The wine had not suffered during the delay between opening and serving. He knew it wouldn't, but it was nice to validate that anyway.

She lifted a forkful of pasta and raised an eyebrow.

"You made this?"

He smiled. True, he mostly bought home take-out, but his mother had drilled cooking skills into him as boy. "Spaghetti Carbonara, and yes, I can cook."

He nudged the engagement ring box toward her. Saw the look in her eyes. Cornered, trapped. This wasn't just dinner. She set the glass down, and her left thumb went to her empty ring finger as if relishing the absence of anything but flesh. His smile froze on his face. This was not the jubilant display of joy he expected. Hoped for.

"Slade, I'm . . ."

How could he have misread things so badly? His palms slickened. It had been years, though, and how long was he supposed to wait? What if he'd waited too long? Missed the opportunity. Turned into a roommate with occasional benefits? Though there hadn't been any of those lately. They'd both been busy. This was meant to change that.

He snatched the box off the table and dropped it in his lap.

"Never mind. More wine?" He held up the bottle. She waved him off. What to do next? Would he move out? He had one suitcase and three boxes when he moved in. There was quite a bit more now, but he could be gone by dinner time tomorrow. He'd been so confident of a yes that he didn't have a contingency plan worked out. Big mistake.

"I'm sorry. I just thought . . ." What else was there to say? He tried a swirled fork of pasta, but it tasted like cardboard.

They sat in silence. He was afraid to put any more words out there. None of the ones he could think of seemed right. At least the wine would numb the pain he felt in his chest, where optimism had once felt so wonderful.

"I have a proposition," Liz said. He looked up. Her eyes glowed. Not with a romantic light, but with a passion, nevertheless. Whatever it was, he'd take it. Anything to spend time with her.

He ate a bite of spaghetti. It hadn't spoiled after all.

"I'm listening."

As she explained her plan, he realized he wasn't in a relationship. She had snared him in a trap. A trap he willingly entered. And would willingly remain in. He'd do anything to be with her.

Anything.

Would he still? Liz had him rattled. One day, she was all over him: the next, cool, collected, and distant. Though the distant days outnumbered the amorous ones lately. Their relationship had shifted, and he struggled to understand why. True, the whole liaison was based on him following her around like a puppy, doing her bidding. As long as she pretended to love him, he had been appeased.

Had been. Those words stuck in his thoughts. *Face it, man, you need to move on.* And quickly. If he valued his skin, he had to return to the safe, embracing shelter of the FBI and a career that, if he kept out of trouble, could lead to promotions.

There was the current mess to clean up. Stella proved to be a liability, and it was up to him to deal with her. That just left Rose MacGillivray. He still had to figure out what to do about her. Then he'd leave the life behind and return to his real, true love. The FBI.

Chapter 39 Rose

~

"I cook with wine, sometimes I even add it to the food." W.C. Fields

Sunday, October 16, 9:00 AM

Fog settled on the Olive leaves and dripped down to the rich soil at their base. After wiping two chairs down with a rag, Rose and Natalie took tea and scones from the local bakery into Rose's back garden. Natalie hadn't stayed the night, a fact that gave Rose hope that her friend hadn't been too traumatized by her stay in jail.

"What was it like being locked up?" she asked.

Natalie took a bite of a lemon poppyseed scone and moaned with pleasure. "For starters, this beats the baloney sandwiches they fed us. It was loud, and bright, and smelled of body odor and disinfectant and that rancid smell a body gives off when drunks dry out. I'm glad to be out and don't want to think about it anymore. Stella is going through way more than I did. Besides, I want to hear about your date. All the juicy details"

The date had been perfect. Frank was a gentleman. The kiss after they'd stopped for a nightcap at a local wine bar – sublime. The memory of his scent lingered.

"Come on," Natalie urged. "First, the date, and then catch me up on what's been happening. I was only gone a week, but it feels like a year."

After a brief description of the musical and the drink afterward, Rose filled her in on all the details. How handsome he'd looked while listening to her talk. How his brown eyes had almost swallowed her whole. What had she said? Hopefully nothing silly.

When she'd run out of date-related gossip, she shared the worry that had crept up on her during the show about Stella being tied up in the crime. It felt like a betrayal, given her current circumstances, but it needed to be said. And discussed.

"You were right. Getting out of this house, away from this corner, my mind was filled with new thoughts. Thoughts I'd rather I didn't have."

"Such as?"

"What if Stella is involved in this? Working with Bolton, I mean. Could we have misread her?"

Natalie set her cup down. "You're saying she wasn't actually kidnapped, but made it look that way? Why?"

"I don't know. It's just, what do we really know about her?" Rose felt that familiar feeling of the shift into self-defense mode. Her muscles tensed. Relax, she told herself. You are not under attack. Instead, she focused on what made her suspicious of her young neighbor.

"They both showed up at the same time, she and Slade, living right across the street from one another, which you have to admit is weird, and why else would she hang around with two old—"

Natalie's eyebrows shot up. Rose corrected herself and continued. "—Er women?"

"Speak for yourself. I refuse to be old, even if I crumble into dust. She hangs around with us because we're interesting! And we're her neighbors, and as you said, she's new and doesn't know anyone else," Natalie said. "Right now we need to focus on finding her. As for your theory about her involvement, I don't agree. And I don't think you do either. You're trying to keep all options in play so you can tell yourself you are being objective."

Did Rose's intuition tell her that Stella was that sort of person? In the bright light of morning, it seemed ludicrous. Natalie had pegged her desire not to let emotions sway her thinking, which annoyed her. She thought she had a better handle on that.

Natalie leaned forward. "It's like in any thriller movie. Money, sex, love, and revenge are the main motivations. You said he overheard the two of you talking about seeing the painting in his garage. If he is involved, that would be a motive to kidnap her."

A look of concern flickered across her face, and she closed her eyes. Rose knew what her friend was thinking. Would any of this help find the young woman? It must.

Natalie inhaled deeply and opened her eyes. "Besides, she's our friend. We need to find her. So, let's think. He got the sex for free; we can eliminate that one."

Rose nodded. "That leaves us with money and revenge. I'm crossing out love because he seemed to drop her a hot minute after your arrest." Unless it was an act, her inner voice said.

Natalie grabbed a scone and broke it in half. "Interesting. Do you think he had something to do with me going to jail?"

Rose remembered the aura of evil at the gala when he mangled her hand in what passed for a handshake.

"I don't know. He was here when they took you away. But then, he lives here, it wouldn't be strange for him to come out to see what was going on."

Natalie nibbled the scone, wiped her hands on a

napkin, and took a sip of tea, with a level of grace that Rose envied. Had Natalie gone to a finishing school? Were there finishing schools anymore?

Natalie looked wistfully past Rose. "He's almost too good-looking to be guilty."

"Looks have nothing to do with it." Rose had known plenty of cheats that could ratchet up a girl's heart rate.

"We're left with revenge, though I can't see how to tie him to that motive where Stella is concerned. Maybe a jealous woman? A really strong amazon?"

Natalie reached over and deadheaded a flower. "We've been assuming that he loved Stella. What if he didn't? Remember, she said he had a picture of Liz in his house. Maybe they were lovers."

A series of images went through Rose's mind. The look of anguish on Stella's face when she told them about finally getting into Bolton's house. The way Liz Bathory avoided answering her question about her relationship with him, and the smug way he implied Stella had been a distraction.

No, he didn't love her. Rose was sure of that. Oh, why did this all go around in a circle? How would any of this help them find Stella.

Natalie must have been thinking the same thing.

"None of this makes sense to me. There must be someone else we aren't thinking of. Someone who had a motive and thought Stella was in the way."

A car roared up the street. Vacation renters. No respect for the neighborhood. Rose remembered how serene it had been when she interviewed the heiress at her impressive villa in the ritzy area on the west side.

She also remembered the shotgun casually bent over the woman's arm and the easy familiarity she'd shown while emptying the chamber.

"When I went out to talk with Liz, she mentioned him, but not in a lovey-dovey way. More in a wish-he-was-dead way."

Then there was Liz's comment that she hadn't expected the small showing in Paso Robles to draw the attention of Slade or the FBI, and the way she'd sidestepped the question of her relationship with him.

Thinking back, Rose decided that Ms. Bathory had reacted the way you would expect a woman to act if she ran into an ex she never wanted to see again. They weren't seeing the whole picture.

She stood up and started to pace in the garden.

"Let's start with means. Stella's tall and strong, so they would have to knock her out, which translates to dead weight. What is she? 125? 130? Slade is at the top of my suspect list. He has the height and strength to do it. But he's such an obvious choice."

Natalie slowly spun her teacup.

"Obvious or not, he overheard her talk. If he had the painting, he'd want to silence her."

"Do you think he would steal a painting and kill someone for Liz?"

"Why her? She's loaded, doesn't need any more art, her walls are covered."

Rose agreed those were good points.

"I'm thinking about what you said. How she spoke about Bolton. Maybe he wanted to do something to impress her, like getting that painting she loved. Their affair could be on the rocks and this was one last, grand gesture. Brad was in the wrong place, at the wrong time. Do you think we had a killer living across the street?"

This town felt safe until all this started. Now it felt like danger crept around every corner.

Rose's chest ached at the thought of Stella in the hands of a kidnapper. They could kill her. So young and full of life. She'd never find her mom…Rose paused, lost in a new thought.

"Do you ever think about kids? I mean, like what it means to have a family?"

Natalie looked up at her with a tilted head. "In what respect?"

A tear threatened, but Rose blinked it away.

"Do you think I would have made a good mother?"

Natalie reached over and laid her hand on Rose's arm.

"Of course, you would. And yes, I occasionally think about what I might have missed. I got pregnant once. Did I ever tell you? It was shortly after Paul and I married. I lost it before it was even anything, at least I tell myself that. Then things got busy with his medical school classes, and well, there wasn't much sex and precious little love. He's lucky I didn't take one of those stupid statues he loved to collect and hit him on the head with it."

There had been an Easter Island statue at the bottom of Bolton's bin.

"Nessa said you identified the statue Stella found in Bolton's trash."

Natalie's face flushed.

"I'm embarrassed to say, I tossed it last week. There were two, and they were cluttering up the garage. I've…I've started painting again and wanted that bad vibe out of my studio space. The darn thing is heavy, so I only tossed one. I still have the other. I'll put it in the can next week."

"We thought it was the murder weapon when we found it."

Now it was just an interesting diversion representing a part of Natalie's former life. Maybe it was time for Rose to let her secret go too.

"I got pregnant once, too." Her voice sounded small and far away, as if someone else was telling the story. Natalie turned toward her with an intense look of concentration, or was it concern?

Tears finally welled in Rose's eyes and slipped down her cheek. She'd held the embarrassment bottled up for so long that she was afraid to let the cork out. She sank into the chair.

"Someone adopted the baby. I honestly don't know the gender. I asked them not to tell me. It seemed—I thought it would be—easier that way."

Salty tears streamed down her face and gathered in the corners of her mouth. She let out a sob.

"You're the first person I've ever told."

She felt lighter. Her fingers gripped the arms of the chair for support. A warm hand settled on her shoulder, and she looked up to see Natalie crying as well. The two women hugged. Natalie patted her back as her mother had so long ago.

Rose sagged down into her chair, relieved to have finally said the words out loud. It made it easier that Natalie had a similar experience, though her child died.

"Have you given any thought to the idea that Stella might be your daughter?" Natalie asked.

Rose had, in the wee hours of her nightly wanderings. The spirited young woman reminded her so much of her own mother and herself. They needed to find her.

"Oh god," she said. "I hope she's alive!"

Chapter 40 Rose

~

Frantoio Olives – an Italian olive from Tuscany. Fruity with a strong aftertaste.

Sunday, October 16, 11:00 AM

The neighborhood felt more complete with Natalie home. Though Stella's house remained dark. A For-Rent sign hung outside Slade's house. Rose guessed they wouldn't see him again unless his picture made the local paper's front page.

Then again, he was FBI. The big bosses would no doubt have something to say about that. Didn't the agency perform background checks on employees and monitor them regularly? He might have touched the bottle at the gala, and then the murderer happened to use the same one to hit Brad on the head. It could be a coincidence, but still, she wouldn't discount it completely.

Rain splashed the front window. A rare early October storm moved in, bringing gray clouds, not unlike in the painting, *Gray Day, Montrose Valley.*

Rose sat at her dining room table and looked at all the notes she'd taken over the last week, using the data to update her timeline. Everyone she suspected had entered the gallery at roughly the same time. Brad came up to them and left abruptly when Evangeline arrived. Then they noticed Liz crying, and Stella and Slade appeared.

Strange how Rose felt like she'd known Stella her

whole life, but they'd only met a week ago.

Liz departed shortly after. Rose and Natalie went home to their respective houses. Natalie heard sounds that might have been a cat. Rose saw someone crossing the street when she awoke in the middle of the night. And Evangeline returned to the gallery at 1 AM.

Throw in a fake anonymous tip and a kidnapping, and she had a proper puzzle. With no clear answer. She stood and paced around the dining table. What was wrong with her? Could age be slowing her down? Maybe she should let the police handle it, as Nessa said.

Rose closed her eyes and took a few long breaths. No. No to it all. No slowing down and no backing out. She sat at the table and scanned the scattered notes.

Despite Liz's strong protest that she didn't steal the painting, Rose felt something was wrong. The heiress had the means and motive for the theft. Find the thief, find the murderer.

She needed to get inside Liz's house again and see if the missing painting was hung somewhere else in the big residence. Yes, that rich lady would hang a stolen piece of art and dare anyone to question her.

The more she thought about it, the more convinced she became. There was something in that house that would help them find Stella and *Gray Day, Montrose Valley*.

Rose picked up her phone and dialed Natalie.

"How about a road trip?"

"It's raining. You know that, right?"

Rose laughed at the hesitancy she detected in her friend's voice.

"We won't melt. Be ready in ten minutes. We're going to Vineyard Drive."

Rose swept all the scraps of paper on the table into a box. A tidy house is a tidy mind.

"Come on, Watson. We're going for a drive." He leaped and spun in circles when she took his leash from the hook.

Watson curled up in the back seat despite the new canine seatbelt Rose installed. Her red sneaker leaned heavily on the accelerator.

"I'd rather get there alive," said Natalie, her hand gripped the door handle so hard her knuckles turned white.

Rose backed the speed down a few miles per hour. Barbra Streisand sang on the radio. Natalie's hand loosened.

"When we get there, I want to get into the house. Liz kept me on the front veranda the last time. You're going to be my distraction. Tell her Evangeline wants to hold another exhibition. That should pique her interest."

"Her collection is legendary. It won't be a lie. But after what happened, don't expect her to go for it."

The windshield wipers swept with steady beat that drowned out the music. Natalie turned the radio off.

"Will you see Frank again?"

Rose gripped the wheel a bit tighter. Would she? Of course, if he asked.

"I'd like to. How long do I wait for him to call again?"

Natalie snorted. "Join the new millennium, Rose, you can call him, you know."

Embarrassed that such a thought hadn't occurred to her, Rose laughed. "So much has changed, hasn't it?"

"Carpe diem my friend. Carpe diem."

Natalie let out a low whistle when they arrived at Liz's Italian-style villa. "Wow, it's good to be rich."

The rain slowed to a mist as Rose parked her Honda next to a silver Porsche Taycan in the circular drive. She opened the door and unhooked Watson's seat belt restraint to let him lift his leg on an ornate concrete urn. Rose wished she could do the same.

"Sorry, Buddy, you have to stay in the car." He jumped back in, and she rolled the window down before shutting the door. No worry about him jumping out.

Their feet crunched on the pea gravel path from the drive to the flagstone steps that led up to the door. Rose pushed the round button in the center of an elaborately embossed metal medallion. The sound of church bells rang from inside the house.

A petite woman wearing a blue shift dress and white apron opened the door. She looked surprised that anyone would come to this mansion. "May I help you?" Her heavy accent sounded Old World. Poland maybe.

Rose smiled. "We'd like to speak with Liz Bathory."

The door opened wider before the housekeeper could answer, and Liz herself glared at them from behind the diminutive maid. "Are you incapable of calling?"

Rose stepped forward. She'd relied, for a second time, on the idea of catching a suspect unaware. "I'm sorry to barge in on you again. I brought Natalie Patel with me. As you know, she works at the art gallery."

Liz's pale blue-gray almond-shaped eyes shifted to Natalie. "Yes, I remember you."

Rose looked from one woman to the other. Given that Natalie had been instrumental in getting the security set up and the exhibit advertised, Liz should well remember her.

Natalie stuck out her hand to shake.

"It's nice to see you again. I understand you have an impressive collection. I'd love to see it."

Liz ignored the hand, but Rose saw the spark of pride and arrogance she'd seen on her first visit. She would let them in to brag about the artwork. Rose was sure of it.

"Also," Rose continued. "I'm sorry, I really need to use your restroom."

Liz stepped back. "It's all right, Valentina."

The housekeeper opened the door wide. Natalie lowered her arm and followed Rose into the great room of paintings, her eyes widening with every step.

"Your collection is . . . gorgeous," she said as she circled in place.

A slight smile played on Liz's lips. "Thank you. I rebuilt after Daddy gave away most of the better pieces. He's been gone five years now. Thank god."

"Powder room is along there." Liz pointed down a long hall at the back and Rose scurried off. Valentina had disappeared. More paintings hung along the corridor.

At the end of the corridor, she found a powder room. A giclée print of a Georgia O'Keeffe sunflower hung over the toilet. Not the real thing. A true art lover wouldn't put a priceless, or at least costly, painting in the loo.

On her return she poked her head into a few other rooms along the hall. One had mirrored walls and rolls of yoga pads. Next was an office with a modern white desk and bright abstract paintings. That must be Liz's office. It screamed contemporary chicness.

On the left side of the hall, there was a door: solid and heavily carved. The keyhole above the wrought-iron doorknob looked ancient and needed a skeleton key. How old was this house?

"What are you hiding?" Rose muttered. She pushed down on the thumb latch to see if the door was, by any luck, unlocked. It emitted a nerve-jangling squeak.

She froze. The voices in the main hall continued as if nothing had happened. She leaned on the door, and to her amazement, it swung open without a sound, though her heart pounded so loud in her ears she wasn't sure if she would have heard a bomb go off next to her.

Floor-to-ceiling brocade curtains darkened the room. A substantial wooden desk dominated the center, with a green leather chair tucked behind it. Matching desk accessories decorated the top surface, but no pens cluttered the square box intended to hold them. Cloth- and leather-bound tomes crowded bookshelves, mostly legal and financial titles. This must be Liz's father's domain. It didn't look like anyone had used the room in the years since he died, though there wasn't a speck of dust, nor did the room smell musty. Valentina must keep it clean out of respect for her former employer.

Rich wood paneled the walls. Walnut, she thought, like the grandmother clocks her father made when she was a child. She tapped on a few to see if they were secret doors, the kind you saw in movies. Miniature gold-framed paintings of hunting scenes lined the walls: dogs and horses with trees and hills in the background. Wall sconces would throw light if she could find the switch. This room was all business.

She walked the perimeter, looking for a hidden recess where *Gray Day, Montrose Valley* might hide. The thick, emerald-green carpet muffled her steps. At last, she had to accept that there wasn't anything to the room other than outdated interior design.

In the hallway, Rose spotted a stairway she hadn't seen before. It had two steps up and then turned to the right, blocking any view of the landing at the top. Did she dare sneak up to see what the bedrooms looked like? Was *Gray Day* hiding up there? No, she'd been gone long enough for a restroom break.

When she rejoined Liz and Natalie in the main room, they'd made their way three-quarters of the distance around and were discussing the impressionist wall.

She searched for the blank hole she'd suspected as the future hanging place for the missing art, but another framed canvas hung in the space. Rose had hoped to capture the vacancy with her camera, but it was too late. And given that the painting now hanging in the space looked perfect there, what did it matter if she had a photo of a blank space?

Rose watched as the two art lovers discussed one painting after another. Rose prowled the room. A strong smell of turpentine and linseed oil permeated the air. None of the windows were the opening kind. How could Liz stand living in such a toxic environment? Hadn't famous painters died because of paint fumes? Or was that the lead? She couldn't remember from her long-ago high school humanities class.

Along the wall a row of wooden crates leaned two or three deep. Ready for what?

They looked like the type Stella described in Slade's garage. A tall stack of folded sheets sat on a long console table that also supported a large, ornate floral arrangement in a stately vase that was probably worth more money than Rose's house. That made two flower vases in one room.

"Rose, this is amazing!" Natalie said. She seemed to

have forgotten why they were there and been swept up in the art collection.

"She's right. Your house is beautiful, Liz. Aren't you afraid of someone stealing these paintings?"

Leather sofas, at least three that Rose could see, were pushed together as well. Was this the way the room usually looked? In the four corners, small black cameras watched silently. Was there a security room somewhere, like in the art gallery? Rose guessed there was.

"I have a panic button that goes directly to the police department. Plus, motion sensors and perimeter security. This is a safe location."

Rose felt a new appreciation for the money it took to have a home like this and art collections worth protecting.

"Evangeline would love another showing at the gallery," Natalie said as she circled the room again.

Liz took a deep breath. "I don't think that will be possible."

"Yes, I can see how you'd feel that way. After what happened. But if you change your mind, call me." Natalie produced a business card from her pocket. "We could focus it on modern art. I think that would go over well. You have a broad selection we could work with."

Liz walked toward the front door. There would never be another showing of her collection, and they were being shown the door.

"We should be going," Rose said. "We've taken enough of your time."

Natalie's expression showed disappointment, but then their eyes met and she nodded.

"Yes, it is getting late."

Rose gave Watson another chance to sniff shrubs before snapping his harness onto the doggy seat belt extension and rolling down the driveway. The car smelled of wet dog.

"That went differently than I expected," Natalie said. "She's very nice."

Rose navigated onto Vineyard Drive and slowed as the first of many windy turns started.

"I searched a few rooms but didn't see anything incriminating. No new threads to follow."

They drove in silence. The windshield wipers beat a tattoo as the rain picked up. Rose thought over what she knew, looking for inconsistencies.

Natalie stared out the window. Stella, well, hopefully, she was still alive. The rain lessened, and several driveways had refuse cans set out for pickup the next day. Rose thought about the black bag full of fast-food wrappers Stella had pulled out of Bolton's trash. She told Natalie about it.

"What were you doing dumpster diving in his garbage can?"

"That's not relevant. There were lots of In-N-Out Burger bags. There's only one in the area. Down in San Anselmo."

"You think Slade kidnapped her and is holding her there?" Natalie asked.

"We know he's been there a lot. Knows the area. There must be some reason he keeps going back there."

Rose gripped the steering wheel.

"Well, they do have good burgers," Natalie pointed out. Rose agreed, but that wasn't the point. Doubts built in her mind again.

"Are we jumping to conclusions? We don't know for certain it was him."

Natalie held up her hand and raised three fingers as she spoke.

"One, he has a car, and I'm sure some great knock-out drugs courtesy of the FBI. Two, he's a big guy and could easily carry Stella. That leaves motive. She saw him with the painting, and he overheard her telling you. He ticks all the boxes. Should we call the police?"

Rose's pale green eyes met Natalie's rich brown ones.

"They're already looking. They have the same information that we do. So far, they've turned up nothing. So really, there is nothing to tell them. There's an old olive orchard in San Anselmo. I heard about it from the Olive Growers, and Nessa said the police knew too. Most ranches have an outbuilding for equipment. That would be a perfect place to hide someone. And it's near an In-N-Out."

Natalie's eyes widened. "Let's go there and do our own investigation."

Chapter 41 Slade

~

Burgundy — a region in France where dry red wines are made from pinot noir grapes and whites are made from chardonnay grapes

Sunday, October 16, 1:00 PM

Slade judged that the operation had gone as close to plan as possible until Stella figured out he had the painting. Damn. They hadn't prepared for so much collateral damage. Or maybe it was just him who hadn't figured on having to kill anyone.

He and Brad had talked. In the park, he remembered that now. People probably saw them. Knight said he'd gone clean. Fool. Didn't he realize you never got out? He might have reported Slade to the cops to polish his new resume. What were the odds that the same guard would be in two different cities where they had planned a heist?

The last time Slade pressed a wad of one-hundred-dollar bills in Brad's hand. This time, though, he refused. If he'd gone along, things would be different. He'd be alive. The knock on the head had been sufficient. He wouldn't have remembered anything. The bullet sealed the deal, though. No snitching on anyone when you're dead.

He could see now that Brad had to die. But it didn't sit well. His gut twisted every time he thought about it. So don't think about it, he told himself.

Sleep eluded him the last few days. Every time he tried, he saw the pool of blood around the guard's head.

Dark red and viscous. Like a miasma that threatened to swallow him, too.

Adding Stella to the victim list seemed a waste. Was he getting soft? A shame, really. If his love for Liz weren't so overwhelming, he'd have gone for a woman like Stella.

She reminded him of the girl from his high school class. Tenth grade. Though it could have been later. Blonde, bubbly, and with a smattering of freckles across her nose. How different he'd been then; clean cut, athletic, and an A-plus student. You had to be, to qualify for the FBI, like his grandfather.

He looked over at the woman he'd drugged. Her head slumped to the side. His grandfather wouldn't even recognize him. Physically, maybe, but inside - never. When did the shift occur from dedicated special agent to art criminal?

Stella moaned.

"You probably think I'm a jerk," he said to the unconscious woman. "It's not what it looks like."

Who was he fooling? It was exactly what it looked like. He'd used her. Had learned where she lived and rented the property to keep an eye on the Patel woman. The one who managed and designed the security system in the gallery, required by the Met, yes, but implemented by her. He didn't know at the time that Stella and Natalie had just met. In the end, it didn't matter. His grandfather would have liked Stella. His dad would have voted for Liz.

Thinking of his grandfather reminded him of Liz's grandfather's diary. The leather-bound book he'd seen on the table the day he moved in with her. Slade awoke one night and couldn't get back to sleep. Liz snored quietly next to him, so he rose and wandered through the apartment.

City lights flickered and traffic signals rotated between red, yellow, and green. Even on the 20th floor, the sound of horns honking and engines revving disturbed what should be a silent night.

She'd left her grandfather's book out. Normally it stayed locked in the drawer. He hadn't seen the key since his first night in the apartment. Slade fought with his conscience for one tour around the floor-to-ceiling windows before untying the string and skimming the pages. It turned out to be a diary he kept during World War II documenting artworks stolen by the Nazis. Here was the proof that Old Man Grossman aided and abetted Goering in confiscating art.

As an FBI agent, he knew this was a treasure trove of documentation that the art historians and museum curators of many countries would pay dearly for. Did the Met know what they had? Some, if not most, of the collection of paintings that Old Man Grossman passed down to his daughter, Annette Grossman, could have been stolen. And should be returned to their owners.

Annette, in turn, married Emmet Bathory, who ignored Grossman's will and assumed ownership of the collection. Liz's mother died shortly after, and no one ever contested Bathory's actions.

That didn't explain *Gray Day, Montrose Valley*. The artist was a California Impressionist from the 1940s. No connection to Germany, Jews, or Nazis. Yet that painting was annotated at the end of the diary. It was specifically to go to Liz, his only granddaughter. Was that why she wanted it so much? Why she staged this viewing in coordination with the Met?

The shed he'd brought Stella to sat far from any

street, surrounded by olive trees that fluttered with feasting blackbirds. So many that at times it felt like a scene from Alfred Hitchocks's *The Birds* as he darted from the car with his bag of food. The old man died five years ago, and what was left of the family didn't want anything to do with it. It meant that no one checked the buildings, though someone still paid the electric bill. He could charge his phone.

The best part was the location, close enough to the highway and several burger joints. He could smell the beef cooking, hear the highway traffic as a stream of cars rumbled down the road, and the occasional honk as someone in a takeout line nudged the car ahead of them.

A familiar ringtone broke the meditative state he'd achieved with a bag of fries. His boss in DC. There was no need for introductions.

"Bolton. What are you doing out there? I'm getting calls from the Paso Robles Police Department asking about your assignments. I want you in my office by tomorrow at noon."

"Sir, I'm closing in on an art forgery ring. It's been years of work." His boss, Jenkins, had no idea how close he was.

"First I've heard of it," Jenkins said.

Damn. Why couldn't the man just accept and forget? Good thing Bolton had decided to go straight. He'd play this up and get kudos from the department.

"I've kept it under the radar, sir. I suspected there might be a mole in the FBI. What I know now is it doesn't look like that's the case." He'd save the diary for the cherry on top of his "busting" of an art ring.

"This should have been brought to my attention, Bolton. Be here tomorrow. Noon."

The line went dead. He threw the phone across the room. It skidded on the concrete floor and landed under a tarp-covered forklift.

Never mind that it was late on Sunday and getting a flight out of this godforsaken part of the country would be nearly impossible. With luck, he'd make the airport by nine. He'd have to leave now and drive like a lunatic to San Francisco or San José to get a direct flight. There was a red eye that might work. His partner would have to pick up the slack.

He gathered what little he had in a duffel bag. A couple of bottles of wine he'd snagged at the local grocery store, his charging cords, and a torn paperback. He fished his phone out from under the machine. A few scratches but no real damage. His clothes remained in the rented house, probably tossed away by now. He couldn't go back and get them.

Stella's head rested on her chest, and her shoulders lifted slightly with each breath. Sun-streaked brown hair fell forward, and he wanted to take a handful and bury his nose in the sweet smell. That would wake her. Maybe he should slip out. She'd die tied to the chair, or someone, probably that annoying old goat, Rose, would find her. She seemed to be getting in his way at every turn.

The Propofol he'd buried in the burger had done the trick. If he were honest, she didn't deserve this. He'd been able to move the paintings before the police or nosy neighbors could validate her story. She'd have been another rando spouting rumors. So why had he kidnapped her?

Because his partner didn't want loose ends. Well, if they wanted everything tied up neatly, they could do it themselves. He was through.

He checked his watch. Almost four o'clock. He could reverse his car to the door, get Stella into the trunk, and be gone before 4:30. A slight detour, and the Stella problem would be solved. That made him feel better about everything. About himself. Maybe there was a path back to being a dedicated agent.

Chapter 42 Stella

~

"Pour yourself a drink, put on some lipstick, and pull yourself togeth-er." Elizabeth Taylor

Sunday, October 16, 3:00 PM

Stella woke when Slade hefted her up into his arms and dumped her into the boot of the car. How daft had she been to fancy a loser like him? She'd been lots of other words that didn't come to her now because her stomach ached, and her head hurt from bouncing on the metal floor of the boot.

Her fingers fell asleep after the first fifteen minutes of jostling. The zip tie around her wrists cut in, and her shoulders ached. She tried to pull her hands around her bottom so that she could get them in front of her, but no amount of tugging or scooting helped.

She focused on turns. Had that been a left at first? Then two more before the ride smoothed out a bit; the highway, she guessed. She managed to slide onto her back, which helped somewhat, but her head bumped onto the deck every time the car hit a pothole or a patch. Wasn't there supposed to be a way to escape these things if trapped? She felt around but couldn't find anything that released the latch. Bolton probably disabled it. Bastard. The smell of gasoline made her stomach turn.

If she'd stayed in South London, she wouldn't be in this pickle. But no, she had to follow some guy who turned out to be a cheater and wind up alone in the States. She'd chased every lead in search of her birth mom and found nothing. One path remained, and if that turned out negative, it might be time to go home. Assuming she lived, that is.

The vehicle slowed and made a left-hand turn.

"Leaving the highway," she said to no one. Then the road became one long jolt after another. Bruises on bruises. Not that it would matter if she didn't survive. How many kidnap victims lived?

When the trunk lid lifted, she saw a figure silhouetted against a dusky sky. Even that low light hurt her eyes. She blinked. A hand moved toward her, holding a cloth. He was going to kill her. The sweet citrus smell stung her nose before her mind went black.

Chapter 43 Slade

~

Barbaresco – an Italian wine made with the Nebbiolo grape produced in the Piedmont Region

Sunday, October 16, 3:30 PM

Slade climbed out of his car and cursed the rain. Even the weather worked against him. He slipped on latex gloves and opened the trunk. Stella's eyes were wide open and wild. After chloroforming her again, he lifted her from the trunk and carried the unconscious woman into the house. Rain seeped down his shirt.

The front door opened as he approached.

"What are you doing here?" Liz demanded.

She was in a cold mood. He couldn't care about that. Somehow, his bosses in DC became suspicious. That was something he needed to quash before it tanked his FBI career. He must get on that plane. His career, even his very life, depended on it.

If he could separate himself from what he and Liz had accomplished, maybe even help get her arrested, redemption might be possible.

She'd blame him. Say it was his doing. But he'd think of something to negate that tactic. If not, at least he wouldn't do this anymore.

The FBI was all he had left.

His mind reflected on the many times they had stolen paintings using his badge. Too many to remember.

Killing the guard on this job bothered him more than anything else. So unnecessary. Boy, he'd changed. Suddenly, death bothered him.

Chilly rain dribbled down his cheek. He needed to get going.

"I've got to be on a plane in three hours. She's all yours now."

Liz's eyebrows arched. "Plane?" She wore a sleek black tracksuit with her dark hair pulled back, exposing a long, white neck. He pulled his gaze from her exposed skin.

"The deputy director is asking questions. I need to do some damage control." He looked around the room. It felt different. Bigger. She stepped aside to let him into the house that she'd inherited from her father, and he'd hoped would be their home forever. But she preferred New York to the West Coast. The walls were naked with faint outlines where paintings had hung for years. All the decorative knick-knacks had vanished.

"Where's all your stuff?"

"I'm redecorating." Her voice sounded nonchalant, but he detected a hint of strain. The telltale sign she had lied. His eyebrows raised as he rescanned the room.

All the furniture huddled in the middle of the room with a clean white sheet shrouding the disarray, erasing the room's identity just as she'd thrown a metaphorical blanket over their relationship, winnowing it down to work. Slade wondered when the forgery scheme had consumed their lives.

He had to admit she was good. The better she got, the less time she had for him. He came to think of the apartment as a crime scene, with their sex life being the victim and her art the murderer.

"Painters will be here in the morning, everything has to come off the walls," she explained. Her eyes watched him. He held her gaze and tried not to transmit any emotion. True, painters would need the walls bare, but something about her stance, the black clothes, and her nonchalance triggered his internal alarms.

He forced a quick nod. Don't let her get to you, he told himself. Though as his Art Crime Team unit made more busts, locked up more art thieves, and traveled to exotic places, which soon meant different women. All kinds, from blond clichés on the West Coast to elegant sophisticates in Paris. Liz didn't seem to notice whether he was there or not. Stella groaned. Time to go.

"Where should I put her?"

Liz pointed to the back hall. She hadn't questioned his arrival with their victim. As if this had been the plan all along.

She had been on reconnaissance this time. Generally, his job, but she'd insisted. He searched his memory but couldn't remember her saying there would be a night guard. The job should have been a clean grab, but it didn't go according to plan. That was on her. She had been on the premises for weeks, setting up the show. Why hadn't she mentioned Brad Knight? What was her game?

He felt bad about dumping the Brit. No doubt she would die tied up in this house. His reaction surprised him. His mother would have been proud to learn that his conscience was alive and well, although squashed down inside him. Time to bring it out of hiding.

In the old man's study, Liz pressed a button under the heavy oak desk. He imagined he could smell the Cuban cigars the guy smoked. A panel of the wall swung open.

"Put her in there." Liz directed.

Inside was a sink and toilet. Stella would die in a small closet instead of a drafty shed. Not really an improvement from her perspective, but it meant that her death was Liz's responsibility. Not his. He moved a straight-backed chair from the room into the closet. She moaned again as he sat her down on the chair. She slumped forward, and her head moved side to side a bit. The knockout drops should have kept her out for a few more hours. Maybe the stuff was old. Did chloroform have an expiration date? He needed to move faster.

"Rope," he said.

Liz left the room. She returned with a thick cord. He lashed the unconscious Stella to the chair, leaving her upright but with her head tipped forward, hands bound behind her.

"Got anything to use as a gag?"

An old blue bandana was found in a desk drawer, probably saturated with cigar spit, and some tape. He stuffed some of the rag in Stella's mouth and then the rest around her head, checking to see that she was breathing. He didn't want her to die while he was here. Somehow that would assuage his guilt. He taped the ends together. Not the cleanest job, but it would work. His fingers lingered on her shoulder. Leaving didn't feel right, but he didn't have a choice. When he stepped back, the panel closed. Stella vanished. He hadn't killed her directly, but she was as good as dead. God, this had to stop.

"After this, I'm out. With the big brass breathing down my neck, it's time to stop. We're through anyway. Frankly, we have been for a while. I don't think you ever really loved me."

Liz's nostrils flared. Her red fingernails against the black tracksuit looked drenched in blood as dark as the blood that pooled around Brad Knight's head. Why had she shot him? The knock on the head would have given them enough time to disappear.

Her eyes softened. She came over to him and wrapped her arms around his neck. That old desire returned. What was it about her that hijacked his reasoning? No, he told himself. Don't fall for this.

"Slade, darling." She snuggled close and leaned against his chest. Warmth crept up his body into his ear tips. She whispered, "Let's talk about this. I know I've been preoccupied, but things will right themselves."

Could she want to rekindle their love? He'd never questioned the spell she had on him, how all his strength ebbed when she was near. Never question it until now. A sharp burning pain stabbed his neck. His legs turned to jelly.

"You should have killed her when you had the chance," Liz said as the room darkened and he sank to the floor.

Chapter 44 Rose

~

Malvasia Bianca -- an ancient, highly aromatic white grape variety originating from the Mediterranean, known for producing diverse wine styles ranging from crisp, dry, and mineral-driven to intensely sweet dessert wines with notes of orange blossom and jasmine and flavors of mango, lychee, and peach.

Sunday, October 16, 4:45 PM

With a mixed feeling of anticipation and dread, Rose navigated the twists and turns of the town's west side, Watson leaning against her shoulder. Through his fur and her jacket sleeve, his heartbeat reassured her. He trusted her to make everything okay again. Not that anything was wrong from his perspective. He had a new home, food, someone to love, and plenty of walks and car rides. Life didn't get much better for a dog.

The humans in the car were preoccupied with thoughts of the difficulty of locating a black car driven at night. The moon vanished behind long, narrow bands of moisture-laden clouds, making the job even harder.

They drove down Monterey Road and passed the elementary school before deciding that it was too far away from the fast-food restaurant. They could get lost out here and Stella's life was on the line. Rose asked the car to call Frank.

"Frank, this is Rose. Where is the Old Bathory place?"

"Why do you need to know? You're not going

there- are you?" His voice sounded stern.

"Not now, Frank. Stella might be there. I have to find her. We're on Monterey Road. Where do I turn?"

"That's a bad idea, you going there alone. I'll call the police and have them meet you. Head back to the highway exit and turn on Graves Creek Road."

"Don't call the police. Yet. This could be a wild goose chase. I'll call you when we know."

With his directions, it didn't take long to find the untended olive farm. Without annual trimming, the trees had shot up, creating a mass of vegetation that almost swallowed the outbuilding at the rear of the lot. Rose extinguished the lights and rolled her car towards it. An owl hooted in the trees. One lone light bulb illuminated the front with stark light and deep shadows. The kind of place horror movies use for the killing scenes.

"Maybe we should call the police," she said. "Let them know we're here."

"Frank knows. And if she's in there, we need to get to her. It will take them ten minutes or so to respond. If this is a bust, then we haven't wasted their time," Natalie said and opened her door.

Rose lowered her window a crack and closed the door. "Watson, you stay."

The little dog whimpered. Natalie fished a flashlight from her purse and switched it on. The beam skipped over the ground as they crept closer to the shed.

"Stop. Shine the light there." Rose pointed to the ground. "Tire tracks. Someone has been around. And recently too. The edges are crisp."

Natalie ran the light along the track and then onto two large stable doors on the side of a corrugated metal building. "Let's get in there."

The door handles resisted a light tug.

"Stella!" Rose called. "Stella, are you in there?"

"Wouldn't he have gagged her?" Natalie asked. That made sense; he wouldn't want her calling out for help. They stood still. If Bolton was in there, he was playing it cool. Hoping they would give up and go away.

"I don't hear anything," Rose said. "He might have gone on a burger run. Which means he could be back at any minute. We've got to get in there now."

She leaned on the door, and with a squeak, it swung open. Natalie shone her light around the interior. The only light came from the flashlight and what little glow the here-then-gone moon generated through the shuttered windows.

An empty straight-backed chair sat in the middle of the room. Dirty footprints littered the floor, and dust motes floated in the light beam. The place smelled of diesel, must, and hamburgers. A trash can overflowed with fast-food bags in the corner.

"They were here," Rose said. "These are the same kind of wrappers in Bolton's trash."

"Maybe it was just him. I don't see anything that indicates she was here."

Rose moved over to the straight-backed chair.

"There are scuff marks around the base of this chair. Someone has been in it." Natalie shone the light on it. Rose bent to look closer. "And wear marks where ropes have been tied. I'm sure she was here."

The flashlight flickered, then dimmed, then died completely.

"Shit!" Natalie swore. "Should have replaced the batteries."

Leaves and twigs clawed against the side of the building as the wind picked up.

What had they been thinking? Coming to this desolate location without letting anyone know. Especially since they now knew the place was empty.

Rose couldn't believe she'd led them into this. Into the whole disastrous mess. It had been her poking around that angered Bolton. Stella had been showing her the box in the garage when the FBI agent overheard.

"I'm sorry, Natalie. This is all my fault."

"I don't believe that for a second."

"The police told me to let them handle things. But I couldn't let it go. I was putting my nose into everyone's business."

"Stella is lucky to have a friend like you who doesn't give up. For that matter, so am I. I'd still be in jail if you hadn't pushed."

Rose heard the words, but they didn't soothe her guilt. "Let's leave," she said. "This place gives me the creeps."

Wind whistled through an air vent in the peak of the roof like a distant train. The door slammed shut. Rose froze. She struggled to get a full breath into her lungs as a feeling of suffocation overtook her. How many feet to the exit?

With her hands extended, she took tentative steps until she felt the door handle, rough against her palm. She tugged.

"It's jammed. I left my phone in the car. Do you have yours?"

She could hear Natalie pat down the pockets of her jeans. "No."

How could they have been so careless? So stupid? Who would even think of looking for them?

Slowly, her eyes adjusted to the dark. There was something bulky in a far corner. Sliding her foot along the ground and groping the void with her arms, she moved toward the glow. Step, slide, grope.

"What are you doing?" Natalie asked.

"I thought I saw something." Rose stopped and stared hard at the pale illumination.

Outside, the wind howled. This sounded more like a Santa Ana wind than a Pineapple Express, but the origin didn't matter as much as the way it shook the structure. A loud screech came from above. A sheet of ragged steel from the shed's roof crashed beside Rose with a mighty thud. It landed on its edge and tipped toward her. Pain seared along her forearm as a ragged piece sliced her arm. She screamed. Crumpled to the floor—hard concrete layered with dirt. Warm sticky blood coated her fingers. Curled up, she held her throbbing arm. How could she let this happen?

"I'm hurt. Don't know how bad, but it stings like a son-of-a-bitch." A flash of lightning lit the shed. Raindrops fell through the newly created hole in the roof. A viable escape route if they could somehow get up there, but when she loosened her grip, the pain sharpened.

The tear in the roof let some light through, and she could see a ladder leaning against the far wall. No stable beam in the ceiling to lean the ladder against, though, and if they did climb up and out, that left them on the roof, outside, in the rain.

Was this how her life ended? They had failed to find Stella. Gotten trapped themselves. She could hear Natalie shuffling towards her.

Rose stifled a whimper as her friend sank to the ground next to her.

"I'm here." Hearing those words eased some of the fear that gripped Rose's throat.

The gash pounded. The ferocious wind scrubbed the Olive trees against the walls. Natalie shifted next to her and put her arm around Rose's shoulders. Rose wanted to cry, but knew that wouldn't be helpful.

"I'll be fine. We need a way out." Rose visualized everything she'd seen before Natalie's flashlight died. A chair, desk, trash, and the big something in the corner.

Blood dripped down her arm. She heard a ripping sound and then felt her friend wrap something around her arm.

"Did you tear your shirt?"

"Well, it was pretty dirty anyway," Natalie said, and Rose detected an attempt at humor in her voice.

"Thanks."

"Do you think that thing over there still works?" Natalie asked.

Rose stood and felt faint. A ray of moonlight beamed through the gap in the roof and landed on the machine, a forklift, like divine providence. Clouds scuttled back in, and the darkness resumed. But she'd seen it. This would work, assuming, like many farmers, that the old guy left his keys in the ignition.

Rose held Natalie's hand, and they shuffled over to the corner. Natalie yanked a tarp off the lift, and Rose ran her hand along its body for the seat and the step to climb up. Once there, she ran her fingers over the steering wheel and the levers until she located the magic that would free them.

"Climb aboard," she said.

"Do you know how to work these things?"

"No. Not directly, but how different can it be from a fancy lawn mower?" Rose had been an only child, and one of her chores had been to mow the grass using the riding mower her mom found at a garage sale.

She turned the key. The engine sputtered and then died.

Natalie groaned. "Cursed with dead batteries."

Rose closed her eyes and thought Please, then turned the key again. This time the engine turned over but stopped after a loud backfire. With luck, they could propel the tines of the lift through the door and wrench it open.

"I still have hope. The battery seems to have enough juice to start, but the engine is balky. The fuel is old, probably fouled, but it might start enough to help."

The old mower was as finicky as a baby. You had to coax it.

She turned the key again. The engine turned over and started to rumble. Loud backfires spewed foul-smelling smoke, but the cylinders kept going. Hopefully, someone will have heard that.

"Hang on." Natalie hugged her around the waist and Rose pushed the gas pedal. With a lurch, the forklift leaped forward. They had to cross the whole width of the shed before encountering the door. The machine accelerated. Rose pulled on the three levers, one at a time, until the fork tines rose three feet off the ground. That should be enough.

Lightning flared outside as the equipment reached the door. Rose could see the tines piercing the metal seconds before she felt the cab slam into the door.

The machine stalled, but the damage had been done.

With a loud moan, the door teetered forward and fell onto the ground outside, a mangled mess. The tines slid out as it went down.

"Yeah!" Natalie cheered. "I can't believe that worked!"

Back in the car, Rose let Watson relieve himself, started the car to get some light, and then found her first aid kit.

"Lucky you have that in your car. Let me help," Natalie said.

Rose dabbed the gash with antiseptic and gasped at the sting. Natalie ripped open the gauze bandage and placed it on the wound. Next, she secured it in place with tape. The pain dulled as Natalie examined her handiwork.

"That will do for now. We should stop by the ER in any event."

Natalie located her phone and checked the battery level.

"Full. At least one battery is good."

Rose returned the kit to the armrest. "I'll live. We need to keep looking for Stella.

Natalie nodded her agreement. "Where do you think she is now? It took us long enough to figure this place out."

Rose didn't have an answer. Her exhausted mind was empty of ideas.

"For a minute in there, I didn't think we'd ever get out." She merged onto the highway just as the first drops of rain splattered on the windshield.

"That got me thinking. I haven't been honest.

There's something I need to tell you."

Natalie hugged herself and leaned back in the car seat. "We all have secrets. You can't leave this life without having things happen you'd rather not relive."

Rose had meant to tell her friend about her name, not being her official identification, since she'd already exposed the existence of a child. But something in Natalie's voice said that she had a secret too.

Thunder rumbled through the night sky, and the rain came down even harder. Natalie drew her knees up and rested her head on her forearms.

"My parents didn't approve of my marriage to Paul. My father insisted I marry someone from India. I did it anyway, and he disowned me. He died before the divorce. I didn't get to say goodbye. Maybe he was right. I don't know anymore. My mother still will not speak to me."

Rose changed lanes to drive around a panel truck that was kicking up a spray of water.

"You win. My secret is silly next to yours."

"Tell me anyway."

"My real name is Winnifred. Like Winnie-the-Pooh. I hated it growing up; all the kids teased me. And Winnifred sounds too stiff. But I was named after my grandmother, and any discussion of another name made my mother angry. So, I lived with it. Then she died, and I moved here. I told everyone my name is Rose."

"I like Rose. I like Winnie too, but I see where you're coming from. Your secret is safe with me."

The weight of deceit lifted off Rose's chest. Granted, it wasn't a big deal; many people went by different names, but she valued honesty more than anything else. After they found Stella, she'd move forward with an official change with the court.

As they drove up the wet highway, Rose's cell phone rang. She checked the time and answered it through the car's hands-free system.

9 pm.

Nessa's voice came over the speaker.

"We just got a call in from our officers on duty. They've discovered a car rented to Slade Bolton at the bottom of a cliff off Willow Lake Drive."

Chapter 45 Rose

~

*Malbec – a French grape with an inky dark color and robust tannins.
One of the Bordeaux grapes.*

Sunday, October 16, 7:00 PM

Rose gripped the steering wheel as a gust of wind buffeted the car. What had the policewoman said?

"He's dead? No, he can't be, Nessa, he's the kidnapper. We just left the shed where he kept Stella."

Static crackled before Nessa spoke again.

"No body yet…forensics has arrived…." Silence.

Natalie leaned closer to the car's microphone and shouted, "What about Stella?"

More crackles before, "No word there."

Nessa had hung up.

If he had been hiding Stella in the shed, why had he moved her? And if he was dead, was she too? If. Such a small word to hold so much hope. Rose didn't have enough friends to lose even one. Then something Nessa said crystallized in her thoughts.

"Willow Lake is out in the direction of Liz Bathory's house," Rose said, not expecting a response. Natalie shrugged.

Two fake paintings, Natalie accused, then cleared, Stella abducted, a wine bottle in her recycling bin, and the smell of turpentine in Liz's house. Evangeline reentered the gallery after she said she'd gone to a hotel with her husband, which was after confessing to an affair with the guard that ended the night he died. So many pieces, so little logic.

"None of this makes sense," Natalie said, as if reading Rose's mind. "I mean, he didn't seem the sort to commit suicide. Stage a suicide, yes. But again, why? Could someone have killed him?"

"Let's not get ahead of ourselves. We don't know for sure that he was in the car. Maybe he did have a thing for Stella, and he's taken her to disappear and have a happy life together."

Natalie snorted. "Like that's gonna happen."

Agreed, thought Rose. Stella would make him pay for everything. The deceit, the kidnapping, and probably for giving her hope that he might be the one.

Slade seemed smarter than that. Whatever he'd done, it wasn't to set up housekeeping with her friend somewhere off the grid. No, there had to be another explanation. Something to do with the gala and the painting. The atmosphere changed when they'd all been standing at the missing artwork, and he and Stella arrived. Like a chilly wind blew in an open door. Then there was the tension between Slade Bolton and the heiress, Liz Bathory. Stella found the picture of them in his rented house. What was going on between those two, and was it something big enough to justify killing him? Possibly.

"There's one person I can think of that might want him dead. Liz. Remember how devastated Stella was when she saw that picture? Slade and Liz have a past. And the way Liz reacted at the gala, it didn't end to her liking. Plus, we're headed to her house now."

Natalie nodded her head the way someone who is digesting a lot of speculation would.

"She did turn cold when he arrived, but might that have been an act?"

"You mean, like they staged a fight?"

Rose resisted that idea, mainly because she wanted to defend women from the Slade Boltons of the world. But if, and it was a big if, they were working together, then Slade might be bringing Stella to Liz's house. Though they could have left her in the shed. If she and Natalie hadn't found it, Stella would have died in a matter of days.

Rose accelerated into the fast lane. Watson barked as the engine howled. Lightning bolted across the sky. Rose started to count. One, two, three…

Seconds later, a sharp clap followed by a rolling rumble echoed through the car. The phone rang again. The name Sergeant Nessa appeared on the screen.

"Is it Stella?"

"No. Sorry, no news there. Liz Bathory called. Someone left the stolen painting on her doorstep. She wants us to get it. I'm on…."

The line went dead. Rose blinked. *Gray Day, Montrose Valley?* The real thing. Or was this another forgery? Another distraction.

Nessa's voice came back.

"…way there. Don't be a nuisance, but find Stella…security tape from the hotel. Evangeline Abbot reenters at 1:35 AM." The call dropped.

Rose stared at the telephone icon, willing it to work. The display reset to show the time and date.

Natalie shifted in her seat to face Rose.

"If Evangeline returned to the hotel before the coroner's estimated time of death-- 2-4 am if I remember correctly-- then she's cleared. Right?"

"I think we can take her off the list. Who does that leave?" Just two people. Slade Bolton and Liz Bathory.

She felt the jolt of adrenaline surge through her muscles. They would find their friend.

"Don't forget to call Frank back and let him know you're okay," Natalie said. Rose felt a flush of embarrassment that she hadn't thought of that. She put the call through and left a message. Hopefully, he wasn't out looking for them. It felt strange to have someone worried about her, yet now wasn't the time to dwell on it. They had a mystery to solve. She pressed down on the accelerator. Storm or no storm, they needed to get to the west side. Fast.

Chapter 46 Rose

~

Roussanne — a white wine grape originally grown in the Rhône wine region of France. The aroma is often reminiscent of a flowery herbal tea with flavors of honey and pear, and full body.

Sunday, October 16, 7:30 PM

Red beacons pulsed on the roofs of the patrol cars in the driveway of the Italian-style villa. A boxy crime scene forensics van had backed up toward the door, its doors swung wide. The house stood open, light streamed out, glistening on the steps. Officers milled around the entrance.

Rose and Natalie stepped over the crime scene tape and splashed through the rain, Watson at their heels.

A tall, broad-chested sheriff came up to them, rain dripping off his campaign hat. Underneath his yellow rain slicker, Rose saw the small metal nameplate read Johnson.

"This is a crime scene, ladies. You'll have to leave." This seemed like a lot of police presence to pick up a stolen painting. What else did they hope to find? Then she remembered Bolton's car at the bottom of a cliff. Empty.

"We're looking for a friend," Rose said.

He blinked as if this was the craziest thing he'd ever heard. And maybe it was. Once the words left her mouth, Rose realized they might have a problem getting inside.

His phone rang. While he listened to the caller, Rose looked at the blank walls of the living room. Had Liz misled them the entire time with her poor, misunderstood heiress routine?

A sharp jab of pain made her wince. She forced herself to ignore it.

"Are you Rose and Natalie?" Johnson asked when the call ended.

Nessa came through for them.

"Yes," Rose said.

He tucked his phone in a pocket.

"Okay, you're cleared to go in. You, not the dog. Stay on the designated paper path. Do not, I repeat, do not touch anything. Got it?"

"Of course, Sheriff," Rose and Natalie said at the same time.

At the entrance, they stopped and stared. Lights blazed against bare neutral walls. Where were all the paintings she'd seen earlier? The wooden boxes that had been leaning on the wall were gone. A white drop cloth covered most of the furniture, grouped to one side of the large living room. A paper pathway led through the room to the back hallway. Plain-clothed detectives, with notepads at the ready, prowled the space, conferring with each other and pointing at items of interest with pens.

Liz had fled. Whatever version of *Gray Day, Montrose Valley*, she claimed had been left was certainly another forgery.

Johnson followed them in. He pulled off the rain slicker and shook the water off on the patio before folding it over his arm.

"Where's all the art?" Natalie asked. He looked from them to the walls, like he had no idea there had been anything in there at all.

He pointed to Rose's bloody makeshift bandage. A rivulet of red dripped down.

"We have a medic here who can see to that."

Rose put her hand over the bandage.

"I'll be fine. Thank you."

They didn't have time to deal with a cut. They needed to find Stella. Rose thought she could smell her young friend's perfume. Or was that a projection based on hope? Could be the scent of Liz Bathory. Mr. Bolton might like his women to smell the same.

Johnson shook his head. "It's your call. Mind the path."

A tall, gangly junior officer approached, and Johnson turned to talk with him. Rose ordered Watson to "stay" where he sat and hoped he knew that command. Then she turned to step on the white runway.

A technician took pictures of everything in the room. Another tech dusted for prints. What had she touched? The bathroom, so her prints would be there. And the doorknob to the study. She should have worn gloves. Need to get some in her purse. Turns out you never knew when they might come in handy. Would the maid, Valentina, wipe those off in her cleaning routine?

Rose hoped so. It might get awkward explaining her presence in this house.

Between the click of the camera, the conversation among workers, and the squawks of police radios outside, it was hard to focus her thoughts.

"Where would Liz go?" Natalie asked. "That was a lot of canvases to move."

They went to the end of the path, which stopped at the hall. Rose peered down toward the powder room. The focus of the investigation appeared to be the main room. The corridor was empty.

"She'd have to have private arrangements to ship them."

"In the last twelve hours?"

The paper trail didn't extend down the back hall. Rose turned to ask someone if they could check there, but no one paid any attention to them. Two silver-haired women blended into the walls. Watson sat in the doorway watching her. He was a clever dog. What luck finding him. Rose sniffed the air again. The faint smell of turpentine persisted. Her nose was good, but Watson's was better. She patted her leg, and he dashed in unseen.

Rose dragged Natalie by the arm around the corner and out of sight until Watson joined them.

"I want to see her father's study."

They inched down the hall, careful to mute their footsteps with a sloth-like pace. At the closed door, they stopped. Rose pressed the latch slowly, hoping to prevent the screech she remembered from before. Bless Valentina, she'd oiled the hinge, and it moved with a silence that matched the room. The big desk still occupied the center.

Natalie switched on her flashlight and shone it on the walls. Every painting was gone. Liz Bathory had packed up her life and moved on. The room smelled of lemon furniture polish. And something else. A hint of -- what was it? Cooked hamburger?

Rose walked the perimeter of the room, her ears pricked and her hand pressing on books and knocking on walls. Watson followed her. He stopped and sniffed the carpet. Rose bent down and used the light from her phone to check. A dark stain had drawn Watson's attention. She touched it with her finger. Damp. Smelled of iron.

"Found something. Blood, I think."

Natalie joined Rose and shone the flashlight on the dark spot on the carpet.

"Oh god, I hope that's not Stella's."

Their eyes met. Rose shook her head.

"Don't go there." She sat back on her heels to think. "Slade Bolton is missing, too. Remember? They found his car but not him."

Watson moved on to something that interested him more. He sat staring at the wall, his head tipped to one side. When they approached, he yipped. Not loud enough for the police out in the main room to hear, but loud enough for Rose. She put her ear to the wall. A faint noise primed her to jump. Watson pawed at the paneling. Then she heard muffled moans.

"There's something here," she said as she knocked on the wood paneling.

"Sounds hollow. Hidden room perhaps?"

Natalie came over and placed her ear on the wall section. "Maybe it's Liz. Someone came in, stole all the paintings, and locked her up."

Rose stood back. "Or Bolton."

This could break the case open.

"I'll be right back."

She returned with Sheriff Johnson.

"Get that dog out," he said in a gruff, authoritative voice.

Rose ignored him. "The sound is behind that wall." She pointed to the spot Watson had sniffed at.

"Watch out for that spot there," she added and indicated the blood stain with the toe of her shoe.

"It's fresh."

Johnson stepped around and, placing his palm on

the panel, leaned in to listen. His brows puckered, then he looked at Rose.

"Well, I'll be." He leaned his head toward the mouthpiece hanging from his shoulder and called for more officers.

"And bring forensics, their evidence on the floor."

Three men arrived carrying a large crowbar.

"There's someone in there," Rose cautioned. The sheriff nodded. "Start with a light tap, see what we're working with."

Everyone stood aside as the men advanced on the wall. They tried to leverage the thin end of the pry bar between sheets of the paneling, but the tip kept skittering off. Finally, the brute force method was all that remained. It took two hits for the hidden door to spring open. Inside the gloom, tied up and gagged, sat a haggard, tear-stained Stella.

Chapter 47 Stella

~

Tannat – a red wine grape, known for its powerful tannins and deep, dark fruit flavors – think black cherries, plums, and even a touch of leather and licorice.

Sunday, October 16, 11:40 PM

Stella groaned. Everything hurt. Her head, especially. She'd kicked the wall with her feet for hours. No one responded. This was where she died. She knew it now.

Her nose was stuffed up from crying, and with the gag in her mouth and the tape holding it in place, breathing was hard. The smell of mildew, piss, and sweat turned her stomach, but weirdly, she liked it because it meant she was alive. As long as she could still smell things, there was hope.

With a loud crash, the door swung open. Light flooded into the tiny space and hurt her eyes, forcing her to squeeze them shut.

"Stella! Oh, thank god!"

She recognized Rose's voice. A wave of relief spread through with such intensity it made her nauseous.

When she could open her eyes, she saw Rose, Natalie, and a room full of police. Tears welled in her eyes. A salty deluge streamed down her cheeks.

Watson jumped into her lap and licked her face.

A sheriff's deputy pulled the rag from her mouth and untied the ropes. Feet and hands prickled as blood surged into numb tissues. She ran a dry tongue over parched lips.

The deputy called to someone in the room, "Get an ambulance." Then he cupped his hand under her elbow. "Let's get you out of this closet."

When she stood, her legs wobbled before giving way. She sank to the ground and passed out.

Chapter 48 Stella

~

Mourvèdre -- a red wine grape variety grown in many regions around the world. It's known for bold, full-bodied flavors of blackberry, plum, and black cherry, spicy notes of black pepper, cinnamon, and clove, and earthy, savory elements like smoked meat, game, and leather.

Monday, Oct 17, 4:30 AM

Stella woke up in a hospital emergency room. Rose sat at her side, holding her hand.

"Where am I?" she asked. Her head felt a bit better. Drip lines descended from hanging bags into her arm. "What's this?"

"Electrolytes. You're severely dehydrated. 48 hours without liquids almost killed you. You're lucky to be alive." Rose's smile sent a tender sentiment through Stella. She leaned against the pillow.

48 hours. It felt like years.

Rose's eyes were red. Had she been crying?

"I was so worried," Rose said. "When we couldn't find you, I…" She shut her eyes, and tears fell from the corners. "When you were taken, well, I almost broke. You're such a brave woman to survive."

There had been moments where surviving didn't seem possible, but one thing kept Stella going. Her quest to find her birth mom.

"I would like it if you were my bio mum. But you never had kids."

Color flushed Rose's cheeks. "A long time ago I, I had a child." She paused, shut her eyes, and rubbed them.

Stella wanted to pounce on Rose's words.

Something told her to wait. Let the truth come out in its own time.

"I was foolish."

"Boy or girl?" Stella asked quietly, hoping for the answer to be an adorable little girl with curls.

Rose sighed, letting out so much air that Stella worried that the older woman might faint.

"I don't know," Rose finally said. "I didn't want to know, and the baby was adopted."

Adopted.

She was an adoptee.

Didn't Rose want to find her child? Or was that just the child, looking for a link to their family history? Not just medical information, but to the connections that defined history. Personal history and world history.

The nurse returned and checked Stella's vitals.

"Considering what you've been through, you're in surprisingly decent shape. Once we get some fluids into you, we can send you home."

Stella wasn't sure she wanted to go to her house. Would she ever feel safe there again?

Rose watched her with such intensity that it made her hold her breath.

"You were telling me about the child."

Rose flushed red on her cheeks.

"I've only told one other person. Natalie, and that was just a few days ago. I've been feeling a connection with you, and I think it I need to tell you about —"

Rose tucked the blanket around Stella's side.

"About the baby. Your eyes, hair, and even the way you laugh, remind me so much of my mother. I lost her a year ago, and at first, I thought I was projecting her onto you, but the more time I spent with you, the more the clues felt real."

Stella hadn't seen the connection with Rose's mother because she didn't know the woman. What she'd seen was in Rose. Her tenacity. Independence.

"Do you ever think about what became of the child?"

Rose's gaze drifted beyond Stella's shoulder to the white board on the wall listing the name of the night nurse and festooned with a smiley face in green marker.

"Every once in a while. But it makes me feel sad, so I try not to dwell on it. Besides, it was a long time ago, thirty-three years."

Stella's head cleared a bit. Had she heard that right? Thirty-three years?

She was thirty-three.

Rose's fingers rubbed the blanket. She startled when the nurse came in and fluffed Stella's pillow.

"Sorry for eavesdropping, but we do have a DNA test available. It wouldn't be covered by insurance, as it is not medically necessary, but we can run it if you want a definitive answer."

Stella gasped and looked at Rose. She wanted an answer, but would it jeopardize their friendship if the answer was no?

Rose smiled a sad smile. "I know how much this means to you, but you might be disappointed. I'd love it if you were my daughter, but prepare yourself. The chances are pretty small."

Stella brushed stray hair out of her eyes. She didn't think the chances were small at all. The ancestry work she'd done told her that she'd find her bio mum in California, and Rose and Stella shared mannerisms.

"I'm willing to take that chance."

She turned to the nurse. "Yes, we'd like to run that test."

Rose patted her arm. "I'll keep my fingers crossed."

The nurse bustled out to get the necessary test kit. She returned, and each woman rubbed a swab around their mouth and inserted the stick into a vial. Slipping the vials into a plastic bag and sealing the opening, the nurse said, "This will take a few days. I'll ask for an expedited analysis. The results will be emailed to you at the address in your record."

"Thank you," Stella said. The nurse refilled her water jug as a woman internist strode into the room. The doctor swiped through pages on a tablet before looking up at Stella and Rose.

"How are you feeling?" Her words were clipped and fast.

Stella sat up straight. "Much better, thank you."

"Your vitals look good, fluid levels are normal, heart rate stable. I think we can let you go this afternoon without admitting you for further observation. However, if you start feeling worse, get to the nearest emergency room."

Rose hugged Stella before she went off to pick up some clean clothes for Stella at home. They had tossed the outfit and underwear she'd worn during her captivity. Stella sat alone in the curtained mini-room and listened to the rapid pace of ER technicians, nurses, and physicians saving people's lives. Like they'd saved hers. She whispered a short prayer that the DNA tests would give her a resolution to her search.

Rose returned with clean underwear, tights, and a large t-shirt. After changing, Stella signed the final paperwork before Rose escorted her to the silver Honda.

"Let's get you home. I thought you could stay with me for a bit."

"Can I use your shower? I must reek, and I want to stand in hot water for an hour."

Rose laughed. "Certainly, and you don't smell as bad as you think. The nurses gave you a sponge bath."

"Glad I was asleep for that."

Rose reached over and hugged Stella.

"You're safe now."

Yes, Stella thought. I am at last safe.

Chapter 49 Stella

~

"There comes a time in every woman's life when the only thing that helps is a glass of champagne." Bette Davis

Monday, October 17, 4:00 PM

Stella finally came down the stairs into the kitchen at close to four o'clock. Rose needed to return the car to the rental place, but wouldn't leave her young friend alone. The pizza steam reached a crescendo as Rose pulled the pie from the oven.

"Hmm. That smells amazing," she said as she perched on a stool by the island.

"How do you feel?" Rose asked. Stupid question, she thought. She probably feels like crap. I know I would.

"I've been better, but then, I've also been worse." She wrapped the borrowed robe tighter around her.

The doorbell rang.

"Do you feel up to celebrating?" Rose asked as she sliced the pizza into wedges.

"I'm sure I look a wreck, but I'd love to see Natalie."

"I've invited Nessa as well," Rose piled napkins and paper plates on a tray.

"Nessa?" She couldn't remember meeting someone by that name.

"The young policewoman."

"Oh, yeah." The doorbell rang again.

"Insistent, aren't they? Eager to see you, I'm sure." Rose picked up the tray and headed for the front door.

"I want to put something on other than a robe." Stella dashed up the stairs.

She'd changed into jeans and a pink sweater that set off her eyes and assessed herself in the mirror. Pale, but who wouldn't after going through what she'd endured? Her wrists had ugly red cuts around them, and one eye bore a purple bruise. Hopefully, they wouldn't notice. She grabbed her computer bag and headed down.

The women gathered on the veranda. The sun dipped behind the mountains, leaving an apricot glow on the remaining clouds.

Rose settled in next to Stella on a couch. With a slice of steaming veggie deluxe slice in her hand and a glass of Malbec in the other, Stella raised a toast. "From the bottom of my heart, thank you for finding me. I couldn't ask for better friends. When I was stuck in that boot, I, well, I thought if I survived, I'd go home. But I don't have friends there like you guys."

And," she went on, "I promise to listen to your advice about men."

"Hear, hear!" Natalie cheered.

Rose nudged a tall glass of water toward Stella. "More of that than the wine," she said. "You're still dehydrated."

"Yes, Mother," Stella said with an eye roll and sarcastic overtone. Soon she would know if Rose was her mother, and she found herself wishing it were true. She set her wine goblet down and dutifully drank some water. Then she settled into her chair.

"Seriously, I had a lot of time to think. Just before my evil boyfriend chloroformed me, I got an email from Evangeline. I got the bookkeeping job after all."

Another round of clinking glasses.

"Thank you, thank you. Anyway, she sent links into her payroll software, which, if it's anything like other systems, might have a back door into hidden parts of the computer hierarchy. And I happen to be a bit of a hacker. All legal, but still…"

"You were able to find the raw security footage?" Natalie asked, a new note of hope in her voice.

Stella nodded. "Bingo."

"I take it that isn't common knowledge at the gallery, that there are two places the video is stored?" Nessa asked Natalie.

"I didn't know about it, and I doubt Evangeline has a clue," Natalie replied.

Nessa closed her eyes and sighed.

"The forensics guys didn't say a word about this. I'll be recommending some new training classes for them."

Stella pulled her laptop out of the soft carry bag and switched it on. While it went through its start-up sequence, Rose cleared away the pizza platter and dirty napkins.

The computer played a little jingle that signaled it was ready. Stella opened the email and clicked on the link. Once that screen opened, she went back to her email and opened another.

"This isn't a tight security protocol, Natalie, but we'll work on that later," Stella said

Everyone leaned in close to the screen.

Stella's fingers typed so fast it was hard to follow

what she was doing at first. Using her new access as their bookkeeper, she navigated through the software, which took them from the payroll screens to a general menu, and then into the security system.

Rose didn't see anything that looked like backups, until Stella pressed on a folder icon that was labeled Utilities. Inside that folder was another one labeled with a series of numbers, which turned out to include the year, month, and day, along with a unique identification code. And there it was, hidden in plain sight: backups of the raw footage, labeled with the date.

"The new cameras must automatically upload the video here," Natalie said. They opened the folder with Friday night's Gala. Multiple views of the gallery appeared on the screen. One covered the front door and another the central aisle.

"I never knew this was here," Natalie said. Rose could tell the admission cost her proud friend.

"The camera in the main lobby is highest-resolution. Check that first."

The last camera captured the security computer room. Stella moved the cursor to the menu selection for the main room and pushed play. She set the speed to one-and-a-half real-time.

Liz Bathory stood looking at the painting. Then Slade showed up. Liz's head turned toward him slightly. She took a micro-step toward him, then stopped. Moments later, Liz left. Slade turned to Stella, and his lips moved.

"He's saying we should get a drink at the cocktail lounge down the street," Stella explained.

Then Bolton bumped into Natalie's shoulder, and her handbag tumbled to the ground. He bent to help her pick up all the things that fell out. A lipstick, keys, a package of tissues, and her security access card.

Everything went into the bag except—Natalie gasped.

Nessa leaned forward. "Did he slip the card up his sleeve?" The key card disappeared like a magician's trick

"That would explain why you couldn't find your keycard, Natalie. He staged the accident to steal it," Rose said.

"And that's how he got in," Natalie said.

It took another glass of wine and about an hour of watching to get to the end of the Gala. At last, the cleaning people finished and left. The box of empty wine bottles sat in the corner. Brad circled the gallery, checking into every room. When he finished his circuit, he went to the temporary guard station erected for the event. A figure entered from the back. The timestamp read 1:00 am.

"Enter Evangeline, stage left," Natalie said. The diminutive owner approached Brad, and an animated discussion occurred. It would be nice if the tape had audio.

Rose explained what they saw.

"She's trying to convince him to continue with the affair. She'd already come clean to her husband, Carlos, but maybe she figured that now he wouldn't be suspicious of her long hours at the gallery. She doesn't know Brad told his wife about it too and committed to leaving if Evangeline didn't put him on the day shift."

On the tape, Evangeline turned and stomped out. Brad Knight was alive.

He conducted another circuit and checked the front doors by tugging on the chain wrapped around the push bars.

At 3:06 AM, Slade Bolton entered. He wore dark pants and a dark jacket.

Brad approached, and a conversation with hands waving ensued. A second thief clad in black clothes came through the security door.

Rose asked, "Who's that?"

The second thief turned away from the camera. Long dark hair flowed out from under a balaclava.

"Could that be Liz?" Natalie asked.

Rose studied the figure. Slight. Tall. Most likely a woman, based on the body-hugging jumpsuit. Could that be the heiress? The video quality in this part of the gallery wasn't good enough to see much, just the balaclava covering the person's entire face and a pair of boots.

"Those are Dior boots. Oh, how I want a pair of those. Too pricy though," Stella moaned.

Why would an art thief have expensive boots, unless they lived a luxury life, like Liz Bathory certainly did.

Bolton walked over to the box of empty wine bottles, picked one up, and held it in his hand as if evaluating the weight. He picked up another one and started toward Brad. All four women leaned toward the computer.

"Oh, no," Natalie said. Slade raised his arm and swung the bottle at Brad's head, connecting at the temple. Even without the sound, Rose imagined she could hear the dull thud as glass met bone. Brad's head snapped to the opposite side, and his legs collapsed. When his big frame hit the ground, his head bounced on the concrete floor. Blood started to seep. He'd be unconscious, if not dead.

The thief, who could be Liz, handed Slade a handkerchief. He held the bottle by the neck and wiped it down, then slid it into his pocket.

Later, when he discarded it in Rose's recycling bin, trying to frame her, no doubt, he redeposited his fingerprints on the weapon. Was it enough to convict him?

The figures moved into the Met gallery. Both thieves approached *Gray Day, Montrose Valley*, lifted it off the hanger, and lowered it to the floor. They spoke; then Bolton picked it up and headed for the back door. The second thief pulled a small handgun out, aimed at Brad, and shot.

"He might have been alive!" Stella cried. "Why shoot him?"

Rose was convinced now the thief was a 'she.' And the only woman who met that description was Liz Bathory.

Was Knight dead when she shot? Or did Bolton kill him? What did the coroner's report say? Blast, she couldn't remember. The way his head bounced off the floor meant he was probably dead then, but he was for sure dead after the bullet.

Rose patted Stella's hand.

The thief went into the security room, which had a camera discreetly hidden in the ceiling tiles. With quick movements, they typed commands, and the security displays flickered off. She pulled a thumb drive from a pocket and plugged it into a port on the computer. A few more keystrokes and the cameras resumed their function, though the screens all showed empty spaces.

"I've seen that done in movies," Natalie said.

Stella said she had too. It was a trope used in many films.

"They had a loop to insert, so their actions weren't there. Too bad she made a mistake, several, actually. One was allowing us to see Evangeline enter, but not leave. The second was not knowing that she only affected the connection between the camera and the security monitors. Not the live stream to the cloud."

Rose sipped her Malbec and then set the glass down. She faced Nessa.

"Given that Bolton took Stella to Liz's house, I think the assumption that the second person on the video is Liz is right. And," she paused, closed her eyes, and took a deep breath. "It then stands to reason that Liz killed Slade, for some reason we may never know. Does that make sense to you?"

Nessa seemed reluctant to answer. At last, she said, "Speaking for myself, and not the department, yes, it does."

"And if Liz killed Slade, then she probably intended to kill me too," Stella added.

"You were all but dead already," Natalie said. "If we hadn't found you, dehydration would have killed you in a day or two."

Tears welled in Stella's eyes.

"Natalie!" Rose admonished. "Was that necessary?"

Natalie dropped her chin to her chest.

"I'm sorry, Stella. But it's the truth."

Rose put her arm around Stella's shoulders.

"Don't dwell on that, it will mess with your mind. You're alive and safe. We don't know if Bolton is dead for sure."

Stella wiped the tears that spilled down. "Don't forget, Liz also shot Brad. What happens next?"

Nessa pulled her phone out and dialed.

"Sir, I've seen evidence that Liz Bathory and Slade Bolton stole the painting and killed Brad Knight."

She listened while the sergeant spoke and said, "Understood, sir."

The three women looked at her with expectation. She clicked off the phone and placed it on the coffee table.

"I need to go. Under no circumstances are you to leave this house. Understood Rose? "

"Where are you going?" Rose asked.

Nessa stood up and smoothed down her dark blue policewoman shirt.

"Chief says we have an MOU with the FBI, and Paso Robles PD will take the lead. They also have a BOLO out for a woman meeting her description. It mentions that she owns a boat docked in San Francisco."

"What's an MOU?" Natalie asked.

Nessa looked annoyed at the interruption.

"Memorandum of Understanding. It's the official way we work together."

She glanced around as if looking for something she'd set down and lost.

"I'm due out at the Bathory villa. I mean it, Rose. Stay here." With that, she strode down the steps and drove away.

Rose paced the veranda. The three women watched in silence, mulling over what they'd learned. The FBI expected Liz to flee to San Francisco, but she wouldn't leave the art behind. It was too much a part of her. So, what would she do with twenty or so paintings?

Think, Rose, think. Patience was one of those traits labeled a virtue. Give things time to develop, she told herself. Liz Bathory was on the run. Slade Bolton was probably dead. Logic dictated that the FBI would catch the heiress and retrieve the stolen art. It's what they are good at.

When she stopped and looked at her friends, she found three sets of eyes watching her. Two women and a dog. Should they eat pizza, drink wine, and hash things over again?

Patience be damned. Liz had fooled them all for too long. It was time to get the upper hand.

Rose smiled at her audience, feeling confident for the first time in weeks.

"Let's see if we can help."

Chapter 50 Rose

~

Sparkling wine – a wine with significant levels of carbon dioxide, making it fizzy.

Monday, October 17, 8:00 PM

Details like curves, trees, and traffic signs flew by. Rose drove her car without regard to the speed limit, eager to get to the villa. If they got there fast enough, there was a chance she could catch Liz Bathory in the act of what she wasn't exactly sure.

Natalie gripped the door handle. Stella waited at Rose's house with Watson, having been deemed too fragile and worn out by her ordeal to ride along.

"In the three months I've known you," Natalie said. "I've been arrested, trapped in an abandoned building, and subjected myself to your dangerous driving. I'm not sure knowing you is good for my health."

Rose realized that for the first time since the drive-along with Nessa, she wasn't bored. The search for Stella, her efforts to clear Natalie, all of it had excited her.

A Hunter Moon shone brightly over the vineyards and big-budget houses on the west side of Paso Robles. The legends around this October full moon foretold of successful hunts. She hoped that it would hold true today.

The clock showed 8:30 pm. Few lights sprinkled the landscape.

The exception was the mansion itself.

It appeared that every light in the house was on. Police vehicles littered the long drive up to the building. After Watson detected Stella in the walls, Rose had no doubts that they were taking the house apart.

"Is that where we're going?" Natalie asked.

Rose shook her head, though Natalie wouldn't be able to see that inside the car with tempestuous clouds overhead that shielded the moon completely. "I don't think there is anything to be learned from Liz's house. We need to figure out where she took the paintings. It had to be somewhere close, and I think I know where."

The road bent to the right as they passed by the glowing villa, and a tunnel of vegetation enshrouded them. Would they get there in time? Should she have taken another route? Maybe the highway would have been faster, though, when they headed out, the whole plan hadn't come to fruition. Focus, she told herself. Keep your wits in check. Her cell phone rang. Before she could say anything, Natalie pushed the accept call button.

"Rose? This is Frank. I've been worried about you. You're not doing anything foolish are you?" His voice was hard to hear over the road noise.

"Not now, Frank. I'm a bit busy. I'll call you later." She disconnected the call. She didn't owe him any explanations. At least not yet. They weren't serious. At least she wasn't. it wasn't fair, she knew, to blame Frank for the entire male sex, but that didn't stop her from doing just that. It was a man who brought her career to an abrupt halt. She didn't want a man to ruin her retirement. Best to keep him at arm's length for now.

She could sort out what to do next when she wasn't driving on a twisty road in the rain.

"I can't focus on anything else right now, foolish or not," she said and eased the car forward into a straighter part. Natalie released her hold on the door handle.

"Looking back," she said. "Liz planned to move things. Remember those crates? I wish I had said something at the time."

The crates had been nagging Rose ever since they'd seen them. Could all those paintings fit in the few she'd seen?

"Could she have packed everything up that fast?" Rose asked.

Natalie shifted in her seat. "She'd need help. To properly conserve them and safeguard transportation, they would need to crate and seal them. We saw them at 11:30 Sunday morning, and they were gone by the time we found Stella."

Twelve hours. What had there been? Twenty paintings? It seemed reasonable to Rose that all the artwork could be boxed up and ready to go in that amount of time. But was it enough to leave the area? Especially given that the heiress had called to report the original of Gray Day had been returned. It was like she was taunting them. Pretty gutsy to challenge law enforcement like that.

She entered the traffic circle at the intersection with Highway 46 and took the first exit down Vineyard Drive as it wound through more vineyards, orchards, and palatial estates. As the miles rolled under the car, she became more convinced she knew where Liz and the paintings were.

"Now will you tell me where we're going?" Natalie asked. "Oh, wait—isn't this the back way to—, wait, weren't we just there. It doesn't seem like a place to take precious art. Why would you think that's where she is?"

It had been right in front of them the whole time. Rose braked to negotiate a sharp turn. "Last week I was volunteering with the Olive Growers at the Craft Market. Nessa stopped at my table, and we talked. The growers are concerned about an orchard that has been abandoned. She said she'd heard about it and called it the old Bathory place. My guess is the shed Bolton took Stella to wasn't a random selection. He knew about it. Knew no one would come looking."

She drove around a horseshoe bend and entered a stretch of road where the trees arched over to create a tunnel. When they came to the desolate drive to the shed, she slowed and turned onto the gravel, switching off her headlights. The car crept along until the building came into view. The crunch of gravel and dirt under the tires sounded as loud as a cannon.

A white panel truck sat where Rose had parked before. The forklift remained where they'd left it. Two other dark sedans were side by side near the trees. Rose stopped the car, shifting into neutral to shut off the taillights, and rolled down the windows. With luck, no one would notice them.

Two stocky men argued in Spanish as they climbed onto the machine and tried to start it. The motor wouldn't even turn over, having exhausted its last bit of life busting through the door so Rose and Natalie could escape.

Another person carried a flat box with two hands underneath it as if presenting a tray of canapés, and handed it to someone in the panel truck. They were loading the art crates for transportation. Liz had everything organized. This wasn't a quick flight to escape.

"Should we call the police?" Natalie whispered.

When Rose picked up her phone, the screen glowed brightly. She held it to her chest to shield the light. Her hands shook. She tightened her grip to steady them.

"We need proof. We need to see Liz," Rose whispered.

"We'll never see her in this dark."

One of the men went into the building and returned with a long wrench that glinted in a shaft of moonlight. He lifted the cowling and banged on the engine. They tried to start it again. Rose thought for a moment they might be successful, but the thing coughed and went silent. They hadn't noticed Rose's car parked in the shadows. At least Rose hoped they hadn't.

A taller, thinner figure emerged from the storage space, pushing a furniture dolly carrying a large crate. Someone from the truck hopped down to collect the cargo. The guys on the forklift gave up and climbed down. A big, burly guy kicked the tire, and his face turned toward Rose and Natalie.

"Hide." They slid down in their seats. Rose's heart felt like it jumped around inside her. She inched up enough to see out the side window. This new person acted like they were in charge. The men jumped off the folk lift and trotted over to—by now Rose was convinced it was—a woman.

"Hurry up!" The voice was strong and arrogant. And female.

"That's her!" Natalie said in a hoarse whisper. "That's Liz. I know it."

Rose dialed. Nessa answered on the first ring.

"Rose?" Her voice held accusation. Rose would apologize later.

"Liz is at the shed on San Anselmo Road." She

spoke as softly as possible, hoping the policewoman could hear her.

"How do you ---?

The tire kicker took a step towards them.

"Hey!" he called out.

"They see us," Natalie said. "We've got—Rose, we need to go—now."

Rose looked over and saw a man heading towards them. He raised his arm. Work lights glinted off the barrel of a gun. In the glare, Rose saw that his head was covered in the same tattoos as the Fresno gang member she'd seen on the internet.

"Duck!" Rose cried, and they both slid down. A bullet smacked through the windshield, spidering the glass and leaving a hole, grazed Rose's head, and hit the rear window.

"Oww!" she said and held her head on a gash above her right ear. Warm, sticky blood coated her fingers. That can't be good. The rear window now had an exit hole, as well as a mosaic of cracks. The roar of a transmission under stress came closer and pulled up beside them on the passenger side. Rose tried to get ahead of them, but her trustworthy sedan wasn't a speed demon. The accelerator pedal was already to the floor. Then Natalie screamed. The gang members had gotten alongside them and one had grabbed Natalie's arm. She was halfway out the window, squirming to free herself, when Rose slammed the gears into reverse and stomped on the accelerator. The car jerked back. The sudden movement caused the man to loosen his hold on Natalie's arm, and she yanked it free.

Crouched down low, Rose could barely see over the steering wheel. Not that seeing helped much with the glittering window. Hopefully, they wouldn't hit a tree. She felt the tires reach the solid road and spun the steering wheel tight to spin the car around. She'd seen it in a movie. Damn if it didn't work. They drove off into the darkness as fast as the curves allowed. Blood rushed through the arteries in her ears and throbbed where the bullet creased the skin. She could barely hear Nessa's voice shouting from the phone's speaker.

"Was that a gunshot?"

"They're shooting at us!" Natalie yelled. "We were at the shed. Liz is there with the paintings. I think they hit Rose."

The glow of headlights in the rear-view window lit the car's insides. Rose could feel her heart banging away in her chest. "Damn, they're behind us." All thought of the bullet wound vanished. She pushed the accelerator further down, and the car surged forward. The dark vehicle behind them continued to gain.

"Where do we go?" Natalie asked as she gripped the door handle.

Rose counted on testosterone and ego to drive the men in the car behind her. She wanted them to follow her and was banking on their blind allegiance to Liz to draw them into a trap.

"Nessa? You still there?" she called out.

Natalie fumbled with the phone and finally pushed the speaker button.

"What's happening?" Nessa yelled.

Rose reached the traffic circle. Installed to stop the succession of fatal accidents at the intersection, it required drivers to slow down almost to a stop.

She didn't have that luxury.

Her tires squealed as she braked, turned, and accelerated around the curve. She leaned out the driver's side window to see the road better. Fortunately, the hour was late, and tourists were sleeping off the day's wine-tasting adventures.

When she reached the other side, she straightened out and stomped on the accelerator. The car sped up and clipped a shrub on the side of the road. It was hard to navigate when the front window was an abstract design with a prism of geometric shapes. Rose adjusted their trajectory and felt the paved road under their tires once again. If she kept the left side of the road in view, they wouldn't hit anything else. She calmed down a bit. "Men are chasing us. We're bringing them to the villa."

"Is she with them?" Nessa asked.

"Damn!" Rose swore as she scraped a tree that grew close to the road. Her method wasn't working.

Natalie's knuckles were white. "We don't think so."

"Shit," was all Nessa said.

"She's at the shed," Rose said before the line went dead. Mountains play havoc with cell coverage along the road.

The villa appeared on the right. The bad guys came up behind her as she turned up the villa's driveway. Did they not see where she'd led them? Idiots.

She drove through the phalanx of police cars along the drive, but the vehicle carrying the gunman found itself surrounded and stopped.

When she reached the turnaround where Liz had stood holding a shotgun, Rose parked.

They exited the car in time to see their pursuers

crawl out with their hands in the air, then turn and place them on the car hoods for frisking. After cuffing the men, one policeman shone a flashlight in the face of the man with the skull cap of tattoos. Two dark permanent teardrops fell from his right eye.

Had they released the burglar from her ride-along? Or were more of the gang members that Brad took down here in Paso Robles? Maybe that was why Brad had to die. He would recognize the gang markings and go to the police.

Rose took a deep breath of relief. Her innards felt wobbly. She had never been so scared, but strangely, she'd never had so much fun.

"I don't see a woman," Natalie said.

"If she's not at the shed, she's on her way to San Francisco," Rose said.

The two men were pushed into the cage of separate police cars.

A police cruiser pulled into the driveway, lights flashing. The cars wound up the long drive and parked next to Rose's battered Honda.

Hernandez and Nessa got out. In the back seat, hard to see at night with the darkened windows, sat Liz Bathory. Nessa spoke with the FBI agent in charge and, after conferring with him and the Sheriff, handed Liz over for booking.

Rose and Natalie sat in the car watching. As a cruiser containing the woman who had caused so much death drove away, Rose picked up her phone and dialed Stella.

"It's over. They caught her."

Stella's cheers rang over the phone until Rose cut off the call.

"I guess we can go now," she said.

"Looks like the excitement is over."

The door squeaked a loud objection as Natalie opened it and slid out. "I'd rather not drive home in your car. Look at it. You were driving blind."

She's right. The car needed a new windscreen and back window.

Nessa walked over and gaped at the car. "You drove that?"

"Drove is a generous word," Natalie said. "We flew like crazy people with those creeps chasing us. They shot the windows!"

"Yeah. Well...obviously we'll need a ride home," Rose said.

Officer Nessa Gomez dropped Rose and Natalie off and drove to the police station. There was a chance they would let her sit in on the Liz Bathory interview. Chief Donneley stopped by her cubicle carrying a grocery bag, while Nessa was typing up her action report.

"You've earned a seat in the interview room. Be ready in ten minutes."

"Yes, ma'am." It took all her self-control not to giggle.

"Gomez?"

Nessa looked up to see the Chief eyeing her.

"How much did that old lady help?" Old lady? Did she mean Rose?

"Rose isn't old, ma'am. She's got enough energy for two of me. She phoned in some information that proved to be useful. And it was Rose, and that dog of hers, that found the hidden cubbyhole in the wall. I think she saved Stella Richards' life. So yes, she helped."

The chief studied her for a long minute.

"Well, despite all that, all we have is a circumstantial case against Liz unless she confesses. The video is inconclusive, but she doesn't know that. If she were the one who altered the record, she wouldn't expect us to even have it. We'll stop the video at the point where you can see her head but not her feet. Then we'll show her these."

She pulled a pair of black knee-high boots and dangled them for Nessa to admire. The supple calfskin glowed in the overhead lights like moonlight on a dark lake.

"I think we can rattle her into confessing," the chief said.

"Are those hers?" Nessa asked, pointing to the Dior boots, knowing that using a fake article often worked to overcome resistance in a witness or suspect.

"Found them in her closet. Guess she forgot to pack them when deciding what to wear while fleeing the country."

The plan was simple, detective 101. Set a trap, lock her into a statement, and then watch her try to squirm her way out.

Nessa finished her report and drank half a bottle of water before stepping over to the coffee machine and pouring a cup into a paper cup. Liz Bathory would want a stimulant. Whether Nessa would give it to her or not depended on how the interview went. As she waited for the booking to finish and the interrogation to begin, she thought about Rose. Was she an old woman? Nessa would never say so. Rose MacGillivray was a force to be harnessed.

Chapter 51 Liz

~

"The peoples of the Mediterranean began to emerge from barbarism when they learned to cultivate the olive and the vine." Thucydides

Tuesday, October 18, 4:00 A.M.

Liz Bathory rattled the handcuffs secured to restraint rings welded to the center of the interrogation table. This was all his fault. Bolton must have double-crossed her.

Overhead lights made her complexion look sallow, especially where the skin was bruised from the cuffs. A TV sat on a tall stand in the corner with equipment boxes on the lower shelves.

She didn't belong here.

If the cops knew the truth about *Gray Day*, they would understand. It was hers. And it wasn't what it appeared. She'd learned that years ago when she'd discovered her grandfather's diary while going through a box of her mother's belongings that had been hidden in the family mansion. Her father didn't know about it because if he did, he wouldn't have given *Gray Day Montrose Valley* away so easily.

Had Slade figured it out? He knew about the diary.

The door opened, and an older Black woman and a young Hispanic policewoman entered. The older woman carried a paper bag. The younger cop carried a gray folder and a steaming cup of coffee. Liz's stomach gurgled. It was late, and she hadn't eaten.

She should be aboard her yacht and out in international waters. Eating something Chef Susan would have ready for her.

The younger woman set a voice recorder on the table and pressed the on button. Both women sat down opposite Liz. The older woman spoke first.

"Ms. Bathory. I'm Police Chief Donnelly, and this is Sergeant Gomez."

The younger woman nodded her head, which Liz took as a greeting.

Liz considered them. Local cops. It should be easy to fool them.

"Where's the FBI?" she asked.

The police chief nodded slightly. "They'll be here shortly. You were read your Miranda rights by the arresting officers. Is there anything you don't understand?"

Liz had memorized the standard reading of the rights. As a precaution. Not for one second did she believe she'd get caught.

And if she did, her father's name protected her.

"No questions," she replied.

"You noted the words, then, that you have the right to an attorney? Yet, I don't see an attorney present." The chief lifted her eyebrows, causing parallel creases to line up across her forehead.

"They are on their way. We may commence, though, I've done nothing wrong."

The chief pressed on. "You agree to this interview without legal representation?"

"As you well know, my last name is Bathory. Lawyers clean up after us. They don't advise us in advance."

The chief looked over at Gomez and shrugged her

shoulders. When she turned back to face Liz, her eyes were hard.

"We will proceed then. Noting for the record that the suspect has declined to have an attorney present."

Gomez opened the file and removed two photographs. She slid one across the table until it sat in the middle. A full-color photo of *Gray Day, Montrose Valley*.

"Tell us about this painting," the police chief said.

Tears stung Liz's eyes. Damn. If she closed her eyes, she could almost see the image under the painting. The Renoir. Just as her grandfather's diary said there would be. Of course, she had the painting evaluated by that ex-con art dealer, and once she verified the truth, she killed him. That secret she would take to her grave.

"What is this?" she asked.

"You tell us," Gomez said.

The policewoman's tone let Liz know she took this personally. Could she use that in her defense? She felt more in control now. What evidence could they have? The security system had been hacked the night of the theft. She'd worn a balaclava to hide her face. She'd pin the whole thing on Bolton; they had nothing on her. She'd play their game. And she'd win.

"Well, let's see. The artist was a woman, Nell Walker Warner, not overly famous but known in her time."

Gomez pushed the photo more toward Liz. "We already know that. Tell us something I couldn't find in an internet search."

Liz reached out with a finger and touched the photo. She needed a convincing lie. One that she could pull off because she grew up believing in it herself. Though growing up she hadn't known about the painting's hidden secret.

Even today, she didn't know which Renoir lay beneath the dour landscape.

"My mother... she bought it from the artist...at a showing sometime in the late forties. They became fast friends, and this was, without a doubt, her favorite work of art." This was the story her mother had told her and she'd believed it wholeheartedly, until she read her grandfather's diary. Had her mother known? Had Grandfather Grossman gone so far as to have the artist "sell" the painting to her mom without knowing it was stolen?

The tears were threatening again. She. Would. Not. Cry.

"She promised it to me. Grandpa promised it to me."

Gomez nodded as if she suspected as much and just wanted to hear it.

"Yet, your father gave it to the New York Metropolitan Museum."

Liz looked up and slapped the table with her bound hands. The sound echoed off the concrete walls.

"That bastard! That painting is mine. He gave it away without permission, and I have every right to get it back, by any means necessary."

That outburst would cost her. She sat back and calmed herself. Slade would know how to finesse this. What would he say? He'd notice that the younger officer's eyes held a glint of understanding. Maybe she could leverage that. But how?

Gomez slowly spun the coffee cup. "Any means necessary? Stealing and killing? Both of which are illegal." The thread of hope Liz held frayed a bit.

The Chief nodded, and Gomez pushed the second

photo toward Liz. The gallery guard's body lay where it fell. The pool of blood had turned dark by the time the photographer snapped the picture.

Liz nudged it over to them. "You can't tie me to that."

The chief stood and walked over to a TV monitor, placing a CD into a slot. Black and white images appeared on the screen. Grainy but clear enough to see Slade and Knight. Enough to see Bolton's face. He'd been a fool not to cover his head with something. His mouth moved. Knight's hand moved toward his flashlight. A flashlight! Another idiot.

That was supposed to be erased. She'd done it herself. Where did this tape come from? Reality dawned on her slowly. Backups. Most computer systems had backups, and they hadn't had the time, nor frankly, the know-how, to delete those as well.

On the TV, she watched herself enter. The police couldn't know it was her. Chief Donneley froze the video when her covered face filled the frame.

"This is you," Nessa said.

"You can't prove that," Liz spat back. Maybe she should wait for the attorney to arrive.

The young police officer stared at Liz without blinking. The metal chair felt hard and cold, and the handcuffs cut into her wrists. No one said anything. Then, with slow, deliberate movements, the chief walked towards her and pulled a bag out from the table. Liz could see that Gomez was trying to hide a knowing smile. The chief pulled out a pair of boots. Her boots. And set them on the table.

She should have burned them. A thought that would have been better had a few days ago, rather than now, when they could use them to prove she was there. Her head lowered to her chin, and she took measured breaths. What was her best play here?

The chief resumed the video, and they all watched Bolton hit the guard with a bottle, and the big man crumpled to the floor.

Seeing it again, she realized the blow probably killed the man. Slade got so angry with her for the shot, but she didn't believe in leaving loose ends.

Gomez cleared her throat. "As you can see, we do have evidence. We know Bolton was involved because we have DNA on the bottle used to hit Knight."

On the screen, the two figures entered the gallery where Gray Day, Montrose Valley hung.

"And visual evidence that you and he were in the gallery during the time of death," she continued.

One of the figures turned and revealed a ponytail. That wasn't definitive. Nor were the boots. She'd get a lawyer to create doubt about that easily enough. "You can't prove that's me."

"Lastly," Gomez said as if Liz hadn't spoken at all, "we have the evidence of Stella Richardson, kidnapped by Slade Bolton and hidden in a wall of your villa. It's pretty damning when you add it all up."

That stupid female distraction! All sweetness and charm, Liz had realized the Brit would be a problem, but hadn't figured out how to solve it when Bolton turned up with the unconscious woman over his shoulder.

The chief turned off the television and returned to her seat. Liz stared at her hands, clasped on the table. A painter's hands. Delicate and yet strong.

But not strong enough to bend the metal ring or

the handcuffs to free herself. She needed another strategy. Deflection. Her father had taught her that when backed into a corner, make it someone else's fault. Say it enough, and people will believe it's true. She'd already handled Bolton to her satisfaction; time to throw shade at the guard.

"You make it sound as if Brad Knight was innocent," she said.

"Go on." Gomez waved her hand in a circular motion to indicate that Liz should keep talking. The younger woman glanced at the police chief as if looking for a slap back, but received none. Liz remembered being young and nervous about stepping out from under her father's shadow. The bastard never understood her need to be independent.

Gomez sipped her coffee. Liz stared at the cup. She needed a caffeine hit more than any drug. Is there good coffee in prison? She sighed. None of this was going according to plan. *Think!* she admonished herself. *You're smarter than this.*

"He knew Slade," she finally said. "He'd been a cop in Fresno when we pulled a small job."

"Please describe that job," The chief asked.

"It's so simple I'm surprised none of your kind ever figured it out. The FBI certainly didn't. We'd case a museum, select the most expensive painting, the easiest to fence, and I'd paint the forgery." Liz stopped, a rush of panic running through her.

Had she just confessed? She's said 'we'. What an idiot she was! She closed her eyes and tried to rein in her emotions, but to use a phrase her father liked, that horse had left the barn. And with that thought, she knew she'd have to live with prison coffee for a long time.

"We'd break in and substitute the painting, then

vanish. Knight caught us in the switch, took our money, and kept his mouth shut. Otherwise, he'd have been dead a long time ago."

"But not this time," Gomez said.

Should she feel guilty? No. That guard brought it on himself. "Slade thought it would be enough to knock him out. Knight said he'd started over and was clean. Idiot. He was a loose end."

"So, Bolton knocked him on the head with the wine bottle, and you shot him." The policewoman's voice was flat and factual.

"Brad Knight was a threat. So yes, I shot him. We had a sweet scheme going. The galleries never knew they had a forgery, and we sold the real thing on the black market."

The scheme worked for over five years, but their luck was thinning. It was time for her to vanish. Take everything and disappear somewhere in the world. Somewhere she hadn't even figured out, thinking that would make it more difficult for anyone to find her. But first, she needed to get the Renoir back.

"Why didn't you replace *Gray Day Montrose Valley* with a forgery at the time of the theft? Like maybe the one we found in Natalie Patel's garage after an anonymous tip, or the one you kindly left for us to find at your villa," Gomez asked.

Liz stared at the two interrogators for a long ten seconds. Why indeed? Bolton had lobbied for that approach; they had even gone to the trouble of creating the fake. She had vetoed the idea.

She wanted her final theft to be an announcement to the world of how she'd tricked them all these years. Museums and galleries, all over the world, would need to examine their stock to see if any were forged. If she didn't leave a blank hole on the wall, no one would know.

The key had been finding someone like Slade Bolton. She needed a mole in the FBI Art Crime division to provide intel and cover. Someone with the right credentials and a flexible moral code. It was easy to convince him she loved him. Maybe she had. Once hooked, he proved a real talent for deceit. Until he wanted out. Was he so naive to think she'd let him walk out and go on with his life?

"But you didn't plan to sell *Gray Day*. Did you?" Gomez asked.

Liz took a deep breath, feeling the adrenaline ebb in her muscles.

"Once I had her in my possession, the fire left me." It was true. Not the whole truth, but enough of one to get by. Maybe even lessen her sentence.

Gomez made notes on a sheet of paper in the file. The Police Chief sat back, arms crossed against her chest. This was Gomez's show. The young officer would gain rank with this case.

"What happens next?" Liz asked.

"I have one final question," Gomez said as she closed her folder and set down the pen. "Why did you call us and report the painting found? I'm assuming it was another forgery."

Yes, thought Liz, that had been her last mistake. Possibly the biggest.

"My mother loved that painting. More than me, I think, and certainly more than my father. I wanted the world to be able to see it."

The steel door opened, and a blue-suited man with

salt and pepper hair stepped in. Liz recognized the standard FBI uniform.

Chief Donnelly stood. "Special Agent Gordon, she's all yours. We'll file murder charges and send a copy to you. You can add it to your complaint. I'll also send you a copy of the audio and video."

The suited FBI man stuck his hand out to the chief, and they shook.

"No problem. Excellent job getting the confession out of her. Felony art theft, forgery, and murder will put her away for an exceedingly long time."

"Oh, and..." the FBI man said as Donnelley and Gomez moved to leave. "We brought a portable X-ray machine up from the Getty. Turns out that *Gray Day* was painted over a long-lost Renoir. Worth tens of millions. Possibly stolen during World War II."

Liz's head, which dropped down to her chest, whipped up. They knew. In the end, her father won. She'd never get her grandfather's bequest. Damn him. Tears stung her eyes, but she wasn't about to let them know how much it hurt.

Nessa would remember the look on the heiress's face for the rest of her life. Defeat and yet, defiance. She'd get good lawyers, would throw money at the problem, and get herself off somehow. For now, though, the satisfaction of catching Brad Knight's murderer felt good. Even better than knowing the insignificant painting this whole murder had been about was hiding a Renoir. It helped settle the motive question, which had bugged Nessa from the beginning.

Though the department would never admit it, the credit went to Rose. Nessa could never tell the chief just how much she'd come to trust her. Though she suspected the chief knew. It was Rose's insistence on Natalie's innocence that pushed Nessa to test the painting found in the garage. And Rose's dogged determination to find Stella uncovered the shed and the hole-in-the-wall hiding place where Bolton and Bathory had stuck Stella.

Maybe this would lead to a promotion. Who knows. Maybe her dream of being Chief someday wasn't so crazy after all.

Chapter 52 Gloria

~

"For we are like olives: only when we are crushed do we yield what is best in us," by Bohumil Hrabal

Thursday, October 20, 12:30 PM

Local news channels ran the story of Liz Bathory's capture repeatedly. It was the biggest thing to hit the news desk in years, and all the national news shows wanted to cover it. To Gloria Knight, it was the end of a nightmare. Yes, her husband was dead, and she still had no idea if she needed to move, but at least she didn't have to worry whether those goons from Fresno were going to show up at her house.

She had no one to care for. Her life was her own. The thought both terrified and exhilarated her. Brad had proposed to her the day after her high school graduation. He had finished the police academy and two years of service. She went from living at home with her parents to living in a small walk-up apartment with Brad. Heaven. They shopped for their modest home and bought rugs and pillows. Curtains and a bedspread. It was the real version of playing house. Brad had a decent job, and they were off and running as a couple. So what if it meant she had to give up on college? Art? Her own identity. Oh, yes, all the magazines she read while he was at work said she could have her own life and still be a good wife, but she never managed to see how it could be so. The apartment was too small for her paints and canvases, so they went into the closet. Then, eventually, into the trash, as the paints hardened and the boots and brooms damaged the canvases.

The clock in the hall chimed nine. Had she really slept that long? She rolled over. Why get up?

Car doors shut and engines rumbled down the street. Then panic struck. Her heart raced; her palms felt clammy. She couldn't pay the mortgage beyond the upcoming installment. Her life revolved around Brad. Had revolved. Without that anchor, there was no reason to get up. Put clothes on. So, she didn't.

Hunger pangs got her out of bed at noon. She ate a slice of toast and stared out the window. How many times had she done this? Looked at nothing and wondered if someone from Brad's history had caught up with him. He wasn't a dirty cop, at least not according to him, but there were rumors that reached her ears. Wives of other officers talked at potlucks. When she asked him about it, he blew up. Yelled that she wasn't loyal.

It scared her so much that she went to stay with her mom for a week. After she returned, he announced that he was leaving the force and had found a job as a security guard. Was she happy now?

She always wondered if he had really left the force on his own. Fear kept her from asking. The move to Paso Robles seemed like a promising idea, a fresh beginning. Then the affair started. She made coffee and powered up her tablet. The bottle of prescription sleep medicine sat next to her cup. Last night was the first in a long time she hadn't needed them. The first news story in the local paper was, again, about the capture of Liz Bathory as the person who had killed Brad. Gloria picked up the bottle of pills and tossed them in the trash. Then she fished them out and vowed to take them to the drug store and discard them properly. She felt a lightness in her chest. Yes, her husband was dead. But it wasn't by her hand. It also wasn't at the hand of the woman she'd been blaming for all their troubles.

An overwhelming desire to confront Evangeline washed through her. To forgive her. She cleaned up the kitchen, went upstairs, and dressed in her nicest jeans and a flamboyant top, then got in the car and drove to Galería de Arte. It was time for Gloria to move forward.

A bell chimed as she pushed in the door and entered the hushed gallery. Sunlight streamed in through the large, glass panes, creating playful shadows as it curved around sculptures and paintings. Where had Brad stood during his shift? The place wasn't huge; she could see the entire main hall from the entranceway. Smaller pocket galleries were harder to see into. He must have been bored out of his mind here, after the excitement of working as a beat cop. He had done it for her, yet the mundaneness of the job had driven him to Evangeline's arms. The idea that he'd chosen the older woman over her unsettled her enough to deny it could be the truth.

She saw a woman with shoulder-length dark hair who had streaks of platinum blond from scalp to tip. Artsy, she supposed. Her own standard haircut framed her face with light brown tresses. Yes, she colored it, but who didn't these days?

"Welcome."

The sound of a human voice startled Gloria. The woman she'd observed now stood beside her. Her smile was so bright it looked fake. Probably veneers. That fit with the opinion Gloria was forming of the gallery owner.

"We had an incident here last week, and the third gallery on your left is closed, but everything else is open. Please, have a look around." The speaker's face was all smiles and openness.

Evangeline Abbott. Homewrecker.

"I'm Brad's wife…his widow."

The woman's face fell an inch or so, causing bags under her eyes and wrinkles around her mouth.

"Oh. I'm sorry. I'm Evangeline Abbot. Would you like some coffee?"

Without the fake facade of cheeriness and hospitality, the gallery owner exuded fatigue. Gloria couldn't muster up enough anger to sustain a bad mood. "No, thank you. I just want to look around at where he worked. Where he—" Gloria's gaze stopped when she saw the chalk outline on the floor. Orange cones and yellow tape surrounded the grisly vision. Really? They hadn't thought to clean that up?

Evangeline moved to block the view. "I've asked them to make that go away, and they've promised to do it as soon as forensics decides they got everything they can. Though some have suggested leaving it as performance art."

"It's dreadful," Gloria said and turned away.

"I agree." There was an uncomfortable silence. "Well…"

"I know about the affair. He didn't tell me directly, but I knew. I also didn't know about his job at the olive ranch."

Gloria wasn't sure why she was telling this woman things that she normally would have hidden away. Maybe it was the path forward. One had to go through first. She pointed to a multimedia piece hanging on a nearby wall. Its bright colors and mix of textures, cloth, toothpicks, and cotton-ball fuzz were a nice distraction. "I remember how much fun it was to create things like that in art class."

Evangeline took a step closer to the canvas, then turned to look at Gloria.

"You went to art school?" Gloria detected a hint of disbelief in the question. Was it so hard to believe that the wife of a security guard had once dreamed of being an artist?

"Briefly. I had dreams, once."

Brad had encouraged her. She'd give him credit for that. But the constant worry that he wouldn't come home or she'd get a call from the hospital robbed her of any creative spark that lurked in her heart.

She wandered down the hall to the next piece, an elaborate realism of a ballet slipper, done in oranges and reds. A stylized logo slashed across the toe of the shoe, a commentary on how corporations had invaded everything, including the fine arts.

Evangeline moved with her. "We're always looking for new artists. Do you have any work I could see?"

Gloria thought about the few pieces hidden in the garage. She'd always meant to toss them in the trash when there was room, but each time she picked up one of the small canvases, she felt an almost electrical connection with it and carefully put it back into its slot.

She shook her head.

"Nothing I'd share with anyone."

She moved to the next wall. A large watercolor hung by wires from the top of the wall partition. Dried grasses, a whitewashed barn, and collapsed buildings with rusted metal roofs.

Evangaline followed her.

"All of our artists are local or have a strong connection to the area. What do you paint?"

Why didn't this woman leave her alone and let her absorb Brad's essence, whatever tiny bit of it there might be here? Hadn't the gallery owner done enough to ruin her life?

As if she'd read her mind, Evangeline took a step back. "I'll let you enjoy on your own."

Enjoy? The word felt harsh in Gloria's ears. She could get some enjoyment out of looking at the art and experiencing the creativity, but that wasn't why she was here. She listened for the echo of Brad's last words. Did he cry out? Call her name, or Evangeline's? She circled the outline of his body on the ground. Whoever suggested keeping it was right. It was almost an art installation. *Fallen Man,* she would name it.

His arms splayed out to his sides, giving her the impression he was hugging the floor. He wasn't a hugger, at least not once the wedding ceremony was in the past.

He must have been unconscious by the time he fell. That thought gave her some comfort. The initial whack would cause pain, but from that point on, to death, he would be blissfully unaware. She tried to picture his actual body filling the outline, but all she could manage was a white-sheet-covered form. Just as well, since tears stung her eyes, and she didn't want to cry in public.

She turned and headed for the exit. A ringing bell announced the entrance of an older couple, obviously tourists. He wore a navy-blue blazer over a white shirt, open at the collar, and khaki slacks. The wife dressed in a cream pantsuit with taupe kitten heels.

Not only did they look like art lovers, but they also had the money to spend.

"Check out the back gallery," Gloria said. "It has some beautiful pieces." It would be her tribute to Brad if they bought something. She smiled at them and then dropped her head and continued toward the door.

Evangeline emerged from the gift shop.

"Welcome to the Galería de Arte. Please enjoy yourselves. Gloria, would you mind joining me in the gift shop?"

Gloria stopped with her hand on the door, reluctant to reenter the building. The visit had been what she needed. A way to close out a chapter. But she didn't want to prolong her time here. The art pulled her in. How long she'd wished she could return to her drawings. To spend a day painting without a care. She turned and followed Evangeline into the gift shop.

"Look," Evangeline said when they'd gotten far enough in to speak in private. "I know there is nothing I can say or do that will ease your grief."

When Gloria didn't respond, she continued. "I heard what you said to those people. It was truly kind. I need to hire someone for the gallery, someone to work here, the gift shop, and to help buyers in each of the private spaces if their owner isn't here to handle the purchase. I sense that you have an eye for art, and I could use you."

Stunned, Gloria took a step back. A job? The woman her husband had an affair with was offering her a job. She opened her mouth to deliver a resounding NO, but the word wouldn't come. She needed a job to augment her wages at the grocery store.

The mortgage wouldn't pay itself, and while Brad had a life insurance policy, it wouldn't cover everything. If the call she'd made that morning to the Fresno PD asking about Brad's pension turned out favorably, she might even be able to quit the grocery store.

She looked around the gallery with new eyes and imagined her art hanging on the walls. Maybe even her own pocket gallery filled with her vision of the world. This could be a happy, peaceful refuge for her. The stinging of tears returned, but not tears of loss. This time, she cried for her new beginning.

"I'd love to. Thank you."

"I have another new artist in mind as well. Natalie Patel," Evangeline said. "She works here part-time and had stuff here years ago. I haven't seen her latest work yet, but I sense that it will be exceptionally good. I'll get you two connected. You have a lot in common."

Gloria nodded. Having female friends wasn't something she'd ever done well. It would be nice to try.

"Of course, where Natalie goes, her friend Rose comes along. You'll just have to deal with that."

The nosey, question-asking woman who visited her the day Brad died. She had exuded empathy, so maybe they could be friends.

"I heard that Rose was the one who helped solve Brad's murder."

Evangeline grimaced. "Yes, she's proved herself to be quite the little detective."

Chapter 53 Rose

~

Champagne – a French sparkling wine usually (but not always) made from Chardonnay, Pinot Noir, or Pinot Meunier grapes. Only sparkling wine made in the Champagne region of France may be labeled Champagne.

Friday, October 21, 5:30 PM

A cool breeze hinted at the colder temperatures predicted for the rest of the week. Winter was coming with its rain and wind. Bottles of champagne were set out on Rose's veranda. Rose and Stella crowded around Stella's computer, sitting on the kitchen counter.

The email had arrived.

"I'm nervous," Stella said. "I've been looking so long, and this is the first time I've felt like it might pay off."

"No matter what it says, it won't change who we are."

Rose felt anxious, too. For years, the question of what happened to the tiny life she brought into the world had lingered in her thoughts like an unwanted ghost. She'd never gone looking. Now an answer sat tantalizingly close.

Stella clicked on the email.

A report popped up with columns of numbers and lines of DNA factors. At the bottom was a summary of the percentage chance of Stella and Rose being related.

99.9999999%

"That's a lot of 9s," Rose said. "Statistically, that's one hundred percent."

Stella was her daughter. Rose felt a fluttery feeling in her stomach.

"I don't know what to say. Should I apologize? Are you upset?"

Stella clasped her hands over her chest, and Rose could see the younger woman close to hyperventilating. "Are you kidding? No, I'm not upset. I'm chuffed to bits. You gave me life and saved my life."

Then she asked the one question Rose couldn't answer.

"Who is my dad?"

"Someone I met at a conference. I was young and reckless. We bonded over Bertolucci's Last Tango in Paris. The idea of being anonymous lovers was overpowering. Like the characters in the movie, we agreed not to share anything personal about each other, including our names. At the end of the week, he left to go back to his life, and I was pregnant."

It seemed such a pathetic excuse for an adoption, but at the time, she wasn't mature enough to make the hard decision. Though some would say that carrying the baby to term and letting someone else raise it was hard enough.

"Stella. I don't know what to say. There's nothing I can do to make up for the missed time, except that we will get to know each other better. I promise."

Stella hugged her. It felt warm and forgiving.

"I can live with that. It wasn't a love union. Fairly sure I'd do the same thing."

"You must understand that my career was all I had. I've come to realize that was a mistake."

Eventually, she pushed Stella away to look closely at her daughter's face.

The broad smile told her everything she needed to know. Stella did understand.

"No, not a mistake. We all make choices. It doesn't help to second-guess decisions we made with the best information and intentions. Your career made you the woman you are."

"I'm going to say that your wisdom is genetic, and I'll take credit for that," Rose said, though she wondered how wise she had been over the last few weeks. Prowling around in dark so deep that even the flashes of lightning had trouble penetrating, entering derelict, abandoned buildings and putting her friend at risk, then driving like a maniac with people shooting at her. Shooting at her! None of that fit the old Rose. Wait, she cautioned herself. It didn't fit the old Winifred. Rose was a new person; someone she was starting to recognize. One thing she did know, Rose had a daughter.

"We need to tell Natalie and Nessa."

Stella laughed. "That should be fun."

Amazing!" Natalie said when told of the test results after arriving with multiple boxes of pizza. "You are both so lucky."

Luck was a flimsy word compared to the emotion Rose experienced.

"Well, it's not a secret anymore. I plan on telling everyone I meet. I have a daughter."

Stella beamed. "Like I said when we met, I've been looking for you for a good long while." She took a slice of pizza from the veggie pie on the coffee table.

"My mum in London will love meeting you, all of you."

"I'd love to meet her, too. Does she know you've been looking?" Rose asked.

How wonderful to have a friend become a daughter, a wonderful daughter who forgave. She sat down. Watson jumped into her lap and curled up as if to remind everyone he was there first.

Natalie lifted the lid of a pizza box, and the scent of cheese and sausage wafted out,

"Hmm. That smells good," Stella said.

Nessa parked her green hatchback at the curb and took steps two at a time up to the veranda.

"I brought cake!" she said and handed a white pastry box to Rose. She wore jeans and a pale blue sweater, which made her look younger than her work uniform.

With a glass of bubbly in hand and a slice of cake on a celebratory paper plate, everyone sat down. Watson moved from lap to lap, pawing hands to keep the scratching going until he reached Stella. There he curled up and lay his head on her lap.

"Thanks, Watson. You saved my life. Oh my god, I promised myself I wouldn't cry tonight. I've done enough of that already."

While Stella petted Watson and spoke with Nessa, Natalie leaned close to Rose and whispered, "What about Frank? Have you heard from him after basically telling him to shove off?"

"I've called, but we haven't spoken. I'm not good at apologizing. Yet another thing to practice."

"Well, take a cue from his approach. Ask him for coffee. It can't hurt," Natalie said. Rose nodded. It would be her move to make. She resolved to take that step.

Nessa pointed to the house across the street.

"So, you had a thief living right across the street."

"Did they ever find Slade Bolton's body?" Natalie asked.

Nessa took a sip of sparkling wine and nodded her head. "Yes. Stab wounds to his lower back probably severed the spinal cord. He was tossed in a ditch not far from the villa and bled out."

Rose had never liked the man. Especially after he insulted her. But no one deserved to die in a ditch.

"I overheard a phone call with his boss," Stella said. "He put it on speaker. It didn't sound like they knew he was in Paso Robles. Slade sounded panicky. And after they shoved me in the closet, I heard him say he wanted out. I guess that Liz Bathory wouldn't allow that."

"Can you prove she killed him?" Rose asked Nessa.

"Forensics has the knife with her fingerprints and his blood," Nessa said. "It's enough to charge." She turned to face Rose. "We couldn't have done it without you."

In her heart of hearts, Rose agreed. But she also knew she didn't do it alone.

"Don't sell the SLPD short. And I had help." Rose lifted a glass to toast. She, Natalie, and Stella had a knack for investigating. They couldn't make arrests, but they could ferret out the narrative. Something she had enjoyed immensely.

"Despite all that happened, I wouldn't mind doing it again," Natalie said.

Nessa's eyebrows raised. "Not many people say they enjoyed being in jail."

"Well, not that part, certainly, but the figuring things out. Collecting clues. Rose is a natural at it."

"I read a lot of mysteries and followed Sherlock

Holmes and Hamish Macbeth's advice." Even so, she had a talent for sleuthing. She took in this collection of women. Her first real friends. While working her way up the ladder in her career, she'd dreamed of having companions who understood her. Women who supported her, uplifted her spirit, and made her laugh. Here they were, finally.

Natalie leaned forward in her seat.

"I was serious when I said I wouldn't mind doing it again. Thinking through everything was good brain food."

Rose thought about her literary sleuth heroes. A mix of amateurs, cops, and self-employed detectives. Could the three of them do the same?

"I'm sure there are lots of mysteries that the police don't get involved in that we could help solve. We don't have to make it an official business; we can think of it as a private club. Just for fun."

Nessa pulled a folded paper out of her pocket.

"I spent some time on the internet this afternoon following a hunch."

She handed the paper to Rose.

"If you started a private investigator business, you'd need to register, and experience is required. But as unpaid amateurs, you can search public records, social media, and the web, talk to people, and use your critical thinking skills. Those sorts of things. As long as you follow legal and ethical considerations by respecting people's privacy and documenting what you're doing, you should be fine. Oh, and bringing us in when you find something."

"What would we call ourselves?" Stella asked. "We'd need a name."

"We wouldn't be advertising," Rose pointed out.

"Still," Natalie said, "I propose—" She held up her

glass, "I think we should call ourselves The Wine and Pizza Knitting Circle."

"But we don't knit!" Stella argued.

"That's not the point," Natalie explained. "My great aunt belonged to a sewing circle for sixty years, and they never sewed a stitch. We don't have to knit, but I do know how and could teach you if you'd like."

Rose thought of the skeins of yarn sitting in a basket upstairs.

"I want to learn; it always looks so peaceful to see someone knit."

Stella laughed. "It looks boring as hell!"

"Lots of young people knit; many have videos on the Internet showing how. Give it a chance," Natalie said.

As Natalie and Stella discussed what things they could make, and Nessa chimed in with a wish to learn as well, Rose pondered the word knit. Their friendship knitted them together. Only weeks ago, she'd stepped out of her comfort zone and signed up for a ride-along with a police officer. That experience introduced her to the notion that her professional background had a new focus.

She settled into her chair feeling reborn, full of purpose, with a daughter, friends, Watson, and a beautiful place to live. Retirement proved to be more exciting than she could have imagined, and she still had to harvest her olives.

Epilogue

~

Two months later, Rose had five quarts of hand-produced olive oil bottled and resting in her pantry. It had taken five of them to bring the harvest in. Natalie was there every day of the two weeks it took. Stella and Nessa joined them when they could, and even Frank put in a few appearances when his schedule allowed. Margery Wheat proclaimed her a bona fide olive grower and producer when Rose presented her with a bottle of the precious oil.

The Wine and Pizza Knitting Circle had met weekly to discuss local events and rumors and had yet to knit anything. Stella managed to get her bookkeeping business on steady feet and into the red, which kept her busy most weekdays. Her biggest client, the Galería de Arte, recovered from the shocking murder and theft and reveled in the increased tourist visits to see the blank space on the wall that Gray Day Montrose Valley had once hung. A placard dedicated the spot to Brad Knight, Security Guard and Victim.

Rose and Frank had gone on seven dates. Progressing from exploratory conversations about background, family, interests, and dreams, to laughing about the time they went to Moro Bay and a seagull grabbed Rose's beach bag, hoping to find edible goodies inside. She'd finally seen the tattoo. His entire upper body, in fact. It was a simple compass rose. Something he said reminded him to stay pointed to true north. And now he said it was to remind him of her. His compass Rose.

All in all, life was good. In the middle of the night,

when Rose and Watson did their walkabout to discuss things—like when she'd see Frank next; Watson was a big fan of Frank, who always had a dog treat in his pocket, and how wonderful it felt to have a daughter, she wouldn't consider herself a mom as she'd done none of the maternal business— Rose wondered if things were too good. Then she remembered that every time her favorite Scottish constable, Hamish Macbeth, expressed pleasure in his lazy, crime-free life, a murder occurred. For the present, though, things were good enough.

Acknowledgments

As hard as writing a novel is, the acknowledgement is harder. So many people contribute to the development of plot, characters, story arcs, and the list goes on. It is impossible to thank them all or even know who some of them are. The snatch of conversation I overhear at a coffee shop, or while trying to reach something on the top shelf at the grocery store are remembered, but not who said it.

That said, there are people I want to mention. First up is the Cambria Writers Workshop. These dedicated, empathetic, creative, and honest people have heard every word of this story and provided constructive criticism along the way. They keep me grounded and call me out when my literary train goes off the tracks.

This is my first mystery and hopefully not my last. Fortunately, I've had little experience with the police. I must thank Jose Ceja for his insightful corrections to all the scenes with peace officers. Thank you, thank you, thank you. You helped make this as authentic as a work of fiction can be.

I also want to thank Officer Vanessa Gomez of the Paso Robles Police Department. We might not have had the exciting ride-along depicted in this book, but I enjoyed our ride and loved meeting a strong, independent woman.

My dear friends, Anetta and Stefan Gesterkamp, provided invaluable proofreading skills and caught many inconsistencies, along with excellent suggestions. You have my heartfelt appreciation for helping to make this book the best it can be.

Lastly, I'd like to thank my husband, Ken. The man who makes me breakfast every day, and who brainstorms plot holes and studies editing and storytelling so he can make his contributions useful. They are, and more.

This story takes place in Paso Robles, California. Officially, El Paso de Robles. The Pass of the Oaks. It is a real place and is just as magical as I've tried to make it sound. However, the names of the coffee shops, art galleries, analytical labs, lakes, and the people and houses are fictional. There is no abandoned olive farm, so don't bother looking for it. Slade, Liz, Rose, Natalie, Stella, and Nessa are fictional characters and not representations of real people.

I hope you enjoyed this story and want to hear more because I love these characters and hope that you do too. If you feel inspired to leave an honest review on Amazon, Google, Goodreads, or any of the book review sites, I would be eternally grateful.

Till next time,
Linda

ABOUT THE AUTHOR

The writing bug bit L. G. Reed after winning a creative writing contest sponsored by The Detroit News in high school and having her story published in Teen Magazine. Following a successful career as an advertising executive and aerospace engineer, she redirected her energy toward her lifelong passion for storytelling. Reed has authored two middle-grade novels and one young adult book. Her non-fiction credits include articles in *Edible SLO* Magazine and the award-winning Society of Women Engineers *SWE Magazine*. She resides in California's Central Coast.

www.authorlindareed.com